"My deep, deep, gratitude to Melody Carlson, the contributing authors, and all others involved for their generosity in dedicating the royalties for this remarkable book, *The Storyteller's Collection,* to The *JESUS* Film Project.

As of January 1, 2000, The *JESUS* Film Project is produced in 502 languages, has been viewed in every country of the world, and has touched the lives of over 3.2 billion people!

For every book purchased, one person will be introduced to Jesus Christ through the phenomenal work of The *JESUS* Film Project."

DR. BILL BRIGHT, FOUNDER AND PRESIDENT,
CAMPUS CRUSADE FOR CHRIST INTERNATIONAL

"This captivating collection of short stories will take you from the most remote corners of the world to the deepest recesses of the human spirit. These pages are alive with emotion and pull you along—from the pulsating drama of Randy Alcorn's secret police, to Neta Jackson's poignant account of a Chicago Bull's T-shirt in Albania. This is a good one!!! Buy it! Buy it! Buy it!"

PAUL ESHLEMAN, DIRECTOR, THE JESUS FILM PROJECT

TALES *of* FARAWAY PLACES

the STORYTELLERS' *Collection*

COMPILED BY MELODY CARLSON

Multnomah® Publishers *Sisters, Oregon*

This is a work of fiction. The characters, incidents, and dialogues are products of the authors' imagination and are not to be construed as real. Any resemblance to actual events or persons, living or dead, is entirely coincidental.

THE STORYTELLERS' COLLECTION
published by Multnomah Publishers, Inc.

International Standard Book Number: 978-1-57673-822-1

Cover images by Photodisc
Cover image of suitcase by Swanstock

Printed in the United States of America

For information:
MULTNOMAH PUBLISHERS, INC.•POST OFFICE BOX 1720•SISTERS, OREGON 97759

Library of Congress Cataloging–in–Publication Data
The storytellers' collection : tales of faraway places / compiled by Melody Carlson.
ISBN 1-57673-738-1 (hd)
p.cm. **ISBN 978-1-57673-822-1 (pbk.)**
1. Christian fiction, American. 2. Short stories, American. I. Carlson, Melody.
II. Title. PS648.C43 S77 2000 813'.01083823–dc21 00–008991

146033670

Table of Contents

FOREWORD ONE

JERRY B. JENKINS INTRODUCES SOME WRITING FRIENDS

Your favorite Christian novelist just may be found within these pages, experimenting with one of the most challenging writing forms. Short stories are to novels as poetry is to prose. Everything is telescoped, shortcuts have to be taken, yet the result must appear seamless in order to succeed. Judge whether the man or woman you love to read most succeeds. In the process you may learn; and find yourself delighted, inspired, challenged in your own walk with Christ.

In God's economy, a thousand years is as a day. So, in light of eternity, the oft times endless seasons of our own lives are mere short stories to Him. Perhaps from the magnifying glass these writers train on the stuff of life, you'll sense God's own perspective as He watches over and cares for your life, which is as a vapor, appearing for an instant and then vanishing away.

JERRY B. JENKINS

FOREWORD TWO

ANGIE HUNT EXPLAINS CHILIBRIS

Last spring, Terri Blackstock, Lori Copeland, and I tossed a few e-mails back and forth, toying with a unique idea: Why not unite Christian writers who feel called to share Truth through novels? After all, special organizations exist for mystery writers, romance writers, and children's writers.

ChiLibris was born on a sweltering Sunday afternoon in July 1999. Nearly two dozen Christian novelists met in a crowded loft in an Orlando restaurant and discovered that we have much in common—we spend long hours alone in quiet rooms, we read voraciously, we hunger for good stories. Through the magic of the Internet, we began to connect and share our hearts, our prayers, and our encouragement. The number has grown from that initial two dozen to over sixty—and every member is a published Christian novelist who desires to glorify God through the measure of talent he or she has been given.

Our ChiLibris community had only been in existence for a month when we began to see the potential in our little network—how could we make a real difference in our world? The first possibility was obvious—we're writers; we can write.

With a sense of joy and purpose we set out to create a collection of short stories that would focus your attention on things beyond your everyday world. No one thought of material gain—not a single author asked for a royalty. Melody Carlson generously volunteered to collect the stories, edit them, and oversee the details of the project.

You are holding the results of our first collaborative effort in your hands. I'm delighted to present you with stories by authors you may know well, and introduce you to others you have yet to discover. These are wonderful stories by skilled artists...and I am honored beyond measure to call them friends.

ANGELA ELWELL HUNT

FOREWORD THREE

RANDY ALCORN EXPLAINS THE *JESUS* FILM PROJECT CONNECTION

From the beginning of this project, we ChiLibris authors decided we wanted all royalties to go to world missions. We considered a number of fine organizations before settling on The *JESUS* Film Project. The *JESUS* film is likely the single greatest evangelistic tool in history apart from the Word of God itself. It's now being used by 1,000 denominations and mission agencies worldwide in 233 countries. More than three billion (that's not a typo) people have seen the film, and at least 110 million of those have indicated a decision to trust Christ. Tens of thousands of churches have been planted through film showings. The film is in 600 languages, with a new translation completed every three days.

I've had the privilege of being part of six different showings of the *JESUS* film in three countries. Four were in the open air, two in private homes. One of these was in a "closed" country with thirty-seven people in a tiny house, crammed in front of the television. Every word Jesus speaks in this film is from the Gospel of Luke. It has the power and authority of God's Word, living and active, able to penetrate minds and hearts. It ends with an invitation to receive Christ.

Nearly 50 percent of the world's population can't read, even if the Bible has been translated into their language. But all of them can understand the *JESUS* film. I've seen the delighted looks on children's faces as they watch Jesus onscreen, and hear Him speak their language. I've seen elderly men and women gasp, cover their mouths, and wipe their tears as they see for the very first time Jesus being nailed to the cross. Then I've seen their broad joyful smiles when He appears after His resurrection, and watched as they absorb the gospel presentation and press forward, indicating they've embraced Jesus Christ as their Lord and Savior.

As contributors to *The Storytellers' Collection,* we're honored to partner with The *JESUS* Film Project. We encourage readers to pray for and consider supporting this wonderful ministry. For information, see **www.jesusfilm.org** or contact The *JESUS* Film Project, 910 Calle Negocio, Suite 300, San Clemente, California 92673 (949-361-7575).

RANDY ALCORN

The Lesson in the Shells

Jerry B. Jenkins

I was on my way back to the United States after a trip to Irian Jaya to observe relief efforts after a 1976 earthquake. The jumbo jet landed on a runway that dominated a tiny South Sea island—one of those inexplicable stops neither for picking up nor dropping off passengers, or even taking on fuel. Airline personnel herded us under a wind- and sun-faded wood canopy where we sat on benches with our cameras and our fatigue. On three sides of us lay hundreds of yards of shell-strewn sand and the beauty of the endless sea. Behind us wound a few narrow streets of squalor. Almost immediately, we were besieged by the island's bronzed children. They had long, jet black hair, dark eyes, and gleaming teeth. With their hands full of shells, they hard sold everyone.

"Dollar!" they would say, and when people looked shocked they laughed.

"Nickel!" they would then say, giggling.

Some people bought shells they could have picked up themselves only a few feet away.

"Don't do it," an older man said wearily. "These kids are supporting their parents' drug habits." I had been so used to declining the beggars of Irian Jaya that it was easy to turn away these little paupers. One boy started at a dollar and went to fifty cents, then a quarter, a dime, a nickel, and even a penny before he gave up. I didn't need or want any shells, and though I enjoyed him and smiled at him, I shook my head. He moved on to success with someone else.

At the edge of the tiny sales force stood a little girl with a face so radiant I can still see it two decades later. She couldn't have been more than five years old. When the rest moved on, she continued to stare at me, then she approached, her tiny hand crammed with three shells, each about the size of a golf ball. She smiled and held out her merchandise. I smiled and shook my head. That's when she said the word in her own tongue that I could not understand. I assumed she was saying "cheap," or "dollar," or "deal." I shook my head again and she reached closer.

She pleaded with me now, repeating the word over and over. How these kids had been trained to pull at heartstrings! Yet I would not be moved. I shook my head again and saw her tears form. Very well done, I thought. Almost worth a sale. But no, I was too sophisticated for that. She moved away, shoulders slumped and tears streaming. She squatted nearby and cried, not looking at me.

She had me; she had won. I pulled two dollars from my pocket and went to her. What was this? She wept even more, and now it was she who was shaking her head. And she repeated the word. Confused, I interrupted a missionary's kid involved in another conversation to ask her what the word meant.

"It means 'free,'" she said, turning back to her conversation. I was stunned. The little girl looked at me warily. I pulled my hands from my pockets and showed her my empty palms. Then I repeated the word as a question, and she beamed as she handed me the shells.

ABOUT THE AUTHOR

Jerry B. Jenkins is a novelist and biographer who has written six *New York Times* bestsellers and whose work has appeared in *Reader's Digest*, *Parade*, and dozens of Christian periodicals. He is the writer of the best-selling *Left Behind* novel series (Tyndale), soon to be a major motion picture and *'Twas the Night Before* (Viking Penguin), soon to be a CBS TV movie. He and his wife Dianna have two grown sons and live with a third in Colorado. Although most people think of Jerry as a fiction author, this story happens to be true.

So Shine

Terri Blackstock

It's been said that suicide is painless, but I say that whoever believes that has never tried it.

It's the most painful thing I've ever experienced, even more painful than when Butch, my husband, died two years ago. I thought I'd never get over that, and it, of course, is what led me to the suicide thing. But I'm getting ahead of myself now.

I'm not the melodramatic type. I didn't choose to do it on a Panama Canal cruise because of any theatrical element. I didn't much care that people back home would wag their tongues about my returning to the scene of Butch's death, right there in Guatemala, to end my own life. I guess curiosity just overwhelmed my need to make a clean exit. I wanted to see where he died, just get a glimpse of what he'd gone through when the tornado, spawned from a hurricane, had destroyed the building he was in. I wanted to picture it in my mind, not to end the pain I'd carried since his death, but just to bring closure to his life and mine. I had chosen to die in Puerto Quetzal, simply because that's where I'd be when I reached that closure.

But I never intended to go with a group of Christians. All I told the travel agent is that I wanted to travel cheap. Next thing I know, she's telling me I can get a group rate if I hook up with this single's group from Something-or-Other Church that just happens to be going on this Panama cruise. The rate was actually lower than the cost of flying to Guatemala on my own, so I jumped at it, emptying every penny of my meager savings account to purchase the ticket. I figured it wouldn't be so bad traveling with that group since I had no intentions of joining in their festivities anyway. But imagine my surprise when I unlocked my cabin door and found a roommate inside.

She was cute, in a church mouse sort of way, with big eyes that looked startled and a smile that ate up half of her face. "Hi!" she practically squealed when I came in. "I'm your roommate." She stuck out her hand. "Mitsy Carpenter. They told me you were new in the group and that you were from Chastain, and I grew up just down the road in Montclair, so I thought it would be fun. I'm a nurse at St. Francis Hospital. Oh, that's such a cute blouse. Where in the world did you get it?"

My life flashed before my eyes as I gaped at her. "Uh...Sears, I think. I'm not supposed to have a roommate."

Her expression crashed. "No? Well, they told me this was my room. You are Sharon Jones, aren't you?"

"Yes."

Her smile snapped back across her face. "Well, then there's no mistake. We're roomies! Don't worry. I promise I won't get in your way. My hair is short so I don't have to spend a lot of time in front of the mirror, and I'm flexible on when to take showers and things, and I don't snore."

I just stood there, wondering how this could have happened. I imagined her wanting to stay up all night talking and trying on my clothes. I'd had visions of spending the time alone, writing a few letters to people who would feel betrayed at what I was about to do, thinking about my husband and how the pain would soon end. I wondered how I could get rid of her. I looked around. "No offense, but this place is just not big enough for two people."

"Sure it is. See? Two beds."

"But we can't breathe in here. Really, there must be an alternative."

"Actually, there's not," she said with a look of apology. "Every cabin on the ship is booked. Your only choice is to switch roommates, if you want. But I'd understand if you wanted to do that. Really, I'd be fine with that."

The catch in her voice suggested that the very thought of my switching could warp her for life. I dropped my bag on the bed and sank down next to it. I should have known. It never occurred to me to ask if I had a private room. I just assumed I did. But I had asked for a cheap trip, and the travel agent had given me one.

As Mitsy busied herself putting her things in the tiny closet and her drawer, I tried to run back over my options. I could get off the ship and find another way to get to Guatemala. Or I could forget my need for closure, and just end things back at home. The final option, of course, was to bite the bullet and stay. After all, how bad could it be? We'd be at Puerto Quetzal in just a couple of days, and then it would be over.

I glanced up and saw Mitsy looking at me with her eyebrows arched like a child persuading her mother to play Barbies. "Stay, Sharon, and I'll do my best to stay out of the room as much as possible. Mostly, I'll be with my other friends on deck. We'd love to have you join us. We have this great speaker who came with us, and he's going to be leading us in Bible study every night."

"Bible study?" I asked with disdain. "You came on a cruise to do a Bible study? Couldn't you have stayed at home and done that?"

"Well, most of us don't drink or gamble, and believe it or not, I love to study my Bible, especially with a teacher like this one." She pulled a dress out of her bag and slipped it on a hanger. "I've always wanted to take a class from him. It's like a dream come true for me. Why don't you come with me?"

I sat there, almost amused. "No, thanks. I don't think so."

Her disappointment was like a neon sign on her face. I hoped I wasn't that transparent. "You probably have other friends on board, huh?" she asked.

"Actually, I don't know a soul," I said, almost defiantly. I got up and unzipped my bag and irritably started unpacking it. She came near, as if to help.

"Are they bringing your suitcase up?"

"Nope," I said. "This is it."

Mitsy gaped at the duffel bag. "Boy, I wish I could travel that light. You don't look like you've got more than one or two days' worth of clothes."

"Actually, I don't. I'm only going as far as our first port."

"Really?" she asked. "They let you do that?"

"What can they do? I paid full fare. I can get off any place I want."

"Then you'll only be here for two days?"

"That's right." She watched as I pulled out two pairs of shorts, a couple of T-shirts, some rolled-up socks, and a framed picture of Butch.

"Oh, is that your boyfriend?" she asked.

I shot her a look that said her curiosity wasn't appreciated. What was her problem, anyway? I thought of grabbing the Bible off of the television set and thrusting it at her. *Go take a class or something. Knock yourself out.* "No, he's my husband," I said.

"Well...why didn't he come with you?"

"Because he's dead." I knew the words sounded callous, and I didn't say it like that to shock her. But I just didn't have the patience for niceties. Not now.

"Oh!" she said, as if she'd just committed the biggest faux pas in history. The Manners Police would be banging the door down any minute now. "I'm so sorry!"

I looked up at her and saw that her eyes were full of tears. Was this woman for real? Tears for a man she didn't even know? *Bizarre.* I kept unpacking, unfolding and refolding the few things from my bag.

"How...how long ago?"

"Six months," I said. To my surprise the words came easily, without that constricting of my throat or the stinging in my eyes.

She sank down onto my bed, as if we were slumber party pals. "You poor thing."

I didn't want to be thought of as a poor thing. "I'm fine," I said.

"So...are you taking the cruise to get your mind off of things?"

She was nosy, as well as pushy—and I wanted her to go away. I pulled my stationery out of my bag, two changes of underwear, and the big ninety-day supply of my sleeping pills. "You might say that. We had been saving to take a cruise. So I decided to come ahead anyway."

"Good for you," she said. She wiped her tears. "Was he sick?"

"Nope." I opened the drawer and dropped my things in one at a time, with slow, deliberate movements, placing them carefully, as though their position was of grave importance. "He worked for the Associated Press. He was in Guatemala covering the hurricane, and a tornado leveled the building he was in."

"That's awful," she whispered again, as if the drama were unfolding right before her eyes. She looked at his picture as I set it up next to my bed. If I'd known I was going to have a roommate, I probably wouldn't have brought it. But I'd wanted to talk to him along the way. I'd wanted to believe he was on this journey with me, understanding and even encouraging.

I must have gotten that dark-tunnel look on my face because, before I knew it, she stood up and hugged me. My first thought was that she had a lot of nerve, hugging a person she'd never met before, acting like we were best buddies. I resented it and stiffened. But she didn't seem offended.

"My pastor…he deals with grief all the time. People burying loved ones. If you want to talk to him, he's on the ship, too. I know he could help you get through this."

"I don't need help," I clipped. I zipped up my bag and stuck it under the bed. From the look on her face, you would have thought *she* was the one who'd lost a husband.

I picked up the bottle of pills, and tried to drop them into my purse. I must have been shaking, because my hand slipped and the bottle fell to the floor and rolled under my bed. I bent to reach for it, but in a second she was on her knees, reaching under the bed to catch it. "I got it," she said, then held it up to me.

I took it, hoping she had not seen the contents. But her face changed again. "Ambien," she said. "We give this to patients who have trouble sleeping."

I didn't say anything. I was beginning to feel violated.

"That's a big supply," she said. Her voice had hushed to a whisper, and I didn't look at her as I dropped the bottle into my purse. She knew, I thought. She was putting the pieces together, and she was figuring out my plan.

Suddenly, I had to get away from her. "Are you gonna be here a while?" I asked.

Her eyebrows arched hopefully. "Yeah, I guess so."

"Then I'll see you later." I grabbed my purse and started to the door, knowing I had probably hurt her feelings. But she seemed like the type who could get over it.

I bought some stationery in the gift shop because I didn't want to risk going back into the cabin and running into her. Then I found a quiet place on deck and started writing my letters as the boat moved down the coast of Mexico. I wrote to my mother and told her I loved her and that none of this was her fault. She often blamed herself for every negative thing that had occurred in my life. I told her that I simply saw a light at the end of all this darkness, and I was heading toward it. As I sealed the envelope, I hoped that would be a nice thought for her.

I needed to write my sister and Butch's mom and my father, whom I hadn't seen in years. But the letter to my mother had taken a lot out of me. I was glad I had two days to do the rest. I decided to walk around the ship, see what it was like, imagine what Butch and I would have been doing if life had gone differently. This cruise was obviously hosting passengers besides the church group, for the casino was alive with gamblers, drinks in hand, hovering around tables and hunched over slot machines. I glanced into the theater, and saw that a game of bingo was being called.

I passed little bars and cafés of all themes and a man playing guitar at the center of some tables, where couples sat nursing their margaritas. I imagined Butch pulling me to the small dance floor, spinning and dipping me as I laughed out loud. It had been a long time since I'd laughed. I turned and walked away until I could no longer hear the music.

The scent of the world famous meals being cooked below already wafted up the stairwell, advertising that dinner would soon be served. But if I went, I'd have to sit with Mitsy's crowd, so I made the decision to skip eating tonight.

I passed a glass-enclosed room with a bar, and saw Mitsy sitting at a table with about twenty other men and women. They had their Bibles out and were talking animatedly. I stopped and stared, not meaning to, wondering why anyone would want to sit around reading their Bibles on a cruise.

But stopping had been my mistake. Mitsy saw me, and before I could escape, she was on her feet and pushing through the door. "Sharon! There you are! Come in here. I want my friends to meet you."

I backed away. "No, I can't. I was just on my way to...bingo."

It was lame, I knew. I was no more the bingo type than I was the Bible type.

"Just for a minute," she said. "Come on. I told them about you. I hope you don't mind. About your husband and everything. We prayed for you."

I was embarrassed. I felt the others' eyes on me, and I wanted to shrink away. "You what?"

"We prayed."

"I don't need prayer," I said quietly through clenched teeth. "You had no right to tell other people about me."

"Well, I didn't tell them much, because I don't *know* much. But my heart went out to you."

I couldn't believe her gall. "Keep your heart to yourself," I said. "I don't need you or anybody else praying for me, okay?" I didn't know why I felt like crying—I hadn't even cried while packing my bag or writing to my mother.

"I didn't mean to upset you. I just believe in prayer, and that God is listening and watching over you. I know He loves you…"

"Oh yeah?" I asked defiantly. "Then how come He let a building fall on my husband?" I blinked back those tears stinging my eyes and backed away. "I don't need or want your prayers, so tell your friends just to forget about me. Tell them to consider me a figment of your imagination."

"They can't do that," she whispered.

"Why not?" I demanded.

"Because you're not here by accident. Neither are we."

"Well, at least you got that right. I'm *not* here by accident. I have a plan. And you are not part of it."

"That's fine," she said, not at all angry, even though my words had been chosen to cut. "I don't have to be. But if you want something to do—something other than bingo—it's a really great group of people. A couple of them have lost spouses, too. You see that woman sitting at the end, with the red hair? Both her husband and baby daughter were killed two years ago in a car accident. Drunk driver. She suffered horrible grief, but the Lord saw her through it. I know it would help you to talk to her. Maybe I can get her to sit with us at dinner."

I stole a look over her shoulder and saw the redhead actually laughing and talking with the group. Was Mitsy putting me on? Why wasn't that woman rabid with rage? Why wasn't she contemplating her own suicide?

The questions renewed my anger, and I didn't want to feel it. I wanted that numbness to invade me again, to keep me moving according to plan. I had more letters to write. I had more thinking to do. I wanted to be alone.

"Look, I know you mean well," I managed to say. "But I have things to do." With that, I took off walking as fast as I could, as if my life depended on getting to that bingo game.

That night, I might have bought something to eat at one of the snack bars, but I had no money to spend. Except for what I'd left in the bank for my burial expenses, I'd spent all I had on the cruise. The hunger pangs almost felt satisfying, since they'd spared me the irritation of dining with Mitsy. I considered sleeping out on the deck, but one of the porters told me I couldn't. I hung around in a bar until the wee hours drinking only water, since it was free. Finally, just before dawn, I went back to the cabin, hoping Mitsy would be sound asleep.

She wasn't. She was sitting up in bed, reading her Bible under the light of a lamp. She looked up at me as I came in. Man, this woman had problems, I thought.

"Mom, I'm home," I said sarcastically.

"Are you all right?" she asked.

"Fine," I said. I grabbed a big T-shirt out of my drawer, then went into the bathroom and changed. When I came back out, she was lying in bed. The lamp was still on. "We missed you at dinner."

I wanted to laugh. "I bet," I said as I pulled back my covers.

"I brought you some leftovers."

I turned around and looked at her. She had her face to the wall. "You did?"

"Yeah. It's in the fridge."

I looked around and saw the small, square refrigerator at the bottom of our closet. I hadn't noticed it before. I opened it and found the Styrofoam box there. It was full of fruit and rolls, things that didn't need to be heated. "Thanks," I said.

But she didn't answer. I was pretty sure she had fallen asleep. I sat on the floor and ate, wondering why she would have done that for me, why she would have waited up the way she had, why she would have told her friends to pray...

Questions swirled around in my head like the tornado that had taken my husband from me. And as I drifted to sleep, Mitsy's words continued to play through my mind like a warped CD. *"You're not here by accident...you're not here by accident..."*

But that strong sense of resolve returned to me two days later when we reached Puerto Quetzal in Guatemala. By then I had finished all my letters. They were addressed and stamped, and I had safely dropped them into the ship's mailbox. It was my way of sealing my decision, I thought. I couldn't turn back now. In just a few days, those suicide notes would make their way into the mailboxes of those I loved the most. It was final.

Everywhere I went that day, I noticed Mitsy nearby. She never looked as if she were following me, exactly. She was just there, alone or with a friend, fanning herself in the sweltering heat. I decided I was going to have to shake her before I got off the ship. I thought I had managed to do just that, but as I walked down the ramp, I heard a voice behind me.

"You mind if I come along with you?" she asked in that perky voice. "I got separated from my friends somehow."

If you hadn't been playing my shadow, maybe you could have kept up with them. "Actually, I do mind. I really wanted to be alone today." I started walking faster.

"Maybe you think you do," she said. "But this is gonna be painful. Seeing where your husband died..." Her voice broke off. "I'm coming with you."

I stopped dead in my tracks and turned around. "No! I don't want you to come!"

"I know you *think* you don't," she said. "But I'm sure when you get there, you'll wish you had someone."

How could I get through to her? "Read my lips," I said with narrowed eyes. I knew my words hurt her. But I no longer cared. "I want to do this alone."

"Okay," she said. "Then I'll just hang back, and I won't say a word. You won't even know I'm here."

"No!" I said. "I don't want you with me. Get off my back!"

She got tears in her eyes again, but she wouldn't give up. "Look, I know I'm getting on your nerves and that you wish you'd never met me. But I've just got to tell you that God loves you more than you'll ever know, and someone's already died in your place. You don't have to do this. He can help you find the light again."

I wondered if she had read my letters, if she'd shared them with her friends... Then I realized she couldn't have. I had mailed them. They were on their way. But I knew beyond a shadow of a doubt that she had figured out my plan. She had seen the pills and put the few things I'd said together. I never should have told her I wouldn't be going farther than Guatemala.

A crowd came by and I took the chance to cut through it, losing her. I took off running, running, running until I knew that she wasn't behind me. Then, leaning against the wall of an old adobe building riddled with bullet holes, I tried to get my bearings. Trying to catch my breath in the stifling heat, I saw the hills surrounding the town, crowded with tiny adobe houses topped in red tiled roofs. The poverty was visible, an ironic contrast to the tropical beauty and lush colors of the landscape.

I got out my map and tried to find the area where I knew Butch had been found. It was near the coast, I thought, not too far from here. He would have been right around here, staring intently at the ocean, waiting for the eye of the storm. He would have been making sure he got it all—the feel of the winds off the Pacific, the debris flying through the air, the sight of the tornado making its way toward him...

I walked for miles, carefully checking the map and noting the landmarks. I passed a barefoot child who tried to sell me a dead chicken and another who offered to take my picture. Occasional vendors made some kind of tamale in their stands, and cruise tourists lined up for them as if they hadn't eaten in days. A man with a guitar stood on a street corner, singing a song in Spanish. I tripped over the hat he'd set out to collect tips.

At last I found the place I had marked on my map, the place where my husband's life had ended. I looked around and saw the mountains he had written so descriptively about. He'd been captivated by the beauty and power of them, knowing that some were active volcanoes ready to erupt at a moment's notice. After the hurricane, those picturesque hills had caused lethal mud slides, killing thousands. Funny how beauty had such deadly potential.

Evidence of the hurricane remained all around, broken trees and destroyed buildings not yet rebuilt. At last I found the crumbled foundation of the hotel where Butch had been sheltered. My heart began to pound hard as I stepped into it, wondering how and where they had found him. Had he suffered at all? What were his last moments like? Had he thought of me? Had he prayed? Had he run through the might-have-beens? The house we might have bought, the years we might have shared, the children we might have borne?

Regrets and grief and anger flooded over me, literally knocking me to my knees in the stones and dirt. Unexpectedly, I began to cry. I had planned to do this thing easily. To simply come to this place; sit down and tell my husband I loved him; and then with the breeze wafting in from the ocean, take my little pills. I hadn't expected this pain, this ambush of grief, this despair that didn't lessen at the thought of my end.

I had lied to my mother. There really was no light at the end of my darkness. There was only blacker darkness. Maybe I had mistaken the light for a reflection that wasn't even real.

Still, with tears running down my face, I reached into my bag, felt around for my bottle of pills. I couldn't feel them. I searched through my purse—there was my wallet, my sunglasses case, my room key, my passport.

The bottle was gone.

I sat back hard onto the ground. Obviously, Mitsy the meddler had taken it. Rage erupted like molten lava inside me, and I wanted to scream or throw something. Now I wished she *had* followed me so I could turn this indignation on her. She had no right! This was not her life. She didn't have to live it.

And neither did I.

I looked out over the water, saw the rough waves frothing against the shore. I wasn't a good swimmer, never had been. I could walk down that pier, drop off the end, and let the ocean be my grave.

Making the decision, I abandoned my bag there on the dirt. There was nothing in it I would need again. Perhaps some hungry Guatemalan child would claim it—probably before I even hit the water. He would rummage through it, thrilled with his finds.

With renewed energy, I headed for the pier. Each step took me closer to my goal, closer to the end of this pain, closer to the light, reflected or not.

I reached the end of that pier and gazed down into the green foaming waves. I'll jump in, I thought, and swim out as hard as I can, and at some point, my arms will give out and I'll go under, and the current will carry me away. I tried to picture that light, but all I could see, no matter how hard I imagined, was darkness. Smothering darkness, oppressive darkness, unending darkness...

I dropped down onto the pier and wailed into my knees, sobbing just like the night I got the phone call telling me Butch's body had been found.

You don't have to do this. He can help you find the light again.

Mitsy's words came back to me, but this time, I imagined Butch saying them. And I wanted to shout out that no one would ever help me find the light, that it had gone out when he was killed, that there wasn't any more light on this earth for me.

Lift your face. A voice, still and small, emerged from the chaos of my mind. And as if someone's finger physically lifted my chin, I looked up.

There before me, I saw the glory of a Guatemalan sunset, full of vibrant color and moving toward the horizon. Then, like a nuclear explosion that irradiated everything within its reach, the sun burst into flame, coloring the sky in blinding burnt orange light.

He can help you find the light again... You're not here by accident... We've been praying for you...

Suddenly the thought of throwing myself into the darkness seemed so futile, and even the pills, if I found them, held little hope. But here was the light, bright and burning in the sky and glittering off the water, as clear as the hope that Mitsy knew. It was the same light I had seen in her face. The same light I had seen in the red-haired widow's eyes. The light I had witnessed in that group that took so much pleasure in printed words from a sacred book...

In stunned silence, I sat there watching the light until it faded down beneath the horizon. I felt the rage and misery and grief seeping out of me. I felt the beginning of light glowing in my heart, the hope of joy again—the prelude to life. Was it possible that Butch had found this before his death?

Slowly, I rose to my feet. A warm breeze feathered gently across my face, whispered through my hair...like a sweet caress that promised rest and peace.

What if Mitsy was right? What if the Giver and Taker of Life really did love me? Could it be that He had assigned me to a room with her?

Not totally certain whether I had won or lost the fight for my life, I wearily left the pier and went back to search for my bag. Miraculously, it was still there, waiting for life to go on. Waiting for new life to set in.

And as I walked down the coast back toward the boat, I wondered where I might find Mitsy. I needed her to tell me how I might truly find the real light I'd glimpsed today. The light that was bright enough to chase away my darkness. The light I had seen shining in her.

ABOUT THE AUTHOR

Award-winning author Terri Blackstock has published eleven Christian novels since leaving the secular market, where she had 3.5 million books in print under two pseudonyms. Her bestselling projects include the Sun Coast Chronicles series, the Newpointe 911 series, and *Seasons under Heaven*, a novel cowritten with Beverly LaHaye. Terri has appeared on national television programs such as *The 700 Club* and *Home Life*, and has been a guest on numerous radio programs across the country.

Is This the Day?

Randy Alcorn

Is this the day I die?

Li Quon asked himself the familiar question as he wiped sleep from his eyes. Why couldn't he have more courage, like his father and great-grandfather?

He lit a candle and watched Ming sleeping vulnerably.

Pulling himself off the thin bed pad, Quon walked barefoot on the frigid concrete floor to the cot four feet away. He knelt down beside eight-year-old Li Shen, resting his forehead against the crown of his only son's head. He reached out to his pudgy hands, then touched a finger to his pouty lips. How could this thick round boy have come from birdlike Ming?

Is this the day I die?

He'd asked himself the question every day since he was Shen's age. Every day the answer had been no. But his father had taught him, "One day the answer will be yes, and on that day you must be ready."

This was Sunday. It was Sunday his great-grandfather had been beheaded. And it was Sunday his father died in prison after a beating.

"It is time?" Ming whispered, her voice a feather falling upon silk. Candle flame dancing in her brown eyes, she looked just as she had ten years ago, at their wedding in Shanghai.

Quon kissed her delicate forehead, ashamed that he, a lowly locksmith's assistant, was so unworthy of her. Already in this short night he'd dreamed again he held her wounded body—Ming running red through his fingers in a dark rain.

They moved swiftly, silently, performing their 2:00 A.M. Sunday ritual. Ming fed Li Shen two crackers, holding up his wobbly head. Quon wrapped a gray blanket around his neck, then squeezed into his dark green parka. Stuffing 100 yuan into his trouser pocket, he stepped outside and strapped a bundle to the back of his old rusty bicycle. He tied and knotted the bundle, double-tying and double-checking the knots. Ming and sleepy-eyed Shen followed, coats bulging like overstuffed cushions.

Quon positioned Shen on the seat in front of him. The boy put his hands on the bars and closed his eyes, head nodding. Ming peddled beside them, a silent shadow. Face stinging, Quon watched the quarter moon cast shadows on the dormant rice fields. He wished there was no moon—it made the ride easier but more dangerous. He preferred safety over ease.

The road of frozen mud cut between buttresses of naked hills. Even here, ten kilometers outside PuTong, an unnatural silvery dust floated on the wind. He felt the grit on his tongue and spit it out. For a moment the air was God's air, fresh and clean, but then the burning smell of factories assaulted him again, reminding him this wasn't the world he was made for.

Quon bounced over hard ruts, pressing tightly against Li Shen. Seeing shadows ahead, he instinctively began the rehearsal. "Our son is sick," he said to the wind. "We are taking him to my brother's for medicine."

Was that a glint of light behind the tangle of boughs and dead leaves? A policeman holding a lantern? He held his breath, the corners of his eyes freezing shut.

No. The shadows were fence posts. He hung his head, wishing he were a brave man who did not whisper lies into the wind.

They spoke nothing lest the silence, once pierced, would bleed on them, as it had before.

After four kilometers, dark clouds rolled in as if an artist suddenly changed his mood on a canvas. The moon hid from the coming storm. They'd have to ride home in it. But that might be better—storms kept eyes off the streets.

"Slow," Quon said to Ming, as they wriggled blindly onward, the ruts herding them, sky so low now it brushed his face.

At seven kilometers, he saw white wisps of smoke rising from a chimney. A welcome sight, yet if he could see it, so could others. He pushed down his fear to that hollow place inside.

They got off their bicycles in deathly stillness and walked them behind Ling Ho's house. They leaned them against the dark side, by the chicken coop. Quon brushed his hand over other bicycles, counting them. Fourteen.

He walked to the back door knowing they'd crossed the line of no return. From this moment all explanations for being out in the night were futile.

"Ni hao," Quon said, nodding.

"Ping an—peace to you," Ling Ho replied, childlike smile stretching his tight skin in the candlelight. He pointed to two large pots of tea, hovered over by his wife, Aunt Mei, whom Quon's mother always called "Fifth Sister." Mei smiled sweetly and bowed her head. Quon wanted the tea, but since they were last to arrive, he ushered Ming and Shen to the front.

Quon nodded and returned shy smiles to the twenty others, especially three at the rear. He regretted that, as usual, his smiles were forced and nervous. The Li family sat on a backless bench, coats on, leaning into each other's warmth.

The dull luminescence cast an eerie hue over the spartan one room house, bare but for a bench, some chairs, and a bed, and one leafy plant Mei managed to keep alive. When the church was smaller, with ten of them, they'd sat in a circle, but now they had four small rows, the last being the edge of the bed.

Chou Jin stood up. Eyelids heavy, but eyes alert, his upper teeth protruded in a yellow smile, distinguishing him from the wary, prune-faced men of Mao's generation. The draft was a wind upon Chou Jin's wispy hair, a wind that stirred the room, then came out the old man's lips.

"Zhu, wo men gan xie ni feng fu de zhu fu. Lord, we give you thanks for your abundant blessing."

Jin gazed at the church, his children. "Today we speak of light and momentary troubles, which achieve in us an eternal weight of glory."

As he said the word *glory,* lightning flashed in the eastern sky. Moments later God's voice shook the earth, then his tears fell from heaven.

Quon felt a hand on his shoulder, chilling him. He turned to see Eng Lok, who'd been coming only six weeks. Quon didn't know him. He smiled nervously as Lok's palsied fingers passed forward a worn hymnal, paper so thin Quon could read the words two pages back. The church sang, too loudly, Quon thought. "Yesu Jidu, we praise your name forever..."

Is this the day?

Quon's great-grandfather, a young pastor, had been murdered in the Boxer Rebellion, along with 30,000 Chinese Christians and 200 missionaries. Quon's grandfather, Li Wing, then eight years old—Shen's age—watched his father's head fall to the ground. Wing's son, Li Tung, became a pastor and was sentenced to prison during Mao's cultural revolution. Beatings were routine, but one day Quon's father didn't get up. He made Quon's mother a pastor's widow and shy bookish Quon an object of scorn.

Yes, the past had been bloody. But these were new days in China. So everyone kept saying.

"Unless a kernel of wheat falls into the ground and dies, it remains a single seed. But if it dies, it produces many seeds."

Craggy-faced Chou Jin was seated now in an old wicker chair, reading the verse slowly, leaning forward. Specters from the flickering candles cut across his ancient brow. He spoke each word with the gentle obstinacy of a long obedience. "Whoever serves me must follow me.... My Father will honor the one who serves me."

Chou Jin reminded Quon of his father. The old man raised his arms, exposing red, callused wrists. The sight stabbed Quon with the memory of the shame he had felt at his father's imprisonment. Teachers and students in the Communist school had taunted him because his father's faith made him a "public enemy." Father was capped a counter-revolutionary, in contrast to the "revolutionaries," who practiced strict conformity to the Chairman's social order.

Young Quon had tried to disbelieve in God. He had tried to embrace the ideals of the party, to believe the words of his teachers. He didn't want to stand out, didn't want to be noticed. He'd longed to blend into the dark green background of modern China. To this day, he wouldn't wear reds and yellows and bright colors. He was no rebel. He'd even joined the student Red Guards.

Quon had tried hard to not be a Christian. But somehow the wind herded him back. In college, the faith that had been his father's became his own.

"Zhu Yesu Jidu says, 'No man having put his hand to the plough and looking back is fit for the kingdom of God.'"

It was still coal black outside, 3:15 A.M. Curtains were drawn. In some towns unregistered churches met while police looked the other way, but here the Chief always searched for enemies of the state, those he could make an example of.

Quon rubbed the rough scar on his neck. Church must end before the prying eyes of sunrise.

"Stand and we will worship our Lord." The old one began singing a hymn Quon had heard and reluctantly sung many times since childhood: "One day I'll die for the Lord."

Is this the day?

As the church sang, Chou Jin raised his hands again. Li Quon rehearsed every scar on his father's back and arms, the scars he used to run his fingers over before Father went to prison the last time. His father would be Chou Jin's age. If only…

"Bie dong!"

Li Quon stiffened at the shout behind him. The voice rang with the authority of the Gong An Ju, the Public Security Bureau.

Quon swept his left arm over Shen, pulling him close against him and Ming.

With a quick glance Quon said to them both, "Look down, be quiet, don't move." Quon had learned the drill long ago, hiding in house church under his mother's skirt. To his left he saw two green uniforms. To his right two more.

"Do not move," a harsh baritone voice commanded from the back.

At the front right a young policeman held out a Type 54 pistol. Quon had seen one close-up. It had been waved in his face, then struck against his skull. Mao had said it: government by the barrel of a gun.

Suddenly Quon's right elbow was banged by the heavy butt of a Type 56 assault rifle, the PSB's version of the Russian AK-47. Quon often contemplated the irony that China's politics and weapons had come from a "despised foreign power."

Quon's head remained bowed, but he peeked up so he could barely see the PSB captain standing just three feet in front of him. Narrow waisted, with oarsman's shoulders, he reminded Quon of a wasp. The man stared at the twenty-four believers with the pinched eyes of cold assessment. A two-inch scar, rough-sewn in his burlap skin, hung over his right eyebrow. Quon didn't recognize him—there were so many police, transferred in and out. Besides, he never took a close look at them, or they would look back.

Hands tight, with fingers pointing inward like gray claws, the captain was dressed sharply in a green uniform, straight black necktie, pants neatly creased, cap exactly positioned. The only imperfection was the slight tilt of his shoulder badge. This minor flaw comforted Quon, a reminder the government machinery was not so perfect after all.

Scarbrow put his hand on Chou Jin, moved him back against Quon, then took his place in front of the hushed room. His smoked-glass eyes raked the assembly.

"This is an illegal *jiaotang!*"

Quon detected an accent that suggested the villages over the mountains, where he'd probably transferred from.

"This church is not registered with the Bureau of Religious Affairs," he said, stretching his voice ominously as if this were the ultimate offense. "You are not part of the Three Self Patriotic Movement!"

His eyes narrowed and mouth fell into a short-fused frown. He'd spoken the truth—it was against the law to gather for religious purposes except at approved locations.

"You meet in the night like the criminals you are."

He walked across the front of the room as though walking it made it his. His gait was arrogant and sure, like an actor posturing onstage. He looked like he'd walked on the necks of a thousand peasants.

"You have been distributing illegal foreign propaganda."

With dramatic flourish, he waved a thin flat brown object covering his palm, gripped tightly by the ends of his gray fingers. Though unmarked, Quon knew what it was—a compact disk container, and inside, no doubt, the movie. Quon had passed out dozens himself. Last month he and Ming brought eighteen neighbors into their little house, where they watched it. "Jidu speaks Mandarin," the amazed neighbors said. Five became Christians. Three were here this morning. Quon had seen them in the back. Already he'd gotten them into trouble—he longed to turn his head to see them but dared not.

"Criminals!"

Shen's pudgy face scrunched. The dour-mouthed captain lowered his gaze and stared at the boy. Shen's upper lip quivered. He started to cry.

Slowly, Ming took off her silk scarf, blood red, and gently pressed it against Li Shen's lips. Quon peered into his only son's eyes, pleading for quiet, making unspoken promises, knowing he couldn't keep them.

"It is against our law to teach religion to children under eighteen!"

Quon prayed. With the regime's one child policy, Shen was their only future. After she gave birth, the doctor had sterilized Ming without consent. It wasn't as bad as what the Kwans, seated behind them, had undergone—the forced abortion of their second child.

"Brainwashing children! You are a disgrace—traitors to the Republic."

The weapon of *xiu chi*, shame, was as familiar as old shoes, and as painful as those three sizes too small. Ancient, but still effective. When his father was arrested, a teacher fashioned paper and strings, and hung on Quon's neck a sign saying, "Li Tung is a criminal." He'd cried uncontrollably. Even now he felt the humiliation.

A secondary teacher told him to qualify for university he must join the party and renounce his father's faith. He did make it through university, but his Christian beliefs were noted in his record, and he could not get hired for teaching jobs. Finally a locksmith from the house church put him to work.

"You are cultists, devious and immoral, no better than the Falun Gong," Scarbrow said. "Do you think you are above the law? If you must worship foreign gods, there is a registered church!"

The nearest registered church was fourteen kilometers away, in PuTong. Three legal meeting places for a half million people. The Li family had only their two bicycles. But even if they could get there, the pastor had been trained at seminary to censor his messages to the Bureau's liking. Some of the registered pastors were faithful—not this one. There were many infiltrators in the church, who watched and reported. Spies and informants were well rewarded. Even some of the house churches had them.

"China is built on the backbone of hardworking citizens loyal to the superior socialist system."

As always, propaganda followed shame. Spoken with passionate seriousness, the words were formula. Quon could have recited them in his sleep. Sometimes he did.

With a rigid swagger, the officer took three steps to the side, then turned suddenly like an owl's head.

"You are very *bad* people!"

An American visiting the university once told Quon such name-calling seemed childish, laughable. Yet in China it was routine. And though Quon knew it shouldn't, it worked—his ears burned with shame. Perhaps his father felt this way when they put on his head that two-foot-high pointed paper hat that labeled him "traitor, spy, and capitalist."

Shen's mouth hung open, disproportionate to his face. Quon longed to protect him not just from the party's weapons, but its words.

"Jidu followers are traitors. You make me sick." Scarbrow's eyes looked like the points of two ice picks.

In such confrontations, his father had taught Quon to withdraw inside, where men were free, and silently resist the accusations, reason against the "reeducation." He also warned him, "Never sign the bottom of a blank page." Li Tung did that once. A confession was typed over it.

As a fourteen-year-old, Quon had been taken to his father's jail by a watcher, who made him read a plea—supposedly from his family but written by the watcher—to confess his crimes. The memory weighed on Quon's shoulders like an enormous log.

One of the young soldiers approached the captain nervously. They whispered, appearing to disagree. Quon prayed for the boy. Atheism had left a huge void. The people's hearts were empty, seeking to be filled by something greater and deeper.

Quon's father had told him, "Mao Zedong is China's greatest evangelist." His reforms had created a vacuum only Zhu Jidu could fill. In the years following Mao's expulsion of missionaries and persecution of believers, a half million Christians multiplied to eighty million, sixty million of those in illegal house churches.

He had longed to ask his father's forgiveness for having been ashamed of him. He believed it was his father who should be ashamed of Quon.

Eng Lok, directly behind, whispered to his wife.

"Silence!" yelled Scarbrow, drawing Quon's eyes up to his, only for a moment. Pondering what lay behind the smoke in those eyes, Quon heard Eng's wife sob.

"For over fifty years we have fought the western imperialists. We have forged ahead against our enemies and transformed the face of China."

The face, yes. But behind it was something else. Mao had murdered untold millions, more than Hitler, more than even Stalin. The fatalities included Quon's father Li Tung. But Mao had not invented suffering. Dreams about his headless great-grandfather reminded Quon that martyrs ran in his family.

Is this the day?

He looked back at the book on the bench, the precious cargo he'd strapped to his bicycle. He was one of only three in this church who owned a whole Bible. He recalled twenty years ago his mother borrowing a pastor's *shenjing* once a month, hunched over candlelight, copying the Bible letter by letter. The reproduction of different books was allotted to various members of the body. Her first three books were Judges, Obadiah, and Luke. When she was bedridden and his father in prison, one Sunday she entrusted those books to Quon, like precious heirlooms. "When the church gathers," she whispered, "the whole Bible must be present; take these and guard them carefully, my son."

Ten years later, six months before she died, Mother finished copying the final book of shenjing. A leather worker in the church bound it for her. Every day, Quon read his Lord's words in his mother's handwriting. It had nearly been confiscated several times. Would today be the last time he saw it?

"By assembling unlawfully you are subject to imprisonment. But what you deserve is much worse!"

Staring at his shoes while Scarbrow ranted, Quon recalled his visits to his father. They were permitted to see him once a month for thirty minutes. He was often in solitary confinement, because when he was near the other prisoners, many embraced Yesu.

Each month Quon watched Father waste away. Eventually the face that stared back at him was misshapen from beatings, crusted with scabs, puffy with infections. At the beginning of his ten-year imprisonment his face looked mottled and leathery, like the sole of an army boot. Eventually it became a chalky mask.

But the eyes peering through the mask's eyeholes, though hollowed and jaundiced, were still his father's, full of determination and joy. Yes, *joy,* welling up from some subterranean reservoir. Quon hated it when his father looked at him and said, "Your day will come." His mother told him he meant it to encourage him. How, he could never understand.

"Jidu followers surrender state secrets to *lao wai*—foreigners!"

Quon asked silently what his father had asked—"What secrets do you think I know?" A dank musty draft overtook him, the smell of prison. He'd wanted so much to hug his father. But they never let him. "The prisoner cannot be touched."

He had no pictures of his father, not one. They'd all perished when the house burned. He tried to remember his father's face at the dinner table, before the crackdown, but he couldn't. He could only see that tortured mask of his nightmares.

Quon's father wasn't there most of his school years. But he always wanted Father to be proud of him, not ashamed. He never stopped longing to hear Father say to him, "Well done."

"What is that?" Scarbrow pointed at the Bible. Quon swallowed hard. The worst had happened—being singled out of a crowd. Would he have to explain why his shenjing didn't have the government seal?

"What is it?" the man shouted.

"It is...a message from God." He heard his own voice, surprised at its steadiness.

Scarbrow pulled from his pocket a little red volume. "*This* is China's book—not your western imperialist Bible."

The captain was a Mao quoter, from the old school. How many times had Quon been told Christianity was a western religion? Didn't they understand Jidu wasn't American? Scarbrow needed to watch that movie in his hand so he could understand the world of Zhu Jidu was more like rural China than America.

"Our revered father Mao Zedong said, 'The Communist party is the core of the Chinese people.'"

In school Quon memorized the sayings of Chairman Mao. *Bai hua kai hua*—"let a hundred flowers bloom." Somehow the church was never considered one of those flowers.

Mao was the "Great Savior," his picture once hung everywhere. But his experiment failed miserably, leaving underproducing collective farms and a commerce greased by bribes and corruption. But the failure was shrouded under a canopy of words, upheld by professional thugs like Scarbrow and a network of gulags, some of which held 10 percent of their inmates simply for living out Christian convictions. There was endless pushing and herding and reminding of how the state cared for them and protected them from their enemies. Conflicting ideology, Christian faith in particular, was not tolerated.

Since the economic reforms of Deng, Mao's successor, many said it was different. But Quon's nephew was killed in Six Four, the 1989 Tiananmen Square massacre. And Quon had been in a house church raided the next week and two more since. The scars and aches in his neck and inside his head, reminded him things were never what they appeared. They reminded him this world was not his home.

"Do you think we will stand by and allow what happened in Russia and Eastern Europe?"

He'd heard it before—Christianity was blamed for creating the demand for freedom, leading to the regime's loss of control. China now had twice as many Christians as Communist party members. A great wall of repression had been built to prevent Christianity from spreading.

There was much good in China, Quon knew—beauty, history, nobility, and decency, and now economic progress. But the chains of prisoners and free alike had choked this great land, strangled his father and his great-grandfather. One day, Quon sensed, they would strangle him.

Is this the day?

Scarbrow waved his rifle. "We must crack down on all law-breaking activities to safeguard social stability."

Code words for crushing Christians.

"The Chairman said, 'If you don't hit it, it won't fall. Like sweeping the floor, where the broom does not reach, the dust will not vanish of itself.'"

He paused, then squared his shoulders, eyes aflame. "Today we come with brooms!"

Suddenly, in concert, every man in uniform lifted his weapon high.

What's happening?

"We must kill the baby while it is still in the manger. You do not deserve to live!"

Quon had been threatened, strong-armed, and jailed, and he'd heard the "kill the baby" line, but never had he sensed such impending doom. He felt his heart throbbing in the tips of his ears. He'd assumed they'd be given warnings, marks would be made on their records, perhaps he and the other men would be taken to jail and beaten. This had happened to him before. But these soldiers were different. Something else was happening here.

Ming trembled beside him, a tear on her downy cheek. Even Chou Jin, who had spent over twenty years in prison, seemed to shake.

"With these brooms we will sweep away the dirt and filth that threatens China."

Scarbrow stared at every person in the room, one by one, studying them. The captain's eloquence frightened Quon. Educated evil was always the worst. Something terrible was coming.

"There are two sides to this room. All those loyal to the party and people must prove it by moving to the left side and out the door. In doing so, they will declare there is no God, and they do not believe in Jidu. They are free to go and will not be punished. Those who choose Jidu will step to the right side."

Quon looked at Ming, a tempest in her eyes. For a long five seconds no one moved. Then one man stepped to the left, toward the door. Immediately, stoop-shouldered Chou Jin walked to the right. Quon tried to budge his legs, but they felt wobbly, like rusted rain gutters.

"In three minutes," Scarbrow said matter-of-factly, "we will shoot every man and woman—and child—who does not declare himself loyal to the people rather than foreign devils."

Soft groans erupted across the room. Quon turned slightly as Eng Lok's wife put her hands over her mouth. No—this couldn't be. Quon had never heard of such a thing. Killings, yes, of course, one or two at a time, but not this!

The captain looked at his watch, stepped aside, leaned against the wall, and observed, as if guessing who would be left for him to execute.

Ling Ho and Mei came forward and joined Chou Jin on the right side of their home.

"Will they really kill us?" Ming whispered feebly.

"I...think so," Quon said.

Eng Lok, eyes down, walked out the door, his wife two steps behind.

"Two minutes," Scarbrow said with a machine's voice. Clearly this man knew what he was going to do. The only question was, what would the people do?

Quon looked toward the right.

"We must not let Shen die," Ming whispered.

"He is Jidu's gift to us," Quon said. "No, not a gift, a loan. God is his father. He will care for him."

"We must not lose our only son."

"God lost His only Son. He buried His Son in a foreign land."

"I am willing to die," Ming said, voice cracking, "but I cannot bear to think of them killing Shen. Still...perhaps it is the Lord's mercy for us to die together."

"I've always thought I might end like my father and great-grandfather… but not you, not Shen." Yes, he'd dreamed of holding Ming's dying body, but he hadn't really believed it would happen. Quon covered his face with his hands. He felt a small strong grip on his arm.

"Are we not Zhu Jidu's also? Are we not His called and chosen? Why should we not walk the way He has chosen for you? Why should you be considered worthy and not us?"

It had always been this way. Whenever she weakened, he was strong for her. Whenever he weakened, she was strong for him. He leaned over Shen and put his arms around Ming. Then Quon got down on one knee in front of his only son.

"Do you understand what the captain said, Shen?" The child nodded his head slowly, eyes puffy.

"Will you come with us and follow Zhu Jidu?"

He nodded again, face pinched and wet.

Quon started to pick Shen up, but instead held his hand and let him walk beside him.

Wordlessly, the three turned their backs on the door and walked to those standing on the right.

"Sixty seconds," Scarbrow called.

Three families, including three children, joined Quon and the others. Five people stood in the middle of the room, starting to move one way and then the other, as if in the center of a tug-of-war. Quon prayed hard for his three neighbors standing there—Fu Gan, Chun, and their teenage daughter Yuet.

"This is your final chance. Leave now or die!"

A woman he didn't recognize headed for the door, followed by a man. Suddenly the three neighbors walked briskly, young Yuet leading the way. They embraced Quon and Ming, holding tightly. Quon rejoiced. When the three had come to Yesu in their home only weeks before, he hadn't dreamed they would die together in church.

He counted. Eighteen people remained. Five had walked out. One last man stood inside the door, glancing back, as if looking for a third alternative. Scarbrow pointed his weapon at the man, who turned and fled out the door into the cold darkness.

One of the police stepped outside, weapon pointed, looking around. Reentering, he shut the door and locked it. Quon, Ming, and Shen clasped each other's hands. Quon breathed deeply and braced himself.

Scarbrow stepped over to Chou Jin and Quon. He put one hand on each of their shoulders. His face trembled. He dropped his weapon.

"Forgive us, brothers. I am Fu Chi. We have come from AnNing village, across the mountain. We are followers of Zhu Jidu. God is doing mighty things among us. We have much to tell you. But we dared not put you at risk...or our brothers and families at home. Registered and house churches alike are betrayed by spies. We had to drive away the infiltrators. Now you know who they are. You can trust each other. We salute you. For you are the overcomers—more loyal to the King than to your own lives."

Quon stared blankly as his executioner embraced him. He felt the man's powerful torso quiver. Scarbrow, now Fu Chi, knelt and faced little Shen, hands upon his shoulders.

"Forgive us, brave one," he whispered to Shen. "We knew no other way."

Among the eighteen, confusion slowly dissolved into cautious smiles. At Chou Jin's beckoning, the younger uniformed men, heads hung, joined them. Quon knelt down to Shen, Ming alongside. He pressed his face against theirs and felt their hot tears mingle with his.

Chou Jin sang, "Zhu Yesu Jidu, we praise Your name forever." Scarbrow's strong baritone rose. Other voices joined them.

Is this the day?

No. But it would come, Quon knew, whether at gunpoint, at work, or at home in the ease of bed. His day would come.

Quon lifted Shen into his embrace. He gazed into his brown eyes, seeing his reflection in them. But he also saw someone else looking back, eyes he'd last seen behind the holes of a mask.

Quon's insides felt as if hot tea were thawing them. He believed for the first time that when his day came, he would be ready. Then on the other side, in his true home, he would see again the face of the father he yearned to embrace, no longer hidden behind the mask. He would see his father's real face and look into those joy-filled eyes. And he would see another face, the face of one who died for him...and for whom he knew at last he was willing to die.

Quon heard a voice. He turned his head to search for it. He saw only Ming and Shen and the followers of Zhu Yesu.

The voice had said, "Well done, my son."

For the first time in many years, Li Quon—not forcing it—smiled broadly...without fear and without shame.

ABOUT THE AUTHOR

Randy Alcorn is the director of Eternal Perspective Ministries (EPM). A pastor for fourteen years before founding EPM, Randy is a popular teacher and conference speaker. He's spoken in many countries and has been interviewed on over 300 radio and television programs. He's the author of twelve books, including the bestselling novels *Deadline, Dominion, Edge of Eternity,* and *Lord Foulgrin's Letters.* Randy lives in Gresham, Oregon, with his wife Nanci and daughters Karina and Angela.

Saturday Night in the Korca Gym

Neta Jackson

Margo White dribbled the ball in a zigzag pattern toward the goal, taking her time. "Focus! Focus!" Her college coach's drills replayed in her mind like the Albanian language tapes she listened to every day. She focused, shutting out the commotion along the sidelines of the gym until the only sounds she heard were the thudding of the basketball and the soft squeaking of her athletic shoes on the old wooden floor.

She picked up the pace...pulled up, faked a pass...then in two quick steps drove all the way to the board—two points. Her mind's eye saw the crowd leap to its feet. *"Mar-go! Mar-go! Mar-go!"*

"Margo! Give me a hand, will you?"

Lida's voice cut into Margo's solitary replay of that last championship game at Lincoln State University. With a quick glance to see where the ball rolled off to, Margo trotted over to her Albanian teammate, who was struggling with a flimsy ladder. Half the gym floor was already covered with mattresses, and Berti and Petrit, the other two members of their team, were dragging in stacks more. At the other end of the gym, a gaggle of middle-aged ladies—the welcoming committee of Korca's consortium of churches—fussed over a long row of tables holding big pots of coffee and lemonade and trays of sandwiches. Stacks of blankets lined one wall. Everything looked almost ready for their "visitors," as Margo had dubbed the expected busloads of travelers.

Question was, was *she* ready?

"Just stick to the game plan!" said the voice in Margo's head. Right. She grabbed the other side of the unwieldy ladder, and together the two young women got it resting more or less upright against the wall of the gymnasium. Lida—her dark hair, pale skin, and bony shoulders a strong contrast to Margo's sturdy Midwestern build and flushed complexion—pointed upward. "Found another broken window. Your turn to go up."

Margo rolled her eyes. That made five broken windows so far! But tonight, getting the gymnasium ready for overnight visitors was the game, and fixing broken windows was her play. She grabbed a hammer and a couple nails from the tin can, picked out a scrap of plywood that looked about the right size from the pile against the wall, and gingerly made her way up the wobbly ladder.

At least the ten minutes of exercise had sent blood rushing through her cold hands and feet—the temperature inside the cavernous gym seemed little different from the chilly March evening outside—and it had felt good to handle a basketball again. It wasn't *that* long ago that she had played point guard on the women's basketball team at Lincoln State. After a couple offers, her coach had encouraged her to consider turning pro or maybe go into coaching after graduation. But she'd chosen Albania instead, and there was no turning back now.

Margo reached through the rungs of the ladder, positioned the plywood scrap against the broken window, and tried to hold it in place with her left forearm. Why did so many things in Albania seem old, broken, or barely functioning? It had definitely been culture shock to leave her typical Midwestern surroundings and land on the campus of the University of Korca as part of an overseas Christian campus ministry. Albania had only recently reemerged on the world map after decades of isolation under Communism's grip, and everything from the pothole-pocked highways to decrepit buses to basic Bible knowledge suffered sadly from neglect. Why, even the *practice* gym back at Lincoln State was a palace compared to this dump. And this building was the main sports gymnasium in Korca!

The ladder swayed menacingly as Margo tried to pound in an uncooperative nail. "Lida!" she squeaked, grabbing a ladder rung with her hammer hand. "Hold the ladder!"

"Sorry. Thought I heard the buses."

Margo caught her breath and listened. The sound of a heavy vehicle passed the gym and faded. She let out her breath slowly. *"Jo,"* she said brightly. "Besides, they're not due till *nëntë*."

"But it's *nëntë* now!" Lida's voice was high-pitched, anxious. "It's been dark for an hour."

"Lida! Just hold the ladder. It's going to be fine."

It *was* going to be fine, Margo assured herself. After all, as a college basketball player, she'd been conditioned to be prepared for every eventuality. "Practice! Practice! Practice!" her coach had drilled into the team. And even though a campus ministry in Albania was like being on the road rather than on her home court, at least she'd had experience with Bible studies in her dorm, leading Sunday night services in nursing homes, and she'd even served meals to the homeless. All good practice for missions.

Of course, tonight their team was being asked to do a whole new play, and it was hard to know what to expect. Still, they had a game plan—get the gym ready as temporary housing, and make the visitors as comfortable as possible, then look for opportunities to share the gospel. A big job, sure, but all the Christian groups in Korca were working together to reach out to their fellow Albanians from the north. That in itself was a good thing. At least she didn't have to make coffee.

With the ladder steady once more, Margo took aim with the hammer and drove the last nail through the plywood into the worn window frame. A chilly draft still snuck through along the edges, but, well, it was better than before.

Berti and Petrit dropped their last stack of mattresses beside Lida just as Margo backed down the ladder. Petrit flopped on the mattresses with a weary groan. "Did you girls hear? They now think it's going to be *dymbëdhjetë* before the buses arrive."

Midnight! Margo shivered. Three more hours to hang around?

Berti, the older of the two young men, eyed the boarded-up window. "Good job. Maybe by the time they arrive it'll be fifteen degrees in here instead of five."

Margo screwed up her nose and quickly tried to translate Celsius into Fahrenheit. "Oh, hooray," she snorted. Guess sixty degrees *was* better than forty, but not much. Leave it to Berti to see the bright side. But that was the quality Margo loved most in the campus ministry leader. Berti's encouraging words had helped Margo weather bouts of homesickness, frustration with learning the Albanian language, and discouragement at the spiritual indifference of many university students, who'd been raised on atheism. He reminded her of her college basketball coach, who never let a setback affect the team's all-out efforts to reach their goal.

Except this was the game of life, and the goal was to win Albania for Christ, starting with Albania's future leaders on college campuses in Prishtina, Korca, and other major cities. And they *were* inching toward the goal, "one basket at a time," as her coach used to say. After all, there was Lida, who was shy but eager to share her newfound excitement about Jesus with students; and Petrit, the newest Christian and youngest member of the team, only twenty. His odd sense of humor kept them laughing and attracted a lot of students whose stereotype of Christianity was the somber Orthodox priests in their ceremonial robes who had been allowed to function as Communism's nod to religion. And the four of them were leading several Bible studies on campus, and the girls in Margo's study were asking a lot of thoughtful questions. So Margo *was* encouraged.

No, she didn't regret choosing missions in Albania over a career in basketball. Still, this *was* a gymnasium, and it was too cold just to sit around.

"Hey, as long as the buses are going to be late, let's play some hoops." She pulled Petrit to his feet. "Whaddya say? *Vajzat kunder djemve?*" Girls against guys. She laughed.

"Uh-oh, watch out. Miss Chicago Bulls T-shirt thinks only Americans can play basketball." Lanky Petrit struck a ludicrous "muscle" pose. "Has she forgotten Toni Kukoc is from Croatia? Does she know that under this skinny disguise lurks his high flying cousin?"

"*Really* lurking," Margo said dryly. She laughed and ran over to rescue the basketball from obscurity under a table of first-aid supplies, soap, and toothbrushes donated from local shops. "Tell you what, Petrit," she called back. "If you win, I'll let you...um, wear my Chicago Bulls T-shirt for one whole day."

"Ha. I thought we'd have to bury you in that thing when you're eighty-five."

Lida frowned, as if playing ball under the present circumstances was like fiddling while Rome burned. "What about the rest of the mattresses?"

Margo dribbled the ball back to the little group. "We've got three hours to kill, remember? It'll take all of ten minutes to put them down later if we all pitch in. Besides, we need a *little* floor space." She pitched the ball to Berti. "You in? Play to fifty?"

Berti grinned. "Why not?" He grabbed Petrit by the sweatshirt and went into a huddle. Margo did likewise with Lida.

"But Margo," Lida protested, shivering, "I'm not that good at basketball. And shouldn't we pray or something? I mean, what if the buses have run out of *benzinë?*"

Margo felt a stab of impatience. Lida worried too much. But she had a point. "Pray. Absolutely. We will. But, Lida, we're all going to go crazy just waiting unless we do something to take our minds off whatever is delaying them. Come on. Playing a little ball will warm you up. Okay?"

Lida nodded reluctantly.

"All right. Now, don't worry about shooting the ball. You just guard Petrit, try to keep the ball away from him. And don't let *him* shoot. If you get the ball, just pass it to me, I'll move in for the basket. Got it?"

The two miniteams broke. Margo snatched the ball out of Berti's hands and tossed it to Lida as she grinned at him. "Ladies first, right?" He rolled his eyes.

Lida passed the ball in to Margo, who dodged Berti, danced the ball around Petrit, and shot a clean basket.

The older women at the far end of the gym whooped and clapped, which brought a laugh from Lida who yelled, "Go, Margo!"

The four friends played hard. Petrit and Berti were better than Margo had expected, and the score leapfrogged, nip and tuck, but Margo sank the last basket to make fifty points.

Laughing and sweating, they all fell out on the bare mattresses. "Guess I get to keep my shirt!" Margo panted.

Petrit wrinkled his nose. "It's all sweaty now, anyway."

"What time is it?" Berti groaned, spread-eagle on his back.

Lida squinted at her watch. "Um...eleven-fifteen."

Berti pulled himself up to a sitting position. "Guess we better put out the rest of these mattresses. Then let's pray those buses in. Where's the rest of the welcoming committee?"

Petrit jerked a weary thumb at the other end of the gym. The coffee-and-sandwich ladies were nodding off on thin folding chairs sprinkled here and there around their tables.

As Margo had predicted, it only took ten minutes to spread out the rest of the mattresses. She wondered vaguely whether they had too many...or not enough. No one had told them how many were coming.

Maybe no one knew.

Word must have gotten around about the new time of arrival, because several other folks from the Korçe churches were wandering in to be part of the midnight welcoming committee. Margo saw Berti talking to a couple of men—probably local pastors—and soon the welcoming committee had become a prayer meeting at the coffee end of the gym. Lida pulled her down on the floor, and Margo sat, hugging her legs and resting her forehead on her knees.

First one, then another prayed out loud, an undercurrent of murmurs from around the circle riding beneath their voices. Margo's stomach growled—hadn't she earned a couple of those sandwiches?—but she tried to ignore it. She could understand most of what was being said in Albanian—prayers for safety, for servant hearts, for an end to hostilities—but she was a little surprised by the growing intensity. One woman's voice was almost keening, like a grieving mother. Margo raised her head to see who it was. It was one of the coffee ladies, head thrown back, tears pouring down her square, mannish face as she prayed for "justice for the crimes committed against our people!"

Margo squirmed. She hoped they weren't going to get political here. That was out of her league. Albania was a mess, that much she knew. The country was just recovering from months of anarchy and economic instability, and now ethnic hostilities between Serbs and Albanians in Kosovo to the north was creating a flood of refugees across Albania's borders.

Refugees on buses, heading to Korca.

Margo suddenly felt short of breath. *Refugees*...the word provoked images in her mind of naked Sudanese children with bony ribcages and extended bellies or boatloads of desperate Cambodians adrift in the Pacific. Surely the word was too strong.

It was easier to think of the coming busloads as "visitors" to Korca, who needed some temporary food and shelter. They *were* Albanians, after all. This was their home country. They spoke the language. They would be welcome. And her mission was to share the gospel with Albanians. That was the game plan.

She began to breathe easier. Yes, this she could do. Keep focused. Stick to the game plan. She even took a turn praying aloud that the hearts of their visitors would be open to the gospel and felt comforted at the familiar words.

The prayers continued. Margo glanced at her watch. Twelve-thirty, and still no buses!

At one o'clock, the prayer meeting ended, and people stood around talking quietly in anxious voices. Where were the buses?

No one dared leave for fear the welcoming committee wouldn't be there when the buses did arrive. But Margo could hardly keep her eyes open any longer. She followed Lida and Petrit's example and flopped down on one of the bare mattresses, pulling herself up into a cocoon inside her zippered sweat jacket and trying not to think about her empty stomach.

A hand shook Margo awake. "They're here," said Berti quietly.

Dragging herself to her feet, Margo stumbled after her teammates, who were heading for the parking lot outside the gym along with the rest of the welcoming committee. She could hardly focus her eyes, but gradually the face on her watch came into view.

Four o'clock.

Groggily, Margo joined the others outside the gym, hunching her shoulders against the early hour's damp cold. The first bus had pulled in—a city bus pressed into cross-country duty—and another was right behind it. Margo quickly calculated. How many people on a bus? Forty? Times two...eighty people. Well, that was a lot but they had plenty of food and mattresses for eighty.

And then another bus pulled into the lot...and another... and another.

The doors of the first bus opened, and a man in a blue windbreaker got out, turned, and began helping people down the steps. A little boy, his eyes huge and frightened, clung to the hand of an old woman. A mother with a baby. Several teenagers, one holding the hand of a child about three. Two young women about Margo's age, their arms around each other, one of whom was weeping. The people kept coming off the first bus and the second. Some clutched small suitcases or duffle bags with Adidas or Nike in leaping letters across the side; others were empty-handed.

Berti and some of the pastors began shepherding the people inside. Margo stood rooted to her spot. Her first impression of the people getting off the bus was that they looked so...so normal. So ordinary. Polo shirts and Nike athletic shoes. Sweatshirts and windbreakers. Jeans and rumpled khaki pants. Sweater vests and turtlenecks. Like any crowd getting off a bus to see some sports event.

Her second impression was that they looked anything *but* normal.

Exhaustion etched every face. Dark circles framed their eyes. There were no smiles or greetings. Dirty streaks on nearly every child's face betrayed both tears and the lack of a washcloth. The hair of both men and women was lank, greasy, unwashed for how many days? And the smell of old sweat and unwashed clothes clung to them as they passed, cattlelike, through the double doors into the gym.

But it was the eyes of both young and old that troubled Margo the most. Guarded. Frightened. Alone. Almost unaware of their surroundings, yet seeing something, something they had seen and couldn't forget.

And still the buses pulled off the road into the parking lot until Margo lost count.

She knew she should go inside. But she wasn't prepared. Not for this. There had been no way to practice for this. It wasn't just an unfamiliar defensive play. It was a different game altogether! As though she had suited up for basketball, but had been asked to play quarterback in men's football.

"Margo?" It was Berti's quiet voice. "We need you *brenda.*" He jerked a thumb inside.

She found her voice. "But there's too many. Look, the buses are still coming." Still more headlights crawled along the road.

"I know. Just find one family. One family. Help them get settled."

Another bus had pulled up near the gym. The driver and one of the Korca pastors were trying to help an old woman get off, but she was resisting their efforts, fiercely holding to the edge of the bus door and shrieking, "*Jo! Jo!* I don't want to get off! I saw the cross! They'll kill us! Kill us!"

Margo turned bewildered eyes to Berti. "What does she mean? The big cross on the Orthodox church coming into Korca? Why is she afraid?"

Berti steered Margo back into the gymnasium. "She is Muslim." He waved a hand at the dozens of bus passengers already wolfing down sandwiches and dropping their bundles on the bare mattresses. "Most of these Albanians are Muslim. The Serbs who are driving them out of Kosovo are supposedly Christian. Muslim versus Orthodox in decades of bitter conflict over land in Kosovo. Unfortunately in the Balkans, 'religion' is more often an excuse for ethnic hostilities than genuine faith in a reconciling

God." The team leader pushed Margo toward a small group huddled uncertainly against the wall of the gymnasium. "Now go, Margo—there's a family who can use your help." Berti turned and disappeared back outside, where yet another bus was pulling into the parking lot.

Margo walked slowly over to the little group. A hollow-eyed woman in a red pullover sweater clutched a wailing infant in her arms. A little girl around eight years old, dressed in jeans and a Barbie T-shirt, pressed close to her side. Beside the sagging mother and exhausted children stood a dark-haired man, unshaven, his arm around another young woman, probably in her twenties, who was crying silently into his rumpled shirt.

"*Tungjateta.* My—my name is Margo," she blurted, hoping they understood Toskerisht, the dialect common in southern Albania. "*Si e ke?*"

"My name? Shemsi," said the man grimly. "These are my sisters, Bukurie and"—he nodded at the woman with the screaming baby—"Adelina. And Adelina's children, Arianit and Jetmika."

The dialect was different, but with relief Margo realized she was able to understand the basic Albanian words. But if this Shemci was the brother, where was the woman's husband? She looked around. "Are there others in your family you are waiting for?"

At Margo's words, the young woman's shoulders shook even more violently against the man's chest.

When Shemsi spoke again, his voice was flat, heavy. "Adelina's husband—he disappeared before we left Kosovo. And our *baba*..." The muscles worked in Shemci's jaw as he mentioned his father. "He was shot by Serbian soldiers because he did not want to give up his passport. They would not let us stop to bury him."

Margo had been about to say, "Would you like something to eat? Some *kafe?*" but she was suddenly speechless. Sandwiches and coffee seemed utterly irrelevant in the next sentence after "disappeared" and "shot." But she had to say something, *do* something.

"Let's...let's find a couple mattresses for you before they all get taken," she finally managed. On impulse she held her hand out to the little girl. "Would you like to help me lead the way, Jetmika?"

The little girl hung her head but placed her hand in Margo's and let herself be led among the long rows of mattresses until they came to two empty ones together.

"Is this all right?" she asked the child's mother, pushing the mattresses together. "You can put your *bagazh* here."

The family group just stood there. And then Margo realized: *They had no luggage.* Not the man, not his sisters, not the children.

No suitcase. No bags. No purses. No diaper bag for the baby.

No passports. No driver's license. No identification.

Just their names and the clothes on their backs.

Margo wanted to weep. What an utter fool she'd been! As an American she hadn't even been able to imagine what the word *refugee* meant when applied to people who looked like they could be her own brother or sister or father or aunt. She'd thought of them as visitors who needed a little hospitality, and gratefully they'd listen as she shared how they could know Jesus and be saved from their sins.

But how did one share Jesus with a family who had been driven out of their homes, out of their town, out of their country, at the point of a gun, under the sign of the cross?

A tug on the sleeve of her sweat jacket jolted Margo out of her spinning thoughts. It was Adelina. "Please," the woman whispered. "Help me...my baby...see?"

Adelina fumbled with the baby's clothes and began peeling them off. The little romper suit and diaper were utterly soaked and reeked of urine. Margo saw that the little boy's bottom was an angry red and covered with sores, the accumulation of days with no clean clothes, no sanitation, no water for washing.

Again Margo wanted to weep. Water for washing a baby's bottom. How much she took for granted, even here in dilapidated Albania!

Water. Well, at least that was something she could do. She went in search of the washbasins donated by the churches of Korca, and then stood in line for fifteen minutes at the women's lavatory to get water. By now the gymnasium was overflowing with traumatized refugees, and she could hear some of the men on the welcoming committee shouting to one another outside about diverting the remaining buses to the nearby soccer stadium and other emergency shelters. The number of refugees rolling into Korca on this night alone must be into the thousands by now. Thousands of refugees multiplied by thousands of basic human needs.

Margo threaded her way back to where she'd left Adelina and her family, careful not to spill the basin of water. She couldn't think thousands. She had to focus: one family, one baby, one basin of water to wash up a baby's bottom. Hadn't her coach taught her to ignore the thousands of yelling fans or opposition in the stands and just focus on the play? And hadn't Jesus said that even giving a cup of cold water was worthy of God's favor? And that if we welcome even a little child in His name, we welcome Christ Himself?

Well, it was *warm* water, and more than a cup, but this was the next play for Margo White, former basketball player, campus missionary. She almost giggled as she set the basin down on the small space of floor between Adelina's family and the next crowded mattress. Standing in the line at the restroom she had already anticipated the next two small crises: No washcloth. No diaper. But her mind was focused now: give Jesus what she had—just like the boy who gave Jesus his five loaves of bread and two fish—and let Jesus take care of the five thousand.

She bent down, pulled off one of her Nikes, and handed Adelina her sock. "It was clean yesterday," she shrugged hopefully. A slight smile softened Adelina's face for a brief moment as she took the sock and wrung it out in the basin of water.

As Adelina gently washed the baby's angry bottom with her sock, Margo pulled the T-shirt she'd taken off in the lavatory from the pocket of her now zippered-up sweat jacket and held up the Chicago Bulls logo for Jetmika to see. "Do you know what this is, Jetmika?"

The little girl's tear-streaked face lit up in recognition. "Michael Jordan shirt!"

Margo smiled. "*Jo.* Not anymore. It's a diaper."

ABOUT THE AUTHOR

Neta Jackson and her husband Dave are the authors of the Trailblazer series of historical fiction (Bethany House Publishers), introducing young people to great heroes of the faith. Neta (pronounced "Nita") got the idea for the above piece from stories told by her niece Tammy Thiessen, a Campus Crusade missionary in Albania who was among the many Christians who helped receive the Kosovo refugees in March 1999. Although based on true events, all the characters are fictional.

HEARTSTRINGS

Liz Curtis Higgs

No time to break jests when the heartstrings are about to be broken.

THOMAS FULLER

Her father had already broken her heart twice this week. Could he manage to keep from doing so tonight?

Not a chance.

Nellie MacDonald sighed in resignation, staring out her bedroom window at the bright blue Canadian sky. A sunlit breeze, fragrant with pine and saltwater, teased a dozen fine tendrils of hair loose from the ponytail that tickled the back of her bare neck. Distracted, she hummed a slow air she'd been trying to master, then picked up the bow of her fiddle to keep her hands busy and her mind off the hours ahead.

It wasn't that her father didn't love her. Benjamin MacDonald loved her with a fierce and dogged loyalty that would do his Highland ancestors proud.

No, love wasn't the problem. It was his ability to say the worst possible thing at the worst possible time—*that* was what did her in. As if he didn't care that he hurt her. As if the desires of her heart didn't matter to him in the least.

She skimmed a paper-thin coat of fresh rosin along her bow with a practiced hand, remembering their unhappy parting last Friday when she was heading out to play for a step-dance competition in Port Hood.

It had been about seven o'clock, the evening air freshly windswept by a late June rainstorm. She'd already pushed open the rough-planked back door when her father lowered his newspaper and raised his eyebrows, clearing his throat in obvious disapproval.

"Another night thrown away for a song, I suppose?"

She shrugged, not wanting to have another lengthy discussion of her plans for the future. Especially since those plans were more or less nonexistent at the moment.

"You realize, young lady"—how she hated when he said that—"instead of fiddling away your weekends with Robbie and Doug, you could be earning serious money for college up at Glenora Inn."

"Waiting tables, then?" She fought the sarcastic note that threatened to creep into her voice, holding back the tears that waited in the wings whenever confronted by her father. "Would you have me cleaning rooms, Papa? Ringing up gifts for the tourists?"

His slate blue eyes narrowed. "It's honest work."

"Yes, it is," she agreed, pressing the door open farther. "Hard work, too. So is playing five sets of hornpipes and jigs."

Her father's *harrumph!* followed her down the walk.

She'd driven south to Port Hood bearing the weight of his disappointment. But her spirits were buoyed by the sanguine company she kept that evening—two classmates, newly graduated as she was and equally enamored with Cape Breton fiddle music. Unlike her, neither young man carried an ounce of regret on his handsome shoulders.

Robbie Beaton's parents were pleased beyond measure that their son was so proficient at piano. And Doug MacNeil never played his guitar in public that one of his family members didn't drop by to add his applause.

But Ben MacDonald praising his daughter's skills on the fiddle?

Never.

Not from her first go at "Johnny Cope" on a poorly-tuned fiddle borrowed from her cousin Danny, to her fine showing at Broad Cove last July.

He cared for her health, her father often said, but not for her "hobbies." *And not for my happiness, Papa.*

Saturday evening when she'd been bound for a *ceilidh* in Creignish, it was more of the same. "Mind the traffic on Route 19," he'd cautioned. "Tourists are everywhere, flying toward the causeway like bats set loose from a belfry."

She'd frowned as she closed the door behind her. His words had reminded her of something Grandpa Neil might have said—archaic and highly picturesque. But the tone wasn't Grandpa's. No, the tone belonged to her father, gruff and scolding, warning of imminent danger as she'd embarked on another night of doing what he hated most and she loved best.

Tonight would no doubt be a repeat performance for both of them.

Opening her fiddle case, Nellie lifted the worn instrument to her left shoulder and caught a glimpse of herself in her dresser mirror, now brightly lit by the midsummer sun. In spite of it all, she grinned as she tucked the fiddle beneath her cheek. The instrument was an old beauty, handmade by a man in Glace Bay, a more-than-welcome friend at any hour. With a steadying breath and a wink at her reflection, she drew the bow lightly across the strings.

The tuning would do, she decided. What song might chase away her melancholy mood? Grandpa MacDonald's favorite reel, of course: "Captain Keeler."

Nellie struck the first note like a match, certain she heard Robbie's spirited keyboard keeping time in the background and Doug's melodic guitar spilling all around her. Fueled by her undeniable frustration with her father, she attacked the strings until the fiddle was on fire, heating the already warm air with a furious, cut-time rhythm.

On and on the tune burned, picking up speed until the very last note. Finishing with a full-bow flourish, she curtsied to herself in the mirror and laughed out loud. "Young lady, you are making a spectacle of yourself!" She waved her bow playfully at the blue-eyed image, wrinkling her freckled nose in a fair imitation of her Grandpa Neil's larger version. "Is that any way for a good Christian girl to behave?"

"My thoughts exactly."

Nellie whirled around. "Papa!"

Three words and she was reduced to an ill-behaved child, her cheeks warm from the condemnation etched in her father's tightly drawn face.

After an awkward moment, he took a deliberate step inside her room. "So. Is there any way I might convince you not to play again tonight?"

"No," she murmured, knowing what it would cost her. "I *have* to play, Papa. I was..." She swallowed a lump that threatened to pinch off her air supply. "I was hoping...*you* might be there. This time."

His expression softened. Not much, but some. "At the church, you mean?"

She nodded, surprised she'd gotten that far with him, that he hadn't shot her down at the mere mention of the ecumenical service that kicked off the annual Mabou Ceilidh.

He looked at her for what seemed like ages, then lifted his shoulders slightly. "I might be able to come. What are you playing?"

"Two hymns." She offered a shaky smile and added quickly, "'Faith of Our Fathers' and—"

"Let me guess." His features were hardening again.

He would guess correctly. It was the first hymn her grandfather had taught her note-for-note more than a decade ago.

Her father grimaced. "'Lord Jesus, of You I Will Sing,' isn't it?" He practically spat out the words, as if they left a bitter taste in his mouth. "No surprise there." He took another step toward her. This one scared her a little. "If you had your way, Nellie, it'd be your Grandfather MacDonald there tonight to hear you and not your own father. Am I right?"

Her mouth dropped open. "No, Papa!" But the words came one beat late. Her too honest face had already given her away.

It was true. Painfully, shamefully true. Her grandfather had only been gone a year, every day of which she'd spent wishing he were still with her in Mabou. And secretly—*oh, so secretly*—wishing that her father were the one buried at the Hillsborough United Church Cemetery.

She'd rather see me dead.

Ben MacDonald's stomach clenched in a tight knot. There was no denying it; her emotions were scattered all over her wide-eyed face.

You deserve this.

He fought the truth, nearly grinding his teeth to keep from telling her how much she'd hurt him. No father deserved such shoddy treatment from his only child. Now that Grandpa was gone, he was all she had. Didn't she know that?

And she is all you have, Ben.

Another truth, more painful than the last. Except it wasn't Nellie that was the problem, it was her blasted *fiddle!* Most fathers were worried about chasing off beaus. For him, there was only one bow he wanted to snap in two.

Judging by the expression on Nellie's face, it was her heart he'd succeeded in breaking. Again.

Say something, Ben.

"Nellie, I'm sorry that I said...what I said." It wasn't much of an apology, but it was a start. He held up his hands. "Listen, I'll do my best to be there this evening, but I can't promise, d'you hear?"

"I hear." Her sigh was practically a song itself.

"See you at supper. I'm cooking, so it won't be much." He hurried his words, turning away to escape her silent plea for his approval. How well he knew that look. Hadn't his own face worn a similar one the first twenty years of his life?

Only twenty, was it? He shook his head as his feet carried him down the wooden staircase. No, it was every one of his forty-four years, right up until he'd buried his father last May. Even then...even *then* he'd stared down into the yawning grave, aching to hear the much-needed words: "I'm proud of you, son."

Neil MacDonald had that effect on people.

The senior MacDonald's high expectations and low tolerance for mediocrity had driven away both of Ben's sisters. Soon after college, Ginny and Pat gave up trying to please the old man and left the island for good. Many a MacDonald appeared in the Inverness County phone book, but this particular branch of the tree had been whittled down to a mere stub.

And that was the heart of the problem. Grandpa Neil had wanted a quiver full of grandchildren. Ben and his ex-wife, Sandy, had produced one. A fine one, to be sure, but only one.

"My namesake, Miss Nell MacDonald, will be the finest fiddler on the island," the old man had announced from the time she could walk. Although by age four her hands were still barely big enough to stretch around the fingerboard, Nellie took to music like a sail embracing the wind off St. Georges Bay.

Her Grandfather Neil, beaming with pride, took full credit for every note.

Ben wandered into the kitchen, hoping to find something to drink, and discovered a fresh pitcher of lemonade waiting for him in the fridge. *Nellie.* Feeling more than a bit guilty, he filled an icy glassful and gulped down the drink in one turn, then went back for a second.

Above the sink their kitchen clock—notoriously slow—inched

toward three. "Cape Breton time," Nellie called it. Ben smiled at that, putting his glass aside to stroll out onto the wooden porch that stretched across the front of the clapboard house.

The western highlands, covered with white spruce and carpeted with moss and ferns, rose behind him and fell with a sharp, craggy drop into the Mabou River and the harbor beyond it. Ben shaded his eyes and scanned the bright skies, full of seabirds but nary an eagle at the moment.

Unlike Sandy, he could never leave this place. The ancient granite hills were woven into the fiber of his soul. Two centuries ago the MacDonalds had come over the sea from Lochaber and settled in "new Scotland"—Nova Scotia. This was home.

But will it be home for Nellie?

Pulled forward by the perfect weather, he walked across the lawn edged with the wildflowers of summer, then stopped to gaze up at his daughter's bedroom window. She was playing again, the notes flowing from her fiddle like the water over Glenora Falls.

Ben dragged a hand across his rough jaw, reminding himself that a shave would be in order if he intended to go anywhere this evening.

If. He shook his head, disgusted with himself.

What bothered him the most? That her talent would take her beyond Cape Breton's shores, beyond his reach? Or was the problem that she'd taken to the fiddle so easily from the start, shaming his own meager childhood efforts?

Nellie couldn't know—no one did—the pure agony he'd felt when his father had stood behind him nearly forty years ago, one hand helping him finger the notes, the other hand resting on his bow.

"Like this, Benjamin." They would play a few tortured notes together, his father's foot tapping out the rhythm. "Come along, son, you can do it," the older MacDonald urged, as if he could will it so. "You're not applying yourself. Now try again."

Ben had tried again. And again. The gift simply wasn't there, not in his hands and not in his heart, no matter how many kitchen sessions he sat through. The informal gatherings started after supper and lasted until Lyra's harp hung high in the Maritimes sky. His mother played piano accompaniment while her husband enthralled the neighbors with one fiddle tune after another.

There would be stories swapped as well, tales from a bygone day kept alive with the telling. And serious discussions about bowing styles and fingering techniques, the history of certain tunes, where so-and-so had first heard it played and by whom.

When the timing was right, a dancer might take to the floor, his upper body relaxed, arms by his side, with all the movement below the knees, the feet barely lifting off the floor, so swift and subtle was the footwork.

Step dancing appealed to Ben, though he never had the nerve to move forward when the floor was open. If he couldn't fiddle like his dad, he'd just sit and listen, he decided.

His father always brought their house sessions to a close. "Here's a fine strathspey from the Old Country," he'd say with a deep measure of respect. Like all Cape Bretoners of Scottish descent, Neil MacDonald held a fond regard for his ancestors and their music. The greatest compliment anyone ever gave his father after a set was: "He's full of the Gaelic."

And he, Ben, was not. The musical genes had skipped a generation, leaving him the odd man out.

"Aren't you the lucky one, Ben?"

Startled, he spun around to find a neighbor, Janet Beaton, standing close behind him. Her arms were filled with groceries, her sunburned face with a generous grin.

"That girl of yours has a rare talent." Nodding in the direction of Nellie's window, Janet added, "She's better than her grandfather, and that's saying something."

No, it's saying everything.

Ben smiled faintly and listened as she chattered on about the four-day ceilidh events in town that week. "You're coming to the salmon dinner, I suppose?"

"I suppose." *Atta boy.* Another hedged commitment. The afternoon was thick with them. "I'll tell Nellie you stopped by."

"See you over at the church, eh?" Janet didn't wait for an answer but hefted her groceries higher with a slight grunt then hurried toward her one-story house half a block down the road.

"I'll be there, I guess," he called after her.

Had he answered Janet's question...or his own?

Nellie's hands were trembling.

Not enough to affect her playing, but enough to be noticed. She tightened her grip on the bow and pressed her chin into the fiddle with a fresh dose of determination. So her father wasn't coming, so what? She would not let it dampen the joy of playing one tiny bit.

The pews were full. Locals, mostly, along with a spotty mix of tourists. The Mabou-Hillsborough United Church sanctuary was more than a century old, its octagonal spire pointing heavenward, the rolled mouldings around the doors reminiscent of a ship's keel. And why not, with Mabou Harbour down the way?

Long, slanting rays poured through three narrow windows facing west, basking the worshipers with a luminous sort of glow. Clergy from three Mabou congregations hovered in the back of the church, waiting their turn. She was to begin playing the first hymn as they came forward for the official welcome and the opening prayer. A simple enough service on this relaxed summer evening.

Scanning the crowd for friends, she soon spied Robbie and Doug in the last pew, already making faces at her. *Grow up!* she wanted to say, quickly followed by the truth: *Please don't.*

Adulthood was upon them all, and a heavy burden it was. Come fall, all three would go to UCCB in Sydney. Not too far away—one hundred-fifty kilometers by car, a good deal less for seabirds—but far enough to be her own person. A new life apart from the father who didn't understand her, yet knew how to wound her deeply, not sacrificing one hour away from his sacred newspaper and television to come and hear her play.

Her grandfather was sure to be there—in spirit and in her heart.

She would make do with that, then.

From the back, Father Angus pointed a finger in her direction. Nellie lifted her bow above the strings, poised to strike the first note. When she looked up for her cue, she drew in a sharp breath instead.

A familiar set of shoulders darkened the vestibule doors.

Papa.

He had come after all.

She swallowed an unexpected lump in her throat and slowly dragged her bow across the strings. Her eyes focused on her instrument, even as a part of her followed the notes to the back of the church, keeping track of the man who settled quietly into a wooden pew.

The assembled crowd sang loudly, if not on pitch nor in unison. "Lord Jesus, of You I will sing as I journey. I'll tell everybody about You wherever I go."

Yes, I will.

As the words of the old hymn washed over her afresh like living water, they infused her playing with renewed passion. "May all of my joy be a faithful reflection of You."

Yes, Lord!

Leaning into the notes with a keen sort of yearning, she filled the four verses with every bit of herself. Her love for God, for her homeland, for the grandfather who'd been proud of her, for the father who had not been so proud, yet loved her nonetheless.

And finally showed up to prove it.

When the last note resounded against the wooden walls, she lowered her bow, spent but satisfied, and quickly found a seat in the nearly empty front pew. Father Angus patted her arm and offered whispered praise while Father Bernie stepped forward to welcome one and all to another year of the Mabou Ceilidh.

The service was short, but blessedly sweet. From time to time she found a reason to gaze over her shoulder toward the back of the room. *Still there.* He hadn't moved when she rose and turned toward the congregation for the closing hymn. He sat a bit straighter, in fact, as if to see her better. The three verses marched quickly by, followed by a solemn recessional to a piper's tune.

While her classmate played, the congregation stood, almost drowning out the bagpipes with their chatter. Nellie slipped out the side door of the church, wanting to collect her thoughts before she saw her father. What would she say to him? "Thanks for coming," sounded lame, but "Did you like my playing?" was just plain dangerous.

From her perch on the side stoop she watched the crowd disperse along the narrow country lane, their cars parked everywhere. Closer to the front door, Janet Beaton's voice carried above the din. "Tell me, Ben MacDonald, are you proud of your little girl now, playing so fine for us this evening?"

Nellie leaned forward, straining to hear his response.

"She played as well as any of a hundred Cape Bretoners, Janet." His tone was flat, hard, and full of bitterness. "It's about time somebody around here realizes there's more to life than playing a fiddle."

"Well!" Janet's voice rose an octave on that. "Peddle that rot somewhere else this week, Ben, or you'll chase the tourists away. No wonder your wife left you. Poor Nellie, having *you* for a father!"

Poor Nellie.

The words cut to the quick.

Through a fine sheen of tears, she watched their irate neighbor stomp off across the grass, clearly no longer interested in the lemonade and cake being served in the annex. Neither, for that matter, was she. Waving a halfhearted good-bye to Robbie and Doug who shrugged and moved toward their cars, Nellie collected her things and ducked around and then back behind the church, grateful for the quiet company of gravestones old and new, nestled among a copse of trees dressed in their leafy summer attire.

Her feet carried her exactly where she needed to go. "Grandpa Neil," she whispered, stopping at his granite marker, choking on her tears. "I miss you…so much."

Sobs shook her body as she leaned on the cold stone, trying to contain her grief and failing miserably. Only a year and already the soil around the headstone was filled in with grass as though it had been decades instead of months.

If her grandfather had been there tonight, if he'd seen her playing with her whole heart, he would have known what she needed to hear; he would have understood what her music meant to her. God gave her this gift, did He not? How could her father dismiss it so easily, as if it meant nothing, as if it was a worthless thing to be tossed aside without a care?

Grateful to be alone with her tears, she felt a tide of righteous anger swell in her. So her father was disappointed in her, was he? Well, she was disappointed in *him*.

In case he hadn't noticed, she was all he had.

And he's all you have, Nell.

The thought sobered her. With Grandpa gone, her father was her only family on the island. Still, he might have at least *smiled* when their eyes met in the sanctuary. He could have sought her out at the end, said a kind word, agreed with Janet Beaton, *something*.

She appraised her silent, stone-faced audience. Well, if her father wouldn't applaud her playing, she knew someone who would. Brushing away a last stubborn tear, Nellie pulled out her fiddle once more and tucked the instrument in place. "For you, Grandpa." *Because I know you'll listen.*

Ben heard the first notes floating over the treetops.

Go to her.

The plaintive hymn wrapped itself around his heart and pulled, hard. "*Lord Jesus, of You I will sing...*" He groaned at the words that echoed in his heart, torn between wanting to leave and wanting to make things right.

Go to her.

But how could he face her now? Bad enough he'd said such a cruel and cutting thing to Janet, not meaning a word of it, but to say nothing to his own daughter after she played so beautifully...

Go to her.

There was no ignoring it, that was certain. He slammed the car door shut and headed for the graveyard knowing right where he'd find her.

She was kneeling by her grandfather's grave, her fiddle lifted up like an offering. Her slim shoulders swayed to the gentle cadence of the hymn as her cinnamon-colored ponytail swung a quarter note behind.

Oh, Nellie...

The sight broke his chastened heart in two.

He quietly made his way around the old, flat stones, not wanting to frighten her, but needing to be closer. Needing to apologize. Needing to tell her she...she was...

"Papa!" Nellie looked up and the music stopped.

He stopped as well. The air between them was thick with unspoken words.

Gazing up at him, her blue eyes transparent with tears, her cheeks stained with a faint blush, her heart in her hands, she waited for him to speak.

His daughter. His Nellie. *My own.*

"Child, I'm..." He struggled to keep his voice even. His heart slammed against his chest. "I'm...you..." Like the fool that he was, he broke down. "Please, Nellie...please...."

She was on her feet in an instant, placing a slender hand on his shoulder. "Papa? What is it?"

"I'm...sorry." He meant it, too. Why was it so hard to say? "I'm sorry I haven't been..." His thoughts escaped him again.

She tugged at his sleeve. "Been what?"

He ground out the words. "The father you needed." There, he'd said it, the awful truth of it.

"But Papa, you're the only father I have."

Ben stared hard at the ground, undone by her tender words. "So I am." He shifted his gaze to the carved headstone. "Still, I never gave you what your grandfather gave you." Clearing his throat, he read the inscription. "Neil MacDonald: May you always be full of the Gaelic."

He looked at his daughter and for an instant, she *was* her grandfather. The proud set of his chin, the piercing eyes, the long, narrow nose. "That's what *you* are, Nellie MacDonald," Ben said, his voice low, weighed down with a lifetime of guilt. "You are full of the Gaelic, just like my father."

In the evening light, her eyes began to shimmer. "Thank you, Papa."

He watched her for a moment; she seemed wise beyond her years, as if she understood what it cost him to admit that. Then he stuffed his hands in his pockets and stared at the gravestone again. "I never pleased him, you know."

Nellie gasped at that, incredulous. "And I've never pleased *you!*"

It was his turn to be shocked. "Of course you...well, I'm very proud of you."

"And...?" She looked unconvinced.

"And I'm proud of your musical talents as well. You're a natural, Nellie." His chest tightened. "You're...everything I wasn't."

"Grandfather loved you, Papa." She stretched up on her toes and kissed his cheek. "Me too."

"That's good." Except it was more than good. It was a miracle, this love from a daughter he didn't deserve.

Ask her. Go on. "Will you play, then?"

"Play my fiddle?" She acted more than a little surprised.

He nodded to assure her. "Please play something...for me."

"For *you?*" She almost laughed, then caught herself. "All right, if you like." She waved her bow at their surroundings. "In such a somber place, better make it a tune like 'Gaelic Lament.'"

Nellie managed three notes before Ben coughed loudly and interrupted her. "I was thinking of something livelier."

"Oh?"

He grinned, feeling weights like boulders roll off his shoulders. "That tune you were playing earlier today at home."

"The reel, you mean? 'Captain Keeler?'" Giggling, she peeked over her shoulder. "Are you sure we *should*, here of all places?"

He glanced at his father's grave. "Here. Of all places."

She needed no more coaxing. Tossing her ponytail back, Nellie tore into the tune with youthful abandon, hardly noticing Ben sliding his hands out of his pockets to let them hang loosely at his side. His body felt the familiar rhythm almost before his feet did. As the music swelled, he lifted one heel, then the other, barely touching the ground as his feet sprouted wings and began to move in a never quite forgotten dance.

ABOUT THE AUTHOR

A storyteller on the platform and in print, Liz Curtis Higgs is the author of fourteen books, including the bestselling novel, *Bookends,* and is a veteran of 1,400 presentations for audiences all over the world. Her love for the lively fiddle music and rich cultural heritage of Cape Breton increased exponentially after a family vacation to Nova Scotia. One trip around the breathtaking Cabot Trail, and the island staked a claim on her heart forever.

Hannah's Home

Athol Dickson

The Lord *does not look at the things man looks at.*
Man looks at the outward appearance,
but the Lord *looks at the heart.*

1 Samuel 16:7

Hannah lost her adoptive father when a drunken driver wandered onto the sidewalk at thirty-eight miles per hour. A street vender's hot dog cart was also crushed. The woman who had adopted Hannah wept and ate nothing for two days. Hannah felt vaguely unhappy, but she did not cry. She could not forget that the dead man had stolen her from home to bring her to that cold and lonely city. The man and the woman had never made a secret of Hannah's place of birth. How could they? Hannah was dark and short and thick, with hair like strands of silken coal and the sloped forehead, long curved nose, and sensuous frowning lips of a Mayan princess. But the man and woman were tall and fair and slender, with pinched noses and thin, smiling lips. Most of the children in Hannah's school were also pale and thin. Of course, they didn't see themselves that way. They saw Hannah as brown and fat. Wherever she went in the man and woman's world, Hannah stood out. They lived on the fifteenth floor of a towering building packed with apartments in a city crowded with ten million people, but Hannah always felt alone. Long before the man died beside the hot dog cart, Hannah had convinced herself that she was the only human being in a world of pale white ghosts.

Two years later, just before Hannah graduated from Myrtle Simms High School, she decided to find her mother, her true mother, the one who gave her birth. The woman who had raised Hannah took this news quietly, with moist eyes and thin lips smiling. For a graduation gift, she gave Hannah an airplane ticket to Mexico, round trip. There were college details still to be settled—the woman had arranged to send Hannah to the university where her husband had studied for the ministry—so it was a week before Hannah set out for the small village high in the Mexican Sierra Madres where her adoptive parents had served as missionaries years before.

When the day came, the woman rode on the bus to the airport with Hannah, kissed her good-bye at the airport gate, and waved until Hannah disappeared down the runway. It was embarrassing. But after traveling for twenty-four hours by jet, bus, and foot, Hannah entered the village of her birth. It clung to its hanging valley, with narrow winding foot paths instead of roads and whitewashed adobe houses and undulating red tile roofs and riotously colorful bougainvillea at every turn. It was glorious.

Everywhere Hannah looked were small and dark and sturdy people, people just like her. Everyone looked Hannah in the eyes and nodded, their soft brown faces warm and welcoming. A dozen children ran up to her, smiling shyly at first, then boldly touching her clothing and skipping around her like tiny planets orbiting the sun. As she wandered along the interwoven paths between the houses, bathed in the tinkling music of their laughter, a feeling settled onto her, growing stronger with each new friendly face, a sense of something she could not define. It was as if she had crossed a bitterly cold wilderness to find a snug little house aglow with warmth. And then, with a bag in each hand, Hannah stepped from the confines of a winding path between rows of stucco houses and saw the broad, cobblestoned plaza in the center of the village, bordered by the *alcalde's* house on her left with its shady portico, the chapel's bell tower high on her right, and the ancient cast-iron gazebo in the center topped by pigeons and ringed with mimosa trees, and all at once she realized what it was that she had been feeling all along:

Home.

The very next morning as she strolled across the plaza, Hannah encountered an elderly priest tending to a small flower bed beside the chapel. Hannah spoke very little Spanish, and the priest very little English, so their communication was rudimentary at best. But his eyes were merry and he seemed to want to try; so Hannah lingered and they spoke as best they could. Miraculously, she learned he was the one who had arranged for her adoption. The priest regretfully informed Hannah that her true mother had died many years before. Hannah felt the horrible ache of her dreams dying. But the priest's face seemed to light up, as if he had only just then remembered something important.

He motioned for her to wait and hurried into the chapel, returning after a few minutes with a slender book in his hands. Handing it to her carefully as if it were a treasure, the priest managed to explain with a few English words and expansive gestures that the book was her mother's diary, left behind when her adoptive parents took Hannah from the village. The old priest had kept it safe all these years, believing Hannah might return some day. When Hannah expressed surprise that her mother could read and write, the priest proudly explained—again, using sign language and stilted English—that he himself had educated the villagers as best he could. Flipping through the slender volume, Hannah found dates that spanned a few months before and after her birth. The binding was black, with no distinguishing marks. And nestled among the pages was a book mark—a faded red ribbon.

Intrigued, Hannah returned to the tiny *posada* where she had taken a room. As she ate a simple meal in the courtyard, she struggled to read the little diary, but soon became frustrated at her inability to understand. Although her adoptive parents had both been fluent in Spanish and had tried to teach her the language of her ancestry while she was young, Hannah had learned only the basics because of a fear that identifying too closely with her ethnic heritage might make her somehow less of an American. Back then, before she knew the truth about the pale ghosts of the north, she had wanted above all else to fit in. How she regretted her decision that evening on the posada patio! How she wished she had learned the language and ways of her real people.

The owner of the hotel, who was also the cook and waiter, observed Hannah's frustration with the Spanish words and asked in halting English if he could help. Hannah tried to explain her problem, but he did not understand. Holding his thumb and first finger close together before his face and saying, *"Un momentito, por favor,"* he disappeared inside, only to return with a young girl in tow. In strongly accented but passable English, the girl explained that she was Esperanza, the hotel owner's daughter. Could she be of help? So, in the diminutive courtyard overlooking the plaza, Esperanza read a page or two aloud from the book, accompanied by the tree frogs chirping among the mimosas. The words were simple but beautiful:

> *My dearest Hannah. Today I dreamed about you coming to me. How can I tell you what joy I feel to know my dream will come true! God is so generous to grant such a miracle to someone like me, and it is such a serious responsibility… I am filled with doubts. Will I be a good mother? Can I provide the things you will need? I want to give you everything, but there is so little money. So I have decided to give you what I can, by writing all the things I know about life. When you read this, I hope that you will find these words encouraging and helpful. I hope you will be able to avoid the mistakes I have made. I hope you will be happy. So, where to begin? Oh, yes. With God, of course. Let me tell you what I've learned about Him….*

As Esperanza's young voice spoke the woman's words of wisdom, Hannah's vague longing to know her birth mother took on a new, more personal dimension. Where before she had merely felt curiosity, she began to suffer a genuine sense of loss, accompanied by a simmering anger that life—and her adoptive parents—had deprived her of the opportunity to know this wise and sensitive woman. And beneath everything were the unanswered questions: Who was her father? And why had he and her true mother given her away?

The following morning, Hannah asked the hotel owner if his daughter could accompany her to act as a guide and translator while she searched the village for people who had known her mother and father. He agreed, in return for the smallest of fees…say, five pesos per day? And so began a daily routine, with the young girl, Esperanza, and Hannah, barely grown herself, setting out each morning to scour the village and surrounding countryside for people who could tell stories about Hannah's birth parents, then returning every evening to dine by the light of an oil lantern and read the diary. They never read more than half a page or so, because Hannah could not restrain her tears, which caused

Esperanza to mark her place with the faded red ribbon and tactfully slip away. The gentle words of encouragement contained within her true mother's diary encompassed all the love in the world to Hannah. They flowed through her soul like a mountain stream, bathing her heart with tenderness and hope.

> *It's important not to worry, little one. Always there are questions about the future: Will we have enough to eat? Will the rains come on time? What if I get sick? But God watches over you, little one. He cares for you and loves you just as much as I do...maybe even more, if that is possible. And with God on your side, you need never worry about the future. He has wonderful plans for you. I know it because He made you so perfect. And besides, He has told me so. You will have problems and even a little pain (oh, how I pray every day for your pain to be little!), but always remember, your Father in heaven will not give you more than you can bear, and every difficulty is given for a reason. Troubles make you strong if you will only trust the Father....*

These were ideas Hannah had never seriously considered. Her adoptive parents had forced her to go to church, inflicting their religion upon her, but never before had Hannah heard such things expressed with so much loving-kindness. The God of the north had seemed cold and distant. But in the simple words of her true mother, Hannah glimpsed something warm and very close.

During their daily forays into the mountainous countryside, Hannah contemplated the life she might have enjoyed had her mother not sent her away. Life with her American parents had been comfortable and filled with a quiet affection, but still, that existence had been so ordinary. As a simple peasant's daughter, she would have learned to live in harmony with nature, part of the extended family of the village where every old man was a kindly *tio*—uncle—and each old woman a doting grandmother, ready to spoil a child with a taste of *dulce de piloncillo,* so sweet and buttery.

One day, filled with exquisite delight in her parent's world, Hannah followed Esperanza along a trail through a dense forest. Passing beneath a looming banyan tree, she turned to the side and glimpsed a pile of dark orange bricks through a lacy veil of green. She called her little guide back to her side, and together they took a few steps off of the trail to stare up at three towering brick chimneys, almost as tall as the forest canopy. Esperanza told her they were all that was left of the abandoned tin mines which had fed and clothed the villagers for four hundred years. Now the lonely spires had submitted to the tangled embrace of vines as thick as Hannah's arm. Looking up at the smokestacks, she felt a mournful mist settle down upon her heart, obscuring the shining joy she had felt before.

Had her adoptive parents not taken her away, Hannah's life could have been filled with such magic places all along. She could have lived in a world of exotic birds, panthers slipping silently between verdant shadows, the gentle kiss of tropical rains and the history of man slowly crumbling to the forest floor. She turned away, her flat high cheeks awash with silent tears; tears she had not shed for the man who raised her, tears she had not shed when leaving her adoptive mother, tears that came freely now, in the land of her real parents, in the place where she belonged. Hannah cried for her true mother. Hannah cried for herself. How could the northerners have taken her away from all of this?

Each time she entered the cool darkness of another ancient adobe or trailed behind Esperanza along another deep green forest trail, Hannah's sense of loss grew stronger. And each evening as she listened with a hungry heart to the words of the woman who had given her life, Hannah felt an inexpressible melancholy for the mother she never knew...the wise and gentle mother who had loved her so completely.

I have learned that faith is a gift. It's strange, but many people do not know this. In the Bible, there is a man who says, "I believe. Help me to believe!" That is exactly how I feel sometimes. But when I look into your beautiful eyes, my darling daughter, I know somehow that you will be given a very strong faith. You are so perfect, so innocent. It does not seem possible that so beautiful a creation as you could ever doubt the One who created you, but if you do, just ask and He will prove Himself....

Those first few days, the villagers were hesitant to speak about Hannah's mother. She assumed this was due to their natural shyness and perhaps a desire to avoid unseemly praise. But then something strange and terrible happened. As she pressed them harder, the villagers reluctantly began to tell stories of a mean-spirited woman, a woman who bitterly complained that she had been cheated by life, who could not keep a husband, who lived in promiscuity and suffered from the self-induced poverty of laziness. No one could name her father...they claimed there had been too many men to know for sure.

The villagers' stories conflicted so completely with the loving words of the diary; Hannah attributed them to jealousy and resentment. She knew envious feelings were a common response to a truly righteous person. But throughout the village and the surrounding valley she heard the same stories again and again. And always, the villagers apologized and reminded her that she had begged them to speak of such things.

Now Hannah's daily treks through the countryside took on a new, more urgent agenda. She mourned for her true mother who had been so misunderstood and vowed to find someone—just one person—who had truly appreciated her mother's virtuous and noble character. But the village's harsh appraisal seemed unanimous. Then Hannah remembered the priest who had apparently been a friend to her mother. Certain that he, at least, would remember her with kindness, Hannah revisited the tiny rectory next to the chapel on the plaza, where she found the old man watering his meager bed of flowers.

"Why did my mother send me away?" asked Hannah through Esperanza, the little interpreter.

The priest sighed. "Are you sure you want to know?"

"Yes! Of course!"

The priest sighed again. "Very well. If you insist, I suppose I must tell you the truth. Your mother sold you for twenty-five pesos to Pablo Delagado who lived beside the stream in the valley of the mines."

Aghast, Hannah stared at him and said, "But, my parents...I mean, the ones who took me away from here..."

The priest nodded, "Yes. Pablo was not such a good man. He did not feed you well. The missionaries from *Los Estados Unitos* bought you back from him. Pablo boasted for many weeks that he had made a ten peso profit from your mother's stupidity. Many people mocked your mother after the missionaries took you away. Then one night she slipped into Pablo's house with a knife. There was a terrible battle. Pablo slit her throat and ran away. No one has seen him since."

Hannah fled across the plaza. It could not be true! Even the priest in this horrible place told lies about her mother. That night, she had no strength to listen to the words in the diary. Early the next morning, filled with bitterness and anger, Hannah bid Esperanza good-bye and quit the idyllic village of her birth, beginning the long walk down the mountain to the road where she waited for the dilapidated smoke-belching bus which roared north through the mountains two times each week unless it was raining or the driver was too drunk. The next day, staring down from 30,000 feet as her jet passed over the rust-colored Mexican state of Coahuila, Hannah thought she finally knew why her true mother had let her go forever. How could such a loving woman allow her child to live among such an envious people? And she felt sad because the village was not her home after all. That had been a lie, just as her life in the northern city was a lie.

Hannah had no home.

How grievous to be lost in limbo: heart here, mind there, body someplace in-between! But then, flying ever closer to her mundane existence in the north, Hannah remembered the final passage Esperanza had read to her:

> *Forgiveness is the hardest thing. I sometimes ask the Father how He could expect such an act from me. I am not divine, yet it seems that only a god could truly turn the other cheek. Then I remember what I have learned about faith, and again, I ask the Father for the strength I need to do as He wishes. Even such a perfect and innocent soul as yours will endure injustice in this world, my dearest Hannah. When you do, remember to ask your Father for the strength you need to forgive. It will be given to you....*

Oh, how could her mother have written those words? Surely she was a saint.

Back in the city, Hannah buried her emotions beneath a flurry of activity. The many small tasks one must undertake upon leaving for college served to mask her abiding anger. How could so many people have misjudged her mother? The injustice of it was unforgivable. And how could her adoptive parents have stolen Hannah away, to leave her mother alone among such people? Uppermost in Hannah's thoughts was a smoldering resentment that her adoptive parents had separated her from the kindness, love, and faith of her true mother, and left her alone there with those heartless people. The insensitivity and presumption of it reminded Hannah of every slight her northern parents had inflicted: the insistence that she go to their church, the rigid rules about music and movies and television, the ridiculous early deadlines for Hannah's precious few dates.

It would be good to leave her adoptive mother's apartment, once and for all. To never be reminded of the way she had stolen Hannah from her true mother. To clear away that unnatural part of her life, so she could focus on her real heritage: the loving woman Hannah felt she had come to know, high in the mountains of Mexico.

So, one week after she left the little village in the Sierra Madres, Hannah walked away from the woman's modest apartment, never to return. She stood woodenly within the woman's embrace at the bus station, and mutely took a parting gift from the crying woman's hands: a brown cardboard box bound by twine. The box was heavy, and Hannah tried to leave it behind, telling the woman she could send it later in the mail. But the woman insisted pathetically, so Hannah stepped aboard the bus, weighed down by the woman's gift.

Her life in college was remarkably similar to her life in the city. She was alone, always aware of herself as the only dark and dumpy one among a crowd of slender giants. She buried herself in her studies, spending evenings at the university library and weekends working as a waitress in sixteen-hour double shifts. Her roommate was very popular, a svelte blond girl, picked for a sorority after the first semester. In spite of such close quarters, they rarely spoke. When the girl moved to the sorority house, Hannah decided to move as well, to take a room above a garage near campus, where she could distance herself from the mocking looks and whispers of the others in the dormitory. As she packed her few belongings, she discovered the brown box bound by twine, still beneath her bed where she had put it upon entering the dormitory room four months earlier. It was so heavy. Perhaps she should throw it out, rather than carry it all the way to her new apartment. But what if the woman's gift was something valuable? Something she could sell? And so, sitting alone on the narrow bed in her dorm room, Hannah untied the twine and opened the box.

Inside, she found twenty small books, all exactly alike. The bindings of the slender volumes were black, with no distinguishing marks. And nestled among the pages of each one was a book mark: a faded red ribbon. Hannah's pulse roared in her ears as she reached for the first book, the one on the left. She opened it, and on the first page, read these words:

My dearest Hannah. Now that we are home, I have decided to begin writing in English. It seems fitting, just as Spanish seemed best back in Mexico. In all the rushing to get ready to leave, I seem to have left my first diary behind. But don't worry, I remember most of what I wrote. I remember telling you how I felt on the day we heard you would be ours. How can I express the joy I felt at the news! God is so generous to grant such a miracle to someone like me....

Hannah read through the night, devouring the diaries, drinking in the love between those pages, laughing out loud at some of the words, and at others, washing her flat, wide cheeks with tears as she thought of the woman's moist eyes and her thin lips smiling while Hannah told her she was going to Mexico, and the tickets she had bought to carry her there and the way she had waited so pale and slender on the bus ride to the airport and her tears at the bus station that other time, as Hannah had gone away again, gone to college never to return. Hannah imagined the way it would have been for the woman, riding the elevator alone up to the modest apartment stacked with all the others high above the city after pleading pathetically with her adopted daughter to take the brown box bound by twine. Hannah knew that she herself had been right about one thing at least: Her *true* mother was a saint indeed, and there was so much to say and do, beginning one hour after the sun rose bright with the glorious truth, beginning now, as Hannah boarded a bus for the city with the brown box bound by twine strangely light within her arms, going home at last.

ABOUT THE AUTHOR

Athol Dickson is the author of two published novels, *Whom Shall I Fear?* and *Every Hidden Thing*. A third novel, tentatively entitled *Days of Awe* is soon to be released. Regarding *Whom Shall I Fear?*, the *New York Times Sunday Magazine* says: "Readers get moonshine, a crooked sheriff and a redneck crucifixion scene that would put Flannery O'Connor to shame."

A Trip to Senegal

Sharon Ewell Foster

Pinky stood on the street in front of the salon. It didn't look like any salon she had ever seen before. In the salon at the mall, on the upper north side, things were chic, things were decorated, things were wide open.

A padlock dangled from the green-painted iron grid that covered the door. It looked ready to snap into place when business was done. Pictures were taped to the salon's front windows. Poorly taped pictures. The old yellowed strips of cellophane looked like they could, at any moment, retire and let the pictures fall.

Besides that, in all the pictures the women had braids. Some of the braids were wrapped around the models' heads like crowns. Some of the braids hung way down the models' backs. Some of the beautiful, brown, smiling women had little tiny, tiny braids that stood almost straight up. *Dakar Senegalese Braiding*, the sign posted in the window said.

Pinky touched her full lips—that's why people called her Pinky, she knew. Her big pink lips and light skin that blanched pink when she was embarrassed. "Pink girl, pink girl," they had called her when she was young, and the name had stuck.

Could she be like them? Like one of the models? Would her friends and family tease her? "What are you trying to prove? Girl, you know you are too pink for those braids!" Would she look foolish—her light skin and those braids?

She looked from the pictures to a spot on the window that mirrored back her image. Ivory-yellow skin and African features. Gray eyes and thick lips. Long, thick, sandy-colored hair, straight on the shaft, kinky at the roots. Pinky squinted her eyes at the bright light that glinted off the glass. Something about her features, about the combination, looked confused. And that's how she felt: confused. Confused and unsure.

Two women walked past Pinky on the sidewalk. Their brown eyes looked her up and down, but they did not speak, didn't look like they wanted to speak. The two just turned their heads and walked past her. One of them leaned toward the other and giggled. Pinky wondered if it was her clothes, maybe her shoes, perhaps her hair. What exactly was it that told them she was not one of them? What made them think she wasn't a woman they would want to link arms with, tell their troubles to, go try on clothes with?

Pinky's eyes followed them as they walked past the Black Muslim clothing store next to the beauty shop. She kept watching until they turned into the soul food carryout on the corner. Her gaze moved to the street and the scene around her. Cars whizzed by—luxury cars sandwiched in between hoopties and city buses. The sound of a recording of the voice of the Honorable Louis Farrakhan drifted out from the clothing store, and competed with snatches of songs coming from car windows and the voices of passersby.

A car paused at the stoplight and the passenger rolled down her window. "This is a time for you to visualize God coming into your darkness, and breaking the glue, and loosing the shackles and giving you vision..." Jackie McCullough's husky voice exhorted to the accompaniment of a Caribbean rhythm, while background singers sang "Shine Forth." At the same time, a mother bustled by with three children in tow.

"I told you all stop fooling around, now. Hurry up," she told her brood. They rushed to keep up with their mother's stride. Too busy to notice her, Pinky observed gratefully.

She turned her attention to another corner where a man in a revived suit and tie passed out gospel tracts and proclaimed loudly, "Jesus saves!" On the opposite corner, a street entrepreneur flashed an arm full of watches out of his sleeve.

It was like no salon Pinky had ever seen, like no street she had ever stood on. Pinky turned and looked at her image, looked at the smiling photos again, walked to the door, pushed the handle, and stepped inside.

"Hey! What you want, miss?" One of the dark-skinned women

spoke to Pinky while the four other braiders in front of her raised or turned their heads so that they could see her. Their customers turned to look at her if their braids would allow. The braiders stared, but their hands kept working—twisting hair, weaving artificial hair tracks, and burning the ends of braids to seal them in place.

"Hey, miss," the same woman spoke again. It seemed like a different world: Pinky's eyes adjusted to the dim light, while her ears adjusted to the accents. "What you want?" The young woman's accent was very thick. She stopped braiding and placed a free hand on her skinny hip. "You selling something? We not buying anything!" The woman's voice was insistent and impatient.

Pinky shook her head, unable yet to speak.

"You want braids?" Pinky was sure she heard a special emphasis on the *you,* thought she saw skepticism in the woman's expression. "You want your hair fixed?"

Pinky shrugged and wondered why she had ever walked through the door.

"Can I help you, miss?" Pinky turned toward the softer voice that came from over her right shoulder. A dark-skinned woman, slightly older than the first, smiled at Pinky, then looked in the direction of the thinner woman. "Don't worry, Sofi," the woman with the softer voice spoke. "I will take care of her. All right?"

"Okay," Sofi nodded, took her hand off her hip and went back to braiding.

"You want braids?" This woman's accent was just as thick, but her tone was much more gentle. "Here." She motioned toward an unoccupied styling chair near her. "Come. Sit down."

Pinky's feet seemed to be thinking, seemed to walk her to the chair and tell her to sit down. The woman reached her hand out and touched Pinky's hair. "How long since your last perm?" *Perm* sounded more like *pum.*

"Three-three months." Pinky's hands felt clammy.

"Good," the woman smiled. "It's a good time to come, lots of new growth. Must be your first time, eh?"

"Yes-yes. I was thinking...thinking I might try them." Pinky felt foolish, felt she must look foolish.

"Good thing," the woman reassured her. "I'm goin' take care of you, okay? My name is Zuri." Zuri's *is* sounded more like *isss* than *iz.* "Don't worry," she added. "It's a good thing." Zuri stopped and bundled several of her client's long braids in a rubber band. While her patron squirmed, Zuri turned her head toward Pinky and beamed, displayed a mouth full of beautiful, perfect teeth. Then she turned back toward her client. "It's almost over," Zuri told her. "The hard part is over. You get to enjoy, now." The client squinted her eyes shut, drew her knees up toward her chest and held her two outstretched hands near the sides of her head.

"I told you I was tender-headed," the client squeaked out between grimaces.

Zuri continued arranging the braids, seemingly unaware of her client's contortions. "It's a beautiful thing," she said. The patron continued to squirm, seemingly unconvinced. "There, I'm finished." Zuri looked in Pinky's direction. "Looks nice, right? Beautiful, right?"

Pinky nodded in response and watched as Zuri handed the patron a mirror. The patron lifted her braids, turned her head from side to side, then smiled at her image, braids cascading down her back. "Beautiful," Zuri said. The patron appeared to believe.

While the patron paid Zuri and tossed her new hair, Pinky looked around the small salon. The styling chairs looked well worn, and the hardwood floor was covered in a flat redwood-colored paint. What intrigued her most were the pictures and posters on the wall. Images of dark-skinned women with intricately braided hairdos, women in traditional ethnic clothing, women with large almond-shaped eyes. There was something in their eyes, something about their faces that seemed *exotic*. The word surprised Pinky. She had never thought of herself, women like her, as exotic. Yet the women in the posters seemed to know that they were unabashedly beautiful, not haughty, just women comfortable with their beauty.

"Very nice, eh?" Zuri's voice startled her. "Senegalese women." Zuri's smile seemed to have no borders and Pinky realized that Zuri was one of them: a Senegalese woman. Pinky looked at the other braiders and suddenly realized they were all exotic Senegalese women. Zuri pointed at several of the pictures. "You see any you like?" After selecting an attractive style, she followed Zuri back to the chair.

"What kind she gone get, eh?" Sofi called across the room to Zuri.

"A basket."

"Ahhh." Sofi then turned and spoke to the other four braiders in what sounded to Pinky like French. "Ahhh," two of them echoed. All five of them then became engaged in an animated conversation in another foreign language. The exchange ended when Sofi called across the room to Pinky, "So, your mother, she is white?"

Pinky could feel her face warm and knew it must be scarlet. She probably would have left if Zuri had not already started parting her hair. "No," she said. "No, I just, I'm just. Most of my family…well, I'm the only one…" Pinky stopped and then opted for the short answer. "No, both of my parents are black."

Sofi turned back to the other women, obviously interpreting. Pinky took a deep breath and reminded herself not to get excited, not to think negatively. Zuri held plastic-covered packages of hair up to Pinky's hair to match the shades. "This one, I think. This is the color," she said, holding the hair where Pinky could see it.

Zuri walked to the water fountain in the corner and returned with a cup of water and a bottle of aspirin she had retrieved from a nearby table. "You better take these now," she said, extending the water and tablets to Pinky. "It will help you."

Pinky took the aspirin and fought back fear that tried to rise within her. "Lay back," Zuri said and began to shampoo and condition Pinky's hair. She felt her head begin to relax into the massage from Zuri's hands. "My sister—" Zuri nodded toward Sofi—"she didn't bother you, did she? Sofi means no harm. Just talking. Still young, sometimes too quick to speak." Pinky stiffened imperceptibly, then relaxed as Zuri continued.

While Zuri dried her hair and began braiding, the African women questioned her until they found out that Pinky was a grant administrator for several charitable programs. "She gives away someone else's money," Sofi explained to the others. They prodded until they found out her birth order, the number of her siblings, and their names. Found out that she had lived in the suburbs all her life. And after what felt like hours one of the other women said something in what Pinky had by then learned was Wolof. The woman spoke quickly and just as quickly the other women—without speaking—all left their clients, the heads they were working on, then washed their hands and began to set out food on a small cloth-covered table.

The aroma was spicy and unusual. Pinky heard her stomach grumble. Zuri spoke to the other clients. "Lunch now. You better get lunch. You stay." She pointed at Pinky. When the other clients had left to get lunch, Zuri told her, "Come."

"No, I won't take your lunch." Her stomach growled louder.

"Come," Zuri insisted.

When Pinky sat at the table she saw that the women ate from one large communal bowl. Zuri took a large spoon and cut some fish and vegetables from the center of the bowl. The African woman pushed the food onto an area of the bowl that was directly in front of Pinky. "Eat." Zuri motioned with her hands. Pinky scooped up a small amount of the fish, some red-colored tomato-flavored rice, and a small piece of what looked to be sweet potato. The taste made her close her eyes with pleasure.

"You like?" Sofi smiled. When she smiled it was clear that she and Zuri were sisters.

"Yes." Pinky nodded.

"Eat," Sofi encouraged. She reached for a piece of lime and drizzled the juice over the fish and rice. Pinky ate—fish, rice, cabbage, casava, carrot, and sweet potato—and felt herself drifting into a faraway place, a peaceful place. She ate with her eyes closed.

"So, why you wait so long?" Zuri's voice interrupted her travel. "Why you wait so long for braids?"

Pinky thought of a safe response, then decided, instead, to speak truthfully. "I thought I might look foolish. I thought people might make fun of me because of, you know." She motioned at her skin. Zuri shook her head, clicked her tongue, then laid her hand on top of Pinky's hand.

"Sounds like a Moses thing to me," Sofi said.

"How so?" Zuri turned her head toward her sister.

"You know, trying to do good for his people, but raised in the king's palace. So, he speaks the language of the Israelites, but with an Egyptian accent. Kind of like you." Sofi nodded her head toward Pinky. "Speaking the same language, but with the king's accent so your own people don't trust you. Plus you got the wrong *color.*" Sofi pursed her lips and shook her head.

"This is true." Zuri nodded. "Seems to me it bothered Moses so much he wouldn't speak, even when God told him to, even when he could deliver his people. Does it bother you that much?"

Pinky could feel tears spring into her eyes. She was afraid to speak, afraid her voice would break.

"But you know," Zuri said, "the people really loved him. When I think about it, I'm sure they loved him. I'm no priest, but I am sure they must have loved him. They just didn't know how to show it. They were hard because of slavery. They had been taught not to love. And I am sure they had been taught to disapprove of anyone who tried to be different, who tried to rise above. But they loved him, they just didn't know how to show it until he died. He may not have known it, either, until he went to the Lord. Of course—" Zuri shrugged her shoulders—"I don't know for sure, it's what I think."

"Um, um, um." Sofi pursed her lips tighter and said something to the other women in Wolof. "This is too sad," she said. "Too sad. Turn on the music."

One of the other women went to a small boom box in the corner and turned it on, turned up the volume. *"Shine forth! Shine forth! Shine forth!"* Singing voices commanded encouragement from the small appliance.

"It's my song!" Zuri leapt from her chair, pulling the other women with her. She began to move in a way that was as much praise as dance. "Come on," she said. "We will dance away this darkness." Zuri pulled at Pinky's hands while the other women pushed her from behind. "Up! Up!" She did not have enough strength to resist them. "Dance!" She began to move, closed her eyes, and felt the words move into her spirit. *"Shine forth! Shine forth! Shine forth!"*

Pinky danced. Danced and closed her eyes so that nothing could come into her view which would take away the joy she felt in that moment. Danced until whatever it was that had kept her head bowed down was gone. Danced until she felt shiny and new and beautiful and exotic.

"Quick, turn the music down so we can pray. We must pray now." Pinky opened her eyes at Zuri's words. "We must pray."

"But, I'm not Muslim," Pinky objected.

"Neither are we." Sofi seemed amused.

"I thought all Africans were Muslim, or…"

"Not all. We are Christians. Missionaries in Dakar, we learned from them. Some Africans have been Christians for more than a thousand years, some were Jewish at the time of Christ." Zuri nodded. "Enough history, it is time to pray. We shall pray for you. Pray as Moses prayed."

Zuri held Pinky's hands and began to sing and pray, "Let thy work appear unto thy servants, and thy glory unto their children. And let the beauty of the LORD our God be upon us: and establish thou the work of our hands upon us; yea, the work of our hands establish thou it." In the background, the four other women sang softly. "And now, Lord," Zuri entreated, "from this day forward, let her shine. Let her shine forth. Let her shine." And then the women held Pinky, wrapped her in their arms and whispered prayers on her behalf and blessings to her, even as they moved to clear away the dishes.

By the time they had finished, the other clients had returned, impatient that the hour was getting late. "Come," Zuri said and motioned toward the styling chair. For hours she braided as Pinky closed her eyes against the pulling and tightening. "Soon," Zuri said. "It will be beautiful soon." Pinky surrendered to the discomfort and slept.

"Here. Here, my sistah." The tapping on her shoulder awakened her and she looked into the mirror stretched out toward her. "Look, see," Zuri said.

Pinky turned her head from side to side and admired the intricately woven coils on her head. She was beautiful. She was exotic. The copper-colored basket accentuated her gray eyes, gave perspective to her face and lips. She looked into Zuri's eyes and, as she paid her, mouthed the words she could not speak out loud, "Thank you. Thank you."

Sofi and the other braiders smiled and waved. "Don't wait so long to come," Sofi said, then grinned. *"Beautiful."*

Zuri walked Pinky to the door, and the two women hugged. "You are lovely," Zuri said. "And you are loved, you know? Some people don't know how to show it, but don't be like Moses. Look for that love while you are here, alive. Expect love and help them; show them how to love so they can love you back."

Pinky opened the door and stepped out into the summer evening. The sun was bright, brighter than she had ever remembered it being at this time of day. She paused to look at her image in the window and smiled. She lifted her head, straightened her shoulders and walked.

ABOUT THE AUTHOR

Sharon Ewell Foster has more than fifteen years of professional and administrative experience with the U.S. Department of Defense. Her previous publications include a daily wire news column, and several devotionals in *Daily Guideposts 2000.* Her first novel, *Passing by Samaria,* is available now. The mother of a grown daughter, a teenage son, and a chihuahua named Punkin who aspires to be a "real boy." Sharon makes her home in Maryland.

Haiti's Song

Deborah Raney

Sa Bo-Dié sé ré pou ou, lavalas pa poté-l alé.
(What God has laid up for you, the flood will not carry away.)

Haitian proverb

I shifted in my seat and peered out over the murky blue-green waters of the Atlantic. The 757 emerged from a bank of clouds, and I thought I could actually make out the greenish string of islands that made up the Bahamas.

The sigh that escaped my lips was louder than I'd intended and my seatmate looked over at me, mild concern on her face. I smiled in a way that I hoped would convey that I didn't wish to be bothered. I turned back to the window. The cloud cover was thicker now, and I lost my view of the exotic islands where I was to have spent my honeymoon.

Now, the reservations in an elegant seaside hotel had long since been cancelled and the "honeymoon suite" that awaited my party of one was five hundred miles beyond Nassau. Instead of a soft king-sized mattress, my bed would likely be a concrete floor, or if I were lucky, a narrow cot. I prepared myself for the concrete floor. By now it had been well established that I was anything but lucky. Lucky or not, I was determined to view my broken engagement as a mere disappointment—not the tragedy it felt like.

Deep inside, I knew that it was for the best that Will had called off our wedding. Oh, he was a nice enough guy—witty and good-looking and above all, interesting. We had shared a strong faith as well. But I saw now that faith alone didn't make us compatible. And time had certainly proven that we were anything but compatible. I trusted that somewhere down the road I would be able to look back and actually be grateful that I'd been dumped.

Okay, maybe it could have happened before the invitations went out; maybe it could have happened when I was twenty-one instead of three weeks after my thirtieth birthday. But in spite of the lousy timing, I could recognize that even this humiliation was better than an unhappy marriage or a divorce down the road. Still, I couldn't deny that it hurt. Whether he was Mr. Right or not, I had loved William Concannon. Really loved him. And I would be lying if I said he hadn't broken my heart. It was broken all right, and it hurt like crazy—a physical pain right in the center of my chest.

I felt tears, hot and stinging, well up behind my eyelids, and I forced myself to think about something else. I'd had enough humiliation over the last weeks; I wasn't about to break down and spill my guts to a complete stranger in an airplane miles above the ocean. I reached under the seat in front of me and rummaged in my bag until I found a tissue. I blew my nose discreetly, then took my passport from the zippered pocket of my carry-on bag. For the tenth time, I opened the little blue book and took out the sheet of scrap paper tucked inside. I stared down at the address of an orphanage on the outskirts of Port au Prince, Haiti. Some honeymoon destination. Yet I knew this trip would be good for me.

The past months of my life had been some of the most difficult I'd ever known, and yet, I was aware that God was working in my heart in a way I didn't quite understand. I only knew that if I allowed it to be, it would be good. I thought about Will and the dreams I'd had for our future. But that was just the problem. They were my dreams. It wasn't Will's fault that he didn't share those dreams with me. And if I was totally honest with myself, I would have to admit that I had allowed my relationship with Will to continue because—well, because I was desperate. There. I'd said it. I was desperate for a man—any man.

All my life, from my very earliest memories, I've only really wanted one thing in life. Kids. Lots of kids. And, well, it always kind of seemed like a man was a prerequisite. Yes, I wanted a dozen children. I wanted to give birth to six, and I wanted to adopt six more. Oh, sure, as I got older—and began to realize that kids cost money and that they weren't always the beings of sweet delight that I pictured in my imagination—I revised my dream. If necessary, I could be happy with just four or five.

Then my twenties flew by with barely a man on the horizon. As my biological clock ticked away madly I revised my dream again. Finally, my dream became a desperate prayer. *Please, God, I want a child. Just one child to love and to love me in return. Surely that's not too much to ask.* Whenever I read in the newspaper that a child had died at the hands of one of his parents or when our pastor's fourteen-year-old daughter turned up pregnant, I wanted to cry. Okay, I did cry—at the injustice of it all.

And then Will came along. He was handsome and funny and he was one of the few men I'd dated recently who didn't have a dark secret or an ex-wife—or an ex-wife who was a dark secret. We shared a strong faith and we rarely fought. He seemed like the answer to my prayer—until I told him about my dream. It's not that Will had anything against kids. In fact he taught the junior high class in our church for several years. He liked kids. He was great with them, and they seemed to love him in return.

But Will had a dream too, a dream that he, like me, had nurtured from his earliest memories. And fatherhood just didn't figure in his dream. Will was an adventurer. He wanted to travel the world. He wanted to climb every mountain and sail every ocean and jump out of airplanes and throw himself off of bridges to which he was flimsily attached by an elastic cord. His dream, believe it or not, involved dying young. Not that he had a death wish or anything. He was just being realistic.

"Face it, Valerie," he told me on more than one occasion, "if I'm lucky enough to get to live the life I dream of, chances are good that I'll die on the side of some mountain or at the bottom of some ocean. And I honestly can't think of a better way to go...doing what I love to do. But I don't want to leave a bunch of orphans behind when I go. And SRS kind of frowns on backpacking babies to the top of Everest," he'd add, trying to humor me.

I must have tried a hundred times to convince him that fatherhood would be the greatest adventure he could imagine. But he wasn't buying it. He couldn't quite believe that three A.M. feedings and changing dirty diapers would give him the same adrenaline rush that piloting a hang glider off the side of a cliff would. We began to argue more and more, and finally, I guess we came to the end of ourselves and admitted to God and everybody that this marriage would never work. It was a mutual decision. Really it was. But Will is the one who said the actual words. So technically, he dumped me. Still, I'd like to think that if he hadn't, I would have come to my senses and said the words myself: "We're making a big mistake."

I think I was kind of relieved when Will called off our engagement. I know he loved me, but he loved his dream more. And I know I loved him too, but apparently I loved my dream more as well.

I could handle not being a mom because I'd never met the right man. But I don't think I could ever have forgiven Will for marrying me and then denying me the only thing I'd ever wanted in life.

For almost a year now, my days had been spent planning a huge church wedding, being the center of attention at three bridal showers, sewing four bridesmaid's dresses and an entire wardrobe for our honeymoon in the tropics. I'd been busy sewing something else, too. Not just since I met Will, but long before, since my first year of junior high home economics, when I discovered how smoothly a sewing machine handled under my touch. I'd made almost all my own clothes. Most of the girls in my high school wouldn't have been caught dead wearing something homemade, but I was proud of my fashions. And then, when I was sixteen I happened across a pattern at a garage sale for a frilly little sundress, size two. I paid ten cents for it and took it home and made the sweetest little dress from the scraps of a summer shift I'd just finished for myself. It was lime green gingham checks, and I attached a ruffled eyelet slip to peek out from beneath the skirt. I'd spent half my allowance on some tiny lemon, lime, and orange shaped buttons to trim the bodice.

Later, when I took a woodworking class, that little dress was the first thing I put into the hope chest I built. Over the years I'd filled that trunk to overflowing with baby clothes. Boy things and girl things, all shapes and sizes. I guess I figured if I was going to have twelve kids, I'd need a lot of clothes. At night, in my room, when the rest of the house was asleep, I would take each little outfit out of the chest and hold it up and picture my babies wearing it. I'd even prayed for them—my precious little future babies—that God would bless them and keep them safe, and that I might have the privilege of praying with each one of them to ask Jesus into their hearts.

Three days after we broke our engagement, after we'd sent letters to all the guests, after I'd boxed up all the gifts and gotten them ready to return, I took everything out of that hope chest. I folded each little piece neatly and placed it in a cardboard box. Then I sealed up the box—a box containing, quite literally, the last threads of my dream—and mailed it to my sister in Chicago. She had promised to give them to her church's annual rummage sale. The clothes would have made lovely gifts. Hand-fashioned baby clothes had become all the rage. But I didn't think I could bear to see my friends' children wearing my babies' clothes. I shed a few tears that day. But if anything, I think it helped prove to me that Will and I had made the right decision.

I would have been a good mom. I still believe that. But my dream had died and I knew it was time to get the spotlight off of myself and do something for someone else. If I hadn't learned anything else from my years of reading the Bible, surely I'd learned that true happiness comes from helping others.

Which is why, on this January morning that was to have been my wedding day, I was on an airplane headed for Haiti. An orphanage my church sponsored had sent out a call for help. Grossly understaffed and desperately in need of workers, they were eager for help, even on a short-term basis. In the end, I was the only one who signed up for the trip, but the church voted to send me anyway. Of course, because of my aborted honeymoon, I already had the passport, plus time off from my advertising job, and even a plane ticket, which the airline had been kind enough to transfer—with a small penalty, of course. I'd briefly entertained the idea of asking for the airline's bereavement rate but thought better of it. In spite of the reason for my change of destination, it was rather exciting—and a little scary—to be headed to a foreign country. For other than a brief foray into Mexico in my college days, I'd never set foot on foreign soil.

I'd read the newsletter that the American missionaries who ran the orphanage sent to our church twice a year; and of course, once my trip was confirmed, I'd visited Haiti via the library and the Internet. But I really had no idea what to expect of this trip. As the flight attendants moved through the aisles collecting pretzel wrappers and rumpled napkins, I turned in my seat, stretching, and discreetly taking in the other passengers on the flight. Most of the faces I saw were Haitian—neatly dressed businessmen, several families with well-behaved children, returning home from visiting relatives in the States, I guessed. The two dozen or so white faces I saw held the same mix of excitement and apprehension I suppose my own face reflected. I readjusted my seat belt and looked out the window again. A metallic bell tone sounded over the PA system, and the captain came on to tell us that we were beginning our descent into Port au Prince. My heart began to beat noticeably faster and I turned to stare out the window again. *Help me, Lord,* I prayed, suddenly anxious.

When the plane came to a stop quite a distance from the airport terminal, I followed my fellow travelers down the steps and across the tarmac to the outdated building. My immediate thought as I stepped off the plane was, "Toto, I've a feeling we're not in Kansas anymore." Just outside the entrance, a trio of native musicians wearing brightly colored shirts had set up shop. As we made our way into the terminal, they serenaded us with lively music that reminded me of the zydeco I'd heard at Mardi Gras. When our carry-on bags had been cleared, we moved in a herd toward the baggage claim area, located in a section of the airport that looked almost archaic.

Pastor and Madame Nolan Greene, the missionaries who ran the orphanage, had warned me that they wouldn't be able to meet me inside the airport, so after my bags passed customs, I made my way to the front entrance of the airport. The sights and sounds—and smells—that greeted me as I stepped onto the streets of Port au Prince were intoxicating—and not in an entirely pleasant way. My nostrils flared at the strange mingling of frying fish, exhaust fumes, garbage, and over it all, the distinct smell of a sewer.

I held a tissue to my nose and shaded my eyes, searching the crowd for the elderly couple I had only seen in a blurry Xeroxed photograph. There they were! Their silver heads and fair skin stood out like beacons amid the sea of ebony faces that swarmed outside the fence. I waved in their direction and they motioned for me to go to an opening in the fence a few yards from where I had exited the airport. Once outside the fence I was suddenly surrounded by children, mostly boys. Snow white teeth grinned up at me from shiny coal black faces.

"Madame, one dollar please?" they all seemed to shout at once in their thick Creole accent. "Please, madame," they begged. And it broke my heart. I looked desperately at the couple who were hurrying toward me now.

"Go on, move away," the man scolded the children with authority in his voice that belied his age. "This woman has come to help out. Leave her in peace." Pastor Greene stretched over the heads of the beggars and reached for my hand, smiling. "You must be Valerie," he shouted over the din.

"Yes—" The word was scarcely off my lips before Madame Nolan plowed through the crowd of children and pulled me into a bear hug that nearly knocked the wind out of me.

"We're so glad you are here," she said, pulling away and holding me at arms' length for inspection. Then, as matter-of-factly as if she were commenting on the weather, "You are an answer to our prayers, Valerie." Ignoring the horde of loudly begging children who still swarmed around us, the spry couple led me to their battered Volkswagen van.

Pastor Greene navigated the narrow streets of Port au Prince, weaving in and out of traffic, honking and dodging automobiles that didn't seem to care which side of the street they used. We drove with all the windows open against the sweltering heat. Colorful tap-taps, Haiti's version of the taxi cab, raced by us, tooting their horns and looking as if they were having a contest to see which of them could cram the most people—and chickens and pigs, for that matter—aboard. Many of the tap-taps carried passengers precariously on their rooftops. I peered out from my seat in the back of the van, feeling, in spite of the bumper-to-bumper traffic, as though I had gone back in time.

In this part of town the streets were lined with simple buildings apparently cobbled together with cement blocks and tin and whatever other materials were handy at the time. Many of the shops had open doorways, and every available space was occupied by a business of some type. Sometimes it was no more than a blanket spread on the sidewalk, on which the proprietor displayed his wares—plucked chickens, fish fried on site, bananas, hats, and sandals. Every pedestrian seemed to carry personal cargo of some kind—the women seeming to prefer to carry theirs atop their heads. Women balanced baskets and bowls overflowing with fruits and breads and shoes, and trays with tin cups, and full pitchers of water which they sold by the drink. Goats and dogs freely roamed the streets, and down narrow alleyways I spied pigs rooting in garbage heaps beside which blossomed stunning magenta bougainvillea bushes. The contrast was startling.

Closer to the outskirts of the city, the landscape changed. Here the countryside was rather barren with sparse palm trees poking up here and there amidst the rubble and rubbish that littered the terrain. But the Haitian people themselves made up for any appearance of drabness. They demonstrated an obvious love of color in the garments they wore, sporting brilliant colors and prints in pleasantly clashing combinations. We drove on, and a few miles into the breathtaking ride—after we'd nearly run down a teenage boy balancing a wheelbarrow filled with cinder blocks—I considered e-mailing Will and telling him that I'd discovered an adrenaline rush unlike anything he'd ever experienced.

I thought the same thing that night as I settled into the nine-by-nine room that would be my home for the next two weeks. I pulled back the thin blanket on my sturdy cot and was startled by what seemed to be an entire colony of tiny black ants. Ants I could handle, but as I brushed the insects from the sheet, my eye caught movement on the wall above my bed. A tiny brown lizard scurried up the wall—to join his much larger cousins, I was sure. I stifled a scream and rubbed my arms vigorously, trying to get rid of the goose bumps that had risen there.

"Lord," I said aloud, "You're going to have to help me here." I shook out my bedding and checked the cot one more time for ants, then in one smooth motion I switched off the light and dove under the covers, my heart beating like a bongo drum. In spite of the stifling heat, I pulled the blanket into a tight tent over my entire body—taut enough, I hoped, to deflect any lizards that might decide to "drop in" on me during the night.

My prayers were answered because the next sound I heard was the chorus of a dozen roosters. Through my window I saw that the sun was just peeking over the eastern wall of the courtyard, but it shone a thin sliver of the most lucent orange I've ever seen on the whitewashed cement walls of my room. Checking the floor and the ceiling above me for lizards, I threw my legs over the side of the cot and slipped into my sandals. I flipped on the light switch but nothing happened. I remembered then reading the caveats on the Internet about Haiti's unpredictable electric service. In the half dark, I rummaged in my bags and found a T-shirt and a wrinkled but clean cotton jumper. Madame Nolan had warned me that breakfast was served at six-thirty sharp, and already I could smell the bacon frying. I took a deep breath and stepped into the courtyard to begin my adventure.

Time seemed suspended in this corner of the world. A week flew by in a whirlwind, and yet there were moments when I felt I had been here forever. For eight days I scarcely gave William Concannon a thought. In truth there wasn't time to think. Pastor and Madame Nolan kept me busy with a list so varied I never knew from one moment to the next if I would be slicing lemons or painting cement blocks or changing diapers. And I truly loved every minute of it.

The children seemed to take to me immediately. Each afternoon when school dismissed, they would hurry to the dormitories and finish their chores. Then we would play games on the playground or under the vine-covered veranda if the sun was too hot. The older girls, fascinated by my fine, straight, blond hair, thought nothing of spending an hour in the evenings, braiding and rebraiding it. They filled my head with ribbons and the tiny, colorful barrettes they loved so much. Sometimes they almost put me to sleep with their gentle brushing and the sound of their rhythmic clapping games and songs. Then I would be startled out of my near-trance by half a dozen little faces giggling and pointing at some silly "do" they'd invented at my expense. I didn't mind though; I'd always loved having someone mess with my hair.

By the time the end of my second week approached, I had grown to love Pastor and Madame Nolan like my own grandparents, I could speak a few Creole phrases passably, and I had even formed a tenuous friendship with the lizards. The closer the time came for me to return to the States, the more oddly unsettled I felt. I had made peace with my circumstances concerning Will; I was on speaking terms with my heavenly Father again. In fact, I'd experienced a rather sweet reunion with Him in this most unlikely of places. Yet, my heart seemed in a strange state of turmoil.

Two days before I was to fly back home, I lay on my cot in the dark, perspiring in the airless room, sleep completely eluding me. Outside my window I could hear the faint sounds of traffic on the streets of Port au Prince, and in the distance the haunting drums of the village witch doctors. I had grown accustomed to this audible evidence of voodoo's hold on Haiti. And though I now felt perfectly safe within the gated walls of the orphanage compound, it still made me shudder to think of the spiritual darkness that covered this people and this land due to the wide practice of witchcraft. I couldn't help but wonder how many of the precious boys and girls within these sanctified walls would be taken captive by this evil religion once they left the safety of Pastor and Madame

Nolan's haven. And what would happen when the Greenes could no longer manage the orphanage? They seemed so young at heart, but we had celebrated Pastor Greene's sixty-ninth birthday less than a week before. He couldn't possibly have enough years left to see the smallest ones—tiny Christlene and Daphney and John-Daniel—safely into the world outside the gates.

I whispered into the darkness, suddenly aware that tears were rolling down my cheeks and into my ears. "Oh, Father, keep Your hand on these precious saints. Give them as many years as they need. Bless each child within these walls. And Lord," I added selfishly, "I know my problems seem so petty and small by comparison, but when I get home, please show me what You want me to do with my life. I love You, Father, and I trust You have something special waiting for me back home. Please just show me Your way..."

It happened in the most unexpected way, at a moment when I was not seeking an epiphany of any kind. All morning I had whitewashed cinder blocks. Before chapel time, I freshened up in my room, working my hair into a quick French braid and changing into a fresh blouse.

When I stepped into the sunny courtyard, I saw that the children had come out to the playground. Out of the corner of my eye I saw a little girl off playing by herself in the shade of a courtyard wall, squatting on lean haunches and scratching intently in the dirt with a stick. She was so tiny—surely not more than two or three years old. I knew her name was Jacquette and had asked Madame Nolan about her the first time I saw her, wondering how such a beautiful child had ended up in a place like this. Madame Nolan had told me that Jacquette's mother had six other children she could scarcely feed or clothe. For a moment I'd fought down the anger that rose in me again—the injustice that allowed this woman to have seven children while I had none. Now I remained at a distance and watched this little girl for several minutes. She seemed perfectly content to play by herself.

Then she looked briefly in my direction and I felt drawn to join her. As I walked closer I could hear, even above the laughter of the other children on the playground, that Jacquette was singing in the sweetest voice I will ever, this side of heaven, hear. The words were Creole, but I recognized the melody.

"Mwen konnen Jezu renmenm', Se Bib la ki di mwen sa..." Jesus loves me, this I know...

I smiled to myself, totally taken by this little ebony-faced beauty. I moved toward her slowly, drawn by a magnetic pull I seemed powerless to resist. When I was still some eight or nine feet away she looked up at me and smiled broadly. Holding my gaze, she rose gracefully from her haunches and held out her stick to me, her jet black eyes sparkling. I reached out to take her offering, but as she toddled toward me into the sunlight, my heart seemed to stop beating. Stunned, I sucked in a sharp breath. I could scarcely believe what my eyes saw. Fearing I might faint, I dropped to my knees in front of the little girl, accepting the stick she offered from her tiny hands.

She started to sway shyly, fingering the skirt of her dress—her lime green, gingham check dress with its white eyelet underskirt. She touched a button on her bodice, tucking her chin down and puffing out her belly so she could see the button's bright yellow shape herself.

Then she looked up at me, beaming. "*Sitro,*" she said proudly. The Creole word for lemon.

It wasn't possible! Yet there, right in front of me, modeled by this round-cheeked, cornrowed angel—the very dress I'd sewn when I was sixteen! The dress with its lemons and limes and oranges for buttons. The one I'd sorrowfully shipped off to a rummage sale an ocean away just weeks ago. How had it ended up here? Then I remembered my sister telling me that my baby clothes had been one of the first things to go at the sale. "An old woman came in and snapped them up—all of them," Beth had told me. "She said she was buying them for some charity."

I know Beth thought it would make me feel good to hear that the clothes had sold so quickly, that they had made a nice profit for her church, and that they were going to help someone in need. But at the time I had felt angry. Furious, in fact. How dare they take the little dresses and nightgowns and playsuits I'd so lovingly created, and just toss them to some little snot-nosed brats who couldn't possibly appreciate what they were getting? Of course I didn't say that to Beth. And to my credit, I was over the whole thing before the sun went down that night. I knew my reaction had more to do with the enormous disappointment I'd just experienced than with the clothes themselves.

Now I wondered. Could it be that this orphanage was the charity the woman had purchased them for? But there were thousands of charities in the world, dozens of orphanages in Haiti alone. How could they have ended up here, of all places? Yet, that had to be it. There was no other plausible explanation.

Pastor Nolan rang the bell, signaling time for noon chapel. My mind still racing, I scooped Jacquette into my arms and went to help the older girls herd the little ones into the sanctuary.

I sang—or rather hummed—the Creole choruses with my eyes closed, soaking in the rich, heartfelt harmonies of this rapturous children's choir, turning over in my mind again and again what had just taken place. After choruses, it was time for devotions. I went to the back of the room to help quiet the younger children who were already growing restless. As Madame Nolan made her way to the front, I scooped Jacquette and another stray toddler up onto my lap. Resting my chin between their two dark heads, I looked around at the dozens of children wiggling in their seats in front of me. And then something else wonderful happened.

Two rows in front of me sat Henri, wearing a brown-and-green plaid shirt sewn from fabric left over from a jumper I made in tenth grade. Down the row from him, little Marie-Andre wore a sleeveless shift of silky flocked magenta. I had ripped the seams in that dress more times than I cared to remember, trying in vain to keep the fabric from puckering. My eyes roamed up and down the rows of benches, and everywhere I looked were little motherless Haitian children wearing the clothes I'd made for my babies.

Madame Nolan's voice droned pleasantly in the background, and the children squirmed in my lap, but suddenly it was as though the Lord and I were alone together in that little chapel. His voice wasn't audible. Instead it was the still, small whisper I'd come to know so intimately over the past few weeks.

"Remember that request you put in for a dozen children?" He asked me now. And I was sure He was smiling. "Remember those babies you prayed for so faithfully when you were barely more than a little girl yourself?"

My throat filled and I choked back tears of joy. I knew in that moment—more clearly than I've ever known anything in my life—that I was home. I looked around that room and I knew I was looking at my children, holding two of them on my lap—the babies I'd longed for and prayed for and waited not-so-patiently for for almost three decades.

It occurs to me now that answers to prayer are even sweeter when you've been waiting for them your whole life.

ABOUT THE AUTHOR

Deborah Raney's first novel, *A Vow to Cherish,* was the inspiration for World Wide Pictures' highly acclaimed film of the same title. The author of several other books, Deb also speaks and presents workshops on marriage and parenting topics. She chose Haiti as the setting for this story because of her parents' longtime involvement with a girls' orphanage near Port au Prince. Deb writes from her home in Kansas where she lives with husband, Ken, an illustrator and author. The Raneys are the parents of four children.

THE WARRIOR

James Scott Bell

Even before we dropped anchor, local natives materialized on the beach. They practically threw their canoes into the green waters around the island.

Slap, rest, *slap,* rest, they paddled out toward us in their dugouts with a rhythm The Rockettes would have envied. I found out later we were the first outsiders to visit in over a year.

It was a couple of days before Christmas 1942, and we'd just reached Auki on the island of Malaita, across the Indispensable Straits, north of Guadalcanal. We were there to pick up some cargo. I didn't know it then, but the cargo was human.

A recent Ensign (thanks to the Navy V-7 program), I'd been assigned to the PC 477, a sleek patrol craft now cruising the Solomon Islands, looking for enemy subs and performing escort duty. And when we weren't doing that we were looking to trade with the island inhabitants.

The little village of Auki lay just beyond smooth, white beaches fringed with palm trees. Thatched-roof huts peered out from great, emerald green trees. Beyond the village lay the jungle rain forest, blanketing volcanic mountains that rose abruptly into the clouds. It was like a scene out of the great Clark Gable picture of a few years back, *Mutiny on the Bounty.* Especially when the Kanakes—hundreds of men, women, and children—reached the ship.

I had visions of myself as the Great American Trader. Maybe I could go back to the States with my very own island in my pocket. I'd call it

Rudy Wannamaker's Paradise, Gateway to the Pacific.

I had a good supply of trade goods from home. I'd asked family and friends to send them. They had responded with all kinds of junk jewelry and trinkets. I also had pocket knives, tobacco, belts, soap, candy, and Skivvies. These islanders loved American underwear.

"Hey, Wannamaker," Al Merce, another Ensign, called to me. "You gonna do better than you did back in Tulagi?"

"You watch me," I said. One of the Kanakes I'd tried to trade with there had taken a pocket knife from me, promising to return with a cane. My mistake had been in trusting him.

"These guys are tough, boy," said Al. "Warrior types all the way back to the Stone Age."

"Hey, I'm from Brooklyn," I said.

"I'll be watching." And then Al smiled that big obnoxious smile of his, which just made me mad. I had to show up Al Merce. Just had to. He was from Philadelphia.

With the canoes all around the ship, I jumped down on the propeller guards and got ready to dicker.

Then I saw my mark. He was a warrior all right, like most of the men in the canoes. They would do all of the trading, while the women sat smiling in the back of the boats. These men thought of themselves as a proud people, even after a century of British colonial rule.

The Kanake I'd picked had deep creases in his forehead. Back in America we'd think that was for worry. Maybe the guy just thought too much. But I could tell he was one of the proud ones. He wore a beautiful *daufe* around his neck—a half-moon shaped, mother-of-pearl ornament, majestic in its own primeval way. Daufes were a sign of strength among these people.

It would be a sign of my strength, too, if I could get it from him. I knew I would. It was just a matter of the right offer. Then Al would have nothing left to say.

I first offered him a wallet, and pointed to the daufe.

"*Nogat,*" he said, shaking his head. Like most Kanakes in the Pacific, at least around the places where Europeans had settled, he spoke pidgin English.

I slapped the wallet again, and once more pointed to the warrior necklace.

He shook his head vigorously. "Nogat!"

A tough one. I pulled out a bar of soap. Lifebuoy.

Now the warrior nodded, but instead of offering me the daufe, he held up a trinket of his own, a bunch of mollusk shells on some kind of string.

"You got to be kidding," I said.

He scratched his head at that one, then suddenly smiled. He had teeth the color of coral. He said what sounded like, "You good fella plenty too much." But I figured he was just buttering me up. The guy would have made a good car salesman back home.

"Soap you give," he said, "I give pull." He held up one of his paddles.

"No dice," I said. "I want that thing around your neck."

He shook his head, and his smile faded quicker than an island breeze.

Out of the corner of my eye, I could see Al Merce on deck, watching.

So I pulled out my pièce de résistance, my most valuable item—a bottle of Sea Breeze aftershave lotion. For some reason these people were enamored of what they called "smell good water." I handed the bottle to the warrior and winked.

He took it gingerly, looking at it like it was liquid gold. Then he handed it to the woman in the back of the canoe, who I presumed was his wife.

Giggling, the woman took it and uncorked the bottle, smelled it, and laughed even harder. She was pleased.

That ought to do it, I thought. But then the warrior held up a paddle and a finely crafted wooden comb.

"No," I said, and hit my chest to indicate the daufe.

The warrior looked at his wife, she looked at the water, then he looked back at me and handed me the bottle.

From up on deck I heard Al Merce laugh. So to save face I chewed the warrior out. "You get gone!" I yelled at him. "No trade with you!" I knocked myself on the noggin with my knuckles. "No trade with you!"

For a second he looked stunned, like this was the last thing he expected. Then, gathering what was left of his ancient pride, he held himself up to his full height. His lean body stood perfectly balanced on the small boat in the choppy waters. And for one, brief moment, I saw him a thousand years ago, facing down an enemy, his look alone enough to dissuade the foe.

Then he sat down and pushed away from the ship. In a blink he turned his canoe around and paddled back toward the island.

"Get much out of him?" Al shouted.

"Shut up," I shouted back.

I went on dickering for another half hour. I traded for fruit—papayas, limes, pineapple, bananas—a comb, a javelin, and a paddle. Not bad, but not great, either. The only really good thing was I didn't have to give up my smell good water. But I couldn't shake the feeling I'd been jinxed, set back by that first warrior who wouldn't deal with me.

Two days later, Christmas Eve, we got down to unloading the rice and barley we'd brought for the islanders.

Before the war, the village had been supplied by small, interisland schooners which brought food and clothing in exchange for copra. Now, with Japanese ships patrolling the waters, even the smallest schooners couldn't get in.

That's why we were here.

When all the food was loaded into canoes, Captain Miller announced we'd be taking on seventy-five Kanake men for transport back to Tulagi. They came onboard under the charge of a British Labor Lieutenant named Stevenson. He told us about the British system of labor and how these islanders got one pound a month (around four U.S. dollars) for working on plantations.

"We're doing these blokes a favor," he said.

I was glad the British labor system wasn't doing me any favors.

It took a couple of hours to get them all signed onboard, these little men averaging just over five feet or so. They were naked except for their lap laps, or loincloths, and sat on deck on their haunches.

Stevenson directed the galley to bring up a mess of rice and barley and then he had it dumped on a big, flat, metal pan in the center of the deck. The Kanakes ate with their hands.

And suddenly, standing there watching this trough feeding, I felt like a slaver. This wasn't the duty I'd signed on for. I thought about the old hymn, "Amazing Grace." My grandmother had taught it to me when I was a kid. I recalled her telling me that the guy who wrote it had been a slaver himself.

I went up to Stevenson and asked him if these Kanake men were being taken against their will.

"Of course not," he said. "These men volunteered. They'll each get three pounds a month this time, for three month's work, improving docks and roads in Tulagi. Then they'll come back to their village."

Some prospect.

I watched for another moment as the men ate their rice. I was just about to go below deck when I saw him.

The warrior.

The one who wouldn't trade with me.

He looked up, his daufe still dangling proudly from his neck. But his look was anything but proud. The fiery eyes I had seen a couple of days ago were now embers on a cold beach.

He recognized me, I'm sure. It's one of those things you just know. He quickly looked back down at the rice pan. Way down. And didn't look back up.

I spent the rest of the day doing odd jobs, charting some courses, meeting with the captain. For some reason, though, the face of the warrior kept coming back to me, floating around in my head the way disquieting memories sometimes do. I kept seeing in his look a melancholy, an encroaching realization that life was no longer a thing to master but an anguish to endure.

Some things are shared by all men, I supposed. Sometimes you get knocked down. Sometimes you don't get back up.

When twilight came I went up on deck to smoke my pipe. The sea air was bracing, and the *fwap fwap* of the water against the hull was the only sound. Malaita Island rose up off the port bow, like some brooding sea monster.

As I lit my pipe I noticed I wasn't alone.

One of the Kanakes was squatting on the edge of the deck, looking at the island. I knew even before I checked that it was the warrior. He was stock still, his arms wrapped around his knees, silent.

I smoked for about ten minutes, watching him. He didn't move once.

Then, as the sun gave its final salute, I made the decision.

I went back to my quarters and grabbed the bottle of Sea Breeze aftershave. When I got back on deck the sky was a dusky shroud.

The warrior was still there. I sat down, crosslegged, next to him.

"Hey," I said.

He looked at me stoically. I held out the aftershave. He shook his head.

"Take it," I said. "Merry Christmas."

"Eh?"

I put the bottle in his hand. "It's Christmas."

"Kissmuss?"

"You know, Santa Claus, ho ho ho, baby Jesus?"

Even in the onrushing gloom I could see his smile. "Oh, Jesus!" he said. "Him good fella plenty too much!"

"That's right," I said, laughing. "You know story?"

"Missionary," he said. "Him good fella too."

"Well, I hope he was American."

"No," he said, shaking his head. "Lime."

"Limey?"

"Yeah, yeah!"

And, as one, we laughed.

I slapped him gently on the shoulder, stood up and turned. He stopped me with a pat on the leg. He stood too, the top of his head even with my chin. Then he slowly removed the daufe from around his neck and handed it to me.

"No," I said.

"Yeah," he said.

"You don't."

"Take, take. Kissmuss."

I took it. And standing there in the darkness I thought about all the Christmas presents I'd received over the years, including the .22 rifle my Dad gave me when I was twelve and the autographed picture of Douglas Fairbanks my mom procured (Douglas Fairbanks Sr. being my favorite movie actor of all time). But flashing back on all that, I couldn't think of a single present that meant more to me than this half-moon necklace I held in my hand.

Suddenly, from way off in the distance, something growled in the sky. In a minute I saw what it was. American airplanes from a bombing raid were returning to Henderson Field on Guadalcanal.

Soon the sky was filled with them, their red, green, and yellow lights almost like a flying Christmas display.

The warrior looked up at them in pure wonderment. So did I.

"Plenty too much," I said.

ABOUT THE AUTHOR

James Scott Bell graduated with honors from the University of Southern California Law Center. He has written over 300 articles and numerous books for the legal profession. A former trial lawyer, he is the author of the Christian legal thrillers *Circumstantial Evidence, Final Witness,* and *Blind Justice.* Jim has taught screenwriting at The Masters College, novel writing at Learning Tree University in Los Angeles, and the art and craft of fiction at various writers conferences.

THE TEST

Gayle Roper

I entered the outhouse and pulled the door shut behind me. The bright sun outside dimmed to dusk. I sighed as I turned the wooden rectangle that served as the privacy lock.

Dear God, I thought morosely as I stared out the ventilation slits at the top of the structure. *I'm not doing very well, am I? I had such high hopes for the week. Lad must be so disappointed in me. I know I certainly am.*

I sighed again as I reached for the toilet paper and froze. My gentle sigh morphed into a gargle of revulsion. There, sitting on the roll of tissue staring at me, was the largest spider I'd ever seen. My skin crawled and sweat popped out all over my body.

Wonderful! Now I'm trapped in the outhouse for the rest of my life. That'll really make Lad proud.

I shrank as far from the creature as I could which wasn't too far even though the structure was a two seater. My back itched because I *knew* the ugly thing had family lurking in the corner behind me, waiting for the signal to jump me at my most vulnerable. Apprehensively I scanned the small structure. The fact that I saw nothing suspicious except my obvious tormentor didn't soothe me much. I knew evil when I saw it, and it had eight hairy legs and was out to get me. I blinked against tears.

When the letter had arrived from Lad's parents with the plane tickets to Canada so we could join the family for one week of their annual month-long vacation at their cottage on Aylen Lake, I'd actually been glad and excited. Lad and I had married in May as soon as we graduated from Penn State because Lad had been given a wonderful opportunity to do graduate work at the Colorado School of Mines in Boulder, one of the only schools in the country that still had a pure metallurgy program. Everyone else had gone to materials science, including all kinds of ceramics and polymers in their programs. But Lad loved metals, and this opportunity was too good to pass up.

So I gave up my bid for wedding of the century and married him quickly in a small ceremony so that I could go with him. It wasn't a hardship. I'd do most anything for Lad. Certainly I'd join his family at Aylen Lake at the southeastern tip of Algonquin Provincial Park in Ontario.

I'd heard Aylen Lake stories since the first night I met Lad at our Campus Crusade group at State. When he took me to his home for the first time, I'd been told more Aylen Lake stories, this time from the point of view of the rest of his wonderful family. I particularly loved the stories his nineteen-year-old sister Marly told, mostly because she made Lad the scapegoat. I loved the way the Winters all laughed at her exaggerations, especially Lad. It showed such a fine spirit and such deep affection. I knew I wanted to be part of a family that loved and laughed like this.

And now I was. Soon I'd have my own Aylen Lake stories.

We flew to Ottawa the first week in August. Pop Winters and Marly met us at the airport and drove us the two and a half hours to the lake.

"The weather's been great," Marly told us. "Sunny and warm. And the water's in the seventies!" And she began telling Lad about who was presently at the lake, who was putting on additions to their cottages, who had been too outspoken at the cottagers' annual meeting, who had preached for the past two Sundays at the chapel, and who was actually putting in septic systems.

"Indoor plumbing?" Lad scoffed. "At the lake? Give me a break!"

"Sounds good to me," I said. I had secretly been wondering how I'd fare for a whole week without a hot shower.

Marly and Lad looked at me in disbelief. Pop eyed me in the rearview mirror, left eyebrow raised. I blushed, but I still thought that a flush toilet sounded like a fine thing.

After a moment's silence, conversation resumed among the three Winterses, and I settled back to listen. I like to listen. Probably that's because I was raised an only child by parents who never stopped talking. Or arguing. They were both lawyers, though thankfully they worked for different firms with different specialties. I shuddered to think what life would have been if they had ever had to go head-to-head in court.

Because they were so abnormally verbal, it became easier to be quiet rather than fight for speaking space. One of the things I loved most about Lad was that he waited for me to state my opinion. Slowly I was learning to speak up, and I was finding it very freeing.

Marly glanced at me and said in no context that I could see, "You needn't worry, Jenn. You won't have any trouble passing the Aylen Lake Test. None at all." And she smiled sweetly.

I blinked. "What's the Aylen Lake Test?"

Marly looked at her father and grinned. "Pop made us promise we wouldn't marry anyone until he or she had been to the lake and proved himself an acceptable Laker. The worst thing in the world would be to have a Winters who wasn't a Laker!"

Lad felt the jolt her statement gave me. He took my hand and said, "Not to worry, Marly. Jenn'll pass." He looked at me, his eyes full of love and trust. "Right, honey?"

"Right," I said with as much assurance as I could muster.

Oh, Lord, let me be a Laker, please!

The closer we got to the lake, the more Lad vibrated with excitement. I could feel waves of anticipation rippling from him like heat shimmers from macadam. The implosion occurred when we reached the turnoff for the lake road.

"Stop, Pop!" Lad called out so loudly we all jumped, including Pop who actually swerved in reaction. "I want to drive the lake road."

Pop pulled over as soon as he made the turn, and we played musical seats. Lad and Pop sat up front, Marly and I in the back. Lad drove and drove and drove. I knew the nine kilometer dirt road wasn't as long as it seemed. It was my nerves, already tight, now strung to breaking with the idea of the Test.

Then we crested a hill, and there lay Aylen Lake. It was so beautiful my breath caught, then whooshed out in pleasure. Sun jewels shimmered on the softly rippled lake, and rank upon rank of evergreens and deciduous trees marched to the shore. A motorboat cut through the water, a foamy white wake trailing like the tail on a kite, and plump white clouds sailed like three masted schooners across a vivid blue sky. Here and there cottages and cabins were tucked into the shoreline. The overwhelming sense was of limitless space and freedom.

"She likes it," Marly said, smiling.

I nodded. "It's glorious." Massive understatement.

We drove to the public dock, unloaded our luggage and put it in the family motorboat while Pop parked the car. Lad piloted the boat across the lake, and soon we were unloading our things and carrying them up to the cottage, a large brown-stained building with windows all across the front giving a spectacular view of the lake.

And so began one of the most wonderful/awful weeks of my life as I tried to prove to the Winterses that Lad hadn't made a mistake marrying me.

The trial by ordeal began moments after my arrival when I faced the outhouse for the first time. I'd never used one before. My mother's idea of roughing it was a Holiday Inn instead of a suite at a five star hotel, so such basic facilities were beyond my ken.

"We've got one of the best outhouses around," Marly boasted. "Clean as a whistle. I know. It's my job to clean it."

As I tried not to breathe while inside, I couldn't imagine what it would be like if Marly didn't clean it. And how did one clean an outhouse anyway?

Then came waterskiing.

I'm as coordinated as the next woman. I like walking and hiking; I love the outdoors; I even like biking in moderation, but I'm not a certified jock. I've always been very happy not being one. Until the Test.

I finally gave up trying to stand on the two fiendish wooden strips when my legs became so wobbly I could barely hold myself upright and my arms were so rubbery I couldn't undo the clips on my life jacket. By this time, I was so full of water that I sloshed when I moved.

"Why don't you just be the spotter?" Lad suggested kindly as he steered me to a seat in the back of the boat after pulling me, exhausted, from the water.

"What's the spotter have to do?" I asked. "Watch out for great whites lurking?"

Lad laughed like I'd made a clever joke, but I wasn't entirely jesting. I was used to the soft sandy New Jersey ocean floor or the smooth hard concrete of a pool. The endless depths of the lake below me as I waited for the tow boat to come rescue me after yet another fall made me exceedingly nervous.

I spotted for Marly who got up on her skis immediately and with grace and ease. She wove back and forth through the wake as we sped from one end of the lake to the other. A black cloud of inadequacy and looming failure sat directly over my head as I watched.

Then I spotted for Lad who was magnificent, skiing with not only one hand but one ski. When we raced back toward the cottage, he skied so close to the shore I was certain he was going to kill himself. Instead he let go of the tow rope at just the right instant and glided to a stop in the shallows where he stepped lightly out of his ski and onto land without even wetting his feet.

Then there was fishing.

I got the hang of casting fairly quickly, my flying hook grazing Lad's cheek only once. And I'm not squeamish. I didn't mind handling the worms. After all, I was a gardener and worms went with the territory. I did however feel each prick as I impaled the poor things on my hook.

But sitting silently in a small aluminum boat staring hopefully at the water? Talk about boring!

"How long will we be here?" I asked Lad after an hour of doing nothing. At least I was doing nothing. Lad had caught two keepers, lake bass he said, and several he deemed too small to keep and had tossed back.

"Don't worry," he said with that magical smile of his. I found myself smiling back in spite of my pique. "We've got plenty of time. We'll stay until dark."

"And how soon until dark?"

"Up here it gets dark later, so about two more hours."

"I should have brought a book," I said with sinking heart.

"What?" Lad was scandalized at the idea. "Don't you enjoy being with me?"

Now there was an are-you-still-beating-your-wife question if I ever heard one.

"I'd enjoy being with you more if we talked, just a bit."

"You can't talk and fish. The fish might hear."

As I said, boring.

I did have a moment of temporary glory on one of our cooking days. Mom Winters has made it very clear that she doesn't plan to spend her vacations in the kitchen cooking for a largely take-it-for-granted crowd, so she has divvied the days of the week among the family.

"Once you turned sixteen, you got a day," Marly told me as she served us pancakes on her day.

Apparently once you got married, you got two days. We had Tuesday and Friday.

I'd planned our meals carefully, and we'd come prepared with a plastic cooler filled with our needs, sealed with more duct tape than was sold annually at Home Depot. The pièce de résistance of Tuesday's dinner was to be a blueberry cobbler made with freshly picked blueberries. The five of us boated over to the small cliff at the south end of the lake where blueberry bushes thrived.

We picked and picked until we had enough for the cobbler and for blueberry pancakes the next morning, Mom cooking. It was appalling to realize how many of the little indigo fruit it took to gather a usable amount. By the time we were finished, my back ached from bending over, and I had a wasp bite on my palm from when a wasp and I went after the same berry. I had a nervous twitch from glancing over my shoulder all morning looking for the bear Marly kept insisting must certainly resent our taking his food, and my left knee was scraped and seeping blood and fluid from the terrifying moment when I'd slipped on a mossy rock and gone down, certain I was about to fall right off the cliff into the lake.

But in spite of my physical impairments the dinner turned out quite nicely, the cobbler a raging success.

That night Lad took me in his arms and said, "You're going to make a great Laker. That was a wonderful dinner, sweetheart."

I felt like such a fraud. Great Aylen Lakers didn't have aching backs, skinned knees, and swollen palms, to say nothing of the new fear of meeting a bear on the way to the outhouse.

The capper to my week of trial by ordeal was our sailing endeavor. Pop Winters had a sixteen-foot day sailer, and Lad decided we should make use of it.

"Bring a book with you," he said. "You can just lie back in the sun and read."

It sounded wonderful to me. I'd brought ten books in my suitcase, and I'd only had time to read half of one. I was going nuts with reader's withdrawal.

"He's taking you?" Marly asked as we came down onto the dock with the detachable rudder and all the required safety gear in hand. My paperback was tucked firmly under my arm.

"Of course I'm taking her," Lad said. "While sisters are wonderful, wives are more wonderful still." And he smiled that glorious smile at me. My heart soared. I vowed I would be the best sailor he'd ever met.

"Lad, maybe Jenn doesn't want to go sailing." Mom was lying on her chaise, book in hand, Coke beside her, sun hat pulled low over her sunglasses.

Lad blinked. Obviously he couldn't imagine such a thing.

"Oh, I want to go," I said emphatically. "I do."

Mom nodded, taking me at my word, and went back to her book.

Lad helped me into the boat and showed me how to pull the rope that lowered the centerboard. "When I give the word, pull as hard as you can until you hear the clunk. Then cleat the rope."

I nodded. I could do that. I settled myself on the gunwale amidships while he seated himself in the back on the opposite side.

"Ready?" he asked.

I nodded, my rope held firmly.

"Here we go!" He pushed off from the dock. "Pull!" he called, and I pulled. I heard the clunk and tried to cleat the rope. As I struggled, I felt the sail fill with wind and the boat begin to move, then tilt alarmingly. I looked up to see the boom coming straight at me. Giving a strangled cry, I backed up and threw myself overboard to escape the lethal swing.

As I sputtered to the surface in about four feet of water, I knew I'd done something wrong. I had no idea what, but I'd obviously made the boat tilt. Another black mark! I looked wildly for Lad.

"I did what you told me!" I shouted as water streamed down my face.

There was a moment of absolute silence as Mom, Pop, and Marly all dry and comfortable on the dock, and Lad, still dry and seated comfortably in the boat, stared at me. Then Marly snickered. She clapped her hand over her mouth to contain the noise, but she couldn't. In a moment everyone was laughing, me included. I could imagine how I looked—a drowned rat came to mind—and how I sounded—my mother, the defense attorney, was apt.

"You're not hurt, are you?" Lad finally had breath to ask.

I shook my head. "I'm fine." Just inept. "What happened? What did I do wrong?"

He had the grace to blush. "You didn't do anything wrong, sweetheart.

It was me. I was so intent on making sure you knew what you were doing that I forgot to attach the rudder. I reached back for it when I pushed off, and it wasn't there. The wind caught us and whipped us 180 degrees."

I noticed for the first time that the boat was facing in the opposite direction.

"I didn't do it?"

He shook his head.

"Really? You're not just being nice?"

"You didn't do it."

I was so relieved that I hadn't accrued yet another failing grade that I climbed back in the boat without a word of complaint. Lad attached the rudder, and this time we sailed off without complications.

"Where are we going?" I asked.

"Nowhere. We're sailing!" He said the last worshipfully. "Just sit back and relax. Read."

But I never got to read a word. I spent all my time pulling ropes at Cap'n Lad's orders or climbing from one side of the boat to the other when we tacked or needed to balance against the wind. Every time I clambered over the centerboard housing, which was every time I moved from one side to the other, I clomped the insides of my legs on said housing as I ducked the swinging boom. I suppose some people might find it fun to bruise their bodies while risking their lives in front of a great swinging piece of metal, but, alas, I wasn't one of them.

And so I found myself, finally dry, sitting in the outhouse, held captive by a spider. Arachnophobia was the final ignominy, the definitive black mark. I knew I had a huge red F imprinted indelibly on my forehead.

I also knew I couldn't sit here forever waiting for the horrible insect to move. After all, dinner was in about thirty minutes, Pop cooking.

With shaking hands I reached down and slid off my sneaker. I grasped it tightly and raised my arm. I swung at the toilet paper with all my might. It went flying across the outhouse, striking the far wall with a muted thud.

But the wily spider had felt me coming. He jumped free at the last moment. I watched with fascinated horror as he now sat mere inches from my unclad foot. I could already feel his fangs as he took a great venomous bite. I could picture Lad's grieving face when he broke the outhouse door down and found me seconds from expiration, panting, writhing in pain, a contented spider sitting on my chest, cleaning his many toenails.

The spider suddenly moved across the floor, and I screamed even as I watched him swagger away from me. He went to a small crack between two boards and slid through.

I sat for several minutes, trying to calm my beating heart. Finally I had the courage to reach for the roll and get myself out of there. I shuddered all the way to the dock.

The westering sun was turning the gentle hills on the far side of the lake golden, and the water had become as smooth as glass. I stood there alone, basking in the solitude, bathed in a strange mix of sorrow and worship, sorrow that I was failing the Test, praise for the obvious proof of our great God.

"O LORD, our Lord, how majestic is your name in all the earth! You have set your glory above the heavens. When I consider your heavens, the work of your fingers, the moon and the stars, which you have set in place, what is man that you are mindful of him, the son of man that you care for him? O LORD, our Lord, how majestic is your name in all the earth!"

I was so lost in my thoughts that I didn't realize Lad was there until he slid an arm about my waist and pulled me against him, my back to his chest. He leaned forward and kissed my temple.

"It's so beautiful," I said. "I could look at it all day. It speaks to my soul."

His arm tightened. "I know."

"I understand why you love it so." The last was a whisper because I could barely speak around the tears clogging my throat. "I love it too. I think that's why it hurts so much."

"What hurts?"

I took a great gulp of air. "I'm so sorry I've failed the Test!"

I whipped around and buried my face in his chest and sobbed. Lad said nothing, just held me until I cried myself out. Another reason to love him. My parents would already have given me fifty reasons why crying was foolish.

When I finally quieted, he took a step back, caught my chin in his hand and forced me to look at him. Not that I was a delightful sight with my runny nose, swollen eyes, and blotchy face.

"Why do you think you failed the Test?" he asked.

"Because I can't do any of the things you like to do." My chin wobbled again. "I'm a lousy Laker!"

He shrugged. "That's not the Test. I already knew you weren't much of an athlete. I was just giving you the chance to try some new things."

I stared at him, confused. "You don't care that I can't ski or that I don't like fishing? You'll still love me even if I don't sail with you?"

"It would be fun if you liked doing those things, but it's not imperative." He grinned. "I think we have what's important in common."

I reviewed the week in my mind, searching diligently for what we had in common. "We both like blueberry cobbler?"

"We both love this place," he said.

I nodded as I looked over my shoulder at the golden hills and gilded lake. "We do."

"Then you passed and with flying colors."

I stilled. "What?"

"You passed."

"Because I love the place?"

He nodded. "Because you love it. Because you can stand here and quote Scripture about how great God is to have created it. Because you can stand here and stare without tiring of the beauty."

I searched my husband's face, looking for a catch, a loophole. All I saw was acceptance.

He smiled at me. "What is the chief duty of a Laker?"

I smiled back at his corruption of the Westminster Catechism.

He answered himself. "The chief duty of a Laker is to love the lake and enjoy it forever."

"I can do that," I said as my heart soared. "I can do that."

What is the chief duty of man?
The chief duty of man is to love God and enjoy Him forever.

ABOUT THE AUTHOR

Gayle Roper has always loved stories, and as a result she's authored more than thirty books, most recently the award-winning *The Decision* (Multnomah) and *Caught in a Bind 134* (Zondervan). Her articles have appeared in numerous periodicals. She also loves speaking at writers conferences and women's events, reading and eating out, adores her kids and grandkids, and loves her own personal patron of the arts, her husband Chuck.

MAREN'S FLAG

Robert Elmer

Grace couldn't finish writing this letter either. She watched another tear puddle form where she had just penned the date at the top.

Oh, but what difference did it make? With a sigh she folded up the onionskin airmail paper and shoved it into the top drawer of the desk, along with all her other notes to Mom.

The ones she could never send.

Copenhagen, December 12, 1947

Dearest Mother,

I'm afraid I've turned into such a complainer in these letters. I never want you to worry about me. But San Francisco was never like this! It is so dark, the days so short. Enough of that. In your last note you asked how the language lessons are coming. In a word? Horribly. *I can't even tell Danes where I live; they don't understand me. One even asked me to spell it out, letter by letter.*

Number 44, K-ø-b-m-a-g-e-r-g-a-d-e. It's the o *with a line through it that gives me all the trouble. Don't worry if you can't pronounce it, either. I believe the Danes intend it that way.*

And I've come to believe it's like standing outside the door to a private club, one you can't enter unless you can say the name of a silly strawberry pudding dessert. Rødgrød med fløde. *Goodness knows*

I've tried, without success. Wasn't there something in the Bible like that, when only the men in Gilead's tribe could pronounce the password?

Shibboleth? *Everyone who couldn't say it correctly was killed, if I recall. If words could kill…*

Problem is, everyone here is like Erik…so sweet, ever so polite, and generous and warm hearted. Quite funny, too, I think. They laugh at their peculiar, quiet jokes, but without me.

Oh, we do have conversations…in English. But in Danish, Mother, it's still so humiliating that I'm almost ready to give up. Here I am, a grown woman, almost thirty years old, and I have struggled with this horrid language now for almost six months. I often feel like an eight-year-old, or worse.

Can you imagine? I'm still saying things in language school like, "This is Lasse. Goddag, Lasse. *How do you have it? I'm glad to make the acquaintance of your purse."*

They smile anyway and tell me it was a good try. "Fantastisk!" *they say, and I can remember that word, but I think they're just trying to make me feel better. My Danish is surely* not *fantastisk.*

And then, Mother, I've told you about Fru *Ipsen.* Mrs. *Ipsen. (Her real name is Maren Kirstine Ipsen, which somehow doesn't seem to fit her.) In any case, she is as cold as the winter sun here, so far away. Yes, she constantly speaks Danish to me, but I fear that's mainly out of spite. Erik tells me she's from the west, and her* jysk *country accent is quite hard to follow. Whatever the case, she seems to resent me for daring to want to marry her Danish son. Imagine the nerve of this young American, trying to change her traditions! How will I ever call her a mother-in-law? It's…*

And that's where it left off, at the bottom of the page, just like all the others.

Stop the silly tears! she told herself, rubbing her eyes. Finally she rose from the desk, still determined not to cry. Maybe some cool air would help her think, clear her head, and help her to know what to do.

One thing was sure: She couldn't go to language classes, not today. For one thing, she couldn't face Erik with her puffy eyelids, not again. Because, not only was Erik her fiancé, he was her language tutor, as well. Maybe that was the problem. Without a word Grace slipped out to the hallway and found her long coat. She held her breath, hoping Fru Ipsen wouldn't hear her leave the flat.

Maren Ipsen sighed when she heard the front door click shut.

"Home by six for dinner, Grace?" she asked the closed door. "We're having *bøf*, and..."

Of course the door didn't answer, and she felt silly—and old, much older than her fifty-two years. She had been planning a nice dinner, though. Yesterday, she'd asked the butcher down the street for an extra portion of ground beef, enough for herself and Erik and Grace. She could do that now since the war had ended. She'd even brought home a fine large onion and four baby potatoes.

So it wasn't exactly like American hamburgers and French fries. But she'd heard Americans ate those foods with their fingers, which seemed horribly impolite. On the other hand, with a little brown gravy (thickened with flour and seasoned with meat juice and piquant smoky browning) and some boiled red cabbage, shredded the way her mother had taught her and seasoned correctly (with just the right balance of sugar and vinegar), this would be a fine little meal.

Or it would have been. If Grace was ever going to fit in, she would have to get used to Danish cooking.

Ah, Grace...Maren kept up her dusting and tried not to care. But the pain welled up inside her again when she brushed the frosty window with her nose and looked down at Vesterbrogade. She caught a glimpse of Grace's cheery red scarf in the distance, past Nikolai's Bakery, which wasn't as good anymore since the younger Nikolai took over. She traced a line in the window fog, trying to capture more of the dim light that filtered through the cold glass.

"Why is this girl so unhappy, Vimpel?" she asked her little caged finch. *Vimpel*, the word for the red and white flag streamers that hung from flagpoles all over her tidy little country. When Jens had given the tiny bird to her at the end of the war—a celebration gift—it had reminded her of a vimpel. It was cute, in any case, with its showy red feathers. Vimpel skittered back and forth on his perch and twittered happily. Of unhappy young Americans, Vimpel had no idea.

"And what does anyone so beautiful have to be so unhappy about?"

Perhaps her son was partly to blame. Erik was unpredictable, she had to admit, just as his father had been. Prone to quick decisions, like coming back from a summer in America with a girl in tow, announcing to everyone they would be married. *An American!*

After she got over the shock, though, Maren had been glad to let Grace stay in the spare room of her flat. After all, she needed company since her Jens died, more than just Vimpel. Nothing against the finch, of course, but Maren imagined she would teach her future daughter-in-law a little Danish cooking, just as her own mother had taught her.

And why not? Jens had always loved her cooking. "My Maren, you're the best cook in all of Copenhagen," he used to tell her. That might have been good enough; what else could she offer, as a perfectly plain daughter of a pig farmer? Children, perhaps?

Not even that. Erik had no brothers, no sisters. He was an accident—no, a felicity, a gift from God. So it was too much, yet Maren had hoped—foolishly, it turned out—that perhaps Grace might turn out to be the daughter she'd never known.

But no. And how not or why not, she'd never quite understood. Never understood very much about the moody, sensitive American girl at all. Never understood how such a pretty young thing could draw back into her star-spangled shell, deeper and deeper, day after day.

All right, then. If pressed, Maren would accept some of the blame, but not all of it. Perhaps the trouble started in part because she had never managed to learn much English. And since she and Grace couldn't speak together, well, their times in the kitchen had dwindled to nothing.

Now Erik, he was the clever one; he spoke enough for the both of them. But he had learned in school, here in Copenhagen.

They didn't do that in my day, she told herself, and certainly not in the little fishing village where she had grown up. Maren could read a bit in English, but painfully and slowly. It was too late to learn.

"I'm sorry, Lord," she blurted out, but the words stopped at her windowpane, turned to fog and ran down the glass like the tears on her cheeks. "What else can I do?"

Vimpel turned his head to look up at her and began singing again.

Only 3:30 P.M. and the sky was already dimming. The feeble little bronze sun hadn't shown itself until ten that morning, and now it was gone, again. More sleet? The clouds overhead were dark enough to deliver, and surely they would.

Fine. Let it rain.

Grace shoved her hands deeper into the pockets of the warm overcoat and snuggled her neck against the fur collar. The coat had belonged to Maren, naturally. This California girl had nothing so warm.

She took the route she'd taken so many times before. Frederiksborggade to Nørregade, past the main library in the direction of Tivoli Park. Past the Anton Berg chocolate store, and she could smell a faint whiff of dark buttery bittersweet, the kind most Danes seemed to crave. Why, she wasn't sure. It tasted bitter to her. And besides, she knew something everyone else in Denmark wouldn't admit.

There's nothing better than a good old American Hershey bar.

She slowed down at the Holmegaard crystal display, elegant and merry for the holidays, only a couple of weeks away. The big Magasin department store was just around the corner, and over there stood Illum, too, decked out for the holidays with immaculately dressed mannequins in the window. Grace would not go inside this time, though. She had somewhere else to go.

Out of the corner of her eye she noticed the street musician playing his hand-cranked organ, tipping his black top hat to anyone who dropped a coin in his basket. A Danish Christmas song, of course. Erik's favorite.

"Det kimer nu til Julefest…" Bells ringing in the Christmas fest…

Fine. Let them.

It was cold enough so the slush from the night before had frozen again, and it crackled beneath her thin boots. She walked on, wondering if her Danish tutor would notice her missing.

So she'd made it for two blocks without thinking of him. A new record? She wasn't sure. But she walked on, wondering how her prince could chase away the dragon chasing her right now.

What dragon? Ever since they'd met again at the Lincoln High School reunion, class of '37, it had seemed as if everything would fall into place in this fairy tale. Erik Ipsen the dashing exchange student returns to San Francisco and falls in love with the girl he'd always admired from afar. He takes her back to his land of castles and they live happily ever after.

Only she couldn't even cross the moat.

It wasn't for lack of trying. And now she could say "I love you" in Danish pretty well. Also "thanks for the meal" and "I'm sorry." Quite a vocabulary, actually. Good enough for starting a fairy tale; perhaps not enough to keep turning the pages.

And the worst part was, Erik just didn't seem to understand her tears. With the patience of a Danish saint he kept coaching her, helping her learn. He was a Danish tutor, after all. But when she watched him laughing and joking with his friends, she knew she was on the outside, looking in.

"You'll learn soon enough," he had reassured her.

Sure, she told herself. *And ugly ducklings turn into swans.*

But how long would *that* take?

Maren moved on to the next room, mentally checking off her chore list. There was no forgetting; it was the same way every time. Not that she was a slave to habit, mind you. It's just that she had tried other ways, when she was younger and a little more prone to being foolish.

But this worked the best. First polish the copper plates, then dust the buffet, then the pictures, then the furniture. From the den to the hall to the bedrooms, in that order and no other. The routine made her feel good, somehow connected, the same way as when she cooked. It was the way her mother had taught her.

In the spare bedroom she stood in front of her brother's old desk, the one Grace liked to use for writing. The drawer gaped open, showing a jumbled mess of papers. No, that wouldn't do.

I really shouldn't, she told herself, and a stab of guilt told her that reading letters not meant for her eyes was wrong, even if she didn't fully understand all the English words. But she couldn't help noticing the trail someone's tears had left across the small, tight letters of the sheet on top.

Should I?

And then she spied her own name.

Thursday, October 22, 1947

Dear Mother,

I will never get used to Maren's food as long as I live. All the odd sandwiches on such dark, thin pumpernickel, the liverwurst, the pickled herring, the raw…I don't know what it is, but I'm afraid to ask.

And the way it's eaten—all with knives and forks, and all in some sort of secret, traditional order. Erik tried to explain it all to me, but it's like trying to perform a play when you can't read the script. FIRST the fish, THEN the meats, finally the roast pork, and cheese at the end. Always the same way, every time. It's just like their language—incomprehensible. And they don't seem to care whether outsiders learn or not.

What's Erik going to do when he figures out I cannot…no, will not *cook the way his mother does? That I will* never *cook like her? That I can't even cook, at all? We haven't talked about it. He still assumes I'm going to learn. He is such a gentle, sweet man in so many ways, but he just doesn't* understand.

And you should have seen Maren's face when she found me eating a jelly sandwich in the kitchen, with my fingers, standing up!

"May I help you?" *In English.*

The girl behind the counter smiled when Grace stepped inside her shop, while the doorbell jingled.

How did she know? wondered Grace. Her Danish shoes came from the Danish department store, made with Danish leather from Danish cows. Even a navy blue Danish skirt, made in Aarhus, though it was hidden under Maren's serious Danish overcoat, which she kept buttoned despite the shop's cheery warmth. This wasn't the first time someone had guessed, but *how* did the girl know? Grace hadn't opened her mouth, and her light auburn features could pass for a Dane's—at least Erik had said so.

But no, the clerk had greeted her *in English.* As if Grace had some kind of Stars and Stripes tattoo waving across her forehead. Come to think of it, maybe that wasn't such a bad idea. It would remove all doubt.

Because it didn't matter how many hours she'd spent in front of a mirror practicing saying *goddag* with just the right tone, just the right little swallowed grunt. Erik called it a "glottal stop." She called it impossible.

She'd also worn a deep groove in that part of the *See It and Speak It in Scandinavian* record, the one her mother had bought as a going-away present and she had packed so carefully into her suitcase, with wads of newspaper. She'd unwadded the *San Francisco Chronicles* and read them over and over again while listening to the record. Play it again.

But she just couldn't play it any more. She couldn't be the wife Erik thought he was getting, she would always be the oddity, the outsider, the wife he would always have to apologize for.

"I'm sorry," he would tell people with his sweet smile, in shops just like the one where she now stood, shivering. "Grace didn't quite understand what you said." And then he would repeat it for her more slowly, in English.

I'm sorry, too, she told herself. *But Erik deserves better.*

She blew into her hands, trying to buy more time to decide. Yes, she loved him. Of course she loved him. But he was making a mistake, and she was it.

Once more she looked over her shoulder, out to the darkening street, just to make sure no one saw her. They would find out, of course, but not until it was too late. And when Erik's mother heard about it, she would be secretly pleased.

The thought nudged her from behind, pushed her to the counter.

"Could you please tell me...how much to buy an airplane ticket?" Grace finally returned the travel agent's pleasant smile.

"To?"

"Home. San Francisco, California." Grace paused and bit her lip to keep it from quivering. "One way."

Maren decided perhaps there wasn't anything wrong with a young woman writing letters to her mother, and quite often she had seen Grace post notes home. But why had she never mailed *these?* The dates stretched back for months. She picked up another.

December 6, 1947

Dear Mother,

Well, I did it again, only this time worse than ever. Erik tells me not to worry about it, but I can't not worry, when his mother is so upset. One would think I'd suggested they cancel Christmas, when all I did was offer to help trim the tree.

Or perhaps that's just what started it. No, she said, the children were not to decorate the tree, and it's not done December 6, oh no. Heaven forbid, and when she heard that's how we did it back home in San Francisco, you'd think she would have a heart attack.

No, it has to be done properly, the Danish way, and that's on the eve of December 23. That's when she'll hang the traditional strings of Danish flags on the tree; that's the day before she will prepare her Christmas goose, stuffed with baked prunes and apples. Everything is in the script. Nothing less will do.

But that's not the problem, Mother. It's the helpless feeling I get when she turns her back on me, when she tells me I'm not good enough. Oh, she doesn't say it in so many words, but I can hear it by what she does. Her disapproving glances. The way she whispers in Danish to Erik. What did she say?

Maren wondered how it might have gone if Grace had spilled out her cares, rather than scribble them all out on paper. And then she cried for the hot shame of knowing that yes, it was her fault. For the guilt of peeking through this window into Grace's unhappiness.

Could she really be the same stone-cold *Fru Ipsen* Grace wrote about? Maren barely recognized herself, only the name.

Fru Ipsen. It's all because of you. She straightened the papers out, took a deep breath, and closed the drawer of her brother's desk. She hoped she hadn't added her tears to the spots already there, but she couldn't be sure.

And for a long while she stared ahead, shaking, praying.

Lord, I didn't know I had hurt her so. She held her hands together to keep them from shaking. *And she thinks I'm an old hag who hates her.*

She knew that part wasn't true. But the other part…perhaps she hadn't done enough. Perhaps she'd kept a foot in the door, holding it open only a crack. What had Grace written? "The way she whispers in Danish…"

But enough. Maren had things to do before dinner. She would think about this as she lit all the Christmas candles, the way she'd done every season for as long as she could remember. The large red Christmas candle, as thick as her wrist, held its place of honor on the dining table. Two more fancy white tapered candles from Illum would spread their cheery glow from the windowsill, framing the pretty red and white Danish flag on its miniature flagpole, right in the middle. With a flick of her wrist her match sputtered to life, then brought a little glow of the faraway sun to her quiet apartment.

Her father's wall clock held the time, as it always had, with a familiar steady beat. She paused a moment, knowing a split instant before it rang four times, anticipating.

Always anticipating. She knew exactly what to anticipate, when to anticipate it. *Forventningsglæde*, the Danes called it. *The joy of anticipation.*

But what joy? She carefully unwrapped the tissue paper from around a little blue and white figurine, the Christmas *nisse* that had belonged to her grandfather.

"There you go," she told the elf. "Back to your usual Christmas spot on the buffet."

She paused a minute at her view of the dark street below, and she couldn't help thinking back to the letters, Grace's letters. And her heart jumped at an idea, a very strange idea. A moment later she heard a knock, and the doorknob turning.

"*Mor?*" called Erik, peeking inside. "Mother?"

She was still pondering her idea.

"*Hahloe?*" He stepped in. "Where's Grace? She wasn't at class this afternoon. We let out early."

"The tree!" Maren knew what she wanted now, and she would have to hurry. She ignored her son's question.

"What are you talking about? What tree?"

"No time to explain." Maren swiveled her son back toward the door and pushed him out into the hallway. On the way she fished a wrinkled bill out of her little black purse on the entry table and stuffed it into his pocket. "You just go get me a Christmas tree, and hurry. Before your Grace comes home again."

"Mor, no." Erik tried to plant his heels, but this time he was no match for his determined little mother. "It's weeks until Christmas. It's still too early."

"No, it may be too late, young man. Now, do as I say. Hurry!"

She slammed the door behind him, bolted it, and looked around. No matter if he thought her crazy. There wasn't much time. She hurried across the room to her kitchen drawer.

"Scissors," she ordered herself. "A little glue. And paper. Red, white, and blue paper."

Grace had already resigned to the early darkness. But by six-thirty that evening, the darkening, wintry kind of dusk had long since turned into a total, light-gulping dark that made her feel like Jonah inside the fish.

Back home, she might have strolled out to Baker Beach to watch the waves and look up at the Golden Gate Bridge. Now she just wanted to get back to the warmth of Maren's apartment. Enough of this walking and brooding.

For a moment, though, she stood frozen to the sidewalk, trying to figure out what was wrong. A little woman in a hurry bumped into her from behind.

"Undskyld," Grace mumbled. *I'm sorry.*

The woman hurried on, buried in her own holiday spirit.

From here Grace could barely see the candles Fru Ipsen would have lit in her window. Two, according to Ipsen family tradition, and a little Danish flag placed just so, in between.

Maren would be bustling in the kitchen, fixing dinner, as always. Erik would be along soon, after his last class.

But every step closer to 44 Købmagergade told her something very odd had happened.

First the window, and that was strange enough. She squinted again. Because instead of the traditional Danish flag, in its place hung a small banner of red and white stripes, and blue at the top.

Once inside the apartment building, Bing Crosby's "White Christmas" greeted her as she took the last few steps up to the second floor landing. She paused and looked around again. Was she really in the right building?

She was even more certain she'd made a mistake when she stepped into the small living room of Maren's apartment. The two worn easy chairs had been pulled back toward the wall, and a five-foot evergreen in the middle of the floor filled the room with the lovely scent of the forest. Vimpel cheeped. Grace gasped.

"Well, come on in and close the door." Erik looked up from the other side of the room. "You're just in time to see my mother finally go crazy. Stark raving mad."

"Erik," Maren called from the kitchen. *"Er det Grace?" Is that Grace?*

"Ja, Mor." Erik grinned at Grace. "What's the matter? Haven't you ever seen a Danish-American Christmas tree before? It's not finished, so you'll have to help us. But don't stand there in the doorway. People will see."

"No, I—" Grace just stared at the fifty candles on the tree, each fixed with a polished brass counterweight to a strong green branch.

Finally she closed the door behind her, stepped toward the tree and fingered a tiny string of construction paper flags, draped between the branches. Only instead of all Danish flags, every other flag was red, white, and blue—enough to make Betsy Ross proud. Grace spied the scissors, the glue, the paper on the floor by the tree.

"We're making new flags," Erik explained. "It was her idea."

Maren stood in the kitchen doorway, her eyes sparkling. She wiped her hands on a sauce-smudged apron and picked up a notepad on the hall table, as if ready to give a speech. And that's what it was.

"Tonight ve begin a new tradition." The words were labored and accented, but reasonably English. Six words. The most English Grace had ever heard at one time from the woman.

Maren looked to her son for approval.

"Rigtigt?" She wanted to know. *Was that right?*

He winked back at her, but she wasn't finished.

"American flags on the tree and in the vindoe." She smiled shyly and pointed. "And American hot hounds...for dinner."

It took a moment for Grace to realize what Maren had just said. Hot hounds? Oh, of course. Usually Grace hated hot dogs—except for tonight. Tonight...

"Hot...hounds sound wonderful." She searched for just the right Danish word, and she gazed at Erik through the fir branches. "Fantastisk."

Grace fingered the airplane ticket in her coat pocket, and for just a moment a wild thought flickered through her mind. Perhaps Maren, with her scissors, could turn it into a proper decoration—a Danish-style woven heart, even, to hang on the tree.

Or maybe another flag.

ABOUT THE AUTHOR

Robert Elmer is the author of the Young Underground series, World War II historical fiction inspired by his Danish family. He's also written the Adventures Down Under, an Australian pioneer series, and the new Promise of Zion (1940s Palestine) youth series, as well as AstroKids.

Bob is a former news reporter and editor. As a full-time writer, he also teaches writing seminars nationwide. He and his wife Ronda live with their three children in Washington state.

Out of Sight

Lisa Samson

To Iain A. Fraser

Lady Luck and I are no longer on speaking terms. In fact not only is speaking with her out of the question, I've given up the entire notion of her existence. She never extended any help regarding plane seats, parking spaces, tables at restaurants. She didn't cast a benign shadow in my relentless pursuit of baking the perfect carrot cake. And her presence lacked any substance whatsoever the night Doug "Can't Make a Commitment" Markovic called it quits after eight years by hoisting a placard in the middle of James Taylor's concert with the Baltimore Symphony Orchestra. I almost dropped my viola when the words "It's over, hon," hovered above the fifth row. But as some emotionally repressed individual once said, the show must go on, and so it did. If I had been honest, I'd have realized that Doug had gone to Carolina, in his mind, years before.

For decades I actually thought Lady Luck might well be responsible for my severe myopia. But now I know better and I do not feel at all compelled to give this good-for-nothing the credit for the most extraordinary day of my life.

I prefer to give credit where it is due.

My story began when I received the summons to play my viola in a studio session for Tad Bream, country music's hottest thing going. Studio gigs were the only consistent work I could muster since moving from Baltimore down to my sister's farm in Nashville (a city that appreciates a good fiddle player). Kimmy, a relatively quiet mother of four ear-rupturing children, lost her husband six months ago to bone cancer.

Tad liked my playing so much he extended another opportunity. And I jumped on it with more bounce than my eldest niece Ashley puts into her backyard trampoline. Recording a Christmas album *live at Westminster Abbey* in September might do a broken heart good.

Kimmy drove me to the airport in the green Econoline van she'd bought with the life insurance money from Pete. With all the kids in school, we stopped at the coffee bar for something guaranteed to percolate our innards and disintegrate our teeth.

Loud, energized cries erupted in the wide corridor that led down to my departure gate. "What's that?" Kimmy asked, brows raised above a foamy mustache, as she thunked down her cup. "Is that Tad Bream?"

I stood on my chair and adjusted my glasses to capture a firsthand witness over the clustered heads of undulating groupies. "Not Tad. No hat. Messy hair, needs a good cut. Really skinny. Doesn't look country." And then I remembered that the Christmas album included somebody else. "No, he's not country at all, Kimmy. I think it's SNAP."

The aging British rocker smiled for crowing fans flapping autograph books, CDs, and even a bra or two to receive his autograph. How disgusting was that?

"From *Great Guns*?" Kimmy stood on her chair, her see-through vinyl purse still dangling from her shoulder. Her face hadn't opened up like that since Pete died. She licked her lips clean. "It *is* him! I'd recognize that boyish face anywhere! Even with crow's-feet! I loved that band before they broke up! He's not going to be recording with you, is he?"

"Unfortunately, he is." The industry had been fizzing about this teaming of twang and shout. Shake it up darlin', now. But if this guy could sing "Little Drummer Boy" on some cheesy charity Christmas album and get away with it, who was I to throw this project on the dung heap?

"I can't believe you didn't tell me, Ursula. I heard he became a Christian a few years back," Kimmy whispered.

I'd heard the same. I'd heard that *Great Guns* had dismantled their interchangeable parts for good for that very reason. I'd heard a lot of things in an industry that's 90 percent gossip. "You'd never know it by his music."

Kimmy jumped to his defense. "Ashley has his first solo album. The sound is the same, but the lyrics are definitely different from when we were teenagers, Ursula."

"Isn't that just ducky?" I tasted vinegar, thinking of all the people he'd influenced in his time with his morose and irreverent lyrics, particularly the song *God on the Rocks.* Now there was a classic, existentialist number if one ever was written! "And now that he's found Jesus, I suppose it's all better?"

Kimmy rolled her eyes at me. "God is obviously big enough to handle SNAP's questions, even if you aren't, Ursie."

Choosing to ignore that comment, I sat back down in my seat. "I heard they've already started laying down tracks over here in Nashville. I guess he's heading to London a couple of days early to visit his family."

Kimmy joined me back down at a lower altitude. "You should introduce yourself if he's on the same flight."

What a joke. "I'm sure he'll be in first class." At least I hoped so. He reminded me too much of Mick Jagger with his jumpy movements. And the way he touched his face when he sang? Yikes. The one good thing I could say about SNAP—all caps, all the time—was that, unlike some other British rockers, he didn't appear to be decomposing this side of the grave.

When it was time to board, Kimmy hugged me tightly and sobbed. My sister cries at everything these days. The craggy bad boy had disappeared from sight, some homemade signs laying on the floor around the trash can the only evidence of the hullabaloo.

"Do you have to leave this early?" Kimmy asked. "Couldn't you just get there for the recording sessions?"

"I want to *see* things, Kimmy," I said, squeezing her tightly. "You'll be fine. I'll be home in less than two weeks."

An arsenal of guilt exploded inside of me as I boarded the 727 for Dulles. So I slept. Five hours later I boarded the 777 bound for Heathrow and slept some more.

When I touched down in London at 6 A.M. Greenwich Mean Time, for heaven's sake, the dream I'd had since I had read *The Little Princess* had ripened to perfection. England and me! Tea and crumpets, if you please. Ivy-covered buildings, crests with lions and unicorns, men in bushy black hats that weighed their smiles down into frowns. The crown jewels. The queen! The queen mum! And the music.

God bless that Rafe Von Williams, too, mind!

After collecting my luggage and standing amidst a flock of beturbaned, sultry-eyed Middle Easterners, I dragged my baggage through customs with much trepidation. Surely, I must be guilty of something. Maybe my mouthwash contained alcohol and didn't a law exist against transporting alcohol? Perhaps they'd pick apart my viola, splinter by splinter, to see if I were really a spy. And what if there really *were* microchips hidden inside? Then what would I do? The urge to scream "I've got a bomb!" grew within me until I bit my moistened lip and prayed for strength of enough magnitude to keep my big, opinionated mouth shut.

But London awaited and my spirits refused to be dampened. By traveling on Heathrow's moving sidewalks, walking all the while, I could probably get to the underground station in no time.

To say I was wholly unprepared for the high speed of the apparatus would be akin to saying a bovine is unprepared to play Liszt. Balancing my viola case, a backpack stuffed with sheet music, a leather purse the size of Wembley stadium and a rolling suitcase, I somehow stumbled onto the wide belt without mishap. Sweat watered my back as, wary, I watched the end of the walkway approaching like the inevitable next bout of nausea during a dogged migraine.

The closer the moment of exit drew, the shakier I became. If I made it safely off this contraption, I would walk the rest of the way on solid ground no matter how long it took. My room at the Royal Sussex wouldn't crumble to bits before I dragged my bruised and broken appendages across its threshold. Harrod's enjoyed the status of a London institution. It surely wasn't going anywhere. And the Tower of London? Good old William the Conqueror had assured my visit almost a thousand years before. No worry on that account.

Sweat beaded on my scalp, neck, the space below my nose. Breathing in deeply, I licked my lips in anxious anticipation, closed my eyes and stepped out. My heart rate spiked. And a low, frightened moan escaped my mouth as my feet left the ground. Bags continued in motion, swinging from straps. My suitcase capsized and my backpack slammed forward into the back of my head sending my -750 prescription glasses flying with a greater velocity than I was now experiencing.

Through the air they wheeled, their spidery silhouette flip-flopping against the bright light. Not that my weak eyes could discern their image for long. And not that it mattered anyway, for sooner than I had gauged,

I found myself splattered across the cold concrete floor.

A few cries, gasps, and oh mys echoed around me and a pair of heels thumped quickly in my direction. Biker boots. Just three inches from my nose. I wanted to cry. Ursula Aitcheson, concert violist, wearer of natural fibers and orthopedic shoes, thrity-five-year-old aunt of four great kids, lover of Dylan Thomas and tiramisu afficionado, wanted to cry.

So I did. Scrabbling to my feet with the grace of a wounded hermit crab, I blubbered like a kindergartner who had been pushed off the monkey bars on dress-up day. My world had been deflated down to a flat, gray paper kind of place. And a picture of creation flashed through my mind, a filmstrip of God snipping away with a huge pair of cosmic scissors creating nothing but foggy silhouettes.

"Lemmie give you a hand, love."

The owner of the boots spoke, the voice broadcast from a closely-coiffed head in front of me, again in silhouette. Dressed completely in dark clothing, this slender man was a solid mass against the sterile light of the windowed tunnel in which the walkways moved in relentless, totalitarian regularity. But the voice held the timbre of middle age, rounded and cozy.

He began to lift my baggage from off the ground beside me. All well and good, but, "My glasses? Do you see them? I can't see a thing without my glasses." My lips took over without my permission. "I'm legally blind without them. I'm just no good without my glasses. In fact, I can't even hear as well without my glasses." I waited for myself to shut up, but it didn't seem to be happening. "Do you see my glasses anywhere? Because—"

"Somebody kicked 'em across the floor. Don't know where they are now. Probably some kid picked 'em up thinkin' Christmas had come a few months early."

"Oh." Could worse news have been given? *Blind in London.* "Great," I said with a groan. "What am I going to do now?"

He touched my shoulder and squeezed gently. "Dunno. Can I get you to the tube? I'm headin' down that way meself. I might be able to help you on your way."

His warm, steady voice reminded me of my old Maytag dryer and so I nodded. "Okay. I'm Ursula Aitcheson, by the way."

"The name's Stan Remington." He shook my hand. The feel of his grasp, firm, coordinated, coolish, delighted me.

"Remington?" I laughed.

He joined in without hesitation. "Me old mum said as how it were a blindin' name for all of her lads. Says we're always shootin' our mouths off! C'mon, then, you goin' up town, or what?"

"To the Royal Sussex."

"Oh yeah, know it. Don't you worry, love. I'll get you back safe."

"But do you have time for this, Stan? And you can call me Ursula. I'm an American, you know."

"I'll make time. And yeah, I did spot you was a Yank." He must have noticed disappointment on my face for he added, "Your accent gave you away, sweetheart."

What a strange experience, putting my trust in a man I couldn't even see. But he was safe. All the signs were present. Helpful, kind, caring, he went out of his way to make sure I arrived at my destination safely. I slid my hand into the crook of his arm and let him guide me. "I don't know why I'm trusting you."

"Sometimes all you've got is Hobson's choice."

"Just promise me no more moving sidewalks."

"Gotcha, love."

To be truthful, Stan's arm was definitely above average, definitely more well developed than Doug Markovic's. And since I had only dated Doug, I didn't have a lot of varied arm holding experience to muddy the waters. But more than just rounded biceps were at issue here. The kindness of a stranger to a foreigner who had lost her way touched me in a place deeper than guys like Doug Markovic knew existed. This was about kindness rendered and made more precious by its timeliness. So what if I couldn't see his face? He was here and now. And he guided my way and I had no choice but to trust him in a place I knew nothing about. A place that should have been beautiful, but just now was nothing more than a blur—talk about your London fog.

Stan guided me onto the train, helping me while I "minded the gap." "Nice one, Ursula."

"Thank you," I said as he led me to a seat. He told me it was 7 A.M. and I expressed my disappointment in missing the sunrise today.

"Blimey, love, there'll be another tomorrow, just you wait and see. You a bit of a sunrise fan too, then, sweetheart?" His voice was even better than his arm.

I shrugged, declaring myself a dedicated early riser.

"Me an' all!" he said, his tones happy.

"Lets me get to my coffee that much sooner."

Again, that wonderful laugh. No one had really thought me funny before this. "Not many of us wormcatchers left these days, are there?" he said, hesitating for several seconds. He blurted out, "You're on then. I'll come down to your hotel in the mornin' and we'll catch a bit of the old sunrise together. Lovely job!"

"But how will I see it?"

"Crikey, Urs, you're right. When we get back to your hotel, I'll make an appointment for you with the eye quack. You'll be right as ninepence by teatime."

Stan guided me all that day, making good on each promise with a smile in his voice. Through breakfast, the eye-doctor appointment, lunch at the Red Lion near Westminster Abbey, his dependable bicep led the way. He took me to places with special sounds. "I'd hate to think of your first day in London banged up in some grotty hotel room," he said.

Victoria Station and a midday choir rehearsal at St. Paul's Cathedral topped our agenda. "Just wait till you get a load of this place, Ursula. We'll leg it back as soon as we get your specs."

And so we talked about music. "Oh yeah, I'm well into music," he said. "I strum an odd chord meself, now and again. Have done for years."

"Really? Where?"

"Smoky gaffs, mostly. Nuffin' in your league, mind."

"It's taken me years to get where I am." I remembered my days back home with the Baltimore Symphony Orchestra.

"I don't mind a bit of your classics," he said. "I reckon Mozart was a bit of a dude."

I told him about my gig with Tad Bream at Westminster Abbey in three days time. "You should come by, Stan. I'll introduce you around. You never know, you may get some studio work out of it back in Nashville. If you don't mind traveling."

I could feel his smile as he said, "Ta, love. I'll keep it in mind."

"I really do hope you'll come. I could use a friendly face around. Especially when SNAP plays." My body shuddered.

"You're not a fan, eh?" he asked. "Straight up? What about that *Great Guns* mob he was with, then?"

"No. I'm not fond of that style of rock and roll. Too much guitar, not enough melody."

"Me sis thinks the sun shines out of him. He's single, you know."

The music of the Hyperion choir echoed around us. I was longing to see the glorious dome above. Who wanted to talk about SNAP while angels sang? "Maybe she should write him. Although I doubt guys like that write back. I have to wonder why he hasn't married yet, though. He's getting pretty old, isn't he?"

The head of Stan's silhouette bobbed up and down. "Late forties, I reckon. Some bloke told us that all the birds were after him for *what* he was, not *who* he was. Just after his money, and that." He laughed softly. "You'd think he'd enjoy having that kind of a problem."

Stan put his arm around me then. I didn't mind. In fact, it assured me, comforted me, gave me a solid place in this fuzzy world.

"I don't know," I said. "I bet a life like that is complicated. I bet it isn't all it's cracked up to be."

"So you reckon you've a simple life, eh?" He pulled me closer in the chilly cathedral.

"I try. I only spend money on books, coffee, and music. I don't have a television and I'm not married."

"That sounds easy enough," he said as the choir disassembled and we got up to leave.

"Uh-huh. I couldn't imagine the life of a rock star."

After cruising down the Thames, Stan talking my ear off the while, we listened to Big Ben strike noon and the auctioneer at Christie's strike the auction block. Stan hailed a cab and we tried to pick up my glasses but they still weren't ready. "We will ensure that your spectacles are forwarded to the Royal Sussex just the instant they are ready, madam."

I was dismayed, but at least these English people were helpful. So I merely smiled and put my hand in the now familiar crook of his lovely, reliable arm.

He took me back to the hotel and had no trouble persuading me to dine with him.

We ate at Boisdale, a clubby sort of place, with a long, red room and a back bar. Or at least that's what Stan said. Thankfully, my lack of vision failed to affect my taste buds.

We each downed two desserts and Stan let me eat all of the Devonshire cream off of his bread-and-butter pudding. Conversation flowed more freely than the coffee. When I asked him why he never married, he said, "I've just never found a bird...em, lady, who loves me for myself."

And I laughed. "You sound like Mr. Great Guns over there!"

"Ain't that the truth!"

Again that buttery voice washed over my aching, Doug-stomped heart like warmed butterscotch over vanilla bean ice cream. And I suggested just one more dessert.

We rambled together in Regent's Park, passing the large mosque with its lacy facade, or so Stan said. Now that darkness had settled, even silhouettes had faced in with the blackness around them. But Stan remained dependable throughout, never wavering, constantly keeping me abreast of the sights I was missing with my eyes.

When he dropped me off at the Royal Sussex, he lingered in the lobby. "That was a lovely day, Urs. We've had a laugh, haven't we, sweetheart?"

"Yes, it's been fun. For a blind girl."

The desk attendant stole our attention. "Parcel for you, miss."

"I'd best be off," he said. "By the way, I haven't enjoyed meself this much in years. It's been smashin'."

"For me too." Better than any day Doug had ever given me.

"D'you want to get together tomorrow?" he asked.

I nodded. "I'd like that."

Reaching out, he squeezed my arm. "Triffic. I'll be waiting down here at six on the dot."

"For the sunrise?"

"Absolutely." His fingers touched my chin and I felt his lips on my temple. His breath comforted me as it brushed the side of my face. At this close range, I could *almost* see him. But he pulled away before I could get a good look.

Much to my disappointment, after I retrieved my package and rested my new glasses on my nose, Stan was gone.

I practiced my viola that night, softly, almost mournfully. The strains of "Amazing Grace" flowed from beneath the bow. *Was blind, but now I see.* Too bad that Stan had run out like that before I could see him...

I yearned to know him better, to understand how he could be so kind, to learn his ways of goodness and grace. No other Stan existed in this world, to be sure. I could only trust that he would return, trust that he would come back to finish what he'd started when he pulled me to my feet that morning. Only seventeen hours ago? Hardly believable.

At length, I slept, dreaming of the sunrise to come.

Dressed and ready, I hurried down to the lobby early the next morning. A man stood at the front desk, chatting to a furiously blushing night clerk. Bearing coffee and a bag of muffins, he turned to face me. "Ursula! I pulled some strings with an old mate at Westminster Abbey." His familiar voice teemed with excitement. "We can watch the sun come up from the bell tower."

I barely heard a word he said. All I could do was stare at the boyish, yet wrinkled face. That famous smile that had been on countless covers of Rolling Stone. Stan Remington...guns...shooting off our mouths. Good heavens!

My face felt hot as I pointed to him. "You're..." It was impossible to get out the word. His eyes were soft—his eyes belonged to SNAP! But where was that awful mop of hair he usually hauled around with him? And where were the groupies? But then, he did look different. So normal.

"Is this a joke?" I asked. "Are you playing some celebrity mind game or something?"

He reached out and touched my chin as he had the night before, shaking his head. "You've knocked me bandy, Urs. I never believed in any of this stuff, mind. Well, not this quick, like. But now...I feel like I know you like me oldest chum."

"I feel..." *Stupid? Big mouthed? Chagrined? Mortified?* Take your pick.

"The same as I do, love?" His large brown eyes, framed by crow's-feet, glimmered with hope.

"But I hate your music!"

"Yeah, I kind of picked that up yesterday."

I wanted to jump in the Thames.

"I'll never go to a concert and like it."

"I'm not askin' you to."

"You said you like classical music, for heaven's sake!"

"I do, straight up."

"But you play that...that...heavy *guitar* music! And it's the nineties! Why?"

"To make things right with some of the folks I led astray." His eyes grew misty as he looked away and set the coffee on the counter. He cleared his throat. "Would you believe it? A woman turnin' me brains to mush after all these years, an all!"

Oh dear God, I prayed, watching the night clerk's eyes grow larger than the clock face of Big Ben. "Not you! I didn't know it was you, Stan! I've always hated people like you."

He laid his hands on my shoulders. "You never knew me back then. And now…it's different, Urs."

"But you're…SNAP, for pity's sake!"

"Me name's Stan. An' I don't mind that you don't love what I do, just as long as you love me for meself. That's all I've ever wanted from a woman."

"*Love?*" I asked. The most difficult, odd, uncomfortable moment of my life was upon me. But this man's eyes, those big brown eyes that I could now see so clearly, were irresistible. They welcomed me. They needed me. His heart called to mine. *But love?*

"Yeah, love. Is that so tough to believe? Odds on when I fell for someone it'd be hard and fast, just like me music. My brothers are going to love this one!"

"And your sister?" I snorted.

"She'd tell you I'm a real diamond and that you should fall in love with me right away."

"Fall in love with you, Stan? I like you. I do. It's just that I've only just met you. I've only just broken up with Doug Markovic, for pity's sake, and I'm thousands of miles away from home!" All fine excuses, true excuses, ones I hoped he'd brush aside.

"Just give me a chance, Urs. Hang around with me while you're here in the smoke. Give me every waking hour."

Stan Remington stood before me looking so completely normal. His graying hair wasn't sprayed up into lethal spikes, but combed neatly to the side. In fact, in his black wool pants, shirt, and black wool blazer, he looked quite respectable. "Is this how you normally dress, then?" I touched his hair. Fine yet thick. Soft. "And your hair?"

He laughed. "This is the *real* Stan Remington. What you see on stage is just some daft geezer in some stupid heavy rock band. In a wig, mind." That smile again. "I always knew who the real me was, even back then. So how's about it, then, Urs?" He held out his hand toward me. "Just let me try and sweep you off your feet."

The night clerk sighed.

The moment of decision arrived. See the sunrise as never before or walk around London by myself. He only asked for a little time. Surely I could give him that. Besides, Stan Remington was the nicest man I had ever met, even if he did fall in love much too quickly.

"Hand me my coffee, Stan," I sighed. "But you know—" I turned to him and felt my face crack open with a smile. "I'd have never trusted you to lead me around London yesterday if I'd known you were SNAP."

"Yeah?" His innocent grin was rather lovely when not screaming those awful tunes for a video director. "Lucky for me you lost your specs."

"Give credit where credit is due," I mumbled, taking a sip of the warm brew as we stepped out onto the street.

"Come again, love?"

"Oh, nothing." I waved the topic away and tucked my hand in the familiar crook of his arm. Together we made for Westminster as the thinning dark of the London sky received its first ray of light.

ABOUT THE AUTHOR

Lisa Samson has loved London since the day she first picked up Frances Hodgeson Burnette's *The Little Princess*. Several years ago, while researching for her medieval series, *The Abbey*, Lisa spent a week in London with her sister and her editor. One day she hopes to take her husband, Will, and their three children there as well. The first place they'll go is the Tower of London. This time Lisa thinks she'll muster up enough nerve to lay her head on the block for one killer publicity photo!

At the Village Gate

Sigmund Brouwer

John 8:1–11

The woman's death had been decided.

And this day was the day of her death, something the children of the village sensed without quite comprehending, soaking in the excitement, and the anticipated horror from the whispered gossip of adults.

So the children followed.

They followed behind the villagers. The villagers, in turn, followed behind the elders in their dusty knee-length tunics. The elders wore their silent grimness like cloaks, their bearded faces straining with the seriousness of their task. All of them followed the woman who walked in front of the elders, draped in a plain, brown-girdled blanket, her hands bound and hanging on her belly, and her freshly shaved head bowed. The children, the villagers, the elders, and the woman formed a small pitiful, dusty procession in a small pitiful, dusty village high in the rocky hills of a small, pitiful, provincial outpost of the Roman Empire.

The death procession was made more grim by the merciless heat. The cloudless sky was white with the glare of sun. Powder rose like talcum as each step of each man's sandal flopped onto the wide path which served as a road between the square plastered houses with palm branch roofs. The walls of the buildings seemed to ripple from layers of hot shimmering air.

The elders walked slowly and ignored the villagers and the children. Leading this entire procession of men, women, and children was a synagogue herald, sweating heavily in his tasseled cassock. Their destination was the crumbling stone walls that formed the town gates.

Near the gates, fist-sized jagged rocks were piled like a cairn.

Every few steps, the herald called out a singsong proclamation of ritual, as if he served an audience of hundreds instead of only the population of a tiny, obscure village. As required by law, the herald called out the same proclamation one final time as all of them neared the gates.

"Jaala Mehetabel, wife of Lachish, the son of Sabian of Beth She'arim, is going forth to be stoned because she has dishonored him and his name through the act of adultery. Nadabb, son of Nodab, and Seth of Kedesh are witnesses against her. If anyone knows anything in favor of her acquittal, let him come and plead it."

No one came forth. The evidence was irrefutable. Late one evening an unidentified and still unknown man had been seen entering her house. This man had not been her husband, for Lachish son of Sabian had been in nearby Japhia for a week-long feast to celebrate a nephew's wedding. The witnesses that night were impeccable and beyond refute: the two town elders, Nadabb, son of Nodab, and Seth of Kedesh. They had immediately undertaken a vigil outside of the house, determined to identify this intruder. Unfortunately, for their curiosity, the seated old men had fallen asleep, each against the other, during their wait to identify the man on his departure.

Within an hour of the sunrise that followed, all the adults in this small village had shared and reshared those scant details through endless hours of gossip. Jaala Mehetabel, wife of Lachish, the son of Sabian of Beth She'arim, had not called out for help, some said, so obviously the intruder had been a welcome guest. Others laughed, saying the man must have been dragged in by rope, for Jaala was no woman of beauty. All agreed, however, it was a shame that the town elders had fallen asleep, for according to law, both the man and the adulterous woman must die.

The subsequent trial had been swift; the judgment rendered as commanded by rabbinic law; the rocks readied. So now the herald and the procession which followed him, continued in the midday heat toward the town gates.

Ten cubits from the place of execution, the herald stopped. As did the entire procession, with the children straining to peer around the larger bodies of the adults. The herald turned to face the woman with the shaved head.

"Make your confession," he commanded her, for ancient law required the statement at exactly this distance from the town gates.

Jaala Mehetabel, wife of Lachish, the son of Sabian of Beth She'arim, raised her head and stared the herald directly in the eyes. She had a square face, the flesh just starting to sag with age. Her eyebrows were thick and dull brown, the same color her thin hair had been before the men had held her down and sheared her no differently than if she had been a sheep to be readied for slaughter. Her lips, like her chunky body, had no curves. She had folded her bound hands together, and the skin showed work scars on red, swollen knuckles. Any beauty she had was in her eyes, which glowed from a mixture of fear and defiance, and strangely, joy.

"Make your confession," the herald demanded again. Everyone expected her to make the ritualistic reply as the occasion demanded. *May my death be an atonement for all my sins.* This would cleanse her of evil; this would cleanse the land of evil.

Her answer instead was continued silence.

"Make your confession," the herald commanded once again, his tone higher with restrained anger.

She did not.

The herald looked to the town elders for guidance.

"Let her die without peace then," a man said at the front of the crowd. He was the largest of them, with the face above his untrimmed beard permanently flushed red from the years of food and wine that had also given him his bulk.

"As you say," the herald said. After all, aside from Moses, who was a greater authority on her punishment than this man, Lachish, son of Sabian, her husband and also her formal accuser?

Lachish waved the men behind him to move forward and push the woman toward the stone wall. They grabbed the woman's arms to force her forward. She shook them off and walked alone to her place of execution.

She faced them, her large hands clenched and straining at the bounds of rope. Defiance finally lost to fear. Tears as thick as blood welled in the corners of her eyes.

Even now, the elders were not ready to take rocks from the nearby pile. Two marched to the woman. Wordlessly, without resistance from her, they stripped the brown tunic from her body and left it at her feet. Because of the watching children, they allowed her undergarments to remain in place. This limited exposure, however, showed the entire village that her body held little attraction for any man. This renewed humiliation brought her head down once more.

The two elders returned to the group.

Lachish, son of Sabian, was the first man to step to the pile of rocks. As accuser, he would be the first to throw.

The other men followed and armed themselves with jagged rocks.

In this moment, wind broke the heat's stranglehold, coming up from the valley and kicking dust. Somewhere from the crowd, a woman wailed. The men of the procession closed their mouths tighter and squinted their eyes against the swirling dust. Neither wind nor mourning would stop them from their duty.

They all waited for Lachish, her husband. The stoning could not begin until he first threw. He hefted the rock in his right hand.

Jaala Mehetabel, wife of Lachish, the son of Sabian of Beth She'arim, raised her head again.

"No," she cried above the rising wind. "Not until I speak."

The men hesitated.

With both bound hands, she raised her arms and pointed at her husband Lachish. "I was sold to this man by my father, a man who drank too much wine and beat me when it suited him. My husband saw fit to continue my father's habit."

"Enough, woman!" Lachish roared. "You have no say."

She ignored him and directed her words to all the town elders. "I have been nothing more to him than a beast, an animal to work his fields and household. I have seen this man pat a mule's neck and comfort the beast with more kindness than he has ever shown me. This is a man who inflicted upon his wife public shame by leaving her behind when he attended a wedding no farther away than a half hour's travel."

The women in the crowd muttered agreement. Many shared her sentiments toward their own husbands and wanted to applaud her anger. But she would be dead soon, and they would have to continue to live with the men who treated them no better than mules.

At the muttering, Lachish raised his hand to throw a rock. The elder beside him restrained his arm.

"It must not be thrown in anger," the elder said to Lachish. "We punish her in duty."

"She has brought death upon her," Lachish snarled. "It is the law."

"Listen to me," the woman cried. "You know how much dishonor there is for a woman to be sent away by her man. Even so, I would have begged him to release me and I would have gladly fled. Yet I had no place to go, no family to take me. So I was forced to stay.

"Listen to me. The women of this village shunned me, and I visited the well alone. Unlike even cows or sheep, I could find no comfort with others like me."

The wind swirled at her feet, pulling at the hem of her undergarments.

"Not once in my life had the warmth of any love touched me," she cried. "Until another man saw beyond this wretched, worn appearance. And I was loved."

Now the tears rolled freely down her plain face.

"Loved," she said. "Loved in spirit, not in body. Loved and respected so much that not once did this man touch me. He gave me a far greater gift. He spoke to me and gave me comfort through long, lonely hours."

She wiped her face awkwardly with her bound hands, smearing dust which had collected on the streams of tears.

"If accepting love and comfort when my own husband treated me as an animal is a sin, then I confess it freely in front of God and His people. If spending cold lonely nights in the company of a man who loved me but did not touch me in an adulterous way is a sin, then I confess it freely in front of God and His people. If death is the price I pay for that comfort and love, I gladly accept it for the short time that love touched my barren life."

Her mouth began to quiver as she fought for more words, until she found new courage. She drew breath and said with a quietness barely heard above the storm. "Stone me if you will."

"Moses has commanded us to purge this evil from the people," Lachish shouted. He wrenched his arm from the man beside him and hurled a rock at his wife.

It struck her in the upper arm, gashing a streak of bright red.

"You want to know who he was," she taunted her husband. "It drives you mad with anger to think any other man might take a possession of yours. In my death, I take satisfaction in knowing you weren't able to kill him alongside me."

Lachish transferred the other rock from his left hand to his right and threw it in full rage. She chose not to duck, and it hit her cheekbone, knocking her to her knees.

"I will not tell you who he is," she said, her words difficult to understand through broken teeth. "You will not kill him with me."

Before any of the other town elders could throw, a man from the small crowd of villagers broke loose and ran toward her.

"No!" he cried. "No! I cannot be among those who watch!"

He was a tiny man with a crippled left arm. Thin. Dressed in rags. He fell to his knees, wrapped his right arm around the broadness of her upper body in an effort to provide her protection with his own body.

"The dung collector!" laughed Lachish, relieved it was not a man of higher stature who had somehow seen an overlooked value in his wife. "Can you do no better?"

Neither the little man nor the big woman gave a sign that either had heard. Each clung to the other, murmuring words of love. He, the man who made a living by searching the rocky hills for dry dung to sell as fuel for cooking. She, a worn childless woman with no friends in the village.

Lachish, son of Sabian, gave the signal. Rocks rained down on both.

The tiny man died on his knees, his arms around her, his face away from the men of the village. The woman's face, however, was clear to the men above the tiny man's shoulder, and showed a smile which remained until the final light left her eyes.

Behind the elders silently intent on throwing the rocks, behind the villagers and older children who jeered the death of the dung collector and the ugly woman, was a young boy, son of Joseph and Mary, born in another village to the south because of a census decreed by the emperor Augustus and enforced by Quirinius, governor of Syria.

Few others around understood what this boy, despite His youth, understood and perhaps even foresaw for Himself on that day in the small, dusty village of Nazareth. Man and law, even armed with death as the greatest and final weapon, can never defeat love.

ABOUT THE AUTHOR

Canadian-born Sigmund Brouwer has written more than forty adult and youth fiction books, including the acclaimed suspense thrillers *Double Helix* and *Blood Ties* (Word Publishing). *Blood Ties* is a crime thriller that explores the mind of a serial killer, a kidnapping case, and an FBI profiler. Sigmund's work has been lauded in such publications as *Library Journal, Booklist,* and many others, and he has received the Alberta Film and Literary Arts Writing Grant twice.

THE FARTHEST COUNTRY

Angela Elwell Hunt

Dayton Jones swayed in indecision as he studied the real estate office. The place looked nice enough—a tasteful black-and-white striped awning covered the wide picture window, and the bright red door beckoned amid a sea of faded storefronts. Through the window he could see two paintings, each mounted on a gilded easel. The first pictured a pretty little white house set amid rolling hills; the second featured a seascape with foaming waters and a rocky shoreline. Both pictures were pretty, he supposed, if you liked artsy things. He didn't, but Marge did, and it was only because of her insistence that he'd come here at all.

For several weeks now, Marge had been insisting that it was time to relocate. The Texas heat bothered her, she said, and the rains, when they finally got around to coming, threatened to drown them in mud. Texas wasn't shy about anything, and she'd had all she could stand of life in the most braggadocious state on the planet. Marge wanted to move, and move far away, which was why Dayton found himself standing before the real estate office that had been recommended by both the good folks at his church and the regular folks at the bar. The folks at the downtown real estate office could send a man anywhere he wanted to go, even to the farthest country.

He paused, looking beyond the window display, and felt himself catch his breath when his gaze crossed that of a man seated behind a desk. The fellow smiled and waved, and Dayton nodded in response as a burning blush began to rise from his collar. He'd been caught checking the place out, so he might as well go in.

Summoning his resolve, Dayton turned the gold knob and pushed his way in. Two men, each of whom sat at a desk in the cavernous room, acknowledged him almost instantly. The first fellow, who wore a blue denim shirt and jeans, stood and thrust out his hand before you could say "jackrabbit." The other fellow would have been as quick, Dayton figured, but he'd been on the phone at the time. He threw Dayton a big grin, though, and lifted a finger as if to say he'd be with him in a minute.

"I'm Gabe, and it's a pleasure to meet you," the first man said, giving Dayton a smile as broad as a Texas barn. "Thinking about moving on?"

Dayton tore his eyes from the other fellow, who kept grinning in his direction. "Yes. I'm Dayton Jones, and the wife and I—well, we've lived a good life here, but she keeps telling me it's about time to relocate. She wants to move to someplace real different."

"We all come to that point." Gabe's smile widened in approval. "Wise is the man or woman who realizes nothing on earth is permanent."

"Except maybe death and taxes." Dayton struggled to smile at his own weak joke. "Anyway, I've heard you guys are good, so I thought I'd come see what you have available. My next-door neighbor bought a lot from y'all last year—"

"Has he relocated yet?"

Dayton shook his head. "No, but he talks about moving every day. I think he's been the one to influence Marge—she's my wife—so she sent me down here to check things out."

He had scarcely finished the sentence when the second agent came out from behind his desk, his hand extended and his eyes alight like a jack-o'-lantern's. "Hi, good to see you! I'm Sam Black, and I have just the place for you!"

The smile vanished from Gabe's face. "He was talking to me."

Sam frowned, his handsome features hardening in disapproval. "But he came in to see *me*. I saw him looking through the window."

Dayton looked from Gabe to Sam. "You two—don't you work together?"

Gabe answered first. "Never. We represent two competing firms, and we work in the same room so people can see the full range of what sort of lots are available in eternal real estate. But you'll either make your deal with Sam, or you'll make it with me. Nobody can negotiate a deal with two agents."

Sam stepped forward and took Dayton's hand. "I'm so glad you came in today, Mr. Jones. We're having a special on lots in a very unique location, and I would *love* to show you some photos. Once you've seen what we have to offer, I know you'll want to sign with ReMorz Realty."

Behind Sam's back, Gabe stood on tiptoe and twiddled his fingers to catch Dayton's attention. "Don't sign until you've seen other options. ReMorz can't come close to matching what we have to offer at Heavenly Homes and Garden."

Dayton felt the corner of his mouth droop in a wry smile. "Um—shouldn't it be Better Homes and Gar*dens*—you know, plural?"

Gabe laughed. "The name doesn't refer to private gardens, Mr. Jones. It refers to *the* garden. Eden. Anyone who secures a home through our organization has access to the most perfect paradise ever created."

Shaking his head, Sam crossed his arms and leaned on the corner of his desk. "Forget the garden, Mr. Jones. Why would you want to hang out with a bunch of fruits and nuts? Our lots have *indestructibility.* Our homes are fireproof and earthquake-proof. Our location is so permanent even the worms in our soil live forever."

"Really?" Dayton asked.

Sam gestured to the computer monitor on his desk. "Just watch this video, Mr. Jones—may I call you Dayton? If you buy a lot from us, we'll certainly be on a first name basis."

"Sure." Ignoring the polite sounds of disagreement emanating from Gabe's corner, Dayton stared at the monitor on Black's desk. An image flickered, then the camera panned over a magnificent mountain, dark and tall, with black rivers running from the crest. Over the floor of what appeared to be a valley, Dayton saw a series of domed stone huts, lined up like petrified gray beehives. There was no denying the power behind the dark and pulsing images of heat and stone, but somehow Dayton didn't think Marge would like living in a black-and-gray landscape.

"I don't know." He kept his eyes on the monitor, avoiding Black's gaze. "It looks a little bleak."

"*Bleak?* How can you not see the beauty in this place? It's a haven for melancholy temperaments. Besides, it can be whatever you want it to be, Dayton." Black's voice fell to a sensuous purr. "Look at it again, through the eyes of desire."

Dayton blinked the images of the oppressive landscape away. Instantly, the scene changed—he saw the quiet Texas countryside of his youth—the long stretch of gently rolling asphalt highway, the slanty barn in the field, the white house with the green-painted porch. Any minute he expected to see his sweet mother push open the screened door and call him for supper—

"Don't believe everything you see, Mr. Jones." Gabe's voice came from the other side of the room. "Remember—pictures and videos can be manipulated. ReMorz Realty has never been known for truth in advertising."

Black ignored his competition and leaned forward to whisper in Dayton's ear. "Our residents are *real,* my friend; there's no room for phoniness in our world. You know those rules and regulations most residential communities enforce? There are no rules in our society. You do *what* you want, *when* you want to do it, and nobody cares."

Dayton felt a light touch upon his arm. He turned away from the tantalizing picture of his childhood home and saw Gabe standing there, a determined look in his blue eyes. "Our community is anything but bleak," he said, jerking his thumb toward his desk. "Come over and see what we have to offer."

Dayton followed Gabe, then leaned on his desk as another video rolled over another computer monitor. The screen filled with images of verdant hills and blue mountains and golden plains, of skies lit with aqua and purple and tangerine lights. The camera then seemed to fly over elaborate mansions outside a shimmering city, and as the helicopter or plane or whatever took these photos dropped lower, Dayton saw people in this development, folks whose eyes were shining with happiness and contentment.

Black's smooth voice broke into his thoughts. "Remember what he said about falsifying video images? Anyone can do it, pal."

Transfixed by the delightful images on the screen, Dayton ignored Black's comments. "This place is beautiful," he whispered. He wanted to close his eyes and fall into the picture, to fly over those fields and join those people in the city…but the hard voice of practicality brought him back to his senses. Marge had sent him to do a job, and she'd want to know about expenses and details and rules. She cared a lot about such things.

"Um—" he approached the subject reluctantly—"does your community have deed restrictions?"

Gabe smiled. "Of course. We understand that perfect happiness springs from submitting to righteous authority. Everyone in our community obeys the Landlord without question. But His yoke is easy, and His burden is light. It's a pleasure to be part of a heavenly community."

The video ended, the monitor faded to black. Dayton blinked the images away and looked up at Gabe. "That's really an incredible place."

Across the room, Sam Black chuckled with a dry and cynical sound. "As incredible as it may seem, it's no place to retire. Ask him about the *work* you'll be expected to do."

Dayton winced. "You expect your residents to *work?*"

Gabe's mouth quirked with humor. "What do you think our people do all day, sit around on clouds playing harps? The Landlord dispenses jobs according to our residents' gifts, and everyone enjoys their assignment. The community is a place of learning, exploration, and serving. Some of our people work in the praise department, others work in the educational system. We even have ministers of fellowship."

Black snickered. "We don't have jobs in our place. No responsibility. No work. Why would you want to sweat through a lifetime on earth and then spend eternity with your nose to the grindstone? We're talking *forever* here, Dayton. I'm sorry, but a million years of singing the 'Hallelujah' chorus is not my idea of heaven."

Gabe lifted a brow. "Our jobs *do* rotate, you know."

"A good job sounds better than a trillion years of boredom. I never minded putting in a good day's work." Dayton put his hand to his chin, thinking. "Okay, but what about the community's population? Marge is a fine woman, but she's not crazy about some of the folks we've had as neighbors in the past. I'd like to know a little bit about the people who will be living in the area."

Sam Black stepped forward, placed his hands on Dayton's shoulders, and firmly turned him around. "I'm so glad you asked. We're a multinational, multiethnic community, Dayton. Equal treatment and equal rights for all—but our accommodations are based upon what a person accomplished in his life. We've got some really extreme quarters for some folks, but you'll find we're a very diverse group and not at all snobby or exclusive. You know what they say—it's the broad gate that leads to our place. We welcome everybody."

Gabe cleared his throat. "Excuse me. The gate to our community may be narrow, but we will be home to a large number of people, more than you might realize."

Dayton turned toward the Heavenly Homes and Garden desk as Gabe pulled a calculator from his shirt pocket. "Let's see," the agent said, "since the creation of the world, nearly forty-two billion people have been born on planet earth. Over the ages, our community has welcomed twenty-eight billion children who died before they reached the age of accountability…add to that the one billion, forty million babies who have entered our gates since 1973—" he glanced up at Dayton—"abortion, you know."

"I didn't know," Dayton whispered.

Gabe turned his attention back to the calculator. "Add to that figure the one billion, two hundred million throughout history who have already made their reservations with us, and it looks like our population will hover around the thirty billion, two hundred forty million mark." He gave Dayton an easy, confident smile. "That's nearly three-fourths of all human beings ever created. Makes sense, doesn't it? The Creator wants to share our place with as many people as possible."

"Hey, hey, let's not get carried away." Sam Black thrust his head into the empty space between Dayton and Gabe. "Sounds crowded, right? Come on over to our place. We've got a bottomless pit; we've got room to spare."

Gabe ignored his competition. "Our capital city, the New Jerusalem, will bustle with folks serving the Lord. The angels will visit there, and the saints, as well as the citizens of redeemed Israel. But the city is foursquare, extending 1500 miles up, down, and across, so it would reach from the northernmost point of Maine to the southern tip of Florida, as well as from the Atlantic Ocean to the western Rocky Mountains. It is a layered city, with one level built atop another. The city planner has designed over eight million miles of beautiful golden avenues."

"You want to live in a crowded city?" Sam snapped. "I know you, Dayton. You're a country boy at heart."

Dayton nodded at Gabe. "He's right. I really do prefer the wide-open spaces."

Gabe smiled easily. "Of course you do, and we don't expect you to live in the city. Our community also features a new heaven and a new earth, so our residents will have an entire universe to explore." He glanced down at a clipboard on his desk. "I see we have an entire subdivision of lots available on the revamped Mars. The atmosphere has been laced with a chocolate chip cookie scent, and residents may choose pets ranging from nonshedding cocker spaniels to tireless Arabian stallions. There's a group of mansions available on the Ocean of Tranquility, each featuring a workless kitchen and gym. Your supernatural, immortal body won't need repair, but some people like to exercise just for the fun of it."

Dayton smiled in pleased surprise. "Well, it certainly sounds wonderful...and expensive. I'm not sure I can afford a place like that."

Sam Black's bony hand gripped Dayton's shoulder. "Hey, that's the best part of my deal, Dayton! Our lots are already paid for! Everything you've ever done has been an investment in our place, and some of your mistakes have really earned a lot in compound interest! Come on over to my desk and let's sign you up. You can go right out and pick up some asbestos skis for the lake of fire—"

Gabe interrupted, quietly and firmly. "Our lots are paid for, too, Dayton."

"Really?" Dayton's forehead knit in puzzlement. "I don't remember doing anything that would earn me dividends in heaven."

"You didn't," Gabe answered. "But anyone who wants a heavenly lot can reserve one. Remember how the United States gave land to homesteaders willing to move West and begin their lives all over again? It's a similar deal." He leaned over, picked up a clipboard, and handed it to Dayton. "All you have to do is accept the gift, agree to become a citizen of the heavenly community, and wait for the summons to relocate. That's it."

"That's still asking a lot," Black said, a hair of irritation in his voice. "And don't forget about your friends and family—most of them have reservations in our community. You don't want to spend eternity apart from your loved ones, do you? Apart even from Marge?"

"Well, I don't want to spend an eternity in hell." Dayton looked at Gabe. "But Marge is the one who sent me in here. Doesn't seem right that I could sign up for a place without making a reservation for her, too."

Gabe cleared his throat, and for the first time Dayton saw a flicker of uneasiness in the agent's eyes. "I'm sorry, Dayton. Our heavenly mansions are available for the asking, but they aren't free. The Landlord's Son is serving as the contractor for the community. He has covered the costs of entrance into heaven, and He has overseen the preparation of each mansion. Since He has done all the work, He has the authority to enforce one stipulation—each individual must claim his or her own lot.

You can't make a reservation for someone else."

Just thinking about an eternity without Marge shattered Dayton. "Surely," he said, catching Gabe's arm, "surely there are exceptions."

"Yes." Gabe nodded slowly. "Babies and small children. The Lord brings them here Himself, carrying them through the pearly gates."

"You see?" Sam Black picked up a brochure and waved it before Dayton's wide eyes. "Your family isn't coming with you, so you might as well come over here and see what we can offer for eternity!"

Dayton tightened his grip on Gabe's arm. "Can't I do anything to be sure Marge and the kids will join me in heaven?"

The grooves beside Gabe's mouth deepened into a full smile. "Prayer works on the heart of God, Dayton, and God works miracles. You can certainly pray for your loved ones. Better yet, you can bring Marge to my office any time. We're always open for business."

Dayton pulled a pen from his pocket and scrawled his name at the bottom of the reservation form. "I'm signing up. And I'm going to bring Marge to see you first thing in the morning."

"Great." Gabe pulled a colorful brochure from his pocket. "Let me show you this wonderful place out in the country. Right across the ocean is an amazing complex, the Last Trump Tower..."

Across the room, Sam Black kicked the desk, then picked up the phone, muttering about other fish to fry. Dayton blocked out the sound of the man's complaining.

"I like it," he said, looking at the color-splashed brochure. "And I can't wait to move."

ABOUT THE AUTHOR

Angela Elwell Hunt began her writing career in 1983. After five years of honing her craft working for magazines, she published her first book in 1989. Since then, she has authored seventy-six books in fiction and non-fiction, for children and adults. Among her picture books is the award-winning *The Tale of Three Trees*, with more than one million copies in print in sixteen languages. She and her husband, Gary, make their home in Florida with their two teenagers, three dogs, two cats, and a rabbit.

THANK YOU, GUSTAF

Melody Carlson

C*ity of Romance*—what a cruel joke! I pressed my path through the busy train terminal and wondered why on earth I'd even stopped here. At last I spotted the hotel information counter and dropped my backpack at the wrong end of a restless line.

"Friday night in Paris," moaned a middle-aged woman up ahead. "We'll be lucky to find a room *anywhere!*" Her male companion just smiled and gave her a friendly squeeze. I pulled my denim jacket tighter around me and looked down the busy terminal. So far my last-minute accommodations had been easy to come by, but I shivered to consider the prospect of spending a night in this drafty train station. October nights were chilly in Paris, especially compared to Kenya, but I was trying to forget Kenya. Or more specifically, Kevin. The purpose of this European side-excursion was to put time and space between leaving Kevin in Kenya and the fact I was returning home, alone. But now my little trip was nearly over and my time and space theory seemed to be a mistake. And Paris was perhaps an even bigger mistake.

At last, the hotel information hostess wearily motioned me forward. She spoke in rapid French and glanced anxiously at her watch. I attempted to explain my need for a room in English—after all, hostesses are supposed to speak other languages. But this one simply threw up her hands and glared blankly back at me. I explained my dilemma again, speaking slowly and using hand motions this time. I wanted to maintain my cool, it was futile to alienate her. But her job was to dispense hotel information, she *must* know what I wanted. Still she merely frowned and obstinately shook her head.

"What do you mean?" I finally demanded, forgetting my earlier reserve to remain calm. "Don't you understand me?" Again the blank look. I wanted to strangle her.

"Excuse me," interrupted the man behind me—the only other person still in line. He spoke to me with a French accent, "My name is Gustaf, and I am French Canadian. May I help you? To translate perhaps?" I quickly sized him up. Slight build, about my height, scruffy dishwater blond hair, honest-looking face, clear blue eyes. Not exactly a knight in shining armor, but he did seem harmless enough.

"Thanks," I muttered as I stepped aside. "I'd appreciate that."

He quickly made inquiries in fluent French, but once again the hostess just shook her head, pointed to her watch, and began putting on her coat.

"She says there are no rooms," he told me with a puzzled expression.

"You're kidding!" I cried. "There must be a room *somewhere* in this city!" I felt hysteria rise in my voice. I wasn't about to spend the night in the terminal! Only last week the Hamburg station had been bombed. Oh, why had I ever come to Paris, and why was I traveling alone? This entire mess was all Kevin's fault!

While I toyed with the idea of a panic attack, Gustaf continued to plead with the hostess, and she reluctantly flipped through her thick directory, made a quick phone call, then scribbled something on a scrap of paper and thrust it into Gustaf's hand. Before we could thank her, she slammed down the Closed sign and stormed off.

Gustaf turned to me triumphantly. "Voilà!" He waved the slip of paper. "It looks like it's not far from here." We both studied the nearly illegible writing, but he seemed able to decipher it. "I'm going to walk, do you want to join me?"

"Okay..." I agreed with reluctance, not entirely sure I wanted to continue this train station relationship, but I glanced around the drafty terminal and realized my other options were growing bleaker by the moment. I threw my backpack over my shoulder and let him lead the way. He was, after all, French—even if it was by way of Canada.

We entered the street, and the sky was a soft, dusky periwinkle, fresh washed by an afternoon shower. City lights started to flicker on, reflected off sleek wet pavement. It reminded me of a blurry watercolor painting I'd often admired as a child—and yes, I remembered, it had been of Paris. For the first time since arriving I felt an unexpected rush. *This was Paris—the City of Lights.* A vibrant charge of energy seemed to surge through the Parisian air, taking me along with it, igniting me with its power. The very streets flowed with life, action, color—unlike any place I'd seen before. Maybe it was the aroma of French cuisine or perhaps the contented faces of workers heading home on a Friday night, but as I strolled along the narrow street, absorbing sounds and smells, I nearly forgot my new traveling companion. And suddenly I realized Gustaf had lagged nearly half a block behind.

"What's wrong?" I called out, wondering if this little French Canadian was going to be an albatross around my neck.

"It's this suitcase," he explained breathlessly as he flopped down on a bench. He retrieved a handkerchief to wipe his forehead.

"Here, let me carry it a while," I offered. "We can take turns." I reached for his large bag expecting some typical male resistance. I remembered how Kevin's macho pride would never allow a woman to carry *his* bag.

But Gustaf simply rubbed his blistered palm and frowned at his watch. "Yes, that's a good idea. The hostess said we must arrive by seven to secure our room. I thought the hotel was closer than this; I hope we're going the right direction." He looked down the street with a baffled expression. "I thought I knew this neighborhood, but I haven't been in Paris for a few years."

All I could think was that he had said *our room* in the singular not plural form. Did this mean there was only *one* room to be had, and we were supposed to share it? I followed Gustaf down a side alley, half carrying, half dragging his heavy suitcase and contemplating the implications here. Even during my engagement to Kevin, we'd never slept together—not because he hadn't wanted to, but because I believed God wanted us to wait until our honeymoon. Our honeymoon which was to have taken place right here—in Paris!

"What've you got in here anyway?" I demanded after lugging his suitcase for a long city block. I stopped and switched hands again. "It feels like a ton of bricks."

"Books," he answered simply, as if everyone carried dozens of books in their suitcases. By then my hand was starting to burn and my shoulder ached. Suddenly this whole bizarre plight took on a comical aspect and I began to giggle like a lunatic. Here I was, lost in Paris, with a little French Canadian. And I was hauling *his* books down a dark alley, with the unwanted prospect of sharing a room with him. Ha! If only Kevin could see me now…Blast Kevin anyway! My amusement quickly evaporated, and I realized Gustaf was now peering at me with open curiosity.

"Here, let me carry that for a spell," he offered. "Perhaps you could hurry on ahead and secure our reservation." He gave me some vague directions and wrote a note in French to give to the concierge. I set off feeling slightly guilty for abandoning him, but at the same time not willing to lose a room—perhaps the only available room in Paris. Besides, I figured selfishly, if I get there first and there's only *one* room, then *I* will get it. After all I'd been ahead of Gustaf in the train station line….

At last I spotted the sign, Hotel La Rochelle—something about the name reminded me of cockroaches, but I tried to wipe that image from my mind as I entered the building, painted a garish pink with bright green trim. And now I noticed it did seem situated in a somewhat questionable neighborhood. The crumbling structure across the street looked like some World War II remains with its boarded up windows and flaking plaster.

Inside the tiny lobby, I quickly learned the matronly lady behind the desk spoke no English, so I mutely handed her Gustaf's note, realizing that the note might say anything. Gustaf could be selling me to a brothel and I'd have been none the wiser. And, in fact, the hotel did slightly resemble a bordello, with its gaudy decor straight out of the forties. Fat cabbage roses clung to yellowed wallpaper and the worn, red plush couch had dangerous-looking claw feet. Even the faded silk lamp shade was complete with tassels.

Finally the woman returned with *two* brass keys, bearing two different numbers. I signed the register and said a sincere merci, then zipped down the alley to meet Gustaf. His smile flashed with happy recognition when I approached. Relieved that he didn't know how I might've snatched the last room and left him out in the cold, I penitently carried his bag in my one unblistered hand the remaining short distance to the hotel.

"And to express my gratitude," announced Gustaf in the lobby, "you must allow me to treat you to dinner tonight." I agreed and he relieved me of his suitcase.

There was no elevator. And when we reached the third flight of the narrow creaking staircase the electricity went out, and we froze on the pitch-black stairway, wondering whether to continue up or go back down. Once again I experienced the haunting feeling that I'd gone back in time;

as if this were a blackout during a Nazi air raid. I could almost hear the warning sirens howling outside.

"This is quite a place," I whispered in the darkness, eager to hear a human voice.

"That's for sure, but why are we whispering?" he asked in a hushed voice. We both laughed, and then the woman downstairs yelled something sounding like French profanity, and the lights flashed back on.

"She knows the magic words." Gustaf chuckled, not offering to translate for me.

Later we met downstairs and reentered the Parisian streets. Free at last of our excess baggage, we roamed and wandered happily and aimlessly like children on holiday. But at last the scrumptious cooking smells and our hunger overcame us, and we decided on a picture-perfect café set close to the curb of a narrow street. There we feasted leisurely on a delicious dinner ordered in French by Gustaf—starting with an amazing consommé and then a plate of tenderly cooked tiny vegetables.

"What brought you to Paris?" asked Gustaf as he took a sip of burgundy wine. "And all by yourself?"

I forked a tender piece of coq au vin and considered my answer. "Actually, I'm just finishing up a three-week tour of Europe. I hadn't really intended to come to Paris at all, but I was so close by that I just decided to stop. I fly out of Luxembourg on Monday; Paris was a last-minute decision—"

"You mean you might not have come at all?" His face was incredulous. "After three weeks in Europe, you might have missed all this?" He swept his hand past the window and the brightly lit street beyond.

I nodded slowly, trying to repress thoughts of Kevin. I swirled the wine in my glass, watching it glow warm and red by the light of the low-burning votive. What would it hurt if I told this guy about Kevin? "Well, you see, I'd been teaching in Kenya for the past two years with a missions group. I'd come over with my fiancé. In fact, we'd actually planned to get married and then honeymoon right here in Paris." I forced a laugh, as if that were the most ridiculous thing. Then I looked around the sweet, little café and tried to imagine Kevin here with me, but oddly enough nothing came. I couldn't even picture him.

Gustaf's eyes widened in surprise and what appeared to be sympathy. "What went wrong?" he asked quietly, intently searching my face.

"Oh, I don't really know when it all began to fall apart. We hadn't really known each other for very long in the States. We'd only met when we both attended an orientation meeting for this mission trip. We were assigned to the same village, the same school, and suddenly it seemed that our fate was sealed." It all seemed so long ago now, another lifetime even. "It was a real whirlwind romance, getting ready to leave, meeting each other's families, and everything. But at the time, I thought we were *both* in love..."

"But you weren't—both in love, I mean?"

I shrugged. "We taught in the same school in Kenya, but it wasn't long until we began to disagree. It started out small at first, just silly things, you know. But our quarrels became more frequent. You see, Kevin had all these stereotypical notions of what women should or should not do and be. Now, I think, it just boiled down to getting his own way. After the first year, he was transferred to a secondary school a couple hundred miles away, and consequently we saw each other a lot less. But we continued to write regularly, and things seemed better on paper."

Gustaf nodded and leaned forward. "So what happened then?"

I hadn't spoken to a soul about this whole breakup. I knew my family would grill me relentlessly when I got home—it was all so sudden, so unexpected...or was it?

"Well, shortly before our two-year term was due to expire, Kevin told me he was in love with someone else. Just like that. Then he said he planned to stay on for another year until her term was up." I forced another laugh—for Gustaf's sake this time. He looked so sad and serious. I wanted to make my disappointment appear light and trivial and *over*. But Gustaf said nothing and so I continued. Maybe it was the wine or just Paris—but the words gushed out of me like a river.

"Her name was Kate, and she was very pretty. You know, in that fragile blond sort of way. She was a soft-spoken little nurse from Atlanta. Probably the kind of woman who'd wear a frilly apron and happily bring Kevin his slippers every night." I laughed again, only this time my laughter was real as I pictured Kate on her knees, slippers in her mouth like an obedient golden retriever.

"So, anyway, here I am—alone in Paris." I sighed. At last, my story was out. And it really didn't feel all that bad. And Gustaf had proved an excellent listener. In all the time I'd known Kevin, he'd never listened to me like that. Kevin usually did most of the talking.

Gustaf sadly shook his head. "I can't believe how foolish your Kevin was. But surely you must realize it was *his* loss, not yours."

I smiled at this sweet little man. "You might be right."

He nodded. "I have a good sense about these things."

I sighed. For the first time in months, I felt so much better—light and free, like I'd just set down a suitcase full of heavy books. "How'd you end up in Paris, Gustaf?"

"I'm an art conservationist," he explained as if I should understand that. "I was just in Amsterdam, working out some problems from a computerized air-control unit in the Van Gogh Museum. I couldn't resist a quick stop in Paris before returning to Quebec."

"I was just at that museum," I exclaimed. "It was fantastic! I could've spent days there."

His eyes lit. "So, you like Vincent?"

"I love Impressionism, and Van Gogh has always been my personal favorite. I even bought some small prints for my new apartment—for when I get settled at home." An apartment I knew I'd never have to share with Kevin now—Kevin, who hated Impressionist art. In Kenya, he had called my Starry Nights poster "palsied paint splots."

"A fellow Van Gogh fan?" inquired Gustaf. "Do you know why my suitcase was so heavy? It's full of the Van Gogh books I got in Amsterdam. I'll have to show them to you later. Say, did you know some of his work is in the Louvre? Maybe I could show you around tomorrow."

I accepted his generous offer, and we talked late into the night about art. We lingered over a creamy dessert and too many cups of strong coffee. But we weren't alone. Others were head-to-head in intimate conversations. No one seemed to be in a hurry in Paris, and no waiters hung about anxiously peering over our shoulders as if waiting to clear our table. I knew I could get used to this.

The next day we toured the city by foot and by subway. Gustaf knew all the best places and the best ways to get there. As we strolled through the Rose Garden, we took time to enjoy the morning sun as it filtered through autumn foliage and created speckled patterns across the immaculate lawn. We even spied some late roses still blooming along the graveled walks. Gustaf led me through the massive Louvre Museum like my own personal guide, pleased to share his vast knowledge of art without pretension.

But that wasn't all Gustaf taught me that October day in Paris. Somehow as the day progressed, his gentleness reminded me that I could have a different kind of relationship with a man—that we could be equals and friends. Not only that, but he made me feel special again—and feminine too. For the past two years I'd put up with Kevin's lukewarm attentions, finally to be cast off for another. My self-image was at an all-time low. Yet Gustaf openly admired me. He was liberal with sweet praise and compliments. Maybe it was just the French in him, but for a delightful change I felt attractive again. As a woman, I felt renewed and hopeful for what was ahead.

From the height of the Eiffel Tower I surveyed this beautiful and amazing city—to think I'd almost missed this! Right then and there I silently proclaimed my newfound freedom from Kevin. And, incredibly, it no longer hurt to think of him. It seemed my anger had evaporated into the blue Parisian sky. And suddenly, I felt anxious to return home. I was ready to get on with my life.

That evening Gustaf sadly escorted me to the train. During the subway ride he begged me to remain longer—trying to persuade me that there were more sights to see, places we hadn't been to yet, one day in Paris was not enough. And, of course, he was right. And I momentarily considered staying; perhaps I could change my flight.... But then I looked in his eyes and saw something growing there, something that looked like it wanted to be deeper than friendship. And while I was flattered, I wasn't ready for it. I remembered that Paris, after all, *was* the city of romance. And I wouldn't hurt this sweet, kind man for anything. I reached for his hand, and struggled for the right words.

"Oh, how can I thank you, Gustaf? You've been such a dear friend to me in Paris. Thanks so much for everything. You have no idea how much our time has meant to me. And whenever I think of Paris, I will always, always think of you."

And I have. Even now, after all these years—I still appreciate his gentle kindness. *Thank you, Gustaf.*

ABOUT THE AUTHOR

Melody Carlson is the award-winning author of over fifty books for children, teens, and adults. As a young adult she enjoyed traveling around the globe, which may have helped inspire the idea for this collection of internationally set stories. Her latest novel series, Whispering Pines (Harvest House Publishers) is set in a small tourist town very similar to where she now lives in the beautiful Cascade Mountains of Central Oregon with her husband, two grown sons, and a chocolate Lab, Bailey.

Broken Wings

Jane Orcutt

Alice Foster awoke one morning, suffocating from life, as though she'd slept all night with the pillow over her head. In reality, she'd left the window open just a crack and the ceiling fan circulating at high speed, as always. Yet the walls pressed around her, stuffy and miserable—stifling—in all their cream-painted perfection.

She threw back the rising dread of routine along with her coffee, scanned the headlines, then dressed in the trim suit she'd laid out the night before. As always. She nodded—ever the polite Southern gentlewoman—to the other occupants in the elevator that took them down, down to what the world optimistically labeled careers but what she more daily thought of as Escheresque mandalas.

Outside, the summer Dallas air clung steamy and thick, like the ladies locker room at the club after an excruciating three sets, but with none of the sweet pain of exertion's aftermath. She headed down the expressway with the Miata's top tightly closed, hermetically preserved in the air-conditioning like an unidentified corpse at the county morgue.

The two-seater was part of the settlement, a payoff, really, for three years of marriage. They had met over the beverage table at the Manhattan wedding of a mutual friend—a former Hockaday prep school chum with whom she'd begun to lose touch but felt compelled to celebrate nuptials. At that time Alice was a young, fresh SMU graduate, ripe for the picking by whatever initial harvester fate employed, whether it be the promising career in journalism she'd long planned or life as the trophy mate of an ambitious young attorney.

His hands had collided with hers over a flute of champagne, and when their eyes met as well, she knew instantly she was on a crash course to a disastrous future, but felt helpless to rescue herself. *Alice,* he'd said, smiling that New York lawyer's smile, sucking the freedom out of her future as surely as her breath. *Dallas Alice.*

Then he'd handed her the glass of champagne, and she'd lost herself in the liquid expression in his eyes that bubbled as well, promising her a lifetime of euphoria but bestowing only a hangover. He'd been as unfaithful as the fleeting effervescence of the bubbles, leaving life after the divorce flat.

Yet her father pulled a favor with an alum, and once again the publishing career was within grasp. She found power in the printed word, power in professional communication between humans that she could not seem to grasp on a personal level. She labored in her editing like a craftsman jeweler, stringing words and sentences as exquisite necklaces for others to wear. Yet she garbed herself with no such adornment of precise communication, preferring the simplicity of solitude and the safety of a grounded life. A life with ruined wings—Icarus, revived.

A failed marriage...no children...a publishing job that only occasionally seemed to divine any meaning from the cosmos...

Alice adjusted her grip on the steering wheel. Such musings on a Monday morning could only be detrimental to her emotional health. The next thing she knew she'd become one of those eccentric old ladies who had no family but housed thirty cats because she couldn't bear to turn one away.

Inside the glass fortress of the high-profile magazine publishing company, she found her daily beeline for the vault of her office circumvented by the appearance of the executive editor. He thrust a large manila envelope in her hands, disdaining any greeting.

Edit this for me, Alice, would you? Promised the daughter I'd handle it—yet another do-good missionary project she's taken on for her church. Easier to throw money at a cause than to embrace it, I say. But thank God somebody goes over and civilizes those foreigners. Brings some hope into their lives, don't you think?

Alice nodded and headed for her office. It was easier to agree with him and get on with the project than to suffer through another speech from the compassionate conservative.

She plopped the envelope down on her expansively tidy mahogany desk, alongside the mosaic coffee mug—a gift from a friend on her last birthday and which she later spied at Nordstrom's for $21.99. Much too expensive to use at work, but it made her presence at the office feel important somehow, so she sipped from it gratefully in the privacy of her office.

Allowing a tiny sigh to escape, she carelessly unhinged the cheap metal clasp on the envelope, releasing a sheaf of crisp white pages onto the shiny desktop.

My Life, she read, and an editor's scan revealed that the pages were paragraph after paragraph, word after word, of a Chinese woman's conversion to Christianity. At the bottom of the last page it read *Submitted in application for admission* and named a local seminary.

Alice tapped a French-manicured nail against her reflection in the lacquered mahogany. She should throw this to someone in copyediting—Marcia, for instance, the earnest young woman who kept a Bible on her desk. Reference material, Alice had always supposed, but now she wondered. Had she overheard Marcia say something about having a husband in the seminary? A brother?

No, the executive editor had given it to her, had complimented her several times for being one of the best editors he'd ever seen. *You got a quick eye and a keen sense of judgment. Real analytical. Dispassionate. That's what makes for good editors in this business, and you've got the gift, kiddo.*

Surely it could not take long to tidy up this woman's heartfelt desire to scratch a match of sincerity against the flint of American religious study and bring a flame back to her homeland.

My name is Fung-man. Fung *means the phoenix, a bird that struggles from fire to get life. Before it dies and is reborn, it has to do lots of struggling.* Man *means "can fly higher." I do not know what struggling my parents thought I would encounter, but I do not believe it has been as they envisioned. And I believe I fly higher than they ever expected.*

Alice leaned with the sheaf of papers back into the slick recesses of her leather chair.

I live in Hong Kong, a land of over two hundred islands.

When I was growing up, I also believed there were many gods that lived around me, as well as my ancestors. I could ask them for help. I always prayed for help before my grandfather's altar at home. Sometimes I prayed before his tombstone when my family went to his tomb, but I always felt empty inside.

One day I was with girlfriends, and someone—a stranger—invited us upstairs to see a film about Jesus. I cannot believe that I went, but it was then that I asked Him to come into my life. There was more to life and I wanted to find out what that was. It was amazing, for after I believed in Jesus Christ, I felt changed. I was free. I could fly.

Fung-man mentioned several Bible books that had made an impression on her life. Old Testament books with serious-minded names that bespoke prophets with long beards. New Testament books with simple names like John and Peter, names that were easier to pronounce but no less fathomable.

Disdaining the possibility of premature wrinkling, Alice rested her chin in her hand. Except for the three interrupted years in New York with her ex-husband, she had lived her entire life in the South, where people openly displayed their Christianity like gun racks on the back of pickup truck windows. Why did these words seem different?

She set aside the papers and moved to the window, feeling like one of the sparrows that mistook the reflective glass for freedom and wound up flattened on the sidewalk, twenty-four stories down. She leaned against the window and stared directly below, as though she could see a bird lying dead on the concrete. All she saw was her reflection in the glass, her head resting heavy against the pane.

My name is Alice. I do not know what it means. I live in Dallas, a city with well over two hundred islands of lost souls.

And I am one of them.

She picked up the empty mug and headed to have it filled. She'd stop by Marcia's afterward, to check the spelling of all those Bible books.

And, perhaps, to talk, and maybe, to stretch her wings.

ABOUT THE AUTHOR

Jane Orcutt's latest novel is *The Living Stone*, which was released by WaterBrook Press in September 2000. Her previous books include *The Hidden Heart* and *The Fugitive Heart*, which were both finalists for Romance Writers of America's 1999 RITA award. *The Hidden Heart* was also a 1999 finalist for *Romantic Times* Reviewers' Choice award. She lives in Texas with her husband and their two sons.

A Passion for Poland

Anne de Graaf

I was afraid to say too much.

Leo had warned me that their apartment in East Berlin was bugged a few hours earlier when he came out to help me empty the car. "What on earth are all these rubbish bags full of?" His British accent still rang strong despite the years living in various countries across Europe.

"Children's clothes for friends in Poland. I've got vitamins and even a little morphine for one particular family. The Dutch coffee and Belgian bon-bons are for you and Marie."

I had just made the six-hour journey from my home near Rotterdam to Berlin. A woman alone in a white Suzuki, I was on a mission, following a hunch, taking a risk. I was searching for my story.

"How was the border crossing?" he asked as we entered the building and started climbing the creaking stairs. I could tell by the smell that cats lived in the basement.

"It took two hours," I sighed. "You know the routine. The guards, the dogs, the watchtowers. I don't like it. Do you ever get used to it? If they had gone through all the stuff in the car, it could have taken another two hours."

Leo paused just outside the door of his apartment and lowered his voice. "No, I never get used to it. Two weeks ago another East Berliner tried to get across no-man's-land. He got as far as the barbed wire, then they riddled his body with bullets and left him hanging on the Wall, crying out as he died. It was ghastly. Finally one of your U.S. guards obtained permission to take the body down. Poor chap, he almost made it."

"How long has the Wall been up now?" I asked, thinking out loud.

"This is 1988, that makes twenty-five years. A quarter century of madness." Leo reached for the door handle and nodded at me. I understood it was a last chance to say anything the *Stasi* East German secret police should not hear. I smiled at him and he swung the door open. "Marie, Anne's here!"

I knew Marie and Leo from when they had lived in The Netherlands. Leo headed the British Reuters news bureau in The Hague, and we had been journalists in the same building, working for different news agencies. The Russian government had thrown Leo out of Moscow a few years earlier and he could speak fluent Russian and German. Marie, his lovely black-haired wife, spoke fluent French and German. And during their year-long assignment in Holland, I had watched in envy as they both soon spoke Dutch with the same proficiency it had taken me five years to achieve.

Marie was always gracious, always listening. That night over dinner, I watched her dark eyes dance as Leo told about two KGB men who had visited his East Berlin office earlier that week. "They just wanted to find out what I didn't know," he chuckled. All three of us knew that statement alone would keep the Stasi busy for a while.

"Tell us about Erik and the children," Marie said, turning to me. "It was lovely seeing them this summer, on your way to Poland for the holidays. And, tell us, Anne, why are you off to Poland so soon again, and this time alone?"

Now I glanced at the ceiling and walls, reminding myself not to mention any names or places. "It's so strange," I began. "When we last saw you, on our way home from that vacation, even then I knew I had to go back. The vacation was a working one. I was sent there by a publisher who wanted a children's book about a child in Eastern Europe."

"And Poland's freer than most places here in the East. At least there some people will talk and you can take pictures," Marie said.

"Those pictures," I smiled. "You know I smuggled those rolls of film out in the dirty underwear bag? I figured no Polish or East German guard would dare put his hand into that." We laughed as I searched my own emotions, trying to find the words to answer Marie's question about my return to Poland.

"The friends we met in Poland through Erik's work with the fisheries, the families of the skippers who have worked for us, their friends and families, the hospitality, the endurance of some of these people, the Christians we've heard about from our mission friends in The Netherlands, the *stories.*" That was it.

"Poland just took hold of me. I've been fighting it all year. I was putting together the thirty-volume children's Bible and still working full time on the night shift as a journalist at the English desk of the Dutch Press Agency. A few months ago I needed minor surgery. Can you believe it? What a mess. What a year!" Marie leaned over to take my hand.

"But throughout it all, something sparked by that first trip began to grow in me. It was that riot in Gdansk. Being trapped in that church courtyard knowing the *milicja* could start shooting anytime. Then the interview with Tadeusz Mazowiécki and Walesa in the same room. Their joint vision, their hope. I know it sounds melodramatic, but when we left Poland and drove home, I couldn't stop crying. Really. When we loaded the car and headed for Holland, I was so angry at Erik for making me leave. We had stayed up the whole night before with Zaneta and two other Polish friends, walking under pines and a full moon, listening to them talk about how they prayed their grandchildren might know a free Poland.

"Marie, these people told me things that touched me, changed me, challenged me. I have to go back and...do something...with those stories." I sighed. It was hard to explain something I didn't understand myself.

"Like a novel?" Marie asked. "That'll be new for you after so many children's books."

"And now that I'm not working anymore at the news agency, it will almost be like getting back into journalism."

Leo said. "Ever since martial law was declared seven years ago, most people have been too afraid to talk, especially with a Westerner."

"I know, but I'm not even sure what I'm after at this point. I visited a publisher in England, a friend of a friend, and tried the idea out on him. I told him how I felt about Poland. How I couldn't let it go. The amazing thing is he encouraged me, even though I didn't know what the story was." I thought back to the publisher's kitchen table, drinking endless cups of tea.

"What else did he say, Anne?" Marie asked softly.

I swallowed. The words had not lost their power over the months since that rainy afternoon in the English countryside. "He told me, 'God plants passion in our hearts for a reason; follow it and you'll find your story.'"

The next morning as I drove out of Berlin, I thought back to my explanation to Marie. The miles rolled by; it was so hot, I saw mirages on the broken concrete slabs laid by Hitler's army and not repaired since.

My trip. This trip. Erik had let me go, somehow he had seemed to understand. But my Dutch friends thought I was absolutely out of my mind. "She's American," was their only explanation, as if being used to driving long distances explained it.

I felt like holding my breath all through East Germany, passing colorless houses and drab farmland, driving southeast until finally after five hours, I reached the Polish border.

I had no problems getting through. Then I pulled out of the customs area and began to actually drive in Poland. I was back! Finally. So strange, I felt like I had come home. There was no explanation for this. I only spoke a little Polish; my family was Irish and Dutch. But I had come home to a place that made my heart soar.

I loved the forests, the open fields, the children waving at me because my car stood out among all the Trabants and Polski Fiats. I loved knowing I was right where I should be, and I even loved not knowing why. I don't know if it was the journalist in me or the author. Whether it was the Christian or the seeker or the doubter, I had to find out what I was supposed to do with my passion for Poland.

My first stop was the home of contacts of a friend who headed a mission group in The Netherlands. The family was expecting me. I already knew they were Christians used to fighting on the front line. For two generations they had been a drop point for Bibles and Christian teaching materials, acting as liaison with various missions in Western Europe. My friend had warned me that the house would be watched, and I should park a street away and walk to the door and not do anything to attract attention to the family.

So when I pushed open the gate in front of the large gray house, smelling the lilies of the valley along the walkway, I didn't know what to expect. I looked over my shoulder at the neighbors across the street, half-expecting to see curtains moving and faces watching.

The door swung open and a smile from here to heaven greeted me.

"Come in, come in. I am Jan." A tall, balding, middle-aged man pulled me inside. "We've been expecting you. You are Anne."

I looked into his deep blue eyes shining with light, and he did not look away. I felt relief that his English really was as good as my mission friend had said. But I also felt a deeper relief, as if I had found someone I had sought for a very long time.

Jan took me upstairs and introduced me to his wife Amy, a tall and slender woman with blue-black hair tied back in a braid, and tired eyes. She welcomed me with a smile, giving me a hug as I entered the kitchen. A two-year-old with eyes as big as her mother's sat perched on Amy's lap. "Welcome to our home, Anne. You must tell me all about our friends in Holland. It's been so long since we've heard from any of them."

Amy was American. She had met and married Jan when working with the same mission group my friend headed. Originally from the American South, her soft accent could still be heard. She had more than proven her willingness to adopt Poland as her husband's homeland. Not only had she mastered the language and all its difficult cases, already she had weathered almost a decade of martial law and shortages.

"Amy, I've waited so long to meet you. I brought the morphine my friend said your mother-in-law could use. He said her multiple sclerosis was worse."

At that moment, I heard the sound of someone retching in the next room. A horrible sound, from deep within the chest. Amy moved the toddler into Jan's arms and left the room with a damp cloth in hand. Jan said, "It's *Mamusia.* She is very sick these days. But she'll be glad to have someone else in the house who can correct her English. And thank you for the morphine," he whispered earnestly. "We can't get much good medicine here, and when they do have painkillers in stock, it's usually the wrong sort." Then in a louder voice he said, "Come meet her. She always loves to meet new people."

I felt like I had entered a new dimension. The house smelled like washing detergent. As I passed the bathroom I saw the bathtub full of laundry soaking. Jan had already explained that his brother's family lived downstairs. They each had two bedrooms and a kitchen for their families. I entered a room bathed in light, doors opening onto a balcony. A cherry blossom tree just outside the door had carpeted the deck with blooms and some had blown inside the room, dotting the tattered carpet with color.

Then I saw a little old lady, hunched in an armchair, propped up with pillows, her arm resting on a board which covered her lap. Her face was a map of wrinkles, her eyes shone so pale I had to look twice before I realized they were gray. She looked up at me and nodded.

"Mamusia, this is Anne; she's come from Holland," Jan said, pointing at me.

"Dzień dobry," I said in Polish.

"You know Polish?" she asked in English.

"No, I'm afraid not. It's an honor to meet you, Mrs. Piekarz."

"Please, call me Hanna."

This was the beginning. Already that first morning I sensed I was on to something as I tried to come alongside this family and draw out their stories.

I spent a week sleeping in a dangerous motel where the door wouldn't lock, the sheets were filthy, and a drunk slept next door and kept trying my door at night, and I had to sit there holding on to the handle, pretending it was locked. Jan and Amy invited me repeatedly to stay at their home, but I could see there was no room. Besides, my time in the motel gave me a chance to madly scribble down notes of each day's conversations. More than once while I was in the Piekarz home, I snuck away to the bathroom and jotted down excerpts of things the family had told me. Sometimes we talked while working side by side in the garden since they suspected the apartment was bugged. It wasn't that they minded me recording their experiences, but years of fear and checking had made them wary of notebooks and tape recorders. If I wanted them to relax enough to talk, I had to interview them as informally as possible.

All that week I showed up at breakfast and left at bedtime, I tried to probe their history gently. I felt myself changing as the week wore on. The stories struck a chord of recognition, deep within my own soul. The chime heard when in the presence of God's own soldiers of gold, tempered by the power of persecution.

The vision I had of my role in all this began to change as I was recast from seeker to tool, someone God could use as a storyteller. I prayed for clear guidance in the questions I asked, acutely aware that I was bringing up painful subjects as we spoke of arrests and beatings, prison sentences, secret Bible smuggling, the death of Jan's father. Still, I was learning to trust God's plan.

My reporter's instinct told me to go after the grandmother. She was my primary source, with two generations worth of tales about everything from surviving the Nazis to suffering under the Russians. She described her husband's internment in a Soviet camp, their miraculous reunion just as Jan was being born, and all that had happened in the closing months of the war as the Germans retreated and the Russians invaded Poland. She also related the daily struggle for personal dignity in a society which placed the ones who refused to join the Communist Party at the bottom of the social ladder and paid mine workers better than university professors.

I spent many hours in that sunlit room at her side, watching the knowing face as we leafed through photo albums. "I used to be quite a sportswoman, you know. Skiing, swimming, and gymnastics were my sports. I even had Tadeusz put up a metal bar out in the garden so I could teach Jan and Piotr how to work out on it."

As she spoke, I was wondering how to get her to talk about her illness. She had suffered from MS for many years. Despite all she had shared with me, this seemed to be a taboo subject. But there was something else too. I sensed she was holding back. We had not yet achieved the same level of communication I had with Jan and Amy. Only the evening before I had shared a rich time of prayer with those two, and again I had been touched by the simple, strong-as-steel faith of these new friends. Still my instincts warned me that Hanna had more to tell. Perhaps the distance she maintained was more than just the cultural and age differences dividing us. Could her illness be the key?

I prayed for discernment. I would have to choose tender words and feel my way, question by question. Carefully, I shared about my own family. "I have an aunt with MS, and she says her best days are when she's been swimming. Has that helped you at all?"

The gray eyes focused on me like an owl's, going deep, looking for the real meaning of my words. I looked away first, even as she answered. "It's kind of you to ask, Anne. Yes, swimming used to help. I must tell you, I have fought this sickness every way I knew how. I've always believed it was a weapon of the enemy to get me down and I battled him with the Word and with prayer and in faith.

"But when my dear Tadeusz finally died, he took some of my heart with him to paradise. The first time I ever was so bad I had to sit in a wheelchair was during Tadeusz's funeral. I have often begged my Lord to let me join Tadeusz in heaven."

At that moment I fully understood what, until then, I had only suspected. *Here was my story.* The woman sitting before me. At the Piekarz family's house, listening, watching, asking, I began to envision my project: based on the true events of this family, woven together with other witnesses' stories, placed in Poland, made accurate by research, proofread by Polish eyes. I foresaw a documentary of integrity, but written as fiction to protect my sources, changed names and places.

Hanna had stopped talking and was staring out the balcony door at the blossoms tossed by the breeze. "You miss him very much, don't you?" I asked. Her refusal to answer reminded me that she still wasn't letting me in. Just then a coughing fit seized her, racking her tired lungs as she bent double with the pain. I held her, supporting her back as best I could. When she looked up at me, tears stood out in her eyes. Was it the pain, or my question which had caused them to surface?

This incident occurred on my sixth day in the Piekarz home. That evening, as I helped Amy peel small, knotted potatoes, she said, "Jan has been called away on an emergency. It's someone in the church. I should really be there with him. I know you were planning on leaving us tomorrow morning, but do you think you could postpone your visit to your friends in Kraków and maybe leave the next morning? We would appreciate it so much, Anne. I wouldn't ask you to do this, knowing how much ground you want to cover in your short time here, but we're a little desperate, I'm afraid. And I have to admit, it's been lovely having you here, you feel like such a sister, already a part of our family. That's why I'm asking." Her voice trailed off in embarrassment.

Inwardly I jumped for joy. This might be the breakthrough I had been praying for. "Amy, of course. It's the least I can do after all your family has shared with me. You've spent your time and a week's worth of food and energy keeping me happy."

"And it's been our pleasure, thank you." She smiled. I looked at her face and could see the worry lines. Amy had paid a price in coming to Poland, but she had no doubts whatsoever that God wanted her here. It was her home, and like Ruth for Naomi, she poured herself into caring for her mother-in-law.

The next day I was at the house bright and early. Amy showed me where Mamusia's clean bedpans and bedding were kept. "Just in case," she said. "We had a rough night, so her other set of linen is in the washer. Have you nursed anyone before?"

"My grandmother, back in Los Gatos. In California," I added. Even saying the words cast an otherworldly pallor on the place I spoke of. Surely the freeways of San Jose belonged to another planet? "When I was going to Stanford, I'd drive down on Tuesday nights and spend the evenings with her. When she couldn't get around very well, I helped her with bathing or going to the bathroom or getting ready for bed."

Amy looked relieved. "Fine. Now, we must go. Remember, Mamusia knows where everything is, so just ask her if you get stuck. Enjoy yourselves," she called to Hanna as she crossed the room to kiss her good-bye. "Anne will take good care of you today, cześć Mamusia."

I looked at Hanna, slouched in her chair. She knew better than I what to expect. In past days of my stay, Amy had handled the nursing while I worked in the garden or kitchen or played with her daughter. But today would be different.

As the day progressed, I had my hands full, cleaning, wiping, lifting, and shifting. But at the same time, I was listening, drawing out, and praying as Hanna answered first one question, then another, then asked me to get out the photo albums again.

This time when I returned from the cabinet, I stopped and pointed at the black-and-white photo of a blonde, thirtyish Tadeusz. It hung on the wall opposite Hanna's chair. "He was very handsome," I said. "A lot like my own Erik, tall, and he looks strong."

"Oh, he was strong. Well, he used to be before he went to prison. After that, he was often so weak. I remember him this way though, young and good-looking."

"Can you tell me more about him?" I asked softly.

She sighed. We both knew that I now knew Hanna was dying of MS, in the final stages. In terrible pain, she couldn't even control her bowel movements. So maybe it was the physical intimacy we had shared that afternoon. But when Hanna sighed, I thought maybe I heard the door opening a crack.

"His anger from the war helped shape him into a real soldier in the Lord's regiments. He took us all by surprise. Many thought he was a revolutionary, just because he preached simply and softly, but so strongly based in the Scriptures. We've had visitors from all over the world, sometimes rich and famous Christians have come here to share in our ministry. They tell us they leave more blessed than they could bless us. I thank God for touching people like that through our home. I don't know how many thousands of sandwiches I've made for all those prayer meetings, always with a lookout for the secret police."

As she paused, I asked, "Tell me about these Westerners who came to visit. Why did they feel so blessed here? I know why I do." I was quick to add, "But what did they say? How did you and Tadeusz used to pray for them?"

"I still pray that prayer," Hanna said. "I pray that Western Christians might recognize the enemy. I think it must be much more difficult in the West. Materialism, the effects of television, so many outside influences. Here it has always been very clear who our enemies are. And we pray accordingly, for the secret police, for the government, for the boys serving in the army. For our enemies. I think the battles Western Christians must wage are much more subtle. For many years we have been praying for your discernment."

She looked at me hard, as if expecting me to defend the Western Christians' predicament. But her words had struck me dumb. I stood convicted, stripped of any claim I thought I had to her particular story. *Who am I, Lord, to write about these people? I've never suffered in Your name.*

As if she read my thoughts, Hanna went on. "There are many promises in the Bible for those who have been persecuted because they believe in Jesus."

I looked away from her, guilty of pride, self-righteousness, and a spoiled lifestyle. My children would never be kept out of university because Erik and I were believers. The government could never force us to live in a two-room apartment and on poverty wages because Erik was prevented promotion due to his beliefs. *Who am I to be in this place now?* the question reverberated through my soul.

At that moment, I felt the smooth skin of Hanna's hand touch my arm. "Anne, I have something to show you. Will you reach into the cabinet behind you? On top of a stack of papers you'll find some pages in English, stapled together."

I looked up. It had been on the tip of my tongue to tell Hanna we should forget the whole project. Whatever I was looking for in Poland, I would find somewhere else. The stories in this home were too precious to subject to the scrutiny of a fickle publishing market.

But I did as she had asked. When I handed the sheaf of papers to Hanna, she held them to her heart and said, "A few months ago I completed my autobiography. I wrote it in Polish, and Amy helped me translate the most important parts into English. Here is a copy. You may use it if it helps you."

I drew in my breath. My breakthrough—a typed English summary of how God had worked in her amazing life. The words tumbled out of me. "But I've just realized, I mean, who am I?"

She fastened her eyes on me critically. "Yes. That has been my question all week. What right do you have to write about us? You're not Polish. You don't even speak the language. Tell me Anne, *why* do you want to write about our family? You know we are not the type who want recognition or acknowledgement for what we do. We give secretly and you should see that it remains so."

"Yes. You see, God has touched me through your stories and I wanted to write them down so He would touch others the same way." I paused, feeling my way.

"'*Wanted?*'" she repeated the past tense. "Don't you want to anymore?"

"Yes." I could hardly get the word out. "But... Well, could you think of me as an interpreter? I translate your story into a form which can be used by God to inspire and challenge others. I would be reporting God's miracles in your life."

Hanna leaned forward and handed the papers to me, saying, "I trust you, Anne. Write as the Lord leads you."

She trusted me. More important, this great warrior for God had given me her blessing. God had confirmed my vision with the sheets of paper I gratefully accepted from the shriveled and swollen hands reaching out to me.

It was a gift, and as with all gifts from heaven, I didn't deserve it. "*Dziekuje,*" I said. "Thank you."

I spent that night back in my funny motel, poring over Hanna's present. I didn't feel worthy. But I did feel the passion more than ever. When we all had said our good-byes earlier in the evening, Hanna gave me a hug. She would not let me go. Neither would her story.

I felt the Lord dare me in those dark hours as I watched the stars fade. He challenged me as Hanna's tone had, with His vision for how this story could be told. I've always ached to write for outreach, touching non-Christians and Christians with words that might cause them to seek further. Now I felt overwhelmed that God's plan was even greater than my own. I had my agent of change.

In the morning as I packed the last of my things, I saw through the window that a group of children had gathered around my car, fingering the Dutch plates. I had parked it beside my room so I could keep an eye on it. As I left the motel and put my bag in the car, the children pushed up against me. They were dark-haired and very dirty, with enormous brown eyes. I felt little fingers going through my jeans pockets. The motel manager had told me these were Romanian gypsies. I was glad I'd hidden my money in several different spots. I quickly slipped into the car and locked the doors.

As I started the motor and backed away, I heard a strange sound. The children were throwing eggs at me, and by the smell coming through the vent, they were rotten. I shook my head, remembering how Amy and I had bought precious eggs one by one earlier that week. I pulled away from the angry children and thought, *It's time to move on.*

In Kraków I had arranged to meet with a friend who'd spent that last summer night with me and Erik. Zaneta initially met Erik two years earlier, when he'd first traveled to Gdansk to hire a Polish crew for the Dutch fishing fleet. She worked for Erik then as interpreter and guide.

When I met her again after my week with the Piekarz family, Zaneta introduced me to yet another circle of friends. She led me through the magic kingdom of Kraków. The city of churches fascinated me with its exquisite architecture and sense of learning and wisdom, a tale itself of forbearance despite the years and the many foreign armies that had marched through its streets. From the lone horn sounding from the market square's church tower to the color of the stone, I fell under the spell of centuries-old traditions. In the Muzeum Narodowe I found an unexpected treat, a painting by Leonardo da Vinci, *Lady with the Ermine.* Zaneta told me first the Germans then the Russians had stolen most of their art. The few paintings still hanging in Polish museums were but a fraction of what belonged there.

Everywhere we went, it seemed we had adventures. I had arrived in the south of Poland during one of the worst petrol shortages in years. A mysterious Mr. Brown at the U.S. consulate gave me an escort to a petrol station supposedly closed for business. With the flash of an embassy pass, his aide obtained enough petrol to fill my tank, as the attendant pocketed his bonus.

Then there was the stooped librarian's assistant who "just happened" to have ridden on top a train going from Kraków to what was then called

Breslau. He made his perilous trip in January 1945, the very date that would begin my first book. He described the packed and panicked conditions in which women and children were forced from cars to make room for German wounded heading west, fleeing the Russian front. He also supplied me with copies of Nazi documents about a secret railway running outside of Kraków during the war. These tracks had enabled the Germans to covertly ship prisoners off to concentration camps. This was priceless firsthand material.

In the weeks to come, Zaneta and I crisscrossed Poland. As I grew to know the country, its landscapes and many faces, I met more and more people, interviewing them, gathering background, scribbling down firsthand accounts, slowly seeing a shape for what would become the Hidden Harvest series of novels.

In the southern mountains near Zakopane we rode the river on rafts and hiked around pristine lakes. In the east I came within twenty miles of what was then the USSR border. In the north, I was reunited with Zaneta's special circle of friends, many my age, university educated yet working two or three jobs, sharing two-room apartments with parents and in-laws, raising small children, and always fluent in more than one language.

As a journalist and an author, the more I heard, the more I became mesmerized by Poland's natural beauty, the rich tragic history, her people, their generosity and hospitality, their fighting spirit and integrity.

That trip in May 1988 was only the first of many trips I would make to research the series. No one knew the miracles waiting just around the corner. At one point in 1990 my husband and I were so moved by the incredible events unfolding in Eastern Europe, we just got in the car and drove east. First to Poland, then south to what was Czechoslovakia and then on to Hungary, talking to whomever we met along the way. The upheaval of nations occurred even as we drove. At one border post, the guards didn't even know who or what they were supposed to be checking because the laws and governments were collapsing that very afternoon.

In 1990 the Communists were ousted from the Polish government. After that, much of the information contained in official archives became public for the first time in half a century, and the "facts" changed yet again. Zaneta helped me navigate this bureaucracy, figure out archaic filing systems and gain access to hundreds of old photos. Without her I never could have written these books. She is a gift and a precious friend. Zaneta interpreted for me. She translated countless diaries, journals, and other books written only in Polish.

I would discover how often British, American, Russian, and official Polish versions of certain events conflicted with more personal accounts. So I sought eyewitness reports.

But this proved a challenge, for the elderly don't live in retirement homes. Instead they live with their families—often three generations share a two-bedroom apartment, and grandparents baby-sit and stand in long shopping lines while the mothers and fathers work.

But Zaneta found people willing to talk. She located elderly people who agreed to share from their history. Many of them admitted to me that they hadn't repeated some of these things to their own children. Fear of reprisals from the secret police had kept them silent for fifty years. They could have lost jobs or been arrested for telling the truth. So the truth had not been told.

Through my promises to write a novel, with no real names or places, I heard painfully honest narratives of what really happened in Poland—incidents that seldom appear in history books.

One white-haired woman told how she thanked God she had been an "ugly teenager" at the close of the war. In even tones she stared straight ahead, sitting as tall as a queen and said, "The Soviet soldiers who 'liberated' Gdansk only raped me eight times in one week. They did house searches throughout the city for young women, street by street, building by building."

Beside her, I felt goose bumps, and didn't know how to respond. Again I asked myself, *Who am I to ask these questions of these people?* "It must have been terrible," I said lamely.

I'll never forget her answer. "All my girlfriends had the same happen to them. We had our faith. We had each other, and we had nothing else. We lived from day to day."

It was such a privilege to hear this woman and the many others who recounted their testimonies of courage, endurance, and most importantly, healing. They healed because they had to, they leaned on God and He healed them. This touched me very deeply. I was confronted with my own weak, spoiled, superficial, complaining background. The Poles I spoke with had only their desire to move on and God. I learned that I didn't have a clue about real suffering. And that even there in the dark terrible places left by war and fear and pain, even there, especially there, God comes to heal.

In the course of this research, I changed from a seeker to the "translator" I'd first described to Hanna. Although I acted on the love God had given me for these people, it was their love and forgiveness that changed me. At last my research transformed itself into a story, and then a book. And finally three books took shape. While writing the Hidden Harvest series, I learned to trust the passion God places on my heart. For I had no choice. I had to write these stories.

Bread Upon the Waters took five years to complete. While writing its sequel, *Where the Fire Burns*, the pages of history literally turned again as Communists regained power in Poland (albeit different Communists and a different sort of power). In May 1999 I finished the final book of the series, *Out of the Red Shadow*.

Now I wonder, *What would Hanna say?* I only met her that once, but her memory remains indelibly with me. When I received Amy's letter announcing Hanna's death, I gave thanks that she suffered no more and had finally returned to her beloved Tadeusz—the two comrades-in-arms reunited. I knew it marked the closing of an era. And as Hanna herself would have been quick to point out, it also marked the beginning of a new one.

On my way home in 1988 I stopped again in East Berlin, halfway home. When I saw Leo and Marie I told them this time, I was afraid I had *too much* to say. They would just have to read the book.

ABOUT THE AUTHOR

Anne de Graaf has sold over four million books worldwide. In 1999, she received the East-European Christian Literature Award. Anne's Hidden Harvest series (Bethany House Publishers) is set in Poland. The first novel, *Bread Upon the Waters,* is about the last year of World War II. *Where the Fire Burns* covers the Stalinist period, and *Out of the Red Shadow,* the rise of Solidarność. The preceding story is an actual account of Anne's adventures as she researched these books. Because her series retells true stories in a fictional style, the names have been changed to protect those who've shared so deeply from their hearts and lives.

PERDONADO

Dave Jackson

"Cortez Selustiano," called the guard. "You got a visitor—some woman."

"Hey, Slew, what's this? How you rate conjugal visits?"

"Shut up, barf face. This ain't California!" Cortez rose slowly from the table where he had been playing cards and pulled down on the short sleeve of his yellow prison shirt, covering the blue blur of the Latin Kings' crown tattooed on his left bicep. He wasn't for flashing it today, not with this visitor. On the other hand, why was he even seeing her?

"Come on, come on," urged the guard. "I don't have all day."

Yes, he did. He had all day, and then he would go home. Cortez wouldn't go home until 2036. He threw the guard a leaden-eyed glance and shuffled toward the door, arriving just as the solenoid buzzed the lock open. Nothing could make him or his time move faster. His shoulders rolled with contempt as he strolled ahead of the guard from his "cottage"—yeah, all concrete and steel—across the frozen yard of the Illinois Youth Center at Joliet. He moved even slower. All too soon it would be the guard's turn...to strip-search him before he could enter the visitation room.

Why had he agreed to this?

It has been a year and a half since that sultry afternoon when Cortez approached some of his homies hanging across from Popeye's Chicken on the corner of Clark Street and Jordan Avenue, just south of the Evanston-Chicago border. "Hey, Rico, what's happenin' man? Who's working?"

"My shorties takin' care of business for me. They already moved four eight balls this morning. They learnin'," said Rico Quiones, the enforcer for the local Latin Kings. He was leaning against the brick apartment building, brazenly smoking weed while a couple of wannabees zipped around, doing tricks on their bikes like flies over chicken. In spite of the warm weather, sixteen-year-old Rico wore an oversized Los Angeles Kings starter jacket.

Rico looked Cortez up and down. Then, pointing with his chin in a way that drew attention to the first few hairs of a hopeful goatee, he said, "Hey, Slew, check out them GDs in that green Taurus."

Cortez studied the ride as it crept by. "They ain't no GDs. What would Gangster Disciples be doing cruisin' with two white guys?"

"I'm tellin' you, man, they're all GDs. Watch this!" With one hand he stabbed the air with Latin King signs, his fingers making the points of the crown. With the other hand, he threw down the GD sign of the devil's fork. The two wannabees joined in the taunting.

The green sedan pulled slowly into the small, Popeye's parking lot, and one of the white teenagers jumped out and ran in. The driver and the two black teens stayed in the car. One of them sneered at the Kings and then gestured with his middle finger.

"There, there! See what I told you," harped Rico.

"See what? You crazy, man. That weren't no gang sign. He just flipped you the bird, man. That's all."

"Nobody flips *this* Almighty Latin King the bird. That was for *you*, punk. You droppin' the flag, man." He turned away and mumbled under his breath, "*Cobarde!*"

Cortez staight-armed Rico in the back, right between his shoulders. "What'd you say, man? What'd you call me?"

Rico lurched forward and almost went down, then turned around slowly. "I'll call *you* anything I want. You gonna do something about it? Besides, anybody who can't recognize GD scum ain't no true King."

"I'm down for the Kings just as much as you are, man, and I ain't no coward. I've seen a couple of those guys at ETHS. We went to school together. They ain't in no gang."

"You're as dumb as you look, Slew. So what if you've seen them at Evanston High? Those guys are from Juneway Jungle. Why else they be cruisin' round here? They're GDs, all right. You just won't admit it 'cause you don't want to do nothing about it. You're *asustado!*"

"*Cobarde! Cobarde!*" the wannabees chanted.

"I ain't scared. Gimme the piece. I'll show you."

"Oh yeah, you'll show us. You can't show us squat!" Rico pulled the 9mm semiautomatic pistol from the depths of his huge jacket and slapped it into Cortez Selustiano's open hand. "So far, you ain't *Slew* nobody. So let's see if you can live up to your street name."

Cortez stared hard at him then turned around just as the door on the green sedan slammed and the car pulled out of the parking lot. Without realizing it, Cortez let out a sigh of relief.

"Now ain't that convenient," sneered Rico. "They're gone, so you don't have to do nothin'. Of course, if you had any guts, you could go after them." Rico nodded at the shorties' bikes. "They won't be gettin' far in this traffic."

Cortez wrapped a handkerchief around the 9mm and dropped it into the cargo pocked on his baggy pants. He glanced up the street and then jumped on one of the bikes.

"Five high, six die," sang the wannabees as he took off.

He rode north between the parked cars and the slow moving traffic. Maybe before he overtook the green sedan, he could duck into an alley, and no one would know what happened. But then he heard Rico peddling hard after him on the other bike.

"Hey, Slew, you gotta hurry, man, if you gonna catch 'em. Let's go!"

"Let's go, Selustiano!" But now it was the voice of the guard ushering him into the small room. "Hurry up. Let's go!" Cortez yanked his arm away where the guard had touched his elbow. If it had to be a strip search, he sure didn't want anyone touching him. He'd heard how some guards tried to turn guys into pancakes. But why mess with inmates? If the guards were kinky, they could get all they wanted on the outside. But Cortez knew why. It was a power thing.

Slowly, as slowly as he could possibly move without getting yelled at, he peeled off his clothes, bent over, went through the routine, and got dressed again. By then he didn't feel like seeing a woman, not *any* woman.

In the visitation room, Cortez waited and waited. If she were here, why didn't they let her in and get this over with? But it did give him time to calm down. He'd be cool. Maybe somehow this would do him some good.

The door on the opposite side of the room opened, and he spotted her. Short brown hair, tanned skin, blue eyes, tall, and maybe a little too thin. A nice looking Anglo, but she seemed younger than he remembered. She came to him and reached out her hand. He scanned away as he offered a limp hand, briefly. He did not rise.

"Hi. I'm Connie Mason."

"Yeah, I know. I seen you in court."

She stood there until he glanced back and let out a sigh. "You wanna sit down?"

Slowly she eased into the chair on the opposite side of the table. "I hope you don't mind." She folded her arms and hunched her shoulders as though hiding her femininity.

Cortez snorted. If she was so uncomfortable with this, why was she here?

"So. Uh...what do you want to do?" he finally asked.

"I want to talk to you, and—" She dropped her eyes and looked around on the floor as though trying to find something she'd misplaced.

"And what?" His jaw stiffened. "Look, lady, I'm sorry. It was just one of those things, you know?"

Her head jerked up, eyes flashing. "No, no, I *don't* know. And don't call it 'just one of those things'!" For several moments she just sat, and he saw muscles in her jaw twitch as though she didn't trust herself to speak. Finally, she took a deep breath.

"I've thought about you often since...since...and I just want to talk."

Cortez shrugged and slouched back in his chair. This wasn't going as he had imagined. But then, just how *had* he thought it would go?

"Many years ago," the woman started, "I made my holy communion at St. Gertrude's Church." Her voice was controlled as though she had pushed the Play button on a tape recorder. "I was only eight, but I was sure that believing on Jesus would keep me out of hell...."

So what was this little confession about? All of the ladies in Cortez's life had been "Good Catholic girls" at one time or another.

He must have rolled his eyes because she hit replay. "No, no, I *really* meant it when I believed in Jesus. But—but life went on—alcoholic parents, school, growing up, my first boyfriend. Although I knew Jesus was with me, I usually ignored Him. And in time I pretty much forgot about Him, and I forgot about who I was. Life became very dark for me with a lot of drugs and sex, even an abortion." Without missing a beat, the prepared speech had turned into a fountain that was overflowing, and tears began to well up in her eyes. "I may have been saved from eternal punishment, but I didn't know what it was to live as a member of God's family."

Cortez watched her lean back in her chair, unfold her arms, and begin fingering the small gold cross that hung from her neck.

"I finally came to my senses when I was twenty-four and a harried mother. Alice was three, and then came Greg..."

Cortez stiffened. Oh no—he didn't need this. Not now, not today, not any day.

She stopped, looked away, and swallowed hard—once, twice.

"I'm sorry. I thought I could do this." She rubbed her nose and sniffed hard.

"I didn't ask you here."

"I know, but I wanted to." She took a deep breath. "I was sitting on the beach along Lake Michigan when a couple of women with their own babies in strollers approached me and asked if they could tell me about Jesus. 'It's a free country,' I said with a shrug. One of them asked me if I knew Jesus, and finally I said sure. After all, I'd been raised Catholic. But then she asked me, 'So how's your life now?'"

With her eyes teary and nose red and running, Cortez's visitor smiled at him for the first time, as if to say, "I'm sure you understand *that* question." But he didn't, or at least didn't want to, and glanced away.

"Anyway, that day on the beach, those words pierced me like acupuncture needles, and suddenly I started pouring out all the details of my miserable life. I couldn't help myself. My days—often twenty-four hours without sleep—were a haze of smoking pot, dirty diapers, TV, coffee by the gallon, and visions of throwing one of my kids out the window. I felt like a flickering fluorescent light."

She paused a moment, and Cortez realized that he had been leaning forward, listening to her story. He slumped back into his chair. What did he care?

"But God had sent those women," she continued, "and they prayed long and hard with me as I recommitted my life to Jesus—making Him my king, my boss, my priest. It was time for Him to run the show! I'd already screwed up bad. I needed help, so I even turned my kids, Alice and Greg, over to God, too."

Greg—yeah, Greg. He'd been the one riding shotgun in the green Taurus that day as Cortez and Rico had raced after it on their bicycles. The red light at Howard Street stopped the Taurus long enough for Cortez to pull up beside it. Maybe he would just yell at them or show the gun and scare the crap out of 'em.

But Rico had pulled up on the other side and started yelling. "Yo, Slew. Don't forget what our great Inca, Amor De Rey, says, 'Cowards die many times before their death; Latin Kings never taste death but once.'"

Cortez's eyes started twitching. If cowards died many times, then he was dying at that very moment as Greg Mason's pale face through the Taurus window was replaced by his own pained reflection. Was he *Slew* or *Cobarde?* Cortez gritted his teeth, reached down, and jerked the pistol from his pant's pocket. Still wrapped in its gang handkerchief, Greg probably didn't even know what it was.

"Do it, man! Do it! Don't be no *cobarde!*"

The blast was deafening. Through the spider-webbed window, Cortez saw blood oozing from Greg's shoulder, but it pumped, spurting, gushing red and frothy from the hole in his chest.

"All right! You did it! You did it!"

The words broke through the ringing in Cortez's ears.

"Come on, man. Let's get outta here. Five-o's be comin'!"

The ringing in Cortez's ears merged into sirens as he wheeled the bike away from the Taurus and sped back down Clark Street. He turned west on Jordan. But he only made it one more block....

"Did you know Greg in high school?" asked Connie Mason as she leaned forward in her seat in the visitation room to stare hard at Cortez.

"What?" Cortez looked at her, his thoughts still screaming.

"Did you know Greg before..."

"Oh. Not really," he muttered. Her looking at him like that gave him the willies, and he looked down, tracing the lines in the tabletop.

For a long moment she said nothing, and Cortez wished she would leave. Just go away and leave him alone, forever. Then she continued. "He was a champion swimmer, you know. He finished number one in the state. And then he started competing nationally. They were getting him ready for the Olympics. He had a real good chance. I used to worry about him all the time when he was away at those meets. Never thought he would die so close to home."

Cortez braced himself for the you-rotten-gangbangers-are-all-going-to-burn-in-hell part.

But her voice softened. "You know, life wasn't a cakewalk for me when I returned to Jesus. But it was getting better. I had hope."

Cortez almost stood up right then and walked away. Instead, he looked up at her and sat rock solid, not moving a muscle.

"But it's gotten real hard lately, harder than I could have ever imagined." Her voice cracked slightly. "I really loved Greg—his murder tore up our whole family." She returned his stare until he broke away. "But I do need to tell you this," she said. "Jesus has been with me through it all. And Jesus is the reason I had to come here and see you."

Cortez felt her warm hands surround one of his. Her touch drew his entire attention, but he didn't look at it.

After a few moments of silence, she said, "Well, I didn't know whether you'd ever be able to ask my forgiveness for killing my son…so I'll go first. I forgive you."

He jerked his head up. What had she just said? Had he heard her right?

She nodded. "That's why I came here. I really do forgive you!"

"But…you can't just…why?" he whispered hoarsely.

She withdrew her hands as though his skin had suddenly become hot. "You killed my son. I cannot bring him back. I could…" Her voice rose and hung there. After a moment, her fingers found the little gold cross again. "But if I do not forgive you," she continued with relief, "the hatred will kill me as well."

Slowly she stood to her feet. As if in a foggy daze, he rose awkwardly. "Besides," she added as tears filled her eyes, "I too have been forgiven." Then she put her arms around him and kissed him on the cheek.

An instant later, she was walking across the visitation room, weaving between the tables with other inmates and their families or girlfriends until she stood at the door waiting for the guard to buzz her out. Cortez sank back into his chair.

She looked back once, flashed a brief, misty smile, and then was gone.

He sat for several minutes trying to take it all in until a guard called, "Hey, Selustiano! This place is for visitation, not meditation. Get out of here!"

It must have been the cold wind that blurred his vision on the way back across the yard. He raked his wrist across first one eye and then the other before entering the cottage.

"Wow, Slew," his card-playing friend intoned. "How was she? You sure took long enough."

"Shut up, barf face. And hey, don't call me Slew no more. Got that? My name's Cortez."

He walked over to the window and stood there a long time staring past the paint-chipped bars into the frozen yard.

That night, with only the security lights on, Cortez lay on his narrow cot trying to ignore the snores and sighs and rhythmic movements around him. Just what had happened that afternoon? What did it matter whether or not he was forgiven if he had to spend nearly forty more years here?

And yet, *Perdonado, perdonado.* If clung to him like a new name.

Though the names and certain details have been changed, this story is based on true incidents. In the Chicago jail I visit each week there are many young men waiting for a new name.

ABOUT THE AUTHOR

Dave Jackson and his wife, Neta, are the authors of *Hero Tales I, II,* and *III,* and the historical fiction series of Trailblazer Books (Bethany), introducing young readers to great Christian heroes. They make their home in Evanston, Illinois, where they attend The Worship Center, a multiracial congregation.

Recent nonfiction by Dave and Neta include *Too Young to Die* (Focus/Tyndale) written with Gorden McLean, a minister to Chicago street gangs, and also *Coaching Your Kids in the Game of Life* (Bethany) coauthored with Ricky Byrdsong, former head basketball coach for Northwestern University. Byrdsong was murdered in a shooting spree by a white supremacist one block from his suburban home on July 2, 1999.

Abundant Life

Kristin Billerbeck

Stacy Whitaker, trembling and numb, hung up the phone. She closed her eyes slowly, trying to assimilate the conversation. Trying to believe the time had really come. "Oh, Grandpa Jesse," she moaned, dropping her head into her hands.

She didn't cry. Not yet. Grandpa Jesse had lived his life to the fullest, and Stacy smiled instead, recalling his many adventures. It was her first and natural instinct. His life was so much more pronounced than his death. She tried to focus on that and where he was now. Although her mother had been asked to come identify him, Grandpa Jesse left word that Stacy was to accompany her. The bond between her and Grandpa was unbreakable, even in death.

In life together, they'd rafted the Colorado River, climbed Half Dome in Yosemite, and most fondly, visited Switzerland for her fifteenth summer. It had been their last vacation together and it was only fitting that his life should slip away atop the Jungfrau. Only her grandfather would attempt to see the Swiss Alps one last time—at ninety-four years of age!

Real life had stolen those carefree vacations with Grandpa Jesse: college, law school, and finally her lawyer position at a top firm in San Francisco. Now the opportunity for *later* was gone, only the memories survived.

A small rap sounded at her office door, "Stacy? Stacy, your clients are here."

Stacy stood immediately, packing her briefcase. "I'm sorry, Mike. Tell them I had urgent business. I have to leave the country."

"You can't possibly leave the country. We've got court in two days."

"Just get a stay from the judge, Mike. These clients have been waiting two years for their day in court, two weeks isn't going to make a difference." Money was all that man ever thought about. If her time wasn't billable, he found it as useless as a three-dollar bill. For Mike Jacobs, life was work. Stacy pondered the thought that perhaps she was turning out just like him.

"Stacy, need I remind you I am your boss? This is a place of business. You can't just go on a whim."

"Mike, need I remind you we're in Silicon Valley, where jobs are as plentiful as the traffic?" Stacy retorted, a newfound boldness within her. Nothing took precedence over Grandpa. Nothing.

"Well, you at least owe me an explanation. Why are you abandoning your clients?" Mike put a fist to his hip.

"I have private business in Switzerland. I haven't had a vacation in four years, Mike, and I don't think I owe you an explanation."

"A client with a private bank account?" he asked hopefully.

"It's personal, Mike." She snapped her briefcase shut and walked past him, unaffected by his sharp glances. There was a reason her grandfather asked her to accompany her mother, and no one was taking her place. Regardless of idle threats, this mission was far too important. She'd find a new job if necessary. She was drained from Mike's unrealistic expectations and finally *this* gave her the strength to do something about it.

Although the flight to Zurich was long and tedious, Stacy was anxious to get to Interlaken. She forced her mother, and their worn bodies, onto a train. As Interlaken appeared, Stacy marveled.

"Oh, Mom, look at this view. I used to argue with Grandpa that this was the most beautiful place on earth. I think I was right." She wistfully stared out the window. With its majestic, snowcapped peaks jutting high into the blue sky, lush green meadows which extended for miles, and of course, the turquoise streams that meandered through town, Interlaken was a sight to behold. She smiled, knowing Grandpa Jesse was in a far more beautiful place now.

"Your grandfather spent his whole retirement trying to find a prettier place. That man wasted every ounce of money he had. I bet there's nothing left in his estate; there probably won't be enough to bury him. I can't believe he had enough to see him through his life. I thought for sure your father and I would be supporting him by now."

"Mom, Grandpa never spent a cent except on traveling. It meant everything to him."

"He never cared a bit about his family. He gallivanted all over the earth, making us worry, and now, travel to Switzerland. Why couldn't he just be a simple old man?"

"Would you rather have him holed up in a rest home, Mom?" Stacy snapped. She never understood her mother's attitude. Ellen Whitaker could find fault in anyone. Stacy just didn't get it. She never heard her grandfather utter so much as a wry comment about his daughter, but Ellen couldn't even find one kind word in Grandpa's death. Their conversation halted, Stacy went back to enjoying the view as it sped by from the train window.

Once at the station, they hailed a cab and headed to the same hotel where she and her grandfather had stayed so many years before. The Hotel Goldey, an elegant family-owned retreat that fronted the quiet river and nestled against the rugged cliffs.

By the time she reached the hotel, Stacy felt ragged. She tried to remember her German phrases, but nothing came. Her mind blank, she searched for something to say.

"Willkommen," the young hotel clerk spoke. Something about him was so oddly familiar, his green eyes so intense.

Stacy blinked. "English?"

"Yes, madam. Welcome. Did you have reservations with us?" The young man filed through his box.

"No, I just stayed here when I was a young girl with my grandfather. I was hoping you'd have space for a few days."

"Miss Whitaker?" he asked tentatively.

"Yes," she stuttered. "Do you know me?" A shiver ran through her limbs and her heart raced. She swallowed hard, "H-how did you—"

"Your grandfather told me you'd be coming. He called me from the hospital just before...well..."

Stacy fought back her tears, then shook her head in disbelief. "Grandpa didn't *know* we'd be coming to this hotel."

"Do you know where the morgue is?" her mother interrupted.

The man ignored her mother's blunt question. "Apparently, he did know you'd be coming here. He left this letter for you, Miss Whitaker."

The envelope shook violently in Stacy's hand. There was something so ominous about the letter. Something that seemed to lack reality, but Stacy knew her grandfather had never been based in reality. He lived in a world of rose-colored glasses and pink gumdrops, a magical place.

"Here's your key; you'll be on the third floor. I'm sure you'd like to rest," he now addressed her mother. "The morgue is closed today, madam. It is Sunday."

"Hmmmph," her mother grunted.

As they walked upstairs, Stacy chastised her mother. "Mom, I know Grandpa was never the kind of father you appreciated, but he's gone now; can't you at least respect his death? You never understood him! You never even tried! He supported you; he saw that you got to college; why do you fault him for enjoying the last years of his life? It's like you wanted him to rot away at home, so you didn't have to worry about him."

"Stacy, you have no idea what you're talking about, so just be quiet. *Where were you?* You had your nose in a court docket, so don't come after me for something you know nothing about!"

Stacy only nodded in response, ignoring her mother's warped idea of the truth. Whatever had happened, Stacy was sure Grandpa Jesse had little to do with it. Stacy had been busy, but never too busy to notice what really happened in her family.

The guest room was just as she remembered it, clean and simple with modern lines. Gentle flesh-toned walls and a white down comforter and small bathroom. All framed by the sliding glass doors which held a magnificent view. Stacy went to the balcony and sighed. In all their splendor, the Swiss Alps were visible in the scarcely clouded sky. If Stacy didn't know any better, she'd assume her grandfather had something to do with that too.

Stacy ripped open the letter with great anticipation, carelessly tossing the envelope aside while her mother checked for dust along the windowsill. Her heart pounded, knowing these were the last words from her grandpa. Her last chance to hear how much he loved her—for she knew she'd always been perfect in his eyes.

Dear Stace:

Well, you made it. I knew you would, and I knew you'd stay here. You always loved this hotel, and you always were so predictable. Remember how you used to hang out in the dining room to flirt with the owner's son? His father probably worried you'd eat their family out of business. Klaus has grown into quite a young man, did you notice? I'm laughing (and the nurse is eyeing me) because I know you didn't notice. When's the last time you had a date?

At least now I have your attention. I bet it's been two full days since you had your head in a law book. Is your mother irritated? She probably thinks I did this on purpose. And maybe I did.

What a week I have planned for you! Since we weren't able to take this trip again together, I want you to take it just as I did. You'd be proud of this old geezer, Stace. I made it atop the Jungfrau, had lunch at the Schilthorn-Piz Gloria, and even took the cog-wheel railway up to Schynige Platte. This place never changes. Too bad my old heart ain't what it used to be. I've been in this hospital for two days now; they give me another couple days before my heart gives out altogether. It's fine. I can almost see Jesus now. The doctor told me (in German to add to the disgrace I suppose) that I was a foolish old man to wander so far from home. Little does he know: I was a foolish young man too!

We understand each other, you and I. From the moment I first held you at the hospital, I knew we had something special in common. You were such a happy little thing and your eyes would just light up at the sight of me. Did this old man good to have you in his life! Now you enjoy yourself this week. And no crying; you know where I am! If you start to get upset, just think about your boss's face when you left. That Scrooge always did think he owned you. I love you, Stace, and I'll see you on the other side. Oh, and tell your mother there's enough money to bury me, I can hear her grumbling already. Grandpa Jesse

Stacy clutched the letter to her heart. *Oh, Grandpa Jesse.* All she wanted to do was pick up the phone and call him. She wanted to tell him just how furious Mike had been when she announced her plans to leave. She wanted to share the pursed lips on her mother's face. Only Grandpa would ever be able to truly appreciate how right he was about people.

"A week," she sighed aloud. "Grandpa expects us to stay the week." As much as she loved Grandpa, she didn't have a week to spend trotting about the Alps. She had work to do back home, clients waiting for her. She didn't care about Mike or his die-hard work ethic, but she did care about her clients. She'd worked two years with them and this case was important to her career. The more she thought about it though, the more she knew her clients would follow her to another firm.

Her mother interrupted her own thoughts. "Well, a week, that's not possible. We've got the funeral planned for Wednesday and it would be appropriate if Grandpa showed up. For once in his life, he's going to be on time for something." She added an afterthought. "What's his letter say?"

"It's my agenda for the week. We're going to travel together, Grandpa and I."

"Stacy." Her mother's voice was firm. "Don't throw away your job trying to please my father's crazy wishes. He was a dreamer, Stace, not a doer. You are a woman of accomplishment."

"So accomplished I can even get another job if I need one, Mom," Stacy replied sarcastically. "Considering it's been four years since my last vacation, I think they'd be hard-pressed to get rid of me now." Stacy nearly broke, her emotions pulled so tight. She loved her mother but didn't understand the block between her and Grandpa. Would she ever change her opinion? Especially now that Grandpa was gone? Why couldn't she just concentrate on the joy he'd brought to those around him? Instead of the self-inflicted pain Ellen seemed to clutch.

After a long, deep sleep, Stacy woke to the dark, 4 A.M. sky, refreshed and comforted by the sweet dreams and memories. A few hours later, her mother stirred, dressed quickly, and left for the morgue alone. Stacy couldn't bear to witness his lifeless body, so she stayed behind.

Coming downstairs, she noticed Klaus, now the hotel owner. Of course his eyes looked familiar; Stacy had gazed at them for hours on end when she was a teenager. His eyes were exactly the same; his hairline had receded a bit, but his eyes held the same sparkle, the same sense of mischief. He obviously had no memory of her. After all, how many starry-eyed American girls must have stayed here in the past twenty years? How many were thunderstruck by his handsome features? She suppressed a laugh at her childishness and strode toward the dining room.

After a hearty breakfast of yogurt, cheese, and rolls, Stacy stepped outside and breathed the clear, fresh mountain air. The gently meandering turquoise waters of the river provided a perfect backdrop for the pathway. She contemplated the bright palette of colors before her. Lavender and yellow flowers dotted the river's edge, the white Alps plunged into the sky and the lush greenery filled in the rest of the colorful landscape. It was all so vivid. Stacy felt her senses come alive. She smelled fresh-cut grass while the glacier stream cooled her to the core, just like standing in front of an open refrigerator. Instantly, her shoulders relaxed and she experienced what her grandfather had, a peace that only came when you left responsibility behind.

At the train station, she purchased a ticket for Junfraujoch, the top of Europe and the highest elevated railway station on the continent. An air of excitement emanated from the tourists on their way to witness a spectacular view of the Eiger, Monch, and Jungfrau peaks from the top.

"Guten morgan." A man addressed her politely.

"Good morning," Stacy responded, unsure whether to try any German.

"An American?" he said with a thick German accent, then smiled. "Dis is my wife, Petra, and I am Franz. You go to top alone?"

"Yes," Stacy said with an enthusiastic smile, relieved to hear him speak English. "I haven't been here since I was fifteen, and I'm so excited. My grandfather arranged this trip for me."

"Grandpapa must be special," Petra replied. "Mit goot taste, too."

"He is indeed special," Stacy agreed.

She smiled happily, delighted by the magnificent cliffs and towns below. To believe a train could make this trip seemed impossible, and she shared her enthusiasm with anyone who could speak English. Even some that couldn't. She suddenly realized her grandfather's pleasure in traveling alone. *To travel alone was to travel with everyone.* To hear tales from all over the world and see people from all walks of life—to meet people like her grandfather—people with a zest for seeing the world.

Once at the top of the railway, Stacy felt faint. She truly was on top of the world. The snow-covered valley was laid out in all its splendor. Thundering waterfalls roared, while the longest ice stream meandered through the sights. Stacy had lunch with her new traveling friends and moaned when it was time to return to the hotel.

Her mother was seated alone in the dining room when Stacy returned. "Hi, Mom. Are you okay?"

Ellen Whitaker wiped a lone tear with the back of her hand. "Your grandfather was a nut, do you know that?"

"Did you have a hard day?" Stacy gently rubbed her mother's back. "Maybe I should have gone with you."

Ellen only nodded and sniffled. "I hated seeing him like that, Stace. I can't believe he's really gone."

"He's not gone, Mom. He's with Jesus."

"Oh, you two and your religion. A lot of good that does for us who are left behind."

"It does me a lot of good, Mom. I know I'll see him again. You can too..." Suddenly Stacy grew hopeful. Would her mother be willing to discuss the Lord now?

"I don't want to hear that God stuff." She straightened in her chair. "Did you know your grandfather was worth a mint?"

"What?"

"Your father faxed me his will this afternoon. Apparently, your grandfather had a penchant for the stock market. Bought a little unknown stock named Intel not too long ago."

Stacy stared in disbelief. How sad that Ellen finally respected her father for something, but it was only money. Of all his attributes, money would have been the least important to him.

"You never expected something like that from Grandpa Jesse, did you?"

A laugh escaped from Ellen. "I suppose I should have."

"Do you want to go with me tomorrow? I'm going to have lunch where Grandpa did, at the Schilthorn-Piz Gloria."

"No, Stacy. I'm going back home. Arrangements have been made. And your father is going crazy without me. He's sick of frozen dinners."

Stacy just shook her head, "Mom, Dad is sixty years old. I think he can manage to feed himself for a couple more days. Besides, he *could* go to a restaurant."

"Your father spend money? Especially when he knows the expenses he's incurring while I'm here? It's not likely, Stacy. You know, I have a responsibility to him."

"Mom, I don't want you to leave until I know what happened between you and Grandpa. Why do you feel the way you do about him? I just can't grasp it."

"You wouldn't understand, Stacy."

"I *need* to understand, Mom. Grandpa was my idol. The man who believed in me no matter what. Why can't you see that?"

Ellen sighed heavily, obviously annoyed. "He *wasn't* my father," she blurted. "What do you think of that?"

Stacy was stunned. "What on earth?"

"My mother got pregnant with me before the war; her beau never returned. Your grandfather married her before he left after the war to rebuild Japan. He married her to spare her embarrassment in town. He wasn't her first love."

"I don't understand; why would you blame Grandpa for that? You could have grown up as an object of scorn!" Still, Stacy struggled with her own feelings. This meant Grandpa wasn't *her* blood relative! But what about *their* close connection? It felt so impossible they weren't really related and yet, Stacy knew it should be of little importance. She knew Grandpa Jesse loved her like no one else—unconditionally and fully. Surely, that should be enough!

"I knew you wouldn't understand, Stacy. Can't you see, he always wanted to get away from us. He only stayed with us *out of duty!* He couldn't wait to get on to his travels. He probably rejoiced when my mother died."

Stacy felt the sting of tears, "No, Mom! Grandpa never did anything *out of duty.* I'll never believe that for a second! Did he take me every summer out of duty? And what about you? Did he struggle to send you to college on a carpenter's salary out of sheer duty? He did it because he loved you, Mom. Any thought to the contrary is just selfishness!" Why couldn't her mother see what was right in front of her nose?

Ellen jumped up from the table. "I need to get packed."

"Mom!" Stacy called. "Forgive and move on."

"I'll see you in the room." Ellen turned and left.

Stacy sank into her chair, unsure of her next move. She knew if her mother could only forgive, she'd have to see Grandpa for who he really was. Just then, she noticed Klaus approaching. Like a foolish schoolgirl, her stomach did a somersault.

"Stacy?" Klaus stood beside her. "You don't remember me, do you?"

Stacy smiled. "Of course, I do. I used to sit right here and gaze at you while you cleared the tables. I thought my life would never be the same when I left for home without the busboy." She giggled.

"Your grandfather told me you'd grown up beautiful. He wasn't exaggerating. Even when you checked in, I remembered you."

The heat rose in her face. "Thank you," she answered with downcast eyes. It had been so long since anyone had told her such nonsense, she was ready, willing, and able to believe it. An uninvited smile broke across her face in full.

"Do you mind if I sit?" Klaus asked.

"Be my guest," she motioned toward the chair.

"Your grandfather gave me this letter for your mother."

He handed her an envelope and she took it.

He paused. "Your grandfather mentioned you're not married." He smiled shyly. "And I found an old picture of us together in the hotel photographs. Do you remember that night you helped me clear dishes?"

"It was almost as exciting as my high school prom," she laughed, recalling Jacob Myers—the only other boy she remembered fawning over.

"Prom?"

"It's a big dance in the States."

"Are you free for dinner tonight?"

"Grandpa didn't pay you to ask me out, did he?" She couldn't help her suspicions. Grandpa certainly wouldn't have been above playing matchmaker.

Klaus laughed. "I would have paid him for the privilege, Miss Stacy. But it's my idea, I promise."

"I'd love to," Stacy answered with all the glee of a teenager.

"Great, I'll pick you up in an hour."

Upstairs, Stacy was greeted by her mother's scowl. "Stacy, you can't possibly stay in a foreign country by yourself. Please get packed."

"Sorry, Mom. I'm finishing out the week. I can't go back to the bondage just yet, not after all this wonderful freedom. Besides, I have plenty of money put aside, if that's what you're worried about."

"No, I'm not worried about that. Your grandfather left you a sizeable inheritance—" Ellen pursed her lips tightly. "'To be used for travel,' he said. Though I hope you're not planning to throw away your life like he did."

"Mom, I can't explain it. I just need to stay here and at least see Grandpa's vision to the end."

"Oh, very well," Ellen sighed.

"Mom, Klaus gave me this letter for you. It's from Grandpa," Stacy handed her mother the letter and waited anxiously, hoping her mother would share the contents. To Stacy's relief, her mother read it aloud.

Dear Ellen,

I know you're upset to be here in Interlaken. You'll probably chalk it up to senility, but my doctors can attest to my lucid mind. I wanted you to see what I came to see, Ellen.

I also wanted you to know that I am your father, pure and simple. I walked you in the middle of the night, took you to the park, and loved you with all my heart. Not only that, I loved your mother. She was my only true love, and I wouldn't have traded one hour with her. I'd always hoped we'd travel together, but when she left us early, I traveled to get away from that lonely house. It was never a home without your mother.

Ellen, I didn't come to Interlaken to die. I came here to live! We don't know how long each of us has on this earth, so make the most of it. Spend some money, and let up on Stacy. She doesn't need money now, Ellen, I've seen to that. Tell her to find a simpler job, give her a life of freedom your mother never had. I love you, my daughter.

Daddy

Seeing Ellen's face, Stacy cried again.

Stacy *hadn't* lived, not nearly enough. She planned to see every last corner of Interlaken—and who knew what after that? With a boldness that could have only come from Grandpa's words of encouragement, she decided she would call Mike and officially quit her job. She knew she had nothing to lose!

Suddenly her heart lifted—the joy of new freedom! She'd go back to the U.S. when she was good and ready. Just then a small knock sounded, and Stacy excitedly turned to her mother, who still looked somewhat stunned. "That's Klaus," she said with a happy smile. "I'm taking Grandpa's advice, Mom. I'm going to live—and I'm starting right now."

Opening the door to Klaus felt like opening a door to her new life. Grandpa lived! And so would she.

ABOUT THE AUTHOR

Kristin Billerbeck has written four inspirational romance novels and three novellas. She lives in the Silicon Valley with her husband and three young sons.

A Reason to Live

Karen Kingsbury

For Austin

Moscow, Russia
February 12, 1999

Lexia Forlov was dying.

In the quiet morning stillness, she glanced desperately around her tiny apartment. The electricity had been off for three days; her icebox empty for the past five. The time had come to say good-bye.

It was the last hour she would ever spend with her newborn daughter.

If life had gone the way it should have, Sergio would have been working, supporting them, celebrating alongside her the birth of their firstborn. Instead Sergio had died of pneumonia three months earlier, the baby had been born at home under starving conditions, and Lexia was finally out of options.

From underneath the door, the cold air stole its way into the boxy room and swirled mercilessly about the mother and child. Lexia worked herself farther into the threadbare sofa and huddled over her newborn daughter.

"It's okay, sweet girl," she whispered in her native Russian tongue. Lexia rocked the infant tightly, willing the child enough strength to cry.

She was still barely able to nurse her, but not for long. Food lines wouldn't open again for two days, and Lexia wasn't sure either of them could survive the wait.

The frigid wind howled outside, and the thin walls of her home shook in protest. Lexia's teeth chattered and her shoulders shook, but she remained hunched over her baby, only vaguely aware of her own condition. She savored the sight of her child and tried to block out what lay ahead. The baby had Sergio's chiseled face. And his wide, sensitive eyes. Hungry eyes.

Had it only been the year before when life was good, provisions abundant? She remembered when visitors had come with food and clothing and a Bible for all who asked. They called themselves missionaries, and they shared about a Savior named Jesus. After accepting the truth about the one they called Lord, Lexia and Sergio finally had a reason to believe, someone to put their faith in. Times were not bountiful, but they were good and she and Sergio had agreed to go on with their family. Never mind the starving towns and villages outside of Moscow. The shortages would never reach the great city. It was impossible.

Now very little was left of those times. Not the missionaries, not the food, not even Sergio. All that remained was her faith. *Father Almighty, grant me the courage to do this thing...for I must do it. I know I must.*

Lexia stared through the darkness at the child in her arms, a child she had named Mara. Not that anyone would ever know. At least not for now. After today she would never hold the child to her breast, never comfort her soft cries, never shelter her from the cold. Icy tears made their way down Lexia's face and she snuggled closer to the baby, pulling the bundle of worn blankets up around the tiny newborn face.

"It's time, my little Mara." She whispered the words in the baby's ear and nuzzled her face against the child, breathing in her sweet scent. *All things work to the good for those who love God....* Lexia forced herself to believe the Bible words she'd memorized after Sergio's death. The promises were all she had left.

An ache grew deep in her bosom and Lexia knew it was her body's way of preparing for the separation. She would rather have her legs ripped from her body than place her baby daughter in the arms of someone else and walk away.

Mara, if only there were another way...

But there wasn't. And what she was about to do required the very deepest of love. The kind of love she'd learned from stories about Jesus. Love that dies to self. *Real love.*

She swept the baby to her chest, wrapped a shawl around them both, and slowly headed out into the snow. This walk would take every bit of the energy she had left. The orphanage was three blocks away, standing like a beacon of hope and health and life for her little one; a symbol of ineffable loss for her.

The headmistress was expecting her. She welcomed Lexia inside and tersely assured her that they would find a suitable home for the baby. Paperwork had been done on Lexia's first visit a week earlier.

"Better not to tarry." The headmistress looked expectantly at the infant in Lexia's arms.

"I…I have a few questions."

"Very well."

"Will the baby be placed here…a family here in Moscow?" Lexia was hopeful, wanting to believe that somehow—if she lived through the food shortage—she might see Mara again, know her, watch her grow from a distance.

But the woman shook her head and her expression grew troubled. "Never. The babies are moved to Kiev. And from there adoptions are mostly by families in the United States."

Lexia nodded. *This was it, then.* "Can we have a moment? Please."

The woman looked impatient. She glanced at a clock on the wall. "Two minutes. We have schedules."

The woman disappeared and Lexia held her infant close one last time. "I love you, Mara. I will always love you." Then in what would be her final act of love, she did the thing she knew she would do every day as long as she drew breath, she prayed for her child.

Lord, place my sweet Mara in the arms of a loving Christian mother. So that one day, by and by, we might be together again.

The silent prayer said, Lexia's tears fell softly on the baby's face and she gently wiped them away. She would never walk hand in hand with this child, never dress her in pretty clothes or tie ribbons in her hair. The loss was almost too much to bear. *Give me strength, great God Almighty, please.* She held the child closer still. "Good-bye, little one."

The headmistress appeared again and this time she was holding a baby bottle filled with milk. She held out her arms expectantly. "I'll take her."

Lexia dug into her skirt pocket and pulled out a folded slip of paper.

"Please. Put this in her file. So that her new parents will have something from me."

The woman nodded impatiently and took the slip. "Very well…the baby?"

Lexia felt her soul tear in half as she held out her arms. All motherly instincts pummeled her from every direction, but she handed her daughter over.

The woman stuck the bottle in the infant's mouth, and through tears, Lexia watched her baby suck desperately. Lexia reached out once more and touched the child's hand. The sweet delicate fingers. Then she pulled herself away and walked out the door without turning back.

A week passed and Lexia prayed for Mara constantly. The cold no longer kept her awake. Instead, she felt her heart slowing. With no more food and no heat, Lexia knew it wasn't long now. She would be with Sergio soon.

She felt herself losing consciousness. *Please, Lord,* she prayed again, *a Christian mother. Please.*

She pictured her baby girl one more time and was pierced again with the familiar ache. And then, nothing but darkness.

VANCOUVER, WASHINGTON
FEBRUARY 12, 1999

For all the blood and glass and rescue workers at the scene, Elaine had been fortunate to survive the accident.

That's what Richard had told her when he arrived at the hospital to find her in the emergency room, with nurses and technicians working over her, taking her vital signs, performing tests to determine the level of internal injuries. Desperately searching for the baby's defective heartbeat. Elaine remained semiconscious throughout the entire ordeal, her thoughts focused on the tiny life within her.

Richard's fingers tenderly stroked the hair on either side of her battered face. "It could've been so much worse," he whispered, his eyes filled with tears. "I heard the call…by the time I got there you were gone." He drew in a shaky breath, his face pale. He'd been a police officer in Portland since before they were married. She knew he'd seen his share of bad car wrecks, but none like this.

"The baby…" Elaine looked past Richard and reached for the white sleeve of a passing nurse. Her words hung in the emergency room like a black cloud.

"We're doing our best, Mrs. Provo. It'll take a while for the test results." The nurse avoided eye contact, and Elaine gripped her stomach as a wave of paralyzing fear washed over her. *Dear God, not the baby.* This child meant everything to her—to both of them. *Please, not the baby.*

She reached for the bedpan seconds before vomiting. Richard put his arm around her and yelled at another nurse. "Get a doctor in here...she needs help!"

Three hours passed and still the doctor had not appeared with the test results. Three hours while her husband sat strangely motionless beside her, his police uniform still starched from the ironing she'd done earlier that morning. He sat there holding her bruised hand and stroking her bandaged head, searching for something to say to make the awful emptiness disappear. But none of it mattered anymore. Not even the doctor's words. There had been no movement in her womb since before the accident and Elaine was certain she already knew the blow the doctor was about to deliver.

The baby was dead.

Three weeks before the birth of their first child—a mere twenty-one days before Alyssa Marie was to come into their happy home—she was gone. The pink ruffled homecoming outfits would never be worn; the painted nursery would never echo with her sweet newborn cries. Baby Alyssa was dead, killed by a teenage driver in a head-on collision that left Elaine wondering only one thing.

Why God hadn't taken her as well?

Elaine and Richard had been believers since they were dedicated as babies in their respective Christian churches. They'd memorized Scripture verses about persevering in trials and about God being close to the brokenhearted. But they'd never had to utilize them personally until Alyssa came into their lives.

First it had been the baby's heart. Three months before the accident, during the ultrasound, doctors had detected a life-threatening heart defect. Further tests revealed Alyssa had a hole in her heart that would require emergency surgery almost immediately after her birth.

"These things happen," the doctors had said. "She'll have the very best care with every possible chance of surviving."

Elaine and Richard researched heart defects and discovered that the team of pediatric cardiac surgeons working out of Doernbecher Children's Hospital in Portland was perhaps the finest in the world. The fact brought them comfort and assurance. Somehow God would pull through, the baby would receive heart surgery and live a normal life. They had been convinced of it. But something had gone terribly wrong and now little Alyssa was—

Elaine startled as the door to her room closed, and she watched as the doctor walked over to them.

Richard squeezed her hand. "Doctor, Elaine's very worried...she can't...the baby isn't moving like before.... A few months ago they found a heart problem and maybe that's—"

Elaine watched her husband suffer through the explanation and she felt herself disconnecting. *Why were they acting out this scene when everyone in the room already knew the ending?* She let her eyes fall to her distended abdomen and wriggled her hand free from Richard's. She moved it protectively over the place where the baby lay absolutely still inside her.

For a moment the doctor hesitated, looking from Elaine to her husband and back again. Then he pulled up a chair, sat down, and released a weighty sigh. "This has nothing to do with the baby's heart defect. I'm afraid trauma from the accident was too severe...the baby didn't make it." His voice trailed off and he stared at the chart in his hands, allowing them a modicum of privacy as they absorbed the full blow.

Elaine remained motionless except for a trail of tears that made its way down one side of her face.

Richard wrung his hands fiercely and moved his head back and forth in quick, jerky movements. "There isn't something...an operation, something...some way to save the baby? If we hurry, I mean..."

What a strange question, Elaine thought, again feeling oddly disjointed. *As if there were a way to bring the child back from the dead.* The doctor said something about the cause of death, but Elaine no longer listened. She rubbed her hand over her belly, stroking the lifeless baby inside. *It's all right, Alyssa. Mommy's here. No one's going to hurt you.* And from someplace deep in her heart where the terrible truth of the moment had not yet penetrated, she began to hum. *You are my sunshine, my only sunshine....* The song she had hummed to this unborn child since the day she learned—after four years of marriage and two years of trying—that she was finally pregnant. The song she had sung in the shadowy darkness of the ultrasound room the day they first learned of Alyssa's heart defect.

When she regained consciousness, Richard stood over her, looking tenderly down, his face filled with anguish, eyes swollen from crying.

"Sweetheart, I love you…" He no longer wore his police uniform, instead he had on sweats and a T-shirt.

Elaine glanced around the room and tried to remember where she was and why she was there. What was happening to her? Something about the baby…her hand shot out from beneath the sheets and onto her belly. It was flatter now, empty of every promise it had ever held. Her baby was gone. The memories came back in a rush. An accident…ambulances and doctors and little Alyssa lying motionless inside her. She remembered it all, now. *Dear God, no, it can't be…* And suddenly she knew the truth—the whole ugly truth.

She hadn't only lost Alyssa. She'd lost her chance at ever being a mother.

And in that moment she could think of only one to whom she could cry out. Her shout echoed over the hum of machinery in her room and down the corridors of the hospital.

"*Why?*" Elaine gripped the bed rails and shouted again. "*Why? Oh, God, why?*"

Time passed slowly and Elaine marked it with imaginary milestones.

Two weeks…Alyssa would have been recognizing her; four weeks…her first smile; two months…communicating in that special language known only to babies and their mothers.

The room remained untouched, like something from a designer baby catalog, pink ribbons looped along the base of the crib, a downy soft pastel quilt draped over the side rail. Her mother's old rocking chair, newly refinished and fitted with a creamy pink-and-white seat cushion. Only one thing was missing. Alyssa Marie.

Still, it was in the infant's room that Elaine felt closest to her and sometimes she would sit there for hours, rocking slowly, staring out the window and imagining what she'd be doing at that very moment if Alyssa were alive. Some days she stayed in there all day. Dishes and laundry and dinner went undone until Richard got home.

"Honey," he approached her tentatively one evening, placing a hand on her shoulder. "Have you been in here all day?"

Elaine nodded, not making eye contact.

"Sweetheart, this isn't...it's not good for you."

She looked at him blankly. He didn't understand her loss. How could he? He'd never felt the sweet warmth of a child growing within him—or the cold emptiness when taken away.

In the haze of her grief, a dense, foglike heaviness settled over her causing her decision-making skills to all but disappear. One morning she opened the refrigerator and found dish soap on the top shelf. Other times she let pans boil dry on the stove, or put dinner in the oven but forgot to turn it on.

She tried to pray, but her depression stole her ability to concentrate. Then Richard began to meet and pray with a handful of police and firemen. And she knew their prayers were always the same, for Richard told her they were praying for Elaine. Praying that she would find a reason to live again.

Next door to the Provos lived Katia Gordelov. Katia was a woman who took her relationship with the Lord as seriously as the air she breathed. At eighty-two she remembered well her Soviet Union days, and how it had been illegal to own a Bible. Oh, Katia always had one just the same, a tattered and cherished old King James version, written in Russian and handed down from her great-grandmother.

The Bible had been her mainstay then, even though it might have cost Katia her life. And it was her mainstay now, as she lived out the last of her days in peace and freedom and the warmth of Christ's comforting arms.

A nurse checked on Katia twice a week, but otherwise few visitors came. Neighbors waved to her upon occasion, but because her English was weak, most did not linger for conversation. None had ever been inside her house. Both of her children were with the Lord now, and the three grandchildren remained in Russia. Katia doubted she would see them again this side of heaven, but she prayed for them daily, the same way she prayed for many people and many situations. In the waning twilight hours of her life on this earth, Katia believed God had assigned her a task of utmost importance—the task of praying.

And lately a majority of her prayers were directed toward her next-door neighbors, Richard and Elaine Provo. Katia wasn't certain what tragedy had fallen upon the couple, only that it was bad. Katia had observed Elaine's abdomen steadily growing large with pregnancy and then—almost overnight—the baby had vanished. Not once since then had Katia ever seen or heard a baby in the Provo's home.

At first Katia's prayers for Elaine were general. *Lord, if there's been a tragedy in her life, please comfort her.* But over the weeks, she began to hear the still, small voice of God in response. And each time His message was the same: *Elaine's baby is in Russia.*

Katia knew those words in her heart must mean something. But they seemed too incredible. How could it be possible that Elaine's baby was in Russia? In all likelihood, Elaine's baby was dead. But then Elaine was young; surely she would have more babies in the coming years. So why had the Lord presented such crazy thoughts? Katia prayed for the answer.

One afternoon, a full three months after she'd been praying faithfully for Elaine and Richard, Katia's nurse brought in the mail and handed Katia a letter from her sister in Russia. Katia read it through tear-filled eyes.

Dear sister,

I fear to tell you of the depth of despair in this, your native land. Hunger is pervasive; bread lines mark the city streets; and children starve. I received word that many of those precious and dear to us have passed on to be with the Lord. My heart cries for them but most painfully for the children. Day after day more babies are handed over to orphanages in Moscow. Although the actions of these women represent the matchless limits of a mother's love, I am disturbed that so many babies will not be placed into loving homes. They will stay at the orphanage and wait for adoption. But to whom? To where? I desperately fear for them—especially those at the orphanage near my flat. I saw a young woman named Lexia enter not long ago and leave without her baby. Not long afterwards, poor Lexia died. My heart breaks for her, for her baby, for us all. And so I ask you to continue in prayer, dear sister. As this is our single means of sustenance.

In Christ, Ana.

At the bottom of the letter, Ana had scribbled the address and phone number of the orphanage near her home in Moscow. Why had her sister included that information? Katia stared at it, rereading the letter several times, praying all the while. Her homeland suffered under starving conditions. Babies filled the orphanages in Moscow. The haunting picture of a mother leaving her baby behind...

The thought dawned on her gradually. Maybe there was a baby for Elaine in Russia. For several minutes, while the nurse finished her exam, packed her things, then left for her next appointment, Katia prayed. And when she finished, she felt convinced that Elaine's baby really was in Russia.

The buzzer sounded twice before Elaine realized someone was at the door. She was in Alyssa's room again, but this time she was reading her Bible. Elaine closed the book and sighed. She didn't want visitors. *I'm trying, God, really. But I need this time alone...I need to just work this thing through—*

Answer the door, My daughter.

Ever since she'd begun reading the Bible again, Elaine had sensed God's voice speaking to her again, and she was grateful. It gave her hope that one day, by some divine sense of miracle, her life would go on. And perhaps like Richard prayed, she'd find a reason to live again.

"Go away," she spoke the words aloud, and stayed seated.

Answer the door.

"What's the point? Everything I ever wanted is gone forever."

There was a loud knock this time, and Elaine pushed herself out of the chair. "All right," she whispered to herself. "I'm coming."

Moving slowly and without enthusiasm, Elaine made her way to the front door and found her elderly neighbor standing outside. She held a small piece of paper in her hand. "Hello, Elaine. I may come in?"

Summoning a strength and interest she didn't have, Elaine stepped back and motioned for the woman to enter. "It's Mrs. Gordelov, right?" The woman nodded and Elaine noticed how she labored from the brief walk. "Sit down, please."

She trudged slowly toward the dining room and took a chair at the kitchen table. "You can call me Katia."

Make her leave soon, Lord. Elaine cleared the breakfast dishes from the table. "Okay, Katia. Can I get you some tea? Coffee?"

"No...I come not for visit." She held up the letter. "I come for God tell me come."

What? Katia stopped and turned to face the woman. *God had told her to come?* Elaine felt a strange sensation inside. "Go ahead, Katia."

The old woman smiled and an unmistakable light shone in her eyes. "God tell me you have baby in Russia."

What? A baby in Russia? Was the woman at the right house? "I...I think there's been some kind of misunderstanding, Katia...we don't have a baby in—"

"I know what story you have. I have prayed many weeks for you, Elaine. I am sorry about baby you carried."

Elaine's mind began to race. *She can't know about that. And what does she mean she's been praying? What did all that have to do with a Russian baby?* "I don't understand...how did you..."

"God tells me what pray and when pray, and late weeks He tell me: Pray for Elaine." She held out the slip of paper. "This is address of orphanage in Russia where God has baby for you, Elaine." The woman reached out and took Elaine's hand in hers. "In my heart I know this thing."

"How do you know there's a baby there?" Elaine had a hundred questions but she spoke the ones first on her mind. "And why would God have me raise a Russian baby?"

Katia seemed to struggle with the question, and Elaine wondered if she had offended her. Finally the woman exhaled heavily and wiped a layer of perspiration off her brow. "Elaine, I know baby is there. And that God has give this baby for you." She pointed to the paper. "Please. Call this place and see what God will do."

Elaine stared at the phone number for thirty minutes and gradually a notion began to take shape. What if the woman really had heard from God? What if there was a baby waiting to be adopted? A child God had intended for her and Richard?

Elaine considered the idea and hope like glorious sunshine pierced the darkness around her heart. *Adoption?* She had never considered raising someone else's baby, but then...the thought of being childless was destroying her. Maybe, just maybe...

I don't know what to do, God. Help me. Is this woman crazy or...?

Make the call, child.

Elaine gulped. She imagined an unclaimed infant, alone and waiting for Elaine and Richard. She closed her eyes and cradled her empty arms close to her chest. She had never gotten to hold Alyssa and her arms ached for the feel of that small, warm bundle of life. Was there really a baby in Russia who could finally fill them? The possibilities flooded her very being, making their way quickly to her heart. Then almost as quickly came nagging doubts. *What if it weren't true? What if there was no baby?* Desperation seized her and she forced herself to stop guessing. *Show me, Lord, if what Katia said is true...or merely the words of a kind, old woman imagining things in the solitude of a lonely afternoon.*

With all the strength she could muster, she crossed the kitchen floor and dialed the number. Because it was an international call, the wait was longer than usual, but finally it rang and someone picked up. There was a faint sound of static in the distance.

"Ahl-law?" It was a woman's voice, thick with Russian accent.

"Yes...uh, hello, my name is Elaine Provo, and I was told you might have a baby currently up for adoption."

After a pause, the woman muttered something Elaine didn't understand. A few moments passed, and another woman came on the line. "I am headmistress at orphanage. May I can help you?" Her tone was businesslike and her accent thick. But at least she spoke English.

"I'm calling about your babies...well, one baby, really." Elaine didn't know what else to say. Were there a dozen babies, children of all ages? *How will I know if this is Your plan, Lord?*

"We have many babies, madam. Of those which do you mean?"

Elaine's mind reeled, searching for something intelligent to say. *What was she doing? Calling an orphanage in Russia in search of a baby from God?* She sighed. "I'm sorry. I might have the wrong information. I was told you have a baby, an infant, who has not yet been adopted. But you probably have lots of—"

"We have baby girl—age three months who is not on hold yet. Is that baby you look for?"

"One?" Elaine felt her heart skip a beat.

"Yes."

"What do we..." She took a deep breath. *How do I know if this is from You, Lord?* "What do we need to do...what's the next step if we're interested in adopting her?"

The transatlantic flight was finally underway and Elaine and Richard sat pensively, holding hands and looking out the window at the cloud layer below.

"You still have doubts?" Elaine studied her husband.

"I don't know...I'm excited, but I still don't understand why God didn't have us adopt a baby in the U.S." Richard took her hand and ran his thumb gently over her knuckles.

They had spent the last two months consumed in paperwork and details, completing the home study and seeking approval from the Immigration Department. The financial cost had been considerable, nearly wiping out their savings. Still, Elaine was convinced that for some reason, the baby girl lying in the orphanage in Moscow belonged to them, had somehow always belonged to them.

Richard lightly squeezed her fingers in his. "You're sure, aren't you?"

Elaine nodded. "I don't know why, but I've never been more sure of anything in my life."

He smiled. "It's so good to have you back, Elaine. There were times when..."

"I know. I was standing on the edge." She leaned back in her seat and stared at the control panel above her head. "After losing Alyssa...I didn't care if I lived or not."

Richard put his arm around her and pulled her close to him. "I've never prayed so much in all my life."

"It was that first day, the day Katia came to the house. After that, I don't know...I guess I had hope."

Richard was silent a moment. "Because God had a baby for you after all."

Elaine nodded. "I don't know why, but for some reason all of this feels like it's from God. Like He has a plan we don't really understand yet."

"Well." Richard lay his head against hers, and his voice filled with emotion. "I guess we're about to find out."

The headmistress met them in the lobby and quietly shut the door behind her.

"I'm afraid there's a problem. We will direct you to different orphanage, another baby. Two days from now officials will meet you at this place." The woman held out a slip of paper with an address on it.

Elaine felt the blood drain from her face. Richard put his arm around her but she felt as if she were falling, losing consciousness. *Not now...not again, Lord...*"What are you talking about? Everything's in order, the paperwork's been—"

The headmistress raised her hand. "I said there's been a problem. The baby girl is not well. She will die."

Elaine collapsed slowly onto a wooden bench, the only piece of furniture in the stark foyer. What was happening? After everything they'd been through, why would God bring them here for a sick child?

Richard looked from Elaine to the headmistress. "We've come this far, ma'am. At least let us see her, hold her."

The woman was heavyset, and she looked like a fortress blocking the way to the room where the children lived. Her expression showed no signs of acquiescence.

Please, God, let us see the baby. Please.

Suddenly the woman's face softened. "Very well." She opened the door in a swift movement.

Thank You, God. Elaine stood, and she and Richard followed the woman through a series of dimly lit rooms to a larger room lined with six cribs. The headmistress stopped near the first one and nodded. "This is the baby girl."

Elaine felt a warm sensation and knew it was her heart melting. The baby was beautiful with honey blond hair and delicate pale skin. She was sleeping, but Elaine reached for her, running her thumb lightly over the child's forehead. "She's beautiful."

Elaine looked to Richard and saw that he was crying. No matter how desperate their life had become before learning of this Russian child, Richard had never cried. He had prayed and encouraged and supported her in even her darkest moments. But since the day they lost Alyssa, he had never shed a tear. Now, they ran down his face shamelessly. Elaine felt her own eyes filling as she stared in wonder at the sleeping baby. *She looks fine, God. She's our baby...*

Richard cleared his throat. "Tell us what's wrong with her. Please."

The woman frowned and crossed her arms sternly. Then she seemed to comprehend their grief and her expression softened. "It is not policy, but I will tell you. The baby has a heart condition. Surgery is not often successful, and she is an orphan. We will let her die in peace."

Elaine's breathing stopped. *A heart problem? Like baby Alyssa would have had if she'd lived?* The words of their elderly neighbor came back in a flood of understanding and Elaine drew a conscious breath. *God has a baby for you in Russia...* She grabbed Richard's hand and stared at the headmistress. "But...where we live there are doctors... We could take her now, today even. We have to try..."

The woman shook her head firmly. "You pay for healthy baby. Russian government will see you take home healthy baby. This baby will die."

"Not if we get her back to the States."

"But there are others, healthy babies at the—"

Richard raised his hand. "My wife and I..." He looked at her, and Elaine knew they were in agreement on what he was about to say. His eyes returned to the sleeping child. "We don't want another baby."

There was a pause. "But this baby is not healthy, she is not worth—"

"She's worth everything to us." Richard's voice brimmed with quiet anger and Elaine knew he was trying not to wake the baby. He ran his fingers over the baby's fine hair and let his gaze linger on her face. His tone softened. "God wants us to have this child, not another."

A sour look flashed across the woman's puffy face. "This is highly unlikely—"

"That's okay." Richard took a step closer to the crib, his eyes still trained on the child. "Tell us what we need to do and we'll do it."

The woman's posture changed and she huffed in exasperation. At that moment Elaine knew they'd won. "I do not agree with your choice. But if you must do this, then there is no time to waste. She is very, very sick and..."

Elaine no longer listened. She moved up against the crib and leaned inside, sweeping the child gently into her arms. The baby stirred and nuzzled against her. *It's her, Lord. This is the one. The baby You had for us in Russia.* Despite her six months, she was barely larger than a newborn. Her features were delicate and perfect, and her eyes fluttered open, big and brown, fringed in soft lashes. Elaine kissed the baby's cheek and the child released a breathy sigh as she stretched and snuggled closer. *She's perfect, Lord. How can something be wrong with her? Maybe the headmistress was wrong. There was a mistake in test results; they'd confused her with another baby.* Elaine scanned the child's arms and legs searching for signs. Then she remembered. The doctors had said there would be something different about Alyssa's fingernails.

Quickly, Elaine found the baby's tiny fingers and saw that the nail beds were a pronounced shade of blue. *Oxygen deprivation.* In that instant Elaine knew the headmistress was right.

They were almost out of time.

They named her Mary Alyssa, and for five straight days their lives became a whirlwind of deprived sleep, countless phone calls, medical arrangements, and lots of prayers. But all that was behind them now as they waited. For nearly six hours, a stillness had hung over the waiting room as the surgeons operated on the tiny child. And Elaine felt like she couldn't bear another minute.

"It's been too long; something's wrong." She stood and paced, folding her arms tightly in front of her. The Russian government had promised that if the baby didn't live, Elaine and Richard could return and choose a different baby. But the thought appalled her. This was their baby, a baby meant for their home, their arms, their love. *Let her live, Lord, please.* And somewhere deep inside, Elaine knew that if Mary Alyssa died today on the operating table, Elaine's dream of being a mother would die along with her.

"Why is it taking so long?" Elaine stopped and stared at Richard.

He was tense, too, his fists clenched, jaw set. "God's in control, Elaine."

She sighed and sat down beside him, burying her head in his shoulder. "Let it be over."

Another thirty minutes passed and finally one of the surgeons appeared. He was smiling, and Elaine leaped to her feet. "Is she okay?"

The doctor nodded. "She came through beautifully. We were able to close the hole in her heart so that we don't expect her to have any long-term affects, no further surgeries. She's a darling little girl."

Richard was on his feet, too, and he and Elaine came together in an embrace. Their baby girl, the one God Himself had given them, was alive. "Dear God, thank You," Elaine whispered in Richard's ear. "Thank You...thank You...thank You..."

"There is one thing..." The doctor interrupted them and they pulled apart. In the doctor's hand was a folded note, lined and slightly tattered. "The agency in Moscow forwarded us her file. We found this inside. It's written in Russian and doesn't seem to be in regard to anything medical."

Elaine hesitated as Richard reached for the paper and opened it.

"It looks like a letter..." He opened it, and Elaine looked over his shoulder. It was written in what Elaine presumed was Russian.

The doctor pulled out another sheet of paper. "Someone at the agency translated it." He handed the paper to Richard. "After I read it, I thought it was something that belonged to the two of you."

Richard took the second paper and glanced at it.

"I'll leave you two alone for a few minutes. It'll be another half hour before you can see her, but I'll come get you as soon as we're ready."

Elaine tore her eyes away from the note and looked intently at the doctor. "Thank you."

He smiled warmly and Elaine thought there were tears in his eyes. "No, thank you." He looked from Elaine to Richard. "There's no question you two saved her life. She wouldn't have lived another week if you hadn't taken a chance on her. Your story is...well...it's nothing short of miraculous."

The doctor disappeared, and Richard motioned for Elaine to join him on the sofa. He glanced over the translated copy of the letter once more and turned to Elaine. "It's from the baby's mother."

Elaine nodded and felt tears gathering in her eyes. When she could find her voice, she nodded toward the paper. "Read it."

Richard's eyes were still on her. "Whatever it says, Elaine, I'll always be convinced that God meant for us to have this baby."

She nodded and he leaned closer, kissing her tenderly on her cheek. Then without hesitating he directed his attention toward the letter and began to read:

"My name is Lexia Forlov, and I am the mother of the baby you now hold. Times have been hard for us in Moscow. People are hungry and cold and dying. First my husband, now me. But I did not want my sweet baby girl to die. I love my baby and so I bring her to the orphanage.

"I am a Christian woman; I serve Christ and only Him and believe that even in this saddest of days, He has a plan. My prayer is this: That you raise my child in the knowledge of the Lord. So that one day..."

Richard's voice broke and he let his head drop. Elaine put her arm around him and hugged him. Although there were tears in her eyes as well, she took the letter gently from him and finished reading. "So that one day my precious daughter will see me again in heaven. I know that God is faithful and that He hears this, my final prayer. Wherever you are, whoever you are...if you are reading this I have to believe that my prayers were answered.

"In my heart I call her Mara. And I thank you for doing what I could not do. For I gave her birth...but you will give her life.

"Until we meet face to face, yours truly, Lexia Forlov."

Elaine paused and her tears became sobs. She wept for the mother who would love her child enough to hand her to strangers in the fervent belief that in the process God would give her a godly home. A mother who would never have the joy of knowing her child this side of heaven.

Richard dried his cheeks and pointed to the letter. "There's more."

Elaine nodded. "It's a note from the orphanage agency. It says Lexia Forlov died one week after giving up her child on..."

"Dear God. Elaine, do you see the date?" Richard took hold of one side of the note and leaned closer. His voice was barely a whisper. "Katia was right. This baby really was meant for us."

"February 12, 2000." How could it be? The same day Alyssa had died halfway around the world, Lexia Forlov walked into an orphanage and put her baby in the arms of strangers. Elaine thought of their gentle neighbor telling her in all certainty that God had a baby for her in Russia. She closed her eyes. *Thank You, God, for directing me to make the call to the orphanage that day...*

They were silent for a moment, their eyes running over the letter again and again. The doctor entered the room again and interrupted their thoughts. "We're ready. She's all set up in the cardiac intensive care unit."

A knowing grin crossed Richard's tearstained face and he helped Elaine to her feet. "Come on, honey...Mara's waiting."

ABOUT THE AUTHOR

Karen Kingsbury is the bestselling author of more than a dozen books including *Where Yesterday Lives, Waiting for Morning,* and *A Moment of Weakness.* One novel was made into a CBS Movie-of-the-Week. She is also the coauthor of the *PRISM Weight Loss Program,* having lost fifty pounds on the program two years ago. There are more than a million copies of her books in print.

She lives in Washington state with her husband and three children, one of whom was born with a heart defect in 1997. After emergency surgery, Austin experienced a miraculous recovery.

If It's Tuesday, This Must Be...Love

Jefferson Scott

"Why do you not kiss her?"

Andy looked at his Asian roommate. "Sai, you don't just kiss a girl you've only known three days."

"Why?"

"You just don't. Maybe in Thailand you do, but not in America."

"We not in Amer—"

"Sai."

"Lynn not from Am—"

"Okay, I get it. Look, I don't want to talk about it." Andy took the trip's itinerary from his jeans pocket. Some things might ride in the underbelly of the tour bus, but he didn't go anywhere without his itinerary. A group like this would probably be at its third stop before they noticed anyone missing.

Sai drew a finger down his long face then shrugged. "This trip only seven days long."

"I know. Oh look, we're going to a lace factory in Amsterdam. *A lace factory.* Like anyone cares." He folded the itinerary away. "Wish we could spend the whole time in Paris."

"Paris is city of lovers."

Andy threw a pillow at him. The roommates continued to joke as they prepared for bed. The Belgian hotel they were staying in was average by American standards. It smelled like his grandmother's attic. But as long as it had two beds, Andy didn't care. He would've slept on the floor rather than share a bed.

Sai turned out the lamp and rolled over. "Lynn is nice to see. Her friend say she want to kiss you. This your vacation. I say kiss her."

Andy lay on his back in the dark. Lynn's face formed and unformed on the ceiling as his eyes adjusted. He rolled onto his stomach. It wasn't that easy: To just kiss a girl like it was no big deal. Not for him. Not since Kim.

He wasn't afraid Lynn had some disease or anything. And he wasn't concerned that a bus-board romance would turn into a foolish long-distance relationship. The girl lived in Australia, for crying out loud. In fact, there wasn't anything about Lynn that he could find fault with. She was certainly attractive. And she was making her attraction for him no secret, either. That was the problem.

He rolled onto his side. Down feathers pricked him through the pillow. Lynn was young. Beautiful. She was out in the great wide world for the first time. She just wanted a little romance to make it a perfect trip. And she had picked him.

He rolled a lot that night.

The next morning everyone assembled for breakfast. Lynn looked radiant, as usual. She and her roommate, Corrine from New Zealand, joined Andy and Sai. Andy got two cinnamon rolls that smelled divine. Sai ate what looked like stale toast—the worst thing on the table by Andy's estimation. Lynn and Corrine nibbled on grapefruit.

The rest of the tour group milled around, laughing and joking like old friends. There was always such a party atmosphere with this lot. Everyone seemed to have bypassed the normal time it took to build relationships and had by mutual agreement skipped straight to instant camaraderie. Even Paula, their guide, sat flirting with Enrico, from Mexico.

"How did you sleep?" Andy asked.

Lynn brushed back her long brown hair and giggled with Corrine. "Would've been better had Jeanine and Billy not been crooning until four."

Andy looked across the restaurant and saw the new couple, one from Malta and the other from Malibu, sitting very close. Sai elbowed Andy.

Suddenly Andy felt Lynn's leg next to his. It wasn't anything provocative, just proximity. But he could feel the warmth coming from her body. He swallowed and concentrated on his cinnamon roll.

The bus driver, a he-man Frenchman named Peter, came into the dining room and said something that Andy had learned meant, "Time to go." People finished up their breakfasts and filed noisily out.

Lynn left a spot for him on the bus, but Andy walked past her and took the next seat back. He saw it hurt her. He slumped into his seat and punched his open hand. This was a problem. He was hurting someone who had shown him affection, all because of... He put his face in his hands and prayed for a way to take the horns of this particular dilemma out of his backside. The hydraulic brakes released with a hiss, and Peter lurched them into traffic.

The first stop was a little shop where the man made wooden shoes for tourists. After the first block of wood became a shoe, Andy lost interest. He stepped out into the chilly Flemish morning. There was a model windmill, like something at a miniature golf course, in the courtyard outside the shop. He walked past it and went to the low fence separating the courtyard and flat pastureland. He needed to think.

They were growing hay in these fields, he decided. Everywhere in Holland he'd seen these great rolls of hay, like tan wheels. Not like the bales from Texas. Another breeze told him there were cows nearby, too.

"She hurt you pretty bad, did she?"

Andy turned around. Lynn was standing a respectable distance away, her light blue jacket clutched at the neck against the breeze.

"How did you know?"

She stepped forward then, looking into the distance. "I'm not blind. Besides," she said, still not looking at him, "I have to believe it's another woman, don't I, or otherwise I might start to think you just don't like me."

"Oh, Lynn." Andy sighed. "It's...it's not that at all."

"Then what am I supposed to think? What's going on?"

Andy smiled ruefully. "Girl, you're right. You are. You totally, completely, 100 percent deserve an explanation. It's just that..."

One glance at her and he zipped his lip. He'd been about to say it was a long story and he didn't really want to go into it. But then he saw this beautiful young woman—this Christian woman who was everything he wanted in a wife; this woman who was, incidentally, pursuing him over all the other guys on the tour—try to hide a tear by flicking it away quickly.

He dried the tear track with his thumb, and she leaned into his hand. He really liked that. He felt a sudden urge to take her into his arms. He knew she wouldn't stop him. But that urge was the very reason he couldn't. He understood it perfectly, had lived with it for years, but she deserved to know why he was spurning her advances.

"Okay," he said. "But it isn't going to be easy. I haven't told this to anyone. I'll probably get it all jumbled." He leaned against the low fence. "Here goes.

"Lynn..." he sighed. "First, let me say that I *do* like you. I'm extremely attracted to you. I mean, look at you! You're...you're everything a man could want. So you have to know that all this doesn't have anything to do with you. It's me. It's all inside me."

Lynn wasn't blinking. She didn't even appear to be breathing. The skin above her nose furrowed. But she was definitely listening.

"You— Well, it's safe to say you bring up feelings in me I haven't felt in—" He felt something like panic welling up inside him. The words came out like a train wreck. "But that's the problem, you see, because I'm not supposed to have those feelings anymore. I can't. Because..."

He growled at himself and brought his fists to his forehead. "Four years ago I was a freshman in college."

"In Texas?" she asked, coming to sit beside him on the fence.

"Right. I had this great roommate. He was my best and only friend—closer than a brother. Anyway, the following year, this great roommate of mine transferred to another college. So there I was, a sophomore with no friends. Not a good thing to be. Everybody seemed to have their own friends established, but those circles didn't include me. I was really, really lonely. You have no idea."

"I might," Lynn said. "So that's when this girl came on the scene, isn't it? Got you when you were down, didn't she?"

"How did you know?"

She blinked. "Some girls smell desperation. They're like sharks."

Andy smiled. "Her name was Kim. She liked me. She singled me out and pursued me." He looked at Lynn with a half smile. "Sort of like someone else I know." He stood up abruptly. "Not that you're—I mean, that isn't what I meant to—"

"Andy," Lynn said sharply. "Andy, it's okay. I'm not offended. Go on."

He laughed at himself. "I'm somethin', aren't I?"

"Mm-hmm. Now: She singled you out."

"Right. And of course I loved it. I'd never been pursued in my life."

"I don't believe you."

He nodded and sat back down. "I knew she wasn't the kind for me. She was about as much a Christian as you are a Buddhist. But I wasn't thinking...I should've known..."

"You were lonely," Lynn said, not without compassion.

He nodded again. "She wanted something from me. I wasn't looking for what she was looking for, but I did want...I wanted to not be alone anymore."

"She was a floozie."

Andy chuckled in spite of himself. "Yeah. You're right. But I wasn't any better. All my resolve, all my great morals, and my commitment to Christ—right out the door in one date. Sure, she seduced me, and what guy wouldn't be flattered by that? But I..." He jabbed both hands forward. "I should've left. I should've run.

"Anyway, I didn't. We were hot and heavy for months. It was built on all the wrong things. We never...you know. We never took *that* step. Not in all the months we were together. But in my mind I did. At that point I didn't care. I was too desperate and she was too willing.

"So for that whole year, I basically worshiped this chick. I'm not kidding. I took God out, and I tried to make this girl, this floozie, fit in His place. I stopped going to church. Stopped having quiet times. Even stopped praying. It was terrible. I was... Well, I'm just so thankful to God I didn't get hit by a truck during that time. You ever wonder what would've happened if the prodigal son had been killed while he was still in his rebellion?

"Anyway, I was a mess. Of course, it didn't work. It's a *God*-shaped void inside us, right? I felt so horrible during that whole time. So worthless. I tried hard to merit her affection. Even so, I felt her slipping away. And why not? I was a total washout. And all she'd wanted from me was a few tussles. I was so needy it was sickening, even to me. I don't blame her for wanting to move on."

Andy tried to judge the look in Lynn's eyes. It might've been concern or maybe anger on his behalf. On the other hand, it might've been disgust. Was he Kafka's bug now? He shrugged. Too late to take it all back. Might as well keep plunging ahead.

"Somehow I knew she was pulling away. Every move she made I interpreted with jealousy. She admitted there had been other guys. She started hinting about seeing other people. But I was like a bulldog. I don't know, Lynn, I think I was a little nuts during that time. I even went to the school counselor and told him I'd been having suicidal thoughts."

A round of applause startled him. The wood carving demonstration was wrapping up.

"She eventually dumped me. Big surprise. Of course, at the time I thought it was the end of my world. Dumped by my goddess—the object of my worship. Fortunately I didn't own a gun at the time." Now, it was his turn for tears. "I was so miserable, Lynn. So wretched. I begged—literally begged her not to leave me. What an idiot."

People flowed from the shop now. Lynn guided Andy to a shaded spot on the side of the building within sight of the bus.

"Now I see it was the best thing that could've happened to me. Praise God she dumped me!"

He risked another look at her. She'd touched his arm tenderly to move him over here. That was something. She could've just gone back to the bus. Her blue eyes never left his and the slightest hint of an encouraging smile tugged at the corner of her mouth.

He went on. "After that, I came back to God like a crazy man. I grabbed onto Him with hands, feet, teeth—everything. I'd seen what I was capable of and I knew how desperately I needed Him."

He took her hand in both of his. "But now, you see, I've got Him and He's got me, Lynn. I just spent three weeks by myself in England before this tour. Do you know who was with me, Lynn? Jesus. He's the only one who'll never leave me. Do you understand what I'm saying? *He's all I need.* I don't...I don't trust myself, Lynn. Do you see? That's why I have to stick with Jesus and Jesus alone."

People were loading back onto the bus now, with Paula doing her head count.

Lynn's blue eyes searched his. "I understand what you're saying, Andy. I truly do. And I respect it."

He sighed relief.

"You're a strange man, Andrew. A strange and wonderful man. Thank you for telling me this." Then she took his arm and led him toward the bus. "I'll leave you alone from now on, all right? But can we still be friends?"

At those words, something began to give inside Andy. He put his arm on her shoulder awkwardly, then drew her into a hug. She fit there so well. Ah, the smell of her hair, the warmth of her body. He just lingered there on her shoulder, accepting her absolution.

Together they walked toward the bus.

"Wait," he said, digging in his jacket pocket. "I want to get a picture."

"Paula's calling."

"It's okay. Just stand right there, right by that funky windmill."

She went over to it. "It looks like a propeller." She put both hands on the windmill blade, as if she were starting up a Sopwith Camel. Andy lifted the camera.

And just then the blade broke off in her hands. "Oh no!"

She fumbled with it for a moment. Then Paula came running, and the shoe carver burst from his shop swearing in colorful Flemish. Lynn broke down laughing.

Andy took the picture.

And just like that he was set free. There in that suspended snapshot moment, he was released from his self-imposed exile. He had passed the test: He had been pursued by an attractive woman, and he had not forsaken his Lord for her. And he suddenly felt giddy. With a hoot, he grabbed Lynn by the hand and fled the irate woodcarver for the bus.

Five steps from the bus door, he stopped. Under the gaze of the group watching from the windows, he gently took Lynn by the shoulders.

And kissed her good.

He followed her up the steps, accompanied by the cheers of his temporary family. His kiss wasn't to start a romance or to seize the moment or to please Sai, Corrine, Lynn, or even himself. He'd kissed her to commemorate the rebirth of something inside him.

Something he would one day give his wife.

ABOUT THE AUTHOR

With "If It's Tuesday, This Must Be...Love," Jefferson Scott takes a break from his usual technothrillers. But this story does continue his theme of real Christians dealing with real issues—and real failures. His first novel, *Virtually Eliminated,* deals with a Christian who has become addicted to his computers. Scott's other novels are *Terminal Logic* and *Fatal Defect.*

SEARCHING ST. PETER'S

Nancy Moser

He will endure as long as the sun, as long as the moon,
through all generations.

PSALM 72:5

Clark...

My late husband's name greeted me on the edge of waking. If he couldn't be there in person to say "Morning, hon," then at least his name...

No. At least, nothing. Thinking about Clark versus having him lying by my side was like comparing glass to diamonds. I pulled the pillow close, but it too was no substitute for a warm body.

It was morning. Another day. I reluctantly opened my eyes—and was immediately confused. This wasn't home. Where was—?

Rome.

The anger returned. How dare Clark die on me? How dare he force me to take this dream vacation alone?

I'm only thirty-two.

Those four words haunted me. Add forty years to that statement and it would have been acceptable—or if not acceptable, certainly within the realm of fairness. But to be young and widowed? I didn't deserve that.

"Promise me you'll go to Rome without me."

In those last days I would have promised Clark that I would go to

Mars if it would have eased his worry. I never meant to keep my promise. And I wouldn't have if the strange letter hadn't come in the mail...

Clark and I were on the mailing lists of car insurance companies, charge cards, and sweepstakes with impossible odds. At our struggling economic level we were not prime candidates for overseas trips or the glossy brochures that advertised them. Our extra funds were spent on repairs for the groaning plumbing and the ancient furnace. But a month after Clark's death, I'd gotten a packet from Travel Italia, Inc. The first odd thing I'd noticed was that it was addressed to me. *Just* me. Our other unsolicited mail still came for Mr. and Mrs., evidence that the news of a dead spouse spread its spider web of sorrow ever so slowly.

I'd sat at the kitchen table and opened it. I'd looked at the pictures of piazzas and ruins, not ever planning to go. I was sure Clark would understand. Someday, but not yet. Besides, I couldn't afford the $3,278. The life insurance money hadn't come in yet, and there were funeral bills and medical bills... Just that morning I'd gathered all of them together and had added them up. $46,722. I would be lucky if the insurance check would cover it. We'd purchased minimal life insurance. After all, there would be a lifetime before we'd need it.

A lifetime which ended at age thirty-two.

I'd glanced at the rest of the mail. The return address of the insurance company caught my eye. I ripped open the envelope. Enclosed was a check for $50,000. The burden of the bills lifted. I drew my calculator close. $50,000 minus $46,722 equaled...

$3,278.

A shiver had coursed through my body from head to toes and back again. Such a coincidence could not be ignored.

And so I'd come to Rome. Alone.

Traveling alone brought about a grotesque combination of pleasure and pain; a reward swathed in punishment. Alone in a busload of strangers who were bound together in smaller groups of two or three. But not one. Never one. Alone.

My fellow travelers were kind enough, including me at their tables at lunch and showing me their shopping bargains, as if such trivialities could make up for the fact that I was a single in a couple world. But I was an oddity and everyone knew it.

I'd considered signing up for a roommate and having the travel company give me potluck. It certainly would have been cheaper. But, I'd been given $3,278, the exact cost for a single room fare; and who was I to mess with the precision of a miracle? Besides, the thought of sharing a room with a stranger repulsed me. The only way to brave this trip was the promise of time alone. Time to think, grieve—and brood. And in the past three months I had elevated brooding to an Olympic event.

My friends back in Steadfast, Kansas, had offered to come along, saying I was being ridiculous to even consider going alone. But I had listened and discarded their opinions with a tolerant smile. This trip was supposed to have been mine and Clark's, someday in the future. Since his future was over, I would do it solo. So there.

Besides, if I was to find God again, I had to do it one-on-one. Do not disturb. Out to lunch. Check back later. Thanks for coming.

I'd lost God at the same time I lost Clark. For some idiotic reason, up until the last moment, I'd held onto the thin thread of hope that Clark would snap out of his cancer, sit up, and say, "Can I go home now?" I felt that way until he drew his final breath—and even for a few minutes afterward as I prayed for a Lazarus miracle. When Clark did not open his eyes and tell me all his suffering had been some sick joke, I rejected the malicious God who would dare force me into such uneasy solitude. Not a morning dawned that I didn't—

Morning.

I looked at the clock: 6:45. A continental breakfast was being served in the dining room. The bus would leave at 8:00 for—

My stomach clenched as I remembered the day's itinerary.

Although I'd loved experiencing the Colosseum with its whispering voices of past carnage, the Roman Forum with the gypsy children eager to pick our pockets, and the Pantheon with its amazing holed dome, today's itinerary was *the* reason I'd come to Rome.

For today was the day I would see St. Peter's. Today was the day I would search for God within the confines of its walls.

Thanks to Clark.

St. Peter's had been my husband's passion. Where some men liked to tinker with cars, Clark had liked to tinker with history. To him, absorbing everything he could about St. Peter's was comparable to learning the ins and outs of a '63 Impala engine. He'd had shelves of books about it and would often punctuate conversation with St. Peter's trivia: *Did you know when they restored Michelangelo's ceiling in the Sistine Chapel, they secured the scaffolding using the same holes in the walls as he used in 1508?*

I would smile and say, "No, Clark, I didn't know that."

"Well, now you do." Then he'd nod as if he'd done a good deed by wising up his history-ignorant wife.

The Vatican, the Sistine Chapel… I'd teased him about being a closet Catholic in Baptist disguise, but he had scoffed. "God called Peter 'the rock' and said, 'On this rock I will build my church.' St. Peter's is the first church—the church that was started for all of us. It is the root of all denominations."

Roots. I needed roots. I needed to feel the connection between past and present—between the God I'd known and the inaccessible God who had moved oh so far away.

With any luck, today would be the beginning of my tomorrows.

"You're looking pretty this morning, Rose."

I smiled at the women seated across the bus aisle. Martha and Mary, widowed sisters from Vermont. Although the women had tried to draw me into their sisterhood of widowhood, I kept my distance. My grief wasn't like theirs; it couldn't be. They laughed. They smiled and joked. Mine was more profound. Real. Fresh.

Yet I *was* pleased they'd noticed the extra care I'd taken in dressing this morning. One did not go searching for God in denim and Nikes. Besides, there were rules of decorum to be followed in visiting St. Peter's. No bare arms, short skirts, or shorts. Our guide had warned us that respect was to be shown or you would not be admitted. I liked that. I respected St. Peter's. After all, it was the key to my future.

"Are you excited about seeing St. Peter's?"

I hesitated only a second. "Yes." It was easier to say a simple yes than explain the intricacies of my feelings.

"I hear you can go to the very top. It's hundreds of steps and the stairway gets real narrow with the ceiling curving right over your shoulder." Martha looked to her sister. "I talked Mary into going. Do you want to go with us?"

Actually, I hoped to find God on the first floor. "Oh…I don't know."

Martha's face deflated at my indifferent response. I had just flaunted my newest fault. Grief had brought with it a bad habit. Rudeness. I leaned toward them to make amends. "The truth is, I have trouble keeping up with you two."

Martha's shoulders shuffled with pride. "Back home we walk two miles a day."

Mary put a hand on my armrest. "Give a holler if you decide to go, Rose."

I nodded and had to stifle a smile as I imagined Martha and Mary giving a "holler" in the sanctity of St. Peter's.

Suddenly Mary gasped and pointed out my window. "There it is!"

I turned my head. My heart fell to my feet. There it was.

St. Peter's loomed on the distant square, huge, white, and majestic. The bus stopped around the corner, and we got out to walk the last two blocks. We followed our tour guide like sheep following a shepherd.

Lead me to God please.

My divine quest was distracted by two beautiful Italian men standing in a doorway, smoking a morning cigarette—Italy was brimming with beautiful men. They blatantly looked me over, and I suddenly wished I weren't a part of this gaggle that branded me a tourist. I felt both pleasure and embarrassment at their attention.

"Buongiorno," one said.

I smiled, nodded, then looked down and combed my brain for one of my handy-dandy Italian phrases. But all that came to mind was *Dove sono i gabinetti: Where are the toilets?* Rather than be their laugh for the day, I kept quiet. It was clear I was not ready to resume the man-woman thing yet—especially carried out in Italian.

Behind me, I heard the giggle of the two college girls in our group. The men's eyes were drawn to the younger prey. I was forgotten. I was also disappointed. A woman's ego is a delicate thing. But I set the disappointment aside. I had bigger quarry to pursue this day. God.

We entered a double row of columns, and I realized we were in Bernini's horseshoe colonnade that circled the square. I nudged my way to the front to see. The ancient Egyptian obelisk stood in the center, the same one that used to crown the spot nearby where Peter, the stubborn apostle of Jesus, had been martyred. His means of death had also been crucifixion, but he'd insisted on being crucified upside down, not feeling worthy to die in the same way as his Lord. Peter, the first pope of the church. St. Peter. St. Peter's. I was here.

It was as if Clark were by my side. A cacophony of trivia flooded back, hopelessly linked to various locations in our Victorian home where Clark had shared his knowledge while painting and spackling and repairing. *To the right of the cathedral is the window where the Pope appears every Sunday at noon.*

Yes, I saw it. And there were the chimneys where the ballots were burned when a new pope was voted on. Black smoke indicated the need for an additional vote. If the smoke was white, a decision had been reached. And there, to the left of the grand stairs were the Swiss guards, dressed in their gaudy yellow-and-navy striped uniforms and plumed hats. Back in 1527 they had sacrificed their lives to save the Pope. In gratitude he had declared that the Swiss would have the honor of guarding all future popes. And they had. For over 450 years.

Like a nervous bride entering the church for her marriage, my legs felt weak as we crossed the cobblestone square and climbed the massive stairs. The sun disappeared behind the statues of the apostles that crowned the roofline.

Our group joined a few hundred other tourists who had come early to beat the rush. I was struck by the different nationalities funneling toward the bronze doors. Our clothing styles were distinct in small, almost imperceptible ways. Geometric patterns versus florals. Muted colors versus brights. But the shoes were the clincher, the flag that waved our various nationalities. Americans sported athletic shoes; Mediterranean men wore delicate, leather dress shoes; socks with sturdy sandals appeared on the Nordic and German feet, and black shoes, so many black shoes. Murmuring voices echoed against the old stones...French, German, Italian, Japanese, and some Slavic languages I couldn't recognize. And the mingling smells...perfumes tinged with sweat, spices, and smoke; the odorous proof of our humanity.

I wanted to look at the people, to marvel in the international moment, but I found it impossible to make more than passing eye contact as we all focused on our goal on the other side of the doors. I caught a glimpse of the inner cathedral over the heads of the crowd. My heart pounded and I felt a catch in my throat.

Then I passed through the portal. The sea of humanity parted. And I was inside.

The long barrel of the nave stretched before me, dwarfing all things mortal. I'd been to other cathedrals, but they were immediately shoved aside, as if they had been built as practice and this one had finally achieved the perfection they lacked. Its immensity was shocking.

I felt Martha's eyes. "What are you thinking, Rose?"

"Wow."

She laughed. "Anything else?"

I tried to pinpoint the wave that enveloped me. The gold, the carvings, the marble...finally, I had it—and the realization made my heart soar. Reluctantly, I pulled my eyes away from their feast to look at her. "If God lives anywhere, He lives here."

"Amen." She nodded, and our eyes returned to the wonder before us.

I heard our guide speaking, "...to our right is Michelangelo's *Pietà*—the statue of Mary holding the body of Jesus. It was created from a single block of marble when Michelangelo was only twenty-one and..."

At his recitation, I was assailed with an undeniable fact. I couldn't listen to him. I couldn't listen to any guide describing what Clark had already described to me in so many ways. I did not want to experience St. Peter's en masse with dates and dimensions swimming through my head. I needed to see it one-on-one. Just me and God.

I wandered away from the group. Martha looked after me, the crease between her eyebrows warning I was a naughty girl and should really get back where I belonged—right this minute.

Like a petulant child, I ignored her. They didn't understand. They were just tourists. St. Peter's was just another building to them. To me, it was a quest.

When the group migrated toward the *Pietà*, I let myself be drawn forward, toward the massive canopy—the Baldacchino—that crowned St. Peter's tomb. I was struck by the incongruity. Peter, a lowly fisherman, buried in a place such as this? Would the humble Jesus approve? Would Peter? Did man build this place for God? Or for himself?

My thoughts were interrupted by the appearance of a shuffling figure to my left. A hunched man was also making his way toward the front. But he was different than the throngs of tourists and clergy pointing at the marvels around them, taking pictures. He was disheveled, his trousers torn at the knees, his beard and hair unkempt.

A bum. Why is he here?

As if to confirm his label, he paused beside a man weighed down with camera equipment. He held out his hand and said something. The man glanced down from the lens of his video camera and shook his head before taking a step away to resume his filming.

The beggar shambled to the edge of a tour group. A mother took one look and quickly pulled her two children closer. The guide flipped his hand. *Shoo! Get away!*

Suddenly, the derelict turned and looked at me. Our eyes locked. I felt a surge of panic. I wanted to hurry away before he came any closer, forcing me to *also* reject him.

The man smiled as if he had just recognized a friend. He stepped toward me. *No! Stay back. Don't come any closer.* My legs tensed. He shuffled faster. I looked away. I turned—

"He lives."

I don't know if I was more shocked by his words or the fact they were said in English. In spite of my apprehension, I turned toward him. "What?"

He was so close I could see the dirt etched into his wrinkles and the glint in his eye. "He lives."

No, he doesn't. Clark is dead. "I don't understand."

He didn't answer, but gave me an odd little bow and backed away like a palace courtier. I stood, transfixed, and watched as he scuttled off to an elderly couple, where he resumed his beggar's plea. They turned their backs on him.

He is trying to survive, just like you.

I blinked at the intensity of the thought. What did dealing with a beggar have to do with St. Peter's? I was here to be awed by the grandest cathedral in the world, not to be perplexed by some bizarre man with a cryptic message. Yet our common bond was biting. He had come to St. Peter's to beg for physical sustenance, and I had come here to beg for sustenance of a spiritual kind.

Enough of this. I moved on to see what I'd come to see. The dome vaulted above me. Certainly it was tall enough to reach heaven. But how did they build this five hundred years ago—without machines?

I heard some harsh words in German and turned toward the noise. The bum was getting called down by a man who had a group of students around him. The beggar was certainly persistent. *How to get rejected in ten languages.*

He looked at me again. *Oh no, you don't...*I had to get away from him.

I looked up. The dome. Was that a man up there? Martha and Mary had mentioned steps leading up...*Up to God?*

And away from strange men.

I was out of breath and headed toward a doorway leading out to a narrow interior catwalk. I walked through it, looked down, and gasped, combining my need for air with awe. I threaded my fingers through the protective grating. I was up in the dome, four hundred feet above the floor. The letters that circled the dome were mosaic—and huge. Nose to tile, I traced a finger along a grout line. Some workman, five hundred years ago, had set these tiny tiles in place. Tiles I was touching now. Time had little meaning as the centuries between each act evaporated.

I remembered Clark telling me what the letters said, "You are Peter, and on this rock I shall build my Church and to you I shall give the keys to the kingdom of heaven." I certainly felt close to heaven now…

I heard organ music and looked down. A group of priests proceeded toward the nave, as small as ants on the ground. Their chants reached my ears like an offering.

The organ, the singing, the dome…*God, is this where I'll find You?* I felt shivers on my back. I turned around to greet the Lord—

But it was not God.

It was the man.

He blocked the doorway. I glanced behind me. The catwalk dead-ended. There was no escape.

He smiled at me, his teeth decayed.

"What do you want?"

"You will not find him up here."

I sucked in a breath, fear and incredulity knotting together in the pit of my stomach. I pushed past him and bounded down the stairs. Forget the rest of the climb to the very top. I didn't want to find myself alone with this wacko on some narrow staircase, or at the top cupola overlooking Rome where the only way out would be to hurl myself over the edge.

I hurried down the stairs, the stone cool as my fingers traced the wall for support. *Were those footsteps behind me?* The hairs on the back of my neck shot to attention. I felt like a child running to bed to escape the bogeyman.

At the bottom, I burst into the nave. I risked a look back. He was not there. I glanced around for my tour group. *Martha? Mary?* Safety in numbers. But they had moved on. If only I'd stayed with them and not been so independent.

A sign pointed the way to the Sistine Chapel. My need to see this wonder merged with my need to escape this man. But his words followed me as I hurried toward the Chapel. *You will not find him up here.*

As if he knew...

In spite of my physical exercise, I felt very, very cold.

Signs. Lots of wordless signs with pictures so all nationalities would understand the rules. *No photographs. No videos. No food. No drink. No talking.*

No talking?

My first thought was relief. *If* the bum followed me into the Sistine Chapel, he would not be able to make any more disturbing comments.

We moved single file down a narrow stairs. Then suddenly, the Chapel opened up before us, long, high, and narrow—built to the same dimensions as Solomon's temple. There were no pews, just wall to wall people, standing, milling about. Looking up.

Michelangelo's masterpiece encompassed the room. The Creation above and the Last Judgment on the crowning wall. The beginning and the end. To think that he didn't want to do it. To think that he did not consider himself a painter...

The noise level grew as people were impelled to break the no talking rule. How could one not comment on what they saw? Ooh and aah were the same in any language. A guard shushed the crowd. We ignored him. A voice ordered, "Silencio!" We were chastised and forced to temporary silence.

I wanted a chair, or better yet a pew where I could lie down and look up to study the finger of God touching the finger of man, an inch separating mortal and divine. I wanted to feel God's touch. I wanted to reach out my hand and have God's electric power encompass me. I wanted—

"He is not here either."

The man stood at my shoulder, his whisper stirring the air between us.

I shoved my way through the throngs toward the exit. I saw a security guard but discounted him. How could I ever explain the situation in my tourist's Italian?

My fear turned to anger. I was being forced to leave the Sistine Chapel. How dare this man cut my time short? How dare he drive me away too soon?

I looked behind me, almost hoping he was following me. I wanted to get him into the open of the cathedral and have it out now. Enough was enough. If I were ever going to find God, I first had to get rid of this pesky man.

I reentered St. Peter's and moved to the center of the nave. Front and center. I made myself visible and available. I turned toward the entrance, looking for him. *Come and get me, buddy.*

But he didn't come.

I felt myself relax. I took a deep breath and lifted my face to the warmth. *Warmth?*

I opened my eyes and realized I was standing in the midst of a shaft of light that flowed down from the high windows, its edges as distinct as if they were made of substance.

My own kitchen held such shafts of light. Clark had liked to move his chair to sit in the midst of them, lifting his face to the heat, just as I lifted my face now.

I allowed the warmth to wash over me like arms holding me close.

"He lives."

I recognized the voice but did not panic, did not open my eyes. In the middle of the radiance, my anger had turned to surrender. I was safe in the sun.

Then I got it, like a mental light going on within the outer light. *God* lived. *He* was alive. And not just in St. Peter's. God lived in His own creation. In the sun that lit the entire world. The sun that warmed my face. The sun that made my heart feel lighter.

I turned to the man—the wise, wise beggar who had helped me see the truth. "He lives," I said. I pointed to the shaft of light. "The sun."

He nodded, then pointed to the top of the Baldacchino. "The *Son.*"

"Right. The sun."

He shook his head and pointed again. And then I saw it. On top of the canopy that crowned the burial place of St. Peter was a cross. *The Son. God's Son. The light of the world.*

"Jesus."

The man smiled, raised his face to the light, and spread his arms in a benediction. "He lives." He did not look like a bum anymore. He looked like—

Before I could complete the thought, he left the light and walked toward the entrance.

"Wait!"

But he did not turn around. The crowd of swarming tourists parted to let him through as if he were royalty, yet their puzzled faces revealed that they weren't quite sure why they were doing it. The man did not look to the right or left, but walked toward the doors with his head held high as if...as if...

As if his objective had been accomplished.

I turned back to the magnitude of St. Peter's. I saw it with new eyes. For this was merely a building—a building built by flesh and blood. God was not hemmed in by walls and roofs—no matter how magnificent they were. St. Peter's was majestic, but far from perfect. For it paled in relation to God's creation. The simplicity and perfection of the sun.

The simplicity and perfection of the Son.

I smiled and knew Clark would be pleased—and amused. For I suddenly realized I never needed to come all the way to Rome to find God. The same sun that shone in Rome shone in Kansas. And the same Son. He'd been with me all the time.

At that moment, in the middle of St. Peter's, I bowed my head and reintroduced myself to God.

He was right where I left Him. In the light of my healing heart.

ABOUT THE AUTHOR

Nancy Moser is the author of *The Invitation, The Quest,* and *The Temptation,* the first three books in The Mustard Seed series of contemporary fiction. She has been married twenty-five years—to the same man. She and Mark have three children. She kills all her houseplants, can wire an electrical fixture without getting shocked, and would love to get locked in St. Peter's for a little one-on-one quiet time with the Almighty.

INNOCENT AS DOVES

Robin Jones Gunn

The only reason I got on the train with Katjia that rainy June morning in 1978 was because she promised we would have an adventure.

I had been working as a cook at a small Bible college in Austria for nine straight months. My expectations of what such a European experience would offer me had been grand. I wanted to taste life beyond my small Indiana town. I planned to see the old country and improve my German. Instead, I rose early every morning only to stare out the kitchen window at the same vegetable garden and stir large pots of oatmeal for all the other American students who came seeking their own adventures.

Katjia was the bright spot in the kitchen. When she asked one gentle evening in May if I would like to join her on a trip to Czechoslovakia, I hesitated. Several other students were spending the term holiday in Italy. Venice sounded like just the adventure I'd been hoping for.

But Katjia lured me with vivid descriptions of Wenceslas Square and the majestic reflection of the Charles Bridge in the Vltava River. She told me few Westerners of our generation had seen Prague's enormous castle, the Hradcany. Even fewer Westerners had visited the believers who met in Underground churches. This was the adventure Katjia promised, and I agreed to go with her.

Five days before we left, my desire for adventure gave way to my nagging doubts. "Are you sure this is going to be safe?" I asked. "What if we get caught?"

"I've been there twice already and look at me. I came out okay."

Of course Katjia came out okay. Her sleek, sun-kissed blond hair and primrose blue eyes were made for flirting with border guards. All she needed was that fresh smile of hers and maybe a chocolate bar. No guard would tell her to turn around and go back home to Vienna. Nothing on her visa hinted at the fact that her American parents ran an Underground mission. No guard would ever guess that Katjia was an experienced Bible smuggler.

"You and I will take the camper," she told me. "We can fit seven hundred Bibles in the hidden floor."

I was whipping the batter for *Kaiserschmarren* as we were talking. Kaiserschmarren is a traditional airy pancake we only served on Sunday mornings along with sweet, tiny strawberries that grew in our garden. Katjia was washing the strawberries. I tried to picture the two of us driving through the border crossing in a camper loaded with contraband. Just me and Katjia, innocent as doves, wise as serpents.

"And then what?" I asked. "What happens to the Bibles after we deliver them to the contact person in Czechoslovakia?"

"They are taken on into Russia. Kiev is usually the first drop-off. Some of the Bibles get as far as Siberia."

"And no one has ever been caught?"

Katjia shook her silky blond tresses. "No. Not yet. That's why it's so perfect for you to go with me. They never suspect American women traveling on a student visa."

The rain had just begun when Katjia and I boarded the train that June morning, destined for adventure. We headed east to the mission headquarters outside Vienna. Katjia's parents were not what I expected. Her mother was beautiful and energetic like Katjia. Her father looked more like a farmer than the head of an international mission. They both welcomed me warmly and for three solid hours Katjia's father drilled me on what to say and not say, what to expect and what to watch for. His final instructions came with a grave expression as he looked over the top of his glasses. "You understand, don't you, that if you are caught transporting these Bibles the penalty could be as much as two years in prison?"

I nodded. Katjia had told me that. But when she said it, she was eating wild strawberries and her eyes were dancing.

Her father's eyes did not dance.

I barely slept that night. The camper was all packed. Our food for the week was ready to go. Katjia had memorized the name of our contact in a small town in the northeast corner of Czechoslovakia. I was not told the names of the contact nor the town. If we were questioned, the less I knew the better. I could tell the truth and say I didn't know.

Katjia's father had stressed at dinner that God's work is not accomplished in His way by liars. "Always tell the truth," he said, shaking a soup spoon at me. "You don't need to tell everything, but tell the truth. God will honor the truth."

I wanted to ask how it was okay to be breaking the law of this Soviet-run country as long as we were telling the truth. But I remembered something Katjia had told me on the train that morning about how she was raised to obey God's laws first and then obey man's laws. God's command was to go into all the world and preach the gospel. Man's law was to close certain borders to the Bible. Obviously God's law superceded man's law in such a situation.

While pondering all this through my sleepless night, I reached into my bag for my flashlight and the pocket-sized New Testament my parents had given me when I graduated from high school. I always carried it but rarely read it. That night, by flashlight, I went searching for an account in the book of Acts that Katjia had referred to on the train. I found it in chapter 5. Peter had been thrown in prison for spreading the news of Christ in first-century Jerusalem. An angel led him out of the jail that night. The next day he was back at it, speaking openly about Christ. When he was arrested again and brought before the counsel, Peter told the officials that he must obey God rather than man. They beat him and let him go.

I did not sleep that night. I kept my eyes open because when I closed them, I saw angels opening prison doors and me sitting under a bright light, telling the KGB that I must obey God's laws rather than theirs.

By the time Katjia and I were in the loaded camper, driving across the not-so-blue Danube River, I felt settled. I won't say I wasn't nervous. But I was settled. We were on our way. No turning back. This was the adventure I had been waiting for.

Katjia reminded me that we should speak only in German. I understood German better than I spoke it. I told her I planned to let her do all the talking and then I leaned against the camper window and waited.

At the two-kilometer mark before the border, Katjia pressed her finger to her lips. I remembered her father saying that some checkpoints had equipment strong enough to pick up conversations several kilometers outside their borders. One team of Bible couriers had been sent back at the border because the guards supposedly heard them praying as they drove up.

As soon as I knew I couldn't pray out loud, I wanted to pray. And I did. Silently. I guessed that Katjia was praying as well because I could see her lips moving as she drove.

The border looked as I expected it would. Barbed wire topped the chain-link fence in exaggerated, rusting loops. A tall tower overlooked the area, complete with two loud speakers sticking out either side of the office like overgrown ears. Uniformed guards wore machine guns strapped over their shoulders. One of the largest guards stalked toward us with a barking German shepherd at the end of a chain.

Katjia rolled down the window and greeted him calmly in German. The fat guard ducked his head and looked at me with an expression so fierce that I bit my lower lip. He demanded our papers, scanned them, and then began asking a list of questions. I understood almost everything he asked. Did we have any radios? Any cigarettes? Any guns?

Katjia merrily answered no to every question until he asked in German, "Do you have any Bibles?" She paused.

My heart pounded wildly. I knew she would not lie.

Katjia repeated the question back to the guard. "Do we have any Bibles?" It seemed she had never been asked that before.

He looked at her suspiciously and repeated, "Answer the question. Do you have any Bibles?"

A terrorizing silence enveloped us and seemed to squeeze me around the middle until I suddenly heard myself spout, "Yes." I even said it in English, which was all wrong.

Katjia turned and looked at me as if I had just pulled out the cornerstone of her father's life work and it would all come crashing down on us.

"I have this Bible," I told the guard in German. I pulled out my New Testament and handed it to him for inspection.

He flipped through the small book and tossed it back to me as if it were nothing. An American good luck charm. It might as well have been a pink rabbit's foot.

Within twenty minutes we were sent on our way to Prague. Neither Katjia nor I spoke for a full half an hour. She was the one who finally broke the silence.

"That was perfect," she said.

I knew what she meant. "That was from the Shepherd, not from me."

We drove through lush, green countryside. It looked like Austria. Every time we passed anyone on the narrow, poorly maintained roads, they stared at us. Two fair-haired young women alone in a German-built recreational vehicle. We were a novelty.

The first time that became a problem was when we arrived in Prague, the capital city, and tried to find a place to park. The only open area where our cumbersome vehicle would fit was in front of the police station. Katjia said we needed to send a telegram. I guessed it was the only way she could let her parents know we made it through the border. We walked the ancient streets to a small building that appeared to be a post office. She dictated her message to the clerk in German, "Happy Birthday, Uncle Edwin." We paid a few *koruna* and were on our way to see the sights.

I wrapped my sweater around my waist as the afternoon sun poured over us on the Old Town Square. Each cobblestone beneath my feet felt locked forever in place in this weary corner of Prague. The tall buildings seemed to smile down with chipped, yellowed teeth. Like a woman long past the age of childbearing, gentle Prague stood before me very much pregnant with life. Twins, it seemed. One old, one new. Both about to wrestle within her. Majestically, with her head held high, I believed she would carry them to full term.

Everything Katjia had told me about the charm of the clock tower, the elegance of St. Nicholas's Church and the powerful presence of the castle were all true. Her words, however, hadn't prepared me for the way I felt as we walked onto the Charles Bridge at dusk. The Karluv Most, built in 1357, rose above the wide Vltava River on massive Gothic arches and was lined with fascinating statues. They seemed to be guardians of the ancient secrets of this city and there they stood, mute. Caught in the amber glow of evening. I wanted to wake them up. To give them breath.

Katjia urged me to hurry. We planned to stay in a campground outside the city that night and Katjia didn't like driving in the dark.

I trotted beside her with my imagination brimming. In one afternoon I had stepped into the courts of ancient Europe, at her very heart, and now with an awkward courtesy, I was content to leave. I could go back to the pots of oatmeal and the view of the vegetable garden because I had experienced the moment of splendor I had hoped for.

But we were not ready to go back to Austria. This trip had a deeper purpose than my desire to acquire mental postcards of regal beauty. Katjia and I were the guardians of a camper loaded with Bibles. It was up to us to make contact with the Underground believers and deliver the goods.

As we rounded the corner to the parking lot in front of the police station, we both saw something that made us stop and reach for each other's hand. Policemen surrounded the camper. The hood was propped up and the side door was open, even though we both knew we'd locked everything.

"What do we do?" I breathed to Katjia.

"Pray," she whispered. Then she took a step forward, pulling me with her.

I didn't think we should approach the vehicle. But I didn't know what else we could do. We couldn't leave. Where would we go? Who would come get us?

Katjia waited for one of the men to address her as she stood before them, doing her best to look indignant at their intrusion. A tall, skinny officer with big ears spoke first in Czech, and then repeated his question in German. Katjia answered him quickly and with confidence, even though I knew she was trembling. Several other officers joined in the conversation and within a few moments a shallow laugh tumbled from Katjia's lips.

They were all speaking too quickly for me to understand everything that was going on. There was something about why we didn't have any men with us. Katjia answered that we were on a holiday so we left all the men at home. The skinny officer then said he would come with us to "protect" us. Katjia laughed and I followed her lead.

She offered them fresh fruit from our limited supply of pears, apples, and oranges. All nine of them gladly accepted and stood around as if we'd just invited them to a dinner party and these were the appetizers. Katjia played it cool. I answered a few simple questions directed at me by the tall, skinny officer. Did I like beer? "No," I told him. Did I like to dance? I answered by looking away. He seemed pleased with my response, as if he had made me blush.

It was dark when the police officers had completed their jovial investigation of the camper. They had looked though every cupboard and taken turns sitting behind the steering wheel, pretending to drive. One of them checked our oil while another demonstrated to his pals the way the water turned on and off in the sink.

Katjia's voice became stern, insisting that we needed to be on our way. One of them demanded to see our passports and visas. He snatched them from us, grinned, and then called us by our names. The others joined in as we left, calling us by our names and waving.

My heart kept racing as I checked the mirrors, certain they would follow us.

"We'll stay outside Karlovy Vary," Katjia said after we'd driven a short distance. "Could you check the map? I think we can get there on this road. It's west of Prague. Karlovy Vary is known for its mineral pools. Tourists often go there."

I found out later that Katjia had the same fears of being followed that I had and so she had changed our course. Our contact was to the north but we delayed our arrival, driving through dozens of small towns and stopping along that way at anything that could be considered a point of interest for a couple of tourists. We snapped photos of statues and fountains while always looking over our shoulder.

Everywhere we went, people stopped and stared. No one was as bold as the police officers in Prague, but one man spoke to us in animated Czech when we stopped for petrol in Plzen. We guessed he was asking for a look inside. Katjia politely answered him with the few Czech words she knew: "Ne, prominte. Na shledanou." Which meant, "No, sorry. Good-bye."

By the time we had made a complete tour of western Czechoslovakia, we were confident we weren't being followed.

Our two nights on the road had been spent at government run campgrounds. Each night our visas were stamped. Katjia said that was so that they would know where we had been. It was the first time she indicated that it might be more difficult to leave the country than to enter. I bought a small storybook in one village and the shop owner also stamped my visa. Authorities could see in a glance where we had been, what we had bought, and with whom we had conversed. Even though we weren't being followed, I felt we were being watched every moment.

Katjia never told me the name of the town where we met our contact.

She never told me his name, either. I drove while she studied the map. When she said, "Turn right," I turned right. It started to rain and she told me to turn off the road and park in front of a cemetery.

"Perfect," she said after I cut the engine. "We have some work to do. Come."

For the next two hours, curious observers were kept inside by the rain. Katjia and I worked quickly, tearing up floorboards and carefully loading hundreds of Bibles into double-thick garbage bags. Some of the Bibles were in Russian. Some in Polish. Some in a Slavic language I didn't recognize. The scent of the freshly printed pages permeated our confined workspace. I felt giddy.

"Let's hope no one wants to take a tour of the camper now," I said.

"I was thinking of all those Soviet guards and police officers who were literally standing on God's Word without knowing it," Katjia said with a giggle. "As soon as it's dark enough, we'll try to meet our contact."

We heated some soup and ate the last of our bread while perched on top of the bulging garbage bags. The rain stopped. We patiently waited for night's velvet cloak to enfold us.

After a final peek out the window, Katjia told me to drive.

"Right at the next corner. Then left and go slow."

I didn't see the man standing behind the tree on the corner, but Katjia did. "Slower!" she ordered, swinging the passenger door open.

In one motion, the darkly dressed, bald man was in the camper, on the floor in front of Katjia and she was telling me to turn left again.

I understood the huddled man's throaty German as he told Katjia how he had waited three nights in a row for us. He had been concerned and thought something had happened to us. He didn't know why the mission insisted on sending such young women.

"We wanted to come," Katjia told him.

"But if you are caught..." the man said with a cluck of his tongue.

"It is much worse for you if you are caught," Katjia said.

"Ja," he said. *"Ich verstehe nicht."*

I knew the phrase he used. It meant that he didn't understand. Did he not understand why Katjia and I were willing to take the risk? Or did he not understand why the penalties in his homeland were now so great for distributing Bibles? I knew that the Bible wasn't outlawed. I saw a huge family heirloom Bible in the small shop where I bought the storybook. However, I also understood when I saw the ridiculously high price that no common person could afford to buy such a Bible. The price was more than the average Czech could make in six months. The storybook was the equivalent of a nickel.

Katjia directed me to keep driving out of town on the main road. We traveled on until all was dark and we were surrounded by vast fields. Our bald companion pulled himself up and sat between us, directing me to drive down a dirt road and turn into an orchard where the trees camouflaged us.

A Soviet-built compact car waited at the edge of the orchard. A man wearing a hat leaned against the car.

For the slightest moment, I was afraid we'd stepped into a trap. Like a black-and-white spy movie, everything around us seemed hazy and mysterious. Why was I so trusting? These people might all be part of the KGB. Even Katjia.

My sudden fears were shoved aside when Katjia told me to stop the camper and turn off the lights. "We must be quiet and swift," she said. "We'll hand them the garbage bags out the side door."

Without words, we went to work as if we did this every night. Katjia hoisted the heavy bags to me one at a time. I stood outside the door of the camper and handed them to the bald man who passed them to the man in the hat. He crammed them into his compact car starting with the trunk and then filling the back seat. In a few breathless moments, the delivery had been made. Completely without words.

I felt myself shivering from nerves and from the chill of the thin mist that hung in the orchard. The slight scent of late spring blossoms mixed with the rich fragrance of dark, damp earth surrounded me and I knew I had never in my life felt so real.

"Danke," the bald man said as he grabbed my shoulders and planted a solid kiss on my cheek. "Danke, danke." His husky voice reverberated in my ear. He said something about heaven. Perhaps he was saying we would meet there one day.

"Bitte," was all I could say back to him. "You're welcome." It had all been so easy. There seemed nothing for him to thank me for.

The man in the hat stepped from the shadow and in the dim light I saw tears streaming down his face. He spoke to me in thick, rapid words, holding both my hands in his. I couldn't understand what he was saying. Twice he broke into choking sobs and then he fell on my neck and wept. That's the only way I can describe it. He fell on me and wept until his tears streamed down my back.

No one had ever cried on me like that before. Certainly not a grown man. And he was crying over Bibles. Hundreds of Bibles. Bibles for which he was now accepting the responsibility to courier them on to places I would never go. My part in the journey seemed so small.

The bald man pressed something into Katjia's hand and then the two men drove away. We hung back so we wouldn't be seen with them. Katjia became concerned that we might lose our way to the main road in the dense darkness of the late night. We decided to stay in the orchard until dawn.

Katjia lit a candle inside the camper and carefully tore the single piece of paper she held in her hand. "I think we should divide this between us."

"Do I want to know what it is?"

"No," she told me. "It is better if you don't know." She folded her half of the paper into a small square and tucked it inside her shirt and then nodded, indicating I should do the same.

"If we are caught or questioned for any reason at the border, eat it."

I chuckled.

Katjia didn't. "I am serious. The guards should not get this list."

I looked at the torn bit of paper before folding it and hiding it in my undergarments. I guessed these were names and addresses of believers in the east; more brothers and sisters in Christ who were willing to accept a delivery from the mission.

Katjia blew out the candle, and I pulled my wool blanket up tight. For hours I lay awake, listening to the silence of the Czechoslovakian night.

By daybreak, we were on our way and didn't stop until we got to Brno. Our gas tank registered on empty for the last forty kilometers. Katjia was driving and I was praying. To this day, I'm quite certain it was an angel's breath that propelled us to the only working gas station between our orchard and the border. As the camper guzzled liter after liter of outrageously expensive petrol, Katjia and I had our visas stamped. I saw a worried look come over her like a shadow. We were back in the camper with the windows rolled up and driving out of Brno before she told me our latest problem.

"We didn't have our visas stamped last night," she said.

"How could we? We didn't stay at a campground."

"Exactly. The guards will ask where we stayed. We can't lie. But if we tell them where the orchard is located, they will ask why we were visiting such an insignificant town."

"What town?" I asked.

"That's right. You don't know, do you?"

I had been looking at the map that morning and I had a fair idea of where we'd been. But I wished I didn't. I did feel safer when I didn't know specifics.

"What do you think we should say?"

"I don't know," Katjia said. She made an unspoken gesture to pray and I began to do so with gusto.

By the time we arrived at the border, we knew our wait would be long. We watched as guards went through the vehicle in line ahead of us, pulling out the backseat, turning suitcases upside down and dumping the contents on the dirt. The car had a Swiss license plate and the two men who had been in the car stood with their hands on the hood while the officers frisked them.

When our turn came, the guards were just as thorough, even though we were women. Our luggage was tossed outside the camper along with cooking gear, silverware, and all our bedding. We stood with our hands on the cold, metal hood of the camper. I watched Katjia. If she reached for her paper and ate it, I would, too. Under such scrutiny, though, I thought that if we moved our hands for any reason, we would be caught.

Just then a guard with a flat stick walked around the camper, measuring the distance from the ground to the inside floor. He suddenly began barking out commands. As Katjia and I watched through the front windshield, two guards rushed into the camper and with the end of their machine guns, they bashed through the false floor and began yelling about their discovery to the leader.

My heart pounded wildly as the uniformed guard grabbed Katjia by the arm and hustled her into the station for questioning. She kept her head turned toward me and I saw that she was chewing fiercely and swallowing. How she had managed to get her paper into her mouth during the diversion was beyond me. I was frozen. Left alone, my hands on the hood, an armed guard stood behind me holding a gun in one hand and the leash to his growling German shepherd in the other. The only thing between my quivering legs and that dog's teeth was the whim of the guard.

I couldn't stop the tears that came.

I kept my head down so he wouldn't see how terrified I was. I stood there, for what seemed like hours, praying with each thump of my heart, accusing myself for foolishly seeking such an adventure. My parents didn't even know where I was. How could I possibly send them a letter from prison saying it was worth it?

But in that moment, I knew that it was. Whatever the penalty, it was worth it to know that a man, whose name I won't know until heaven, had spilled his tears down my neck. And all his tears were over Bibles. Bibles he valued more than his own safety. More than his own life. He treasured God's one book. God's only book. And he was willing to take that written truth into all the world.

I wished I had memorized God's Word while I had the chance. I needed His words right then. I craved it. I wanted to read my Bible and be filled. Filled with God's Word, which I now knew was living and powerful and sharper than any two-edged sword.

In my heart I cried out to God. His Spirit like a calming breath came to me on the evening breeze; drying my tears, stroking my hair, meeting me as I stood before that snarling dog. His Spirit whispered, "Do not be afraid. I am with you always."

Just then Katjia returned, accompanied by a tall, skinny man with big ears. He wasn't wearing his uniform, but I recognized him as the police officer from Prague who had asked if I liked to dance.

"My girlfriends!" he declared in German to the guard who stood behind me. He called us by our names as if we were old friends. With a grand smile and a string of sentences in Czech, he seemed to be endorsing us.

I slowly took my hands off the hood and turned around. The German shepherd stopped barking and sat beside the guard, his long tongue hanging out. A lion turned into a lamb.

Our plainclothed police officer from Prague had his arm around Katjia and appeared to be once again inviting himself to come with us. Katjia offered him a thin laugh, as she had in Prague. He seemed pleased that he rescued us. What that police officer was doing that day, at that border, at that exact hour, we'll never know. But with a flourish of kisses on our cheeks, and apologies for our disheveled belongings and damaged camper, he convinced the guards to send us on our way.

They never even looked at the visas. Nor did they find the list I carried through the border, pressed against my racing heart.

This all happened over twenty years ago. I finished out my year commitment as a cook in Austria. In that kitchen, with a view of the vegetable garden, I worked on memorizing entire chapters of the Bible. My final week there I met an aspiring seminary professor from California. We were married two years later. I never did see Venice. Katjia married a Swede and the two of them are carrying on her father's mission. Every Christmas she sends photos of their three absolutely adorable blond boys.

Last Sunday we had a guest speaker at church. He was from the Ukraine. He said that as a teenager, he had been offered a book by a man on the street in Kiev. There was no charge. The book was free. It was actually a gift. A gift from God. He took the Bible, read it, trusted his life to Christ, and ended up spending four years in prison as punishment for actively sharing his faith at the university.

After the service I waited in the back of the church to meet this man. I told him how his words had meant so much to me. I wanted to say more, but didn't know where to begin. I stood there, mute. Caught in the amber glow of evening. I wanted to wake up the memories. To give them breath.

"Is it possible," I said with fumbling words, "that the Bible given to you came from a garbage bag that..."

He wasn't listening to me. His eyes were fixed on a table beside us. At least a dozen Bibles were spread out; all different sizes and colors. Bibles for babies, leather-bound Bibles, Bibles covered in fancy pink floral fabric with sewn on handles and pockets for pens.

"How wonderful," he said to me. "Your church makes available these Bibles for those who come and do not have one of their own. It was, of course, never this way in my country."

I did not want to tell the truth to this innocent believer.

But I did.

"This is a lost and found table," I said. "These are Bibles that people left here at church."

His face went gray. "They did not miss them? They did not come back to claim their copy of God's Word?"

I slowly shook my head and pressed my lips together.

He seemed unashamed of the tears that spilled down his face. "It would not be so where I have come from," he said solemnly.

My vision blurred as I blinked back my tears. Then to the embarrassment of my husband and two teenagers, I did the only thing that seemed natural at the moment: I fell upon this stranger's neck and wept.

ABOUT THE AUTHOR

Robin Jones Gunn's first books published in 1985, and she hasn't stopped writing since. To date, Robin has thirty-five novels in print with over two million copies sold. Teens who grew up reading the Christy Miller series and the Sierra Jensen series (both by Bethany House) now devour the Glenbrooke series (Multnomah) and the Christy and Todd: The College Years series (Bethany House). She currently makes her home in the Pacific Northwest with her husband, two teenagers, and golden retriever, Hula.

Angel in Gold Fur

Lauraine Snelling

I wouldn't have to swim too far, she thought.

Huddled on a rock just above the spume line, Julia Ransome stared out over the gunmetal chop of Lake Ontario. Gray clouds, gray water, gray rock. But nothing compared to the gray inside. The wind blew off the water and right through her wool jacket, freezing the right breast that no longer was.

She and Miles had loved to sit on this very rock and watch the sunrise. But now he was enjoying eternal sunrises, and all she saw was gray.

So, how far? she wondered. *How long would it take? The water temperature is below forty-five degrees, so that means hypothermia in less than five minutes. Of course, the swimming would be good exercise if I could even lift my right arm far enough for a decent stroke. For that matter, I could just float on my back.*

So, now or tomorrow? What's there to wait for?

Her nose dripped in the cold; February in Toronto was beyond chill. Ice rimmed the beach. If only it were frozen enough so that she could just walk out until the ice gave way and dropped her in, deep enough to be beyond saving. With her luck, some do-gooder would come thrashing out to save her.

She'd have to do it at night.

Julia turned in surprise at the soft sound of a dog whimper. There, next to her rock, sat a golden retriever, head cocked, studying her with warm brown eyes. Gold amid the gray. Quite a contast.

"Beat it." She made shooing motions with her right hand that sent a shock up to her shoulder. "Blast!" She winced. "The cold must be tightening it up." She flexed her shoulder and clasped her hands around her knees, refocusing her gaze back to the gray water.

The dog whined again.

Julia tried to return to her contemplation but she could no longer concentrate.

"What is it, dog? You lost or something?"

The golden tail feathered across the sand, and the dog raised one paw.

"Are you hurt?" Julia reached for the paw and then caught her breath. When would she get used to the pain? The doctor told her to exercise those muscles every day. He'd carefully led her through the whole program, but what was the use when one knew the days were few? She swung her legs off the rock and leaned forward enough so her reaching wouldn't bring on nausea. Even through her gloves she could feel the warmth of the dog's head as she stroked it. A lightning quick tongue kissed the end of her nose.

The right paw came up and rested on her knee.

Julia rubbed the golden ears and down the dog's neck until she found a collar. A dog-bone-shaped tag read Pepper. Turning it over, she found no numbers, neither phone nor identification.

"Pepper, eh?" The tail fanned the sand again and the dog scooched closer. "Well, you better be gettin' on home, Pepper; it'll be dark in a few."

Julia stood and turning, looked up and then down the beach. The boardwalk ribboned along the shore, empty as if wearing signs of no trespassing. Even the sassy black squirrels with tufted ears had sworn off chattering and whisking their way up and down the oak trees in the park. A seagull mewled, its cry a dirge that matched her own. But at least the gull could shriek. Julia had tried that. It didn't help, so she'd sworn off shrieking and mewling.

She'd do something about it instead. She took two strides toward the water lapping the sand and encountered a solid wall of dog, planted between her and the six-inch surf.

"Get! Go on home, you mangy mutt."

Pepper looked up at her with eyes full of...full of what? Warmth, love, pleading?

Julia backed up; the dog came with her.

"Look, Pepper, go home." She enunciated and donned her most dog-obey-me-now tone, the one that always worked with dogs or kids or whomever needed a firm word. But Pepper remained at her side, looking out over the wind-whipped water.

Julia looked up Willow Street, trying to figure which one of the houses might be missing a stubborn and opinionated golden retriever.

"You can't be a stray, too recent a brushing." She ran hands down the dog's ribs, her right arm reminding her that she'd stretched again. "You haven't missed many, if any, meals either. Did you get out of your yard?"

Pepper's head cocked slightly, and with pink tongue lolling, seemed to shrug.

"Well, you surely don't act too worried about it. Scoot now, get on home."

The dog continued to gaze across the lake.

Julia shivered. The blasted wind could turn one's bones to glacier ice. She stuck her fleece-gloved hands into her pockets and glanced once more over the water. *Tomorrow,* she promised herself. *Tomorrow night.*

She started up the street, still feeling slightly off balance since her surgery.

Pepper paced her, step for step at her left knee.

Julia stopped halfway up to Queen Street. "Now, get this, dog. Go on home." She motioned in an arc, giving the dog a choice of direction.

Pepper sat and looked up at her, one eyebrow raised ever so slightly.

"Suit yourself." Julia strode on up the incline, ignoring the click of nails against the concrete sidewalk. At Queen Street, she waited for the light. Pepper sat. When the light changed, she stood and matched Julia's stride as she crossed the intersection.

"Someone sure must be missing a well-trained dog like you."

A kid yelled from the other side of the street. "Hey lady, don't ya know there's a leash law in town?"

"It's not my dog." The words sounded as stupid as she felt. Who'd believe it, a stray that heeled like an obedience champion. Julia walked on up past the meat market to Cedar and turned left. So did Pepper.

"Well, you're going to have to go home; you can't come in, you know." She repeated herself at the top of the stairs to the front yard and again on the wide front porch. Two Italianate urns still hoarded bits of the last snow, as did the north sides of houses and the shaded sidewalks where people had tossed snow from their walks. Dirty, gritty, gray slop now.

Pepper sat in front of the door, as if accustomed to waiting for a key to be found, inserted in the lock…and then what?

"No. You cannot come in. Your family must be frantic by now. Go on home." Julia brushed past the dog, slipped into the entry and shut the door behind her, even refusing to look out the square window shielded by a lace curtain. The storm door gave its final snick.

"There, and that's that." After unwinding her scarf, she placed it and gloves in the basket on the door then hung up her anorak. She closed the door to the closet, which was tucked neatly beneath the stairs, using just the right push to make the stubborn thing click. Miles had always intended to fix that old catch on the door.

After heating water in the microwave, she let her tea bag steep while she flipped through the mail she'd stacked on the counter. The pink begonia that bloomed its heart out year round on the windowsill, hung in limp sorrow over the edges of the pot.

Throw it or water it? She fingered a translucent stem and leaf. At least it wasn't dried and brown. She poured a cup of tepid water on it, then carried her mug of steaming tea back into the living room. Dusk hung in the room. She curled up in the corner of the couch, not bothering to turn on the lamp to banish the shadows. The furnace kicked in with a click.

The Christmas tree still filled the front window, its needles collecting on the white and gold skirt. She hadn't turned on the tree's lights since the night Miles had his heart attack, but still couldn't marshal the energy to take the poor thing down.

"Why, Miles?" she pleaded. "Why did you have to leave like that?" She stared up to the ceiling. "God, if You love me like You say You do, then why—why did You take Miles?" She couldn't begin to count the times she'd asked those questions. Questions that had yet to be answered.

An angel wing, atop the withered tree, glinted from the flash of a passing car's lights. If Miles had become an angel, he'd not made an appearance yet.

But then again, angelhood was just another one of her unanswered questions.

Still it didn't matter, tomorrow she'd find out some of the answers for herself. She'd ask Miles face-to-face.

The streetlights painted tree shadows on her wall. Surely the dog had gone home by now. But on her way back to the kitchen, Julia peeked out the front door, just to see. There Pepper lay on the mat, curled in a tight circle, nose hidden in tail.

"Oh, for Pete's sake." Julia unlocked the dead bolt and swung open the door. "Why didn't you go home, you silly dog? Come in here before you freeze to death."

Pepper didn't need a second invitation. She scooted around the storm door and into the entry hall, tail wagging in approval. A happy sound like a loud purr rumbled from the dog's throat as she frisked around Julia's legs. Pepper gave a little yip before sniffing the entry rug, then glanced curiously at the walnut staircase before she came back to lean against Julia's legs, and the rumbling purr sounded again.

"So you talk, do you?" Julia leaned over to ruffle Pepper's ears, noticing that the dog was a female. She stroked her golden head. "Poor girl. I suppose you're hungry too."

Pepper sat and lifted one paw, her well-shaped head at an angle that seemed to imply approval and all the while her tail swished back and forth across the floor.

"I don't have dog food, you know." Julia considered her cupboard and refrigerator, both singularly lacking in food in general, let alone anything suitable for a dog. She hadn't felt like shopping in weeks. She picked up a can. "Do you like chili?"

Pepper smiled her total agreement.

Julia opened the can and poured the chili into a low bowl before setting it in the microwave. "Might taste better if I nuke it a little."

Pepper just sat nearby watching every move.

When Julia set the warm bowl on the floor, Pepper glanced at it then back to Julia, but made not a move. "Okay, girl, it's yours. Have at it."

Pepper ate daintily, at a steady pace, and licked every trace from the bowl. Then she sat and wagged her tail.

"You need a drink?" Julia filled the bowl with water and set it back down. Once again, when invited, Pepper lapped until satisfied.

The evening stretched ahead of her, empty like all the rest since her son, Darren, and his wife, Cindy, had left after the funeral. They'd both needed to get back to their jobs. She understood how their lives on the West Coast kept them too busy to visit very often. And while her son loved her and promised to keep in touch, the phone calls petered out after a few weeks. Before, the distance hadn't mattered so much. Now even the phone felt too heavy to lift.

"You can sleep in the basement tonight and tomorrow we find your owner, okay?" Julia led the way to the basement, taking an old coat off the hook on her way down the stairs. "This should make you a good bed, and the washroom is plenty warm."

She set another bowl of water down on the floor, arranged the coat and pointed to the makeshift bed. "There you go." Pepper sniffed the coat, then sat in the middle. Julia ruffled the dog's ears and stroked her head, earning a wrist kiss for her efforts. "Ah, you are a sweet dog, aren't you?" Pepper rumbled and raised one ear, her tail wagging all the while.

Julia closed the door, shutting off the lights as she went. She adjusted the heat for the night and made her way upstairs. On many nights the stairs seemed too much of a challenge, and she'd simply doze off on the couch and then awaken half frozen.

She stared around her disheveled bedroom. She should straighten things up in here if tomorrow was really the day. Shame to let Darren come in to such a mess. Should she write a note? That way they'd know what happened and not think it a homicide. Surely, she should set her affairs in order.

Instead, she pulled on her fleecy, footed pajamas. Nights had been so desperately cold without Miles. Lying next to him had been like sleeping with a cozy bed warmer—one with arms and a beating heart.

She clicked on the remote to the TV, flicking through channels like a man. Her thumb coordination on the remote had improved in the last weeks, but that was about the only part of her body that seemed to work these days. As usual, nothing caught her interest. She glanced over at the Bible on her nightstand. At first she'd searched for comfort within its pages but the words seemed as flat and lifeless as the two-dimensional bodies moving across the television screen.

Only the heaving icy lake offered comfort. *Tomorrow night for sure.*

She woke sometime later to a dog's tongue licking away her tears.

"What?" she cried. "Pepper, how'd you get up here?" That familiar purring sound and a cold nose were her only answers as the dog eased down beside her, resting her head on Julia's left shoulder. "You should get down," warned Julia. But the warm body simply snuggled closer. Julia scratched the dog's ears and stroked her silken head. Pepper sighed.

Julia did too. But instead of getting up and pacing the floor, as had become her habit when waking in the middle of the night, this time she remained in bed, continuing to pet the dog until she fell back to sleep. She didn't wake until the chime of the doorbell sent Pepper bounding from the bed and down the stairs. Julia struggled into her robe. Getting her right arm into the sleeve of this loose-fitting garment without pain was yet to be accomplished.

The bell chimed again.

"All right, all right," she called. "I'm coming." The clock showed nine. Must be the mailman. She belted her robe as she descended the steep stairs, careful not to let the back of her slippers catch on the risers. A tumble down the stairs might mess up her plans.

Pepper stood at attention, her nose to the door, tail wagging cautiously. She looked over her shoulder as if to ask, are you coming?

"Pepper, sit."

Pepper obeyed.

Julia brushed her hair back with her left hand, then reached for the doorknob with her right. The pain of the movement made her whimper. Pepper stood at attention, her gaze drilling the door with a protective glance in Julia's direction.

"No, it's okay, girl. Sit." The dog had gone on guard for her, but now sat obediently. Julia opened the door and reached for the slender package. "Thanks."

"Hope you're feeling better," the mail carrier said.

"I'm fine, thank you," she replied, closing the door with a snap. *What a liar I've become! But what else can I say? Thank you very much, I'm so fine that I plan to walk across Lake Ontario today—underwater.*

Pepper sniffed the mail and turned through the arch into the living room, again looking over her shoulder, as if expecting Julia to follow.

"No," Julia answered in a matter-of-fact tone. "I'm not sitting down to read the mail today. You see, I don't read mail anymore. Just like I don't answer the telephone." The stack on the coffee table seemed obvious proof of that.

If anyone heard me justifying myself to a dog...

She dumped the mail on the growing pile and walked through the opened French doors into the dining room and then on to the kitchen. She could write her good-bye letter in the dust on the ancient pine table—or any other flat surface in her house for that matter. She stared at the table. Miles should be sitting there, with his back to the sunshine that often streamed in that window. He loved the warm sunlight on his shoulders, his steaming cup of coffee, his morning paper.

She'd discontinued taking the paper. The sun had discontinued itself.

Pepper stood before the sink, tail wagging, and another glance over the shoulder.

"You're hungry?" The tail wagged faster. "Chili again?" More wagging. The tail brushed softly against her dark fleece robe, leaving long golden hairs behind. "How about going outside while I fix your breakfast?"

The rumble purr again. Assent perhaps? Pepper followed her down the four steps to the back door and slipped out almost before Julia had it open. Within minutes the dog whined at the door until Julia opened it, and then headed directly right for the bowl of chili, lapping it up until the bowl shined. "Today we find your owner," said Julia as she placed the bowl in the sink.

"I'll start with the phone," she announced as she sat down and picked up the phone directory, grimacing at the weight. Pepper rested her chin on Julia's knee as she first dialed the Humane Society, then the local veterinarians, and finally the pet stores to see if there had been any notice of a lost dog. But no one knew anything about a missing female golden retriever who answered to the name Pepper. Julia's tea grew cold, and Pepper stretched out for a snooze, her muzzle now nestled on Julia's feet.

After a bit, Julia's stomach grumbled, the first time she'd noticed hunger since—when? She shrugged. Strange. Not that she'd sworn off eating altogether, but nothing seemed to suit her, and she never actually felt hungry. Perhaps heating that chili had triggered her hunger response.

Unless she wanted the last can of chili, the cupboard only yielded stale water crackers and a jar of peanut butter. Her stomach rumbled again. She could get dressed and go out to get something. The very thought made her ravenous. She had to eat—now! Quickly crisping the crackers in the microwave, she spread the peanut butter, nibbling from one while her tea water heated. Then she took the whole plateful and returned to the living room wondering whom else could she call to uncover the owners of this dog? One by one, she ate the crackers, slipping bits to the dog who watched every bite but never begged once.

"Somebody *must* be missing you, girl! You surely didn't fall out of the sky, did you?" She leaned over and cupped the dog's face in both of her hands, touching her forehead to the animal's. "Ah, you are so beautiful and I—and I—" She stopped herself, wondering what she must do. *I can't care for this dog—why, I can't even care for myself! I don't know how to find her home and she can't stay here—all alone. But how can I abandon her either?*

Her cheek felt a quick lick, and she realized that tears she hadn't even noticed were being swiped by a warm tongue. Sitting upright, she wiped the back of her hand under her eyes. "Thanks, Pepper, but that wasn't exactly what I had in mind." *How come since this dog arrived, I've been crying all over the place again?*

She leaned back into the soft cushions of the couch, one hand still absently caressing Pepper's head. *Ah, God, this hurts so bad. I'm ripped in half—and half a body can't live.*

"I don't want to go on like this!"

Pepper put both paws on her knees and stared right up into her face.

"Get down, girl. Can't you see..." But Pepper whined and leaned forward, her dark eyes so full of love that Julia's tears started all over again. This time she wrapped both arms around Pepper's neck and sobbed into the golden fur. Pepper made her way onto the couch and snuggled right into Julia's lap, leaning, it seemed, directly into her grief.

Sometime later Julia awoke, her eyes burning, but her body actually warm for a change. The golden dog was still stretched out on her halfway, her soft golden fur like a living afghan. *Warm,* how blessed warm felt. She gently nudged the dog. "I think we better go get you some dog food and me some people food, eh, girl? Do you like to ride in the car? Who knows, maybe we'll even find your owner." Julia's brow creased. "And then, well, I'll just give them your food, and we'll send you on home."

But they didn't see an owner or anyone looking for a lost canine companion, and Pepper didn't show the slightest interest in any of the houses they passed as they cruised up and down the streets on both sides of Queen. Besides groceries and dog food, a leash, dog brush, and doggie treats filled the paper bags.

"After all," Julia explained to her new friend, "dogs must be kept on a leash in our town."

By late afternoon, no one had returned her calls with any information regarding the dog or owner. So she snapped the leash onto Pepper's collar and off they went. Gray clouds ghosted the treetops as they walked up the hill, away from the waterfront. No sense going to the lake since she couldn't do what she'd planned anyway.

In the park, Pepper found a stick. Removing the leash, Julia took the stick and threw it. Not an overhand throw like she might've done just months ago. Now she tossed carefully, swinging underhand from the elbow. But her ravaged muscles screamed just the same. Despite the cold, beads of sweat popped out on her forehead. Pepper, tail spinning in delight, retrieved the stick and laid it at Julia's feet.

"You could just hand it to me, you know." But Julia forced herself to bend down anyway. To her surprise, stretching her back and legs felt remarkably good. She threw the stick again—and yet again, wondering if stick throwing was on the list of acceptable exercises for postradical-mastectomy patients? Just the same, she suspected anything she did at this stage would make her doctor cheer.

Back at the house, she put her outer clothing away, then turned in alarm at the sound of Pepper whimpering. Following the sound, she found the dog, belly to the floor and nose pressed against the edge of the sofa.

"What is it, girl?"

Pepper looked over her shoulder then stuck her muzzle beneath the narrow space under the couch next to the carved wooden foot.

"What?"

Another whimper.

Julia slowly got down on her hands and knees, flinching at the effort. She tried to crouch low enough to see what Pepper saw, and the pain increased. Something once so simple now seemed utterly impossible! But Pepper whimpered again, compelling Julia to roll to her seat then onto her back, and finally she rolled over to her stomach. With her cheek against the hardwood floor she spied enough dust bunnies to fill a forest. And way back in the corner sat a bright, yellow tennis ball.

"Pepper, I can't possibly reach that." The dog whined pitifully, tail feathering, a pleading expression in her dark brown eyes.

Julia rolled back to her seat, then pulled her knees into a crouching position and slowly rose up, barely using her arms. Leading with her chin put strain on her other muscles but somehow she made it to her feet. She fetched the broom from the backstairs landing and returned to the couch where Pepper waited expectantly. This time she dropped to her knees and swept the broom back and forth until the tennis ball finally rolled free. Pepper snatched it up and tossed the yellow object into the air. Suddenly Julia recalled how much Miles had loved tennis. Her eyes burned, but the tears stayed at bay.

"So, now I'm supposed to throw that for you, eh? Well, you'll just have to wait a moment." Then she swung the broom back and forth beneath the sofa evicting the errant bunnies along with hundreds of fallen fir needles. She swept everything into a neat pile, and went to retrieve the dustpan, but met another quandary. "Stupid, useless arm," she chided herself. Pepper looked at her, head cocked, panting slightly.

If you'd just done what the doctor ordered...

"I know, I know." She bent from the waist, filling the dustpan and straightening with a loud groan.

Pepper met her in the kitchen, ball in mouth. Julia tossed it down the hall toward the front door, and Pepper raced after it, skidding on the area rug next to the door. Julia felt the strange sensation of a laugh gurgling in her throat. Pepper tossed the ball in the air and caught it in her mouth, tail spinning joyfully. Again and again she brought the ball to Julia, eager for the game to continue. Julia tossed the ball down the stairs, under the dining room table, even bouncing it off the wall and watching the dog leap into the air to catch it. Finally Julia cried, "That's all," and hid the ball in her hands behind her back.

Later in the evening, she showed the dog the makeshift bed in the laundry room once again. "Now, Pepper," she warned. "Dogs sleep down here, do you understand?" Pepper cocked her head, tongue lolling and eyes dancing. Julia glanced at the door, wondering how the dog had managed to escape the previous night. *I must not have shut it securely, that's all.*

Taking time to prepare for bed, she brushed her teeth, washed her face, and even combed her hair, stopping just short of spritzing herself with the fragrance Joy. She stared at the bottle in her hand, remembering how this had been her nightly ritual through the many years with Miles. He loved the aroma of Joy, and he loved her breasts. But when he heard the doctor say "one must go" he'd simply replied that Julia was a whole lot more than a pair of breasts.

Ah, Miles, you worried about my cancer and all the while your heart was ticking to the final countdown. Once again, tears sprang to her eyes, rolling down her cheeks before she could stop them. Her vision blurred with tears as she slipped into her footed pajamas again.

"Ah, Father in heaven, I *hate* this. Let me loose, please, free me." Hearing a sound behind her, she turned in alarm to spot the golden dog gracefully leaping to her bed.

"How'd you get out?" But Pepper simply waited for Julia to join her. Julia shook her head and climbed into bed. The dog snuggled close, her fur absorbing Julia's tears as she drifted off to sleep, her fingers entwined in the soft furry coat.

Once again, Pepper kept her warm throughout the night. And like a living alarm clock, she woke her in the morning for a mercy run out the back door.

Together they walked and played—and Julia even laughed.

And a week later, fresh snow blanketed the city. Pepper put her nose down and plowed a rut clear across the backyard, then she rolled in it, tongue pink and legs kicking. Julia tossed her a snowball and Pepper caught it on the fly, then dropped it and gave her a look that clearly said, *not fair.* Julia laughed.

That evening, Julia stood, hands on hips, studying her forlorn Christmas tree still standing in the living room. It was so pitiful it could even make Charlie Brown's tree look glamorous. "First thing tomorrow, Pepper—you want to help me take that thing down?"

Pepper rumbled in agreement, then nudged Julia's knee, looking longingly up the stairs.

"Are you ready for bed already?"

Tail wagging, Pepper started up.

"All right." Together they mounted the risers.

The next morning, Julia stood at the sink staring out the window without really looking until a new bloom on her begonia caught her attention. "Hey, Pepper, this plant didn't die after all." Pepper looked at the plant then back to Julia, smiling as if she understood.

"Come on, girl, let's take a walk." Julia got out the leash and Pepper grabbed the end, heading for the front door while Julia put on her outer-wear. Leash in place, they paced down the hill this time, instead of up toward the park. Theirs were the first tracks in the new snow that had fallen during the night.

Sunlight kissed the tips of the small swells on a lake so blue it almost made Julia's eyes ache. Cotton puff clouds swabbed the sky clean, and diamond-decked ice lace skirted the rocks in the water.

Julia brushed the top hat of snow off her favorite rock and perched to look over the water. Pepper leaped up and sat by her side.

"Beautiful, eh, Pepper?" Julia turned to see an empty rock. Pepper was gone.

A white-robed figure leaned over to ruffle the ears of the golden dog. "Been on another mission, eh, Pepper?"

ABOUT THE AUTHOR

Lauraine Snelling is an award-winning author of forty novels for both young adults and adults. She now lives in California, but this short story is set in Toronto, Canada. While visiting there, Lauraine cared for her two "granddogs" (her son Brian's pets). Pepper in this story is based on Tanner (pure love wrapped up in gold fur). Tanner loved living near the lake and the black squirrels drove both her and her buddy, Bryce, nutsy.

HOME TO ENGLAND

Tracie Peterson

Helen Myers came awake slowly. The aching in her back prompted a moan, rapidly followed by a sigh. Opening her eyes, she started for a moment—this wasn't her bedroom. *Where am I?*

Smiling at her silliness, she eased her stiff limbs over the side of the bed. "I'm in England," she reminded herself. The tiny hotel room and rock-hard bed did nothing to endear the country to her, but then, she hadn't come here for such things.

Born in England during World War II, Helen had been one of many children sent abroad to live with relatives. She had been one of the fortunate ones with grandparents both willing and able to take her into their home. And she was even more fortunate that they were Americans. Although America suffered with rationing and other hardships of war, compared to England, they had emerged nearly unscathed. There was, of course, Pearl Harbor, and the loss of American boys in both the European and Pacific theaters. Helen's own father, also an American, had been killed while flying escort to a formation of B-17s. Still, America had not suffered the nightly bombings of the Blitz, nor the fear of the enemy only miles away, separated by a narrow channel of water. Helen's mother had been killed during a bombing raid on London, and Helen had remained in America to be raised by her only living relatives, her father's parents.

Sometimes she thought about her parents, like now. Today, she planned to make her way to the small countryside cemetery where they'd both been laid to rest. She looked in the mirror as she put a brush through her salt and pepper hair. Was she doing the right thing? Tired brown eyes stared back from her wrinkled face. Sixty-some years had crept up on her and while she was in perfect health, and fully capable of doing most anything she wanted, time flew faster than she liked to imagine.

She pulled on warm jeans and a thick, pale pink sweater. This trip *was* important. In all the years she'd lived in America, she had planned to make this pilgrimage. Her grandparents had given her vivid details of her father but only sketchy information about her mother and even less description of her original homeland. And, while Helen loved America and wouldn't trade her citizenship for the world, there was a part of her that was forever linked to England. She felt it when a television travel special highlighted the British Isles. And when a woman from London spoke at the college where Helen had served faithfully as a secretary for over thirty years, she'd been overcome with a strange sense of nostalgia.

And now that Helen's two grown sons were married with children of their own, and now that ten years had passed since her own beloved Grant had gone home to be with the Lord, Helen had decided it was time to put her childhood to rest. At last she would visit her birthplace, and she would put flowers on her parents' graves, and she would try to imagine what life might have been like had she remained in England.

Checking the train schedule, Helen realized her daydreaming had cost her precious time. She must hurry if she wanted to catch the morning train. Packing only what she needed for the day trip, Helen was soon seated snug in a cab and bound for the train station. She tried not to be sad about the trip, but part of her held a great sorrow for her childhood losses. Grandma and Grandpa had become loving substitute parents, but they'd died when Helen was hardly more than twenty years old. Still unmarried at the time, she didn't even meet Grant for another five years. She had never felt more alone in her entire life. Just that memory alone was enough to bring her to England. For whatever reason, this trip seemed a necessary comfort.

I'm a silly old woman, she told herself as she boarded the train. *I'm looking for something, and I don't even know what it is.*

The English countryside held her eager interest as the train made its way west. Helen had worried that October might be cold and rainy, but so far the skies were blue; and the day, although a bit crisp, was pleasant.

Nevertheless, Helen had her umbrella, just in case.

The city soon passed by, leaving behind row houses of brick and stone, trimmed artfully with wrought-iron gate work. The country rushed at them with sheep-dotted pasturelands, dense woodlands, and tightly woven brush that formed the most aesthetically pleasing fences. Helen hadn't really known what to expect, but the countryside didn't disappoint her. Still retaining a lush greenness to its autumnal landscape, the Thames valley filled Helen with a sense of peace.

Hardly any time seemed to pass before the train slowed and her destination came into view. From here, she would be on foot. And hopefully by tonight she'd be back in London for a few days of fun and exploration before heading back home to America. It was a quick trip to be sure, but it was enough. Somehow she knew this trip would fulfill all of her longings. In many ways, it was her homecoming.

Consulting a map, Helen made her way from the station. Narrow streets with timber-framed houses and shops lined the way ahead. Helen marveled at the foreign setting, wishing for nothing more than to somehow soak it all up at once. She needed to see everything—to feel everything. This had been the home of her mother and her mother's people. *My people*, she thought. And the idea seemed to comfort her. I belong here just as much as anyone else. This is my homeland, too.

Almost instinctively, Helen found her way around the small town. She paused at a local pub when she spied a sign in the window offering fresh-baked meat pies. The aroma wafting out the open door was too enticing to pass up.

She entered the darkened room and noted the heavy timber framing and dark wood paneling. Small wooden tables and chairs dotted the open room, and a fireplace, big enough to stand in, dominated the far end.

"Why, Maggie Montgomery, what brings you here this time of day?" a woman spoke with a thick British accent.

Helen looked at the woman oddly and just then the woman noted her mistake. "Why, you're not Maggie."

"No," Helen replied. "I'm not."

"Funny, you're the spitting image of her," the older woman said, sizing Helen up.

"I'm from America," Helen announced, not knowing how else to get through the awkward moment. "Actually, I was born here or around here, and my parents are buried in one of the churchyards nearby."

"Well, that explains it," the woman said, smiling. "You must be some relation."

"I don't think so," Helen replied. "My grandparents raised me and they told me I had no one left in the world but them. I was sent to the States during the war, right after my father was killed. My mother died shortly thereafter."

"How sad for you."

Helen remained motionless. "I saw your sign and was beginning to feel pretty hungry. I didn't think to have any breakfast before leaving London."

"Oh, so you came on the train?" the woman asked.

"Yes. I thought a quick trip here and back would make for a pleasant day. I don't have a whole lot of time and figured I'd spend most of it in London."

"Now, why would you want to go and do that, love? If your people are from this lovely land, you really should stay on and explore. Where are your people buried? What are their names?"

Helen smiled and gave her the name of the church. "Oh, and my folks' names are Jeff and Louisa Daniels."

The woman looked thoughtful for a moment. "Can't say as I know that name. Your father was a Yank?"

"Yes," Helen replied. "He flew fighters during the war. I was quite young when he died, and what with the war going and being recently widowed, my mother opted to send me to America with my grandparents. She lived closer to London then. That's how she was killed—during an air raid."

"Oh, how very sad," the woman replied. "A lot of families suffered..."

They seemed to run out of things to say, so Helen announced her desire to purchase two meat pies. The woman quickly retrieved the food and even before she placed Helen's money in the till, Helen took a bite of pie.

"Oh, this is heavenly." She closed her eyes to thoroughly enjoy the moment. "It's just like I thought it would taste."

"I'm so glad you like it," the woman replied, handing Helen her change. She pocketed the money and turned to leave. "Oh, by the way," called the woman. "You'll find the church up the road. Go to the bridge, then turn to your left. Just keep walking—you can't miss it."

Helen thanked the woman and went back into the street. What a lovely place, she thought. People were kind and friendly, and the food was wonderful. She walked up the main road and a feeling of trepidation came over her. What if she couldn't find the graves? What if her grandparents had been mistaken? But of course, they wouldn't have been. Their own son was buried here.

The sky began to cloud over by the time Helen reached the church. A simple stone building, nothing like the stately cathedrals she'd seen on television, rose up to greet her. But the simplicity appealed to her.

She glanced around, wondering for a moment if she should go and talk to someone about the gravesites. It would save time if someone could direct her. But before she did anything, a young man came bounding down the church steps. He seemed to be in a hurry, but when he saw Helen he stopped and greeted her quite respectfully.

"Good day, ma'am; might I help you?"

"I've come to see the grave of a Captain Jefferson Daniels and his wife, Louisa."

The man looked at her strangely for a moment. "I'm not all that familiar with the graves, but let me see if I can help you. This was actually my uncle's church. He passed on two weeks ago, and at the family's request, I've come to conclude his business."

"I'm sorry for your loss," Helen said. The man reminded her of her youngest son and she couldn't help but like him. "You are kind to help me, but if you're too busy—"

"Nonsense," he said in casual manner. "I can surely take a few moments to show you to the graves."

He offered Helen his arm, and laughing, she transferred her partially eaten meat pie to her other hand before accepting his assistance.

"The graves are around here, in back."

"What strange bushes." Helen studied the foliage. Almost as tall as trees, they fanned out like a skirt of green and touched the ground.

"They're yews," he explained. "You often find them in cemeteries. Can't have them much of any place but there and sometimes gardens. They're poisonous, don't you know. If the animals nibble at them, they'll die."

"I see." Helen waited as the younger man opened a short wrought-iron gate to allow her into the cemetery grounds.

"Now, as you can see, there are quite a few graves here. You might want to wander over there, while I look in this direction. Maybe together we can locate your Captain Daniels."

Helen nodded and began to gaze around at the ancient stones. Some of the graves dated back two and three hundred years. It was almost impossible to fathom the age of this place.

"Ah, we're in luck," he announced. "The grave is right here."

Helen looked up to see that he'd paused in front of a rather simple marker. She steadied herself and took a deep breath. *This shouldn't be that hard,* she thought.

"I must excuse myself now," the man said. "I do hope you have a pleasant day."

"Thank you so much for your help," she replied.

"Not at all."

She waited until he'd passed beyond the gate and disappeared around the side of the church. The cemetery seemed unnaturally quiet, as cemeteries usually did. Helen thought of where Grant's body laid to rest. Hers would one day rest beside him, there beneath the shade of a beautiful oak tree. Grant had thought the place looked too pretty to be a cemetery. She'd thought so too, but in the end they'd agreed it was the place they wanted for their own earthly resting place.

Helen made her way past stones and markers to where the young man had directed her. And there it was.

Captain Jefferson Daniels.

She reached down and brushed a few dried leaves from the marker, then touched the engraved words. A sigh escaped her. Was it because she was much closer to the age where she'd be laid to rest than she liked to think? Or maybe, just maybe, it was a sigh from the longings and desires of a child with no conscious memory of a father who had died so young. Why, he was even younger than her sons!

"I wish I'd known you," she whispered.

After a few moments, Helen looked for her mother's headstone. But to her dismay, the stones on either side belonged to other veterans. Perhaps her mother's grave lay elsewhere in the cemetery. She got up and looked nearby, but to her complete frustration, nothing indicated where Louisa Daniels was buried. She searched one end of the cemetery to the other, grateful the entire area was no larger than her backyard. Still, numerous gravesites filled the tiny parcel of land.

"She's *got* to be here," she finally said aloud.

"Elaine told me I might find you here," a woman's voice spoke.

Surprised, Helen turned to see a woman, probably ten years her junior, standing by the gate. Squinting for a better look, Helen made her way across the grounds. "I'm sorry, I don't know any Elaine."

"You met her at the pub," the stranger offered.

Helen drew closer to the woman noting her overcoat and head scarf. "You must be expecting rain," she said glancing heavenward.

"We're due a shower," the woman replied.

Helen stopped in midstep when she came close enough to clearly see the woman's features. She gasped aloud. And the woman appeared equally startled. They could have been twins—or at least sisters.

"Elaine said you looked like me," the woman announced.

"You must be Maggie Montgomery," Helen replied. "She called me by that name."

"Yes, I am Maggie," she admitted. "And you are?"

"Helen. Helen Myers. Originally Helen Daniels."

The woman's eyes widened at this information, and she reached for the gate to support her. "And you've come to see your father's grave," she stated in an even voice.

"Yes," Helen admitted. "My mother's too, although I haven't found it yet."

"Your mother's?"

"My mother, Louisa Daniels, is supposedly buried here as well. My grandparents gave me this information so long ago; however, I might be mistaken." Helen looked back around and shook her head. "My father died in the war and my mother was killed shortly afterwards in a bombing raid on London."

"Your grandparents told you that, eh?" Maggie questioned.

"Why, yes," Helen answered, returning the woman's even gaze. It was hard to get past those familiar features—that combined with standing in the cemetery caused Helen to shudder. Nervous, she hurried to add, "I don't suppose you know where I might find my mother's grave?"

A few raindrops hit Helen's face, causing her to reach for her purse and fumble with her umbrella. When she looked up, she found Maggie watching her oddly.

"I don't know what to say," the woman finally said.

Helen put up her umbrella and shook her head. "That's all right. If you don't know where the grave is, I'll just check around to see if there's a register."

"You *won't* find a grave for Louisa Daniels," the woman said quite seriously.

"Why not?" Helen couldn't imagine what the problem might be.

"Because she's *not* dead," Maggie Montgomery answered.

Helen felt as though she'd been kicked in the stomach. Her knees began to weaken. *Not dead? My mother's not dead?* She couldn't even voice the words. *Dear Lord,* she prayed, *how can this be? What is happening here?*

"I'm sure you're mistaken," Helen said, trying to keep her voice steady. "My mother has been dead for some time. I never even had a chance to know her. Perhaps you're thinking of a *different* Louisa Daniels."

Maggie nodded sympathetically. "I might consider that, except for our appearance. You see, Louisa Daniels married Owen Montgomery after losing her first husband, an American flyer, in World War II. Owen and Louisa Montgomery are *my* parents and I believe that would make you my half sister."

The declaration floored Helen. "I think I need to sit down," she gasped.

Maggie came through the gate and took hold of her arm. "Come with me."

She led Helen to the church steps and helped her to sit. "I'm so sorry to shock you like this. You see, I've known about *you* all of my life. But obviously you had no way of knowing about me."

"This can't be true. My grandparents—"

"Insisted our mother give you up after their son was killed. They said you would be safer in America and encouraged her to do the right thing. They even invited her to come with them, but she had her own mother to worry over, as well as other siblings. She couldn't leave them all. She finally gave in and let them take you, with the promise that as soon as things were safe, they would bring you back. But our mother never heard from them again. She was heartbroken over the loss of her child. She has never stopped speaking of you, even now, so many years later."

Helen didn't know what to say. Her entire life as she had known it, had changed—in an instant. The world she thought she knew, had suddenly become strange and foreign to her. "But my grandparents received a letter—a letter which told of my mother's death in London."

"Apparently a lot of mistakes were made during the war." Maggie spoke matter-of-factly. "We figured your grandparents had disappeared with you; and you figured your mum to be dead."

This news was almost too much for Helen to take in. "So, if she's still—still alive—where is she? Is she close by?"

Maggie nodded. "Yes. She lives with me, and she'll be wondering why it's taking me so long to go for a paper." She smiled. "You must come home with me, Helen. You must come home and meet our mother."

"You don't think it will be too hard on her? I mean, the shock and all?"

"No," Maggie replied firmly. "She has prayed to live long enough to see you again and she faithfully believed God would give her this request. And now He has."

Helen swallowed hard. "I do want to see her. Oh, I can't imagine." Her voice broke. "My mother is *alive*. My mother is here."

Maggie smiled and reached out for Helen's arm again. "Not only that, but prepare yourself." She chuckled. "You also have four brothers and another sister."

Helen shook her head. *"I have sisters and brothers?"* Her heart nearly broke for the lost years. If she'd only known, she would have come to England long, long ago.

"Are you ready to go?" Maggie asked softly. Her dark eyes glowed warmly with compassion.

Helen took a deep breath. "I suppose, as ready as I'll ever be."

She thought about the startling revelation that had just wrapped itself neatly around her life. *She had a family.* Not just the sons she'd given birth to, or the daughters-in-law and grandchildren she loved so dearly. She had a mother and siblings and she was going home to meet them.

The little cottage where Maggie led her was nearby. She escorted Helen up the stone walkway and then paused outside the door.

"I'll go in first," said Maggie sensibly. "And you come behind me. Mum just started eating when Elaine called me, but I imagine she's finished by now."

Helen nodded eagerly, then waited for Maggie to go inside before following her. *Oh, God, give me strength. I don't know if I can manage this or not.* A warm, spicy aroma filled the air; and Helen set her umbrella by the door, then followed Maggie down the narrow little hall.

"Mum," she heard Maggie call out. "I have a surprise for you."

"A surprise?" came the questioning voice of Louisa Montgomery.

Helen's eyes filled with tears. *Her mother was speaking.* She couldn't remember *ever* hearing her speak before. Her memories held no image of the woman, and her grandparents had no photographs to share. Helen moved forward, almost unable to contain herself any longer. She must see her. She had to know what her mother looked like.

Stepping into the snug, little living room, Helen stopped behind Maggie, then her sister moved aside and spoke. "I've brought you a visitor. A very long-expected visitor."

The old woman met Helen's gaze in stunned silence. For several moments, Helen watched her for some sign of recognition. Then at last, the woman, her pale skin so paper-thin and delicate, stood with a gasp of surprise.

"*Helen?* My baby!"

Helen let her tears fall. She had no words as the old woman moved across the room. Reaching up, Louisa Montgomery's gnarled hand touched Helen's cheek.

"Oh, my baby," the woman cried. "*My Helen!*"

Helen managed to speak. "They told me you were dead—" her voice broke—"that you had died in London during the war."

"I couldn't locate you." Louisa stroked Helen's hair. "I wrote letters and even tried to call, but Jeff's parents had moved away. They took you with them and promised to bring you back. But they never came back."

"Oh, Mom," Helen said, reaching out to embrace the woman. "We thought you were dead. They received a letter...a notification."

The woman held her with amazing strength. "All those years," she murmured, "and you were thinking me dead."

"All those wasted years," cried Helen.

Her mother pulled back and gently shook her head. "No, Helen," she said firmly. "Not wasted. You've had a good life, I presume?"

Helen nodded. "Yes, except I always missed not knowing you and Dad." She wiped at her eyes, still stunned to realize she was actually talking to her very own mother. "I prayed and prayed when I was a little girl."

Her mother smiled. "And what did you pray?"

Helen remembered, and suddenly realized God had somehow taken the prayers of a tiny child and answered them. Even if it had taken fifty years to do so. "I prayed that it was all a mistake. That you and Dad were really alive. I prayed you'd come and get me and that we'd all be a family again."

Louisa smiled. "We are a family, Helen. We might not have had the years together, but our hearts were always one. I knew you were out there—somewhere. And I knew that God would bring you home to me someday. I knew it down deep inside—like a promise He had made just to me. Our separation was not our choice or our doing. God knew the truth and now He's brought us back together. Will you stay with us, Helen?"

Helen looked to Maggie who only smiled. There seemed no sign of animosity that a prodigal of sorts had now captured her mother's attention. "I'd like to stay, but I left my things in London. I figured I'd just come here for a quick look at the graves and then return for some sightseeing. Maybe I could go get my things and then come back?"

"Of course," Louisa said, nodding happily. "Maggie could drive you. Then you'd have a chance to get better acquainted."

"Oh, I don't want to be any trouble—"

"No trouble at all," Maggie assured. "I feel like we've been waiting all our lives for you to come home." She smiled and reached out to touch Helen's hand. "Like Mum said, we're a family. It didn't matter that we'd never met you or that you were far away, we always knew you would come here one day. We knew it because Mum was confident in what God could do."

"I'm glad you feel that way," Helen replied. "I want very much to take my place in this family—to know you all better—to let you know me." Her tears began falling again. She sniffed and wiped her eyes once more. She felt the years washing away in the flow of her tears. God had brought her home to the mother and siblings she had never known. God had brought her home to England, and life would never be the same again.

ABOUT THE AUTHOR

Tracie Peterson, award-winning, bestselling author of CBA fiction, makes her home in Topeka, Kansas, with her husband and children. Her fondest wish is that her work might cause the reader to fall in love with God. Visit her Web site at http://members.aol.com/tjpbooks.

Two Brothers and Telemachus

Angela Elwell Hunt

Telemachus was a European monk who, seeking to put an end to the gladiatorial shows at Rome, entered the arena in person on January 1, 391, to separate the combatants. He was killed by the spectators. The act is said to have led the Emperor Honorius to abolish the games.

—The Oxford Dictionary of the Christian Church

In the long-ago days of ancient Rome, two brothers lived in a poor village where the teacher was a man called Telemachus.

Telemachus taught the brothers how to read and write. He taught them about the prosperous cities and peoples of the Roman Empire. He told them about good and evil, right and wrong.

The two brothers liked most to hear about the emperor's capital city where champions trained to fight in the arena. The biggest boy, Justus, wanted more than anything to make a vast fortune in Rome. The strongest boy, Marcus, wanted to be so famous that every man and woman in the imperial city would know his name.

"God will use you if you choose to do right, boys," Telemachus told the brothers. "A man does not have to be rich or famous to make a difference for God."

"Silly old Telemachus," the boys would say as they pretended to duel outside their schoolhouse. "He doesn't know anything about the world outside our village."

Years passed, and Justus and Marcus grew bigger and stronger. One day a stranger called Bittor came to the village. He took one look at the handsome brothers and offered to take them to the majestic city of Rome.

"With your big arms and shoulders, Justus, you could make a fortune in the arena," Bittor said. "And Marcus, with your strength, you would be famous. You could become the two strongest gladiators in the world!"

"Please, boys, don't go," Telemachus begged them. "Choose to do right, and God will use you."

But the boys laughed at silly old Telemachus and packed their few belongings for the trip. While their teacher remained behind, Justus and Marcus journeyed to the royal city.

Rome was unbelievable. Justus and Marcus had never seen such riches or so many people! They ate delicious spicy foods, slept on soft beds by flowing fountains, and wore handsome tunics in vibrant colors.

To pay for these luxuries, Bittor enrolled the brothers in a gladiators' school where they trained to fight like true warriors. At first Justus did not want to hurt his opponents, but Bittor assured him that he would earn thousands of gold and silver coins if he won. When Marcus hesitated, Bittor promised that he would be famous throughout the world if he fought in the arena—and lived.

Marcus and Justus fought every day in the Roman Colosseum. Each morning they sharpened their swords, cleaned their shields, stretched their muscles. Then they stepped onto the sands of the arena while thousands of cheering people threw flowers and gold coins.

Justus thought of nothing but the fortune he had won.

Marcus thought of nothing but how famous he had become.

And every day Telemachus prayed for the brothers, and God kept them alive.

One day Telemachus heard the still, small voice of God speak to his heart: *Go to Rome. Find Justus and Marcus.* Though he did not think he would like the imperial city, Telemachus obeyed.

Once he reached Rome, it was not hard to find the brothers. "Justus and Marcus duel today!" a man called, waving to passersby outside the huge Colosseum. "On this first day of the new year, the two bravest gladiators in Rome will fight each other!"

Telemachus pressed through the crowd inside the stadium and climbed to the highest row of seats. Looking down, he saw Justus and Marcus in the ring. Sweat dripped down their faces; swords swung from their hands. The crowd roared and cheered as Justus and Marcus faced each other.

"What's happening?" Telemachus asked a woman sitting next to him.

"Today Rome will crown a new champion," she said, standing to see over the crowd in front of her. "Either Justus or Marcus will die in this match, and the other will truly be the best gladiator in all the world."

Telemachus sprang to his feet. "In the name of God, stop!" he called, his voice ringing with thousands of others, "Choose to do right!"

No one listened. On the sand, Justus and Marcus gripped their swords and slowly circled each other.

As if he had wings on his heels, Telemachus hurried through the open aisle and down to the stone wall separating the crowd from the gladiators. "In the name of God, stop," he cried, waving his arms toward the brothers. "Choose to do right!"

Hearing the familiar voice, Justus paused. Marcus saw his brother's watchful expression and turned as their old teacher climbed over the wall and landed in a heap on the sand.

"In the name of God," Telemachus called again, rising to his feet in the ring. His eyes filled with tears as he held out his hands toward the brothers. "Choose to do right, boys, and God will use you."

Justus lowered his sword. Marcus hung his head.

And a man in the crowd threw a rock at Telemachus. "Shut the old fool up! He's stopping the contest!"

"Don't let him ruin our fun!" a woman cried. Another rock flew toward the old man, and then another. Justus and Marcus dropped their weapons and tried to help their teacher, but rocks flew so furiously that the brothers could not reach Telemachus in time.

After the shower of stones, Telemachus lay quiet and still in the sand. An astonished silence fell upon the crowd as the two gladiators stood beside Telemachus and wept.

When the Emperor Honorius heard the story of the man who had given his life to stop the dueling gladiators, he decreed that never again would people be allowed to kill each other for sport in the Colosseum of Rome.

Leaving fame and fortune behind, Justus and Marcus carried their teacher's body home to the quiet village he loved.

ABOUT THE AUTHOR

Angela Elwell Hunt has authored seventy-six books in fiction and nonfiction, for children and adults. Among her picture books is the award-winning *The Tale of Three Trees*, with more than one million copies in print in sixteen languages. Angela has always been fascinated by history. So when she heard the true story of the man called Telemachus, she put her writer's imagination to work to create this remarkable story about the boys who grew up under his teaching.

AN AWAKENING

Melody Carlson

Emma leaned into the small plane's side window, watching the tiny treetops grow larger and larger, until at last the plane swept over their tops to land on the airstrip directly below. She felt the bumps in the tarmac as the twin-engine Piper slowed down, her old fear of flying strangely gone now. So, this was Papua New Guinea!

"Welcome to Lae," announced the Aussie pilot, extending a hand as she climbed down from the plane. But the way he pronounced the word Lae sounded more like "lye." These Australians with their thick accents, it was as if they spoke a totally different language. She smiled and thanked him for the informative trip as a small barefooted black man hurried over and scooped up her bags, adeptly loading them onto a rickety metal cart.

"Thanks, Rabo," said the pilot, then he spoke to him in an odd language that sounded almost familiar, yet she couldn't discern a single word. "I told him to call a cab for you," translated the pilot as Rabo scurried off. "Now, go on over there and Rabo will set you up. And good luck to you." Emma felt reluctant to see the pilot leave—he seemed her last link to English-speaking civilization. But telling herself that was ridiculous she followed Rabo over to a corrugated-roofed building and then waited inside. Almost hypnotized, she leaned against the counter and watched the slow moving ceiling fans circulating the warm, moist air. Several idle workers stared openly at her, chatting and laughing amongst themselves. She was the outsider here.

"Meesus, you seet down." Rabo pointed to a bench. "I ring cab man now." He smiled, obviously proud of his loose grasp of the English language. She sat next to her bags and retrieved the address from her purse. She'd flown out of Sydney early this morning and between layovers and delayed flights it had taken all day just to reach her destination. It was after six now and dusky already. Strange how it got dark so early here in the tropics; the warm weather made her think of summer, as if it should stay lighter longer.

"He's here now, Meesus. You come." Rabo waved at her, indicating the waiting cab, then rushed to collect her bags and load them in the beat-up old car that didn't resemble a taxi in the least. The dark man in front turned and smiled toothlessly and she wondered if he was truly a cabby or not. But she seemed to have no choice in the matter, and dumbly she handed him the name of the guest house, hoping he could read.

"Yesa, yesa," he said. "Me know dispela place." She nodded and smiled, hoping that meant he could get her there. After a short drive he pulled up to a two-story complex and let her out. She only had Australian money, but that satisfied him and he quickly left. It was dark now, but the guest house was well lit, giving it a friendly appearance. She walked up to a door that said Main Office and knocked. After a few moments, a heavyset woman answered, tugging her stained apron with impatience.

"Yes? What do you need?" she asked with an Australian accent.

"I, well, I was given the name of this guest house, by a friend—as a nice place to stay."

"Well, we're full up right now. Did you ring for a reservation?" The woman stared at Emma as if she were a vagabond or gypsy of sorts.

"Well, no. I wasn't aware I needed reservations. Uh, do you happen to know of any other place to stay?" Emma turned and looked at her bags piled out on the foot path, then glanced hopefully at the stoic woman shaking her head, and already closing the door.

"Norma, what is it?" asked a tall skinny man. He pushed past the unsociable woman and looked at Emma. His long thin neck reminded her of Ichabod Crane, but he opened the screened door and smiled warmly.

"This lady wants a room, but I keep telling her we're full up." The woman threw up her hands. "Why don't you take care of it, Ed," she called over her shoulder as she stormed off.

"Won't you come in," he offered kindly. "I'm Ed Grimes and that's my wife, Norma. We run this guest house—been doing it for over twenty years now. But Norma's telling you the truth, we are full up. But there's a good hotel in town; I can ring them up for you. Would you like to stay for tea?" Emma didn't want to impose, but the thought of a soothing cup of tea was tempting.

"That sounds lovely, if it's no trouble. I'm Emma Davis; the Millers recommended this guest house to me."

"Ah, well, the Millers are good folks, and tea's no trouble at all. You just sit down, little lady, and I'll tell Norma." Emma settled herself in a stiff plastic chair in the tiny office and waited for what seemed a very long time just to make a phone call and fetch a cup of tea. She glanced at her watch uncomfortably. Had they forgotten her? Her stomach growled and she realized she hadn't eaten a meal since her morning flight from Sydney to Port Moresby.

"Tea's ready," announced Ed, pointing to the door behind him. Emma grew uneasy, she didn't want to intrude into their home.

"Oh, that's all right, I can drink my tea right here."

He looked at her queerly then said, "Well, it's obvious you're a Yankee, but you must be new to these parts." She nodded and he continued. "Yeah, I can always spot them. But come right along, tea's a'waiting." He led her to a large dining room where others were just sitting down to a table full of food. He pulled out a chair for her and grinned.

"You see, Emma, what you Yanks call dinner, we Aussies call tea. So come eat tea with us."

Her cheeks reddened as she unfolded the napkin. She hadn't meant to invite herself to supper. Across the table, a ruddy-faced man smiled at her. He had deep creases at the corners of his eyes and looked like someone who'd worked outdoors a lot. Names were exchanged, but mostly lost on her, except for the man across from her. His name was Ian. For some reason it stuck. But her mind was distracted with thoughts like where she would sleep tonight and how badly she wanted a nice, cool shower. After tea she noticed Ed discussing something with Ian and they both looked her way.

"Ed, here, says you need a ride into town." Ian spoke with a Scottish accent. "And I happen to be heading that way; I could give you a lift, if you like." He glanced down at his heavy hiking boots. Emma sensed his shyness and for some reason trusted him.

"That would be terrific, if it's not a problem."

He looked back up with aquamarine eyes and said, "Not a problem, at all."

He loaded her things into the back of a dust-coated Land Rover, then extended a hand to help her into the seat. "Sorry it's so dusty. I just came down from the highlands to deliver someone into town and to pick up supplies. It's amazing how much dust you can accumulate on some of these roads. Oh, let me move that box so you can sit down." He chuckled slightly. "That's a case of fancy orange marmalade from France, a surprise for Mary. It has to be handled with care, so I buckled it into the seat belt."

"It's so good of you to give me a lift like this." Emma slid into the seat, wondering if Mary was his wife, then questioned why she should even care. Ian didn't seem very talkative, so Emma assumed responsibility for the conversation. She rambled away about how she'd so haphazardly decided to travel to Papua New Guinea—just because she needed to get away and start a new life. He chuckled at the story of how she put her finger on the spinning globe, and Emma suddenly realized how foolish she must sound. Thankfully, they reached the hotel quickly.

"It was nice to meet you, Ian. Thanks so much for the ride." He carefully set her luggage by the hotel door, as a young boy came out to meet them.

"Not a problem. I wish you a nice visit in our country." He tipped his broad-brimmed hat, smiled, and then left.

As promised, Ed had called ahead to secure her room, and to her relief they were expecting her. The first floor of the hotel housed a small restaurant, and the young boy showed Emma to the third, and top, floor. He didn't look more than ten or eleven years old, but he took her bulkiest suitcase before she could protest, and together they trudged up the stairs lugging her luggage with them.

"What is your name?" she asked, speaking the words plainly, unsure whether the boy spoke or understood any English.

"Jonathan," he answered clearly. "My papa manages this hotel, and my mama is the head cook for the restaurant. We have our own room behind the kitchen." He dragged her suitcase to door number thirty-one and inserted the key. Emma noted with amusement that her room number was the same as her age.

"How old are you?" she asked, as he opened the door, exposing a small neat room before her.

"Thirteen years old." He beamed proudly. "There is a lavatory in your room, and the bathroom is at the end of the hall. Can I get you anything, meesus?"

She glanced around. "Everything looks just perfect, thank you. Say, Jonathan, could you find me a map of the town." She handed him what she knew was too large of a tip and his dark brown eyes grew wide, but he grinned and didn't refuse.

She stayed up late, unpacking all her bags and arranging her room. Most of her clothing needed laundering. But she'd have to find out about that tomorrow. Too excited to go to bed, she began pacing in the small room. At long last, she had arrived at her final destination! She had no idea what might be ahead, but at least she was here. Really here! She knew it was going to be one of those nights when she would not be able to sleep, but she got into bed anyway. It was too warm and humid even for the lightweight sheets. It hadn't been nearly this hot down in Sydney. She wondered if it would always be this warm in New Guinea. Would she be able to get used to it? What would she do in the morning? Why had she come? How long would she stay?

Finally, her mind slowed down, and thoughts of home came calling. To her relief they didn't come with longing or regret. She had called Fran the very first thing when she'd reached Australia and was relieved to hear they were all getting along just fine without her. Grandma had finally decided to cooperate with Bernice, and according to Fran, they liked the same TV shows and had even taken to playing double-solitaire for hours at a time. Emma was glad but, strangely enough, also uneasy. Because now, and for the first time, she felt totally removed from them. Before they'd always needed her, and now they realized they could get along quite nicely without her. Suddenly she was expendable, unnecessary. But that had been her goal, and she knew she should be celebrating now. She was cut loose—totally free of them. This had been her original plan, but now it was disconcerting.

The next morning she awoke late, but instantly realized it made absolutely no difference. No one waited for her. No one expected her. Her time was completely her own now; she had no schedule to keep, no routine. No one to please but herself. Outside, the tropical sun shone brightly. She leaned onto the window sill and looked out to the busy street below. What appeared to be an open market was situated across the street, but the people seemed to be packing up their wares and produce already, loading baskets and large string bags and slowly moving away. It looked like she'd have to get up earlier if she wanted to get a better look at that market. On the floor next to her door lay a shiny pamphlet. She picked it up to discover a neat map of the city, along with a handwritten note from Jonathan, listing one by one what he must have considered the local highlights.

As she dressed, she realized that although it was just past nine, her room was already getting hot and humid. And a quick search revealed no sign of any sort of air conditioning. She closed the louvered windows and pulled the shades to block out the light. Perhaps that would help keep it cooler during the day. She noticed, with some relief, that a large ceiling fan hung above her bed. She hadn't noticed it last night. It might help dispel some of the heat.

The little dining room downstairs was empty and Emma wondered if they were still serving breakfast. Just then a short, round, dark woman waved from behind the counter.

"Eets olright, meesus," she said cheerfully. "You come eenside. You can eat now." She showed Emma to a table and handed her a paper that listed three different breakfast entrees. Emma selected the second one and the woman disappeared.

Emma studied her map and began charting her day according to Jonathan's suggestions, and soon the woman returned with scones, bacon, and eggs, complete with the customary grilled tomato, something Emma had actually gotten used to on board the ship.

"Eets olright, meesus?" asked the woman anxiously.

"Yes, it looks very good. Are you Jonathan's mother?"

The rotund woman smiled, exposing a missing front tooth. "Yesa, Jonathan's my boy. He's good boy, works hard."

"Yes, he's a fine boy," agreed Emma. "I'm Emma Davis. Do you know where I can get my laundry done?"

"Yesa, Meesus Davis. We have laundry here. I send Jonathan after school. You sit bag by door."

Emma smiled and thanked her. But something about the way the locals treated her gave her an uncomfortable feeling. They were so solicitous, so overly polite, almost as if they considered themselves lower than her. It reminded her of what slavery might have been like before the

Civil War. And she didn't like it. And she knew she would never get used to it. But for now, she dismissed it. There would be a whole lot to get used to here. Best not to try to figure everything out at once.

She spent the day touring the local sights in the small coastal town. She went to the War Memorial and the beautiful Botanical Gardens where orchids and all sorts of tropical flowers bloomed profusely. Then finally she went down to the shore to see the ocean.

To her disappointment, the sand was dark and gray and the water seemed to match. This was nothing like the clean, white sandy beaches of Hawaii or Sydney. And nothing about this gray beach enticed her to swim or to even wade. No matter that it was extremely hot and humid, and a dip in the water could be refreshing. She had no interest in returning to the hotel for her suit and towel. She had no interest in anything. And so she sat down on a rough wooden bench and stared out across the steely water.

And in that moment she was filled with such a loneliness—far more stifling than the thick moist air that pressed in all around her. The sultry clouds continued to push in from the horizon, low and heavy and gray. What had she been running from? What was she running to? She thought she would discover herself, find her life, and now she wondered if there'd ever been anything to really find.

After an hour or so, it finally began to rain. But still, she didn't leave the bench. The large droplets splashed down on her. But they weren't cold, as one might normally expect of a March shower. Instead, they were about the same temperature as her skin. In fact, she almost couldn't feel them at all. But just the same, as the wetness soaked in, it cooled and even refreshed her. Never mind that her thin cotton blouse clung to her like cellophane; no one was around to see anyway. In fact, it was almost as if she were invisible. She glanced down the deserted gray beach. Perhaps she was the only person on the whole earth. All alone—except, perhaps, for God.

Then suddenly, and for no explainable reason, she stood and stretched her arms up high over her head, as if reaching for the heavens. And looking up into the leaden sky, she allowed the tepid rain to run down her arms, to wash down over her face, trickling into streams down her neck, pouring down her back. Until she was totally and completely soaked.

And then to her amazement, her loneliness just seemed to evaporate.

And somehow she knew in her heart that God had sent this rain just for her. Maybe it was like a baptism of sorts. Or maybe just a shower to refresh her. But somehow she knew it signified a promise, and though she had no idea what that promise might be, and maybe it didn't matter anyway, she knew it was from God. Then almost as quickly as it came the shower ended; the clouds passed on. And the sky returned to a freshened shade of blue. The sun's sharp rays promptly dried her blouse, erasing all traces of the rain—at least on the outside.

ABOUT THE AUTHOR

As a young adult Melody Carlson spent a year teaching preschool in Papua New Guinea, where this story, an excerpt from her novel *Awakening Heart* (Bethany House), is set.

Melody is the award-winning author of over fifty books for children, teens, and adults. Her latest novel series, Whispering Pines (Harvest House Publishers) is set in a small tourist town very similar to where she now lives with her husband, two grown sons, and a chocolate Lab, Bailey.

INTO AFRICA

Anne de Graaf

DAY 1, JO'BURG, SOUTH AFRICA

Into Africa, out of Africa, in me, out of me, around me. If I had nowhere else to go, I would go back there, where my heart is, a place I know every time I go, another place I can call home.

I'll start with the colors. After an eleven-hour flight I looked left and saw the color gold-yellow-autumn amber, soft like Polish wheatfields gold. The color of an African sunrise welcoming me back. Unlike Karen Blixen, I've made it back four times now, and each time I feel so grateful, so privileged to see the world like this. This amber gold follows me throughout that first day. I see it in the trees which still carry autumn leaves in an African winter, mild at day, the chill of the night still hanging in the air around Jo'burg where we go to pick up the 4-wheel-drive. Toyota Hi-lux, where will you carry us to by the end of this trip? All the old emotions and stories of last year wash over me as I open myself to the light, warmth, promises of Africa. The smiles. The children's eyes. Theirs not meeting mine. That's right, South Africa is the place where people look away from you. It was Swaziland where they made eye contact. Old tension still here. Old hatreds, I've seen this generations-old distrust before when living in Ireland. And in Atlanta. It's the spoiled fruit of hatred taught to children.

Still the gold follows me in the color of dry, weather-drought grass.

Eight months since they've had rain. The only sign that it's winter is the frost in the early mornings. Haunting sounds of trees with autumn leaves still scraping together in the breeze while what seems a summer sun shines on it all.

We drive and drive, heading west to Gaborone, Botswana. Sunset's final gold reflects back my sunrise, at 30,000 feet. Mist moves between the hills, soft, soft filtered light, trees, grass, hills, light fog. We cross the border after dark, which comes early, only 6 P.M. Suddenly the sun is gone. Darkness.

DAY 2, GABORONE, BOTSWANA

Next day. We drive and drive north seven hundred kilometers, still on tarred roads. Cross the Tropic of Capricorn and take photos.

We get stuck in Francisville, trying to shop for supplies. It all takes too long, changing money, dollars into *pulis*. Buy bags of cookies for the kids, the sun bakes down onto us. Africa sun, it makes you know you're white-skinned.

In Botswana we can approach blacks and strike up conversations. I do this, to our teenagers' embarrassment. At the market across the street from where the 4-by-4 is parked I ask, "Did you make that yourself? How long did it take you? It's very fine work. No, I can't spend too much or my husband gets angry. Do you have that problem too?"

The woman laughs and touches my arm in a gesture of sisterly understanding. "No, madam. Here, I am the one who tells the husband what to spend." We have a good laugh and she blesses me on my journey. Her words surprise me and I look at her more closely to see if she means it. She nods.

"And God bless you," I say, thinking she'd fit right in with many of my best friends.

At Nata Lodge we're booked in two four-person tents with beds and linen. It's clean and that's all I look for, with good mosquito netting. Thornbush all around us. All dry. We eat outside and now finally, I listen to the song of the stars. In Francisville I bought our fourteen-year-old Daniel astronomy books. (I didn't have enough pulis, so told the bookstore clerk to keep my sixteen-year-old Julia as a deposit until I returned with more money. Everyone but my daughter was amused.)

Daniel's already been out with the flashlight and book. He comes up to our table and takes me by the arm. "Mama, you've got to come see." I've waited a year to see the southern hemisphere's stars again, and I know it will be like walking into a roomful of old friends, all smiling and waiting for me. I follow him out to an open space between the trees and raise my chin.

There they are: the Southern Cross and Scorpio, the Milky Way, striping the night sky in white. Many of these stars I never see in my home up in northern Europe. I look and look until my neck is stiff, turning around and around in the warm darkness, listening to the crickets, feeling the dry air, tasting the light of the stars, stretched literally from one horizon to the next. This sky on the edge of the Kalahari, where will it take me? I wonder.

DAY 3, NATA, BOTSWANA

The dawning sun chases both the cold night and stars away. In their place, sunlight and warm dry air. This is the desert; Nata Lodge occupies an oasis of desert palms, rocks, colorful birds, pool, warm smiles.

When I emerge from the outdoor shower, my skin red with the cold water, three South African bikers are pointing at our teenagers' tent. I walk a little closer and hear Julia and Daniel singing the "Wilhelmus," our Dutch national anthem, as loudly as they can. The bikers strap on their black leather jackets and tune their hogs, laughing at the kids.

They ask me in Afrikaans, "Is that a school camp? Are you their teacher? What's that they're singing?"

I guess the assumption, this close to South Africa, is that if you're white, you speak Afrikaans. I surprise them by replying in Dutch, which they can understand as I can them. The two languages are probably as close as Shakespeare's English is to ghetto talk. "No," I say. "It's not a school camp, and I'm afraid I'm the mother. That's the Dutch national anthem." They laugh and I go into my usual routine of striking up a conversation. They've just come from Maun, where we're heading. Can they suggest a place to camp? They mention Okavango River Lodge. "Will they take wild children?" I ask, since by now the kids are singing the olé, olé victory chant of Dutch football during the World Cup.

"They took us," the men laugh as they speed off into the sunrise.

Not for the first time, I'm grateful for who Julia and Daniel are. She is a tall, long-haired blond beauty, not yet aware of the stares that follow her, much to my Erik's relief. Daniel's body is shooting out in all directions, long legs, long arms. Sometimes he's not sure how to walk, torn between the saunter of manhood and the gallop of childhood. His charming smile and twinkling brown eyes have made me smile since the day he was born. They are my one hearts. Here, all I need to do is point my head toward a bird, or raise my finger toward the bush around the camp, and they stop what they're doing and listen. They know. We all know, this is a place of magic. But you have to be open to it, looking for it, or it will pass you by.

Day 4, Maun, Botswana

On our first day of game driving with an armed guide, we're up at five, breakfast under the trees. Kids constantly making noise. Two hours in an open Land Rover, a 1962 German fire truck. I escaped the wind and slid down beside our guide, Koos (pronounced like *close)* Joubert, a white Botswanan, who went to boarding school and university in South Africa, met his wife there and brought her back. "I'm NOT South African," he said. I laughed. He's a big man, flat nose, dark eyes, tanned strong arms ending in thick fingers. As I went into interview mode, he didn't seem to mind.

Most dangerous moment: When a leopard jumped on him from a tree. A client had injured the leopard and Koos had to go after him. When the leopard sprang, Koos shot point-blank and the bullet entered the animal's chest as its weight knocked Koos onto the ground. When he finally rolled out from under the leopard, he was covered with blood, and thought at first it was his own, that he'd misfired, then realized it was the leopard's.

Most recent accident: A month earlier, when a German tourist ignored the guide's warning to not leave camp and went out on his own to video an elephant. A big bull pulled the man's arm off with his trunk, then threw him into a tree, killing him.

Koos is also a member of the antipoaching defense league and when I told him some of what we'd learned in Swaziland the previous year, he reluctantly opened up and agreed. "It's a war and I have orders to shoot to kill anytime I come across poachers. We even have weapons hidden in the bush so we can attack quickly. And helicopter patrols."

We're in the Okavango Delta, one of the richest wildlife areas in Botswana. It's a country where the people are building a future for themselves and their land, one of the few places I've been in Africa where you don't feel like the government is cheating the people. Here park fees are high, but the money all goes back into local villages, water, and education, those are the priorities. Even the currency is called *puli,* it means *water,* the same word as *life.*

The Okavango Delta is a rich wetland on the edge of the Kalahari, miles and miles of marsh; some birds here can be found nowhere else. Koos brings us to a place where we can slip into canoes made from hollowed-out tree trunks, each with a poler and quietly move through the rushes, alert for hippo or crocs. Now the kids are quiet. I speak to the boy in the canoe I share with Daniel. I ask where he learned to speak English? Koos has told me only 20 percent of the local children go to school.

The boy is Julia's age, sixteen. He says his sister taught him. She's a schoolteacher, he says proudly. "And whenever she comes home, she makes all of us speak nothing but English all during her stay."

We canoe through paradise. The other poler is called Heaven. Really. We make jokes about Heaven on earth. Quiet, rustling, higher grass than in the Mara, Kenya. Gold still following me in light and colors. Paradise water lily, swish through water, so quiet, so green. So still.

During the canoe trip through the Okavango Delta we see one croc, and hippos across a marsh from us, but during lunch, Daniel and Heaven go swimming in a croc-free pool. My son, he'll do anything. The skin of Heaven is so black, black like silk, black like purple-blue black. Really beautiful and hard for me not to stare.

I want to touch Heaven's arm.

At night, the mosquitoes are everywhere, malaria-ridden, long pants despite the humidity. Koos brings his wife Annette and we all sit and talk, getting to know each other. Their children are away at boarding schools in South Africa, and you can tell they enjoy being around Julia and Daniel. He tells stories and gets quietly drunk on vodka and orange juice. He has malaria and is sick several times a year. We exchange addresses, he buys Julia a drink. I'm a sucker for all his stories. That night Daniel breaks out his minispeakers and we put my Africa tape into his walkman. Under the stars we listen to Kansas sing "Dust in the Wind," then the film music from *Out of Africa* comes on. The fire glows on all our faces. The magic is inescapable.

Who are we in this place of vast extremes?

DAYS 5–6, MOREMI WILDLIFE RESERVE, BOTSWANA

We drive north, skirting the eastern border of Okavango, heading for the Moremi Game Reserve which borders the delta. The asphalt ends abruptly in a village of thatched mud huts. Which dirt road to take? Erik squints at the sun and says, "That's north." Off we go. I hate to brag, but this is what I love about my husband. He knows where he's going.

My Erik, glasses, Daniel's laughing eyes, kind, sees all, there before I even know I need him. Solid, stable, and strong, just the way I like my men. That's what I tell him, anyway. And we laugh. For years, we've been laughing and seeking, side by side.

While we're on the subject, part of the magic of the trip is how Erik has arranged it all via Internet and long-distance faxes. I had four travel agencies specializing in Africa tours discourage us from doing this alone. Everyone else takes package tours. No one takes kids into Botswana. No one will rent you a 4-by-4 to go from South Africa to Botswana and into Namibia. You can't do it.

But there we are, checking to make sure the sun stays in the right place, extra petrol, extra water, kids, 4-by-4, maps, and a few faxes. It is so cool to be on our own like this.

The Moremi is ahead of us, and we have read and heard that this would be the highlight of our trip. Unbelievable game, varied landscape, thousands of square miles of bush, all protected.

More dirt roads, deep sand, right, follow the scrawled-on-rock letters: South Gate. I had a professor at Stanford who told us to listen to the stories we tell. When I hear the children and Erik talk about this trip, the story of this night at Third Bridge is the one I hear them tell over and over.

As we make camp, the stars descend and hippos croon and sputter in the river ten feet from our tents. Erik breaks a dead tree branch in half and we build the fire around the first third of its trunk, moving it closer to the fire as it burns, African style. We eat pasta and listen to the movements of Africa all around us. Crickets, jackals, hyenas in the distance.

"Are there lions?" Daniel asks.

I look in the book. "Third Bridge is one of the places the lions can cross without having to get wet." We soak up the night air, the mystery around us, the movements and sounds.

And just before we go to sleep, I warn everyone to bring their shoes into the tents tonight. "No food in your tents. And no matter what, don't leave your tent." We make the usual jokes about his and her bushes, douse the fire, lock everything into the truck, and crawl into the tents. The teenagers in one, Erik and I into the other.

The smell wakes me up. I see the glowing face of my watch and read 4 A.M. Then I heard the snuffling noises around the tent. A hyena calls, another answers—a horrendous, chilling sound, like I imagine near-dead witches make when given a second chance. They couldn't be more than a few feet away.

I shake Erik awake and put my finger over his mouth, then point outside. We can hear the animals, there must be several. Then the hippos start splashing and calling, they're closer too, in the water right beside the tents. I'm sitting up now, trying to peer out the triangle flap I didn't zip closed. Through the mosquito netting all I can see is our log still glowing. But everything else is so dark, I half expect a hyena snout to shove into my face.

Then like an earthquake in the distance, I hear a low rumble. An answering rumble, a groan, a guttural moan. I squeeze Erik's arm in the dark and whisper the word, *"Lions."*

"Yeah," he answers. Then, "The children?" No sign. My only prayer is that they don't panic and leave their tents. The lions must be at the bridge, less than one hundred yards away. The snuffling sound comes closer, I don't dare sit up anymore, somehow I feel safer lying down, snuggled up against my daring Dutchman. There's a digging sound and Erik jerks back his foot away from the tent corner. Neither of us dares to even whisper. The stench from the hyenas is overpowering. Then we hear the bag of extra tent stakes rattling, the sound heads toward the river. "I'm stupid, I should have put them into the truck," Erik says.

"Your foot," I say.

"I know, he almost got it. I felt him." I don't say anything and just lie beside him, relieved that the hyenas are only playing with tent stakes, telling myself we didn't need tent stakes after all, and listening to the lion groans come closer and closer. I looked at my watch again. Five A.M. The lions call back and forth, their sounds growing louder. I hold my breath. They're very close, by the road now. Am I wishing, or do their calls become more distant? Then the birds begin. At 5:45 the false dawn has begun and I can see out the flap. The lions' moans echo from farther away. At six we get up and call the kids.

They have heard nothing; they slept through the entire performance.

Driving east we continue to see more and more elephants. The area is dry, a bonus for us. It means the animals are so thirsty, they all come to the riverside, which just happens to crisscross the dirt track we have to follow. We see two trucks that whole afternoon, and they are package tours.

"Ha! We're on our own," we tell ourselves.

Hippo and Paradise Pools live up to their names. Hippos out of the water, calves between adults, shiny humps looking over their shoulders, watching us as we drive slowly around the perimeter of the lake. Crocs along the shore, slipping quietly into the water, a herd of elephants, the tiniest light gray baby hiding between the protection of its aunts' tree-trunk legs. We spend a good hour in this Garden of Eden, then Erik finally heads toward the main track.

I look out the window just as we skirt a tree and cry, "Windows up!" Three lions, three females, are lying down in the shade, not six feet from where we've stopped the truck. We don't dare move. Now, what to do? We wait. The lions don't look too interested. One of them lies with her head on the stomach of the other, just like our dogs do at home. Erik gets out the zoom lens and we start shooting. VERY slowly we drive away.

Nothing can go wrong now, our trip isn't even half over and already we've seen lions from close up. The safari is a success. In Kenya, four years earlier, we traveled fourteen days through the Masai Mara and saw only one lion. Now these three, plus the crocs and elephants and hippos; Moremi has been good to us.

Day 7, North Gate, Botswana

We're out of the park and back on sand roads, dotted every fifty kilometers with a village of thatched mud huts. Today we want to drive to Savuti and into Chobe National Park. It's called the most beautiful game park in Botswana, but we have our doubts. Nothing can beat Moremi. Chobe is famous for its elephants, more than 35,000, the book says. But first we have to reach Savuti. No asphalt, and the sand tracks get deeper and deeper. It's slow going, even in four-wheel-drive. What's worse, the petrol gets used up faster when the roads are this bad. After a long morning of fighting hard terrain and not seeing any game, we finally pass a few dirt tracks off the main one and know we're approaching the village of Savuti. The countryside around us is elephant devastated. Broken trees, bare trunks, no green, dry and brittle. Even the air is sand choked with the drought.

We're uncertain, almost out of petrol, although we still have our reserve tank. But we absolutely have to be able to buy supplies at Savuti, we have no food. This was exactly what we didn't want happening on this trip. Savuti turns out to be a few goat herds and some mud huts. The so-called campsite is non-existent; "DESTROYED by elephants," the hand-scrawled sign says. It doesn't look like anyone's slept there for fifty years. It's a good thing we stayed at North Gate after all.

There are supposed to be three lodges here. We decide to splurge and go for a lodge lunch. It'll mean a three-course meal, but what the heck, we tease the kids. We all need a little pampering. I look at us, Erik hasn't shaved in two days. Designer stubble, I tell him. "Yeah, Papa," Julia says. "You look like George Michael."

We're feeling better as we pull up to the gate of one of the lodges. It's rich. The book says this place costs $550 per person per night, I read. *Whoa.*

A white guide with a British accent comes out to meet us. *Bad sign,* I think, *old school Rhodesia, rather than Zimbabwe.* I say, "Yes, we'd like to have lunch, please." He looks over our kids. I have to admit, with the dust on their faces and dirty T-shirts, they look like rugrats.

"We don't serve lunch to nonclients."

"Oh. We really need some petrol. Could we please buy some petrol?" Now I think he hears the urgency in my voice.

He looks more sympathetic. "All we have is diesel, for the planes and trucks. If I had petrol I'd sell it to you." I look at Erik. This is not good. We are our worst nightmare. Stuck in the desert with two kids, no petrol and no food.

"What about the other two lodges?" I ask.

"One has closed. You can try the other. Go back down the dirt track, turn left at the water tower, keep right, left at the tree."

Left at the tree? Okay. We're off. I tell the kids, "We should pray. Pray to yourselves." I tell them, "Pray for petrol and pray for food. God honors specific prayer." The kids are quiet. Erik is quiet. I'm quiet, kicking myself for all the things we could have done, should have done to make sure this didn't happen. I'm already thinking of options. We have a reserve tank. We could stay here at the former campsite, but the nearest town is Ngoma Bridge, another two hundred kilometers. And it's already taken us three hours this morning just to drive one hundred kilometers. I'm thinking all this, and praying, when we pull up to Lloyd's Camp. A white woman comes out to greet us. She's not smiling. We're not rich, we didn't fly into the landing strip like all their other clients (this place is only $380 per person per night). I lick my lips and put on my most charming author smile.

"Yes, hello. We were wondering, actually, I'm afraid we're in a bit of a fix here. We've run out of food and petrol. Could you please help us?" I'm desperate now, so I throw in, "We have children with us, anything you can sell us, we'd be very grateful for." The woman looks us up and down and I decide I like the blacks in Africa better than the whites.

"We don't serve lunch. Only to clients."

Uh-oh, I think. "Could we please buy some petrol?" I ask again.

"Yes, but only ten liters. We have our own needs to think of, you know."

Right, I think, and try to stay charming. What she's offering is less than three gallons. I follow her into the complex and can hear Erik relaying the news to the kids. Maybe I can use their disappointed faces, after all. "Excuse me," I call after her. "Can't we please buy a loaf of bread and some cheese from you?"

"Bread? You want bread?" she asks.

Just then another woman shows up. "Can I help you?" she asks as the first woman disappears. I give her our story, "Oh, you poor dears. What a terrible position to be in. I wish I had more, but yes, of course," she says leading me into a cafeteria-sized kitchen. "Here's a loaf of bread—we bake it underground here ourselves—I'm sorry I don't have more—and some cheese. Do you need water? We have plenty of that. And drinks for the children. And I hope your husband is getting the petrol. What a terrible place to be stuck."

I know what she's really saying: YOU'RE not very clever to be in this tight spot. I nod and take her hands into mine. "You have saved us today. Thank you very much." I pay and we're off, feeling like angels must be dancing on our rooftop.

Incredible. There we were, middle of nowhere, no shops or petrol stations for two hundred kilometers and we find the one place that can sell us some food and petrol! God is good.

"Only" two hundred kilometers to go to Ngoma Bridge. That's the border post with Namibia and we can buy petrol there. Then onto the golden highway to Katima Mulilo for fifty kilometers and we should be at Zambezi Lodge. "Tonight," I promise the kids, "we'll swim in a cool pool and have a great dinner." They don't believe me anymore.

It's hard going. The terrain worsens. The sand tracks are sometimes two feet deep. The truck plows its way onwards and petrol gets used up even faster than when we approached Savuti. The dust is unbearable. Dust in the wind, sand, dry, hot, above forty degrees (centigrade), death and dryness all around. At Lloyd's Camp they said the river here has dried up. In another month most of the game here would be dead. Just past the landing strip we pass a cluster of fifteen elephants, gathered around a pathetic puddle of water. "They'll be dead soon," I tell the kids. We're all quiet.

Erik asks what's ahead of us. I look at the map. Nothing but desert. Sand, scrub, thornbush. The first village isn't even for one-hundred fifty kilometers. This area is called the Mababe Depression. "Yeah," Daniel says. "I could get depressed here." The first village will be called Kachikau. Erik gives me one of his looks. He and I both know this is probably the worst place for anything to go wrong. If we have car trouble now, we'll have to walk for help. During the first two hours, we pass no other trucks. Finally we see a tractor sitting on the track. Bizarre, no one is in it, but the motor is running.

Our truck's engine overheats and we have to pull over to turn it off to let it cool down. The reserve tank is almost empty. The harsh terrain is using up way too much fuel. The kids are asleep in the back of the truck. We empty the last jerry cans of petrol into our tank. That's it. Then ten liters of our precious drinking water reserve goes into our motor. We've poured another ten into plastic bottles. We still have twenty liters if we have to walk, we tell each other.

"Okay, now, nothing more can go wrong," Erik says. I don't know if he means we can't afford it to happen or that it really can't go wrong. I don't ask. The heat, the dryness. Dry death drought. Through the sand, hour after hour after hour as the sun climbs from east to west, more sand, more scrub, more dryness.

Impossibly, I doze with the kids, and when I wake up, I look left and see a vision of what this country should be, could be. A delta: the difference between death and life. Rich green, and impala grazing in the distance. The sun is lower; it must be around four. I check the map. This is from the Chobe River; a perennial river they call it, that means it never dries up. The river by Lloyd's Camp wasn't perennial. Soon we see some goats, then some children, finally a few huts. We're in Kachikau, the first village. I check my watch. That day we've spent ten hours doing three hundred kilometers. I'm so relieved I can't stop smiling. Erik's doing the same. I tell him, "From here, the road improves, good enough for two-wheel drive. We'll make better time and use less petrol."

A group of children comes running up to the car. We slow down. They're all smiling at us, calling out for pens and paper for their school. We don't have any, but are looking through the bags and purses when a teenage girl comes out, calls the kids off us, and presents us with a strange fruit. "Would you like to buy this?" she asks.

"Yes." We pay her way too much money and drive off. Unexpectedly, there's a petrol station. We fill up the truck, then splurge on ice-cold Cokes to celebrate survival.

The green grass is still on our left, a vista of endless savanna, green with hope, and rich in wildlife. The Chobe does not disappoint us. We see elephant, giraffe, baboons, impala, water buffalo, greater kudu. Herds of game, water mirroring the African sky, the river winding its way through the landscape like a diamond necklace. Deep gold and green mixing in the harsh African late afternoon light. The villages pass by, the litany of names read like some ancient prayer: Kachikau, Kachikabwe, Seriba, Matabanelo, Kavimba, Mabele, Muchenje, and then Ngoma Bridge, the border with Namibia.

Here two years ago, I joked with the border guard when he asked if I was Erik's wife. "I'm his wife in Namibia," I told him then, "but he has another in Zimbabwe." The man liked that. Now the road is paved, just five hundred yards, mind you, but it is still a little strip of progress. And there's even a flush toilet!

That evening we pull into Zambezi Lodge, and I know from two years earlier that this place has great food, four-person chalets, warm water, a pool. If only they still have space for us. I go to the reception desk and ask. They have room! I practically kiss the woman behind the counter.

"Where did you come from today?" she asks.

I laugh, looking at my dust caked hands, filthy fingernails, and imagine the raccoon marks left by my sunglasses on my face. "North Gate, Moremi," I answer. She's amazed.

"No one does that stretch in one day," she says. Then the kids troop in. Dirty, hair stiff with dust, dumping their backpacks on the smooth oak floors. The fans groan above us. "With children?" she asks. I nod.

"Yeah, we're crazy," Julia says in her pretty British-English.

The woman just shakes her head. "You're lucky," she answers.

It doesn't matter now. *We're safe.*

I think of the smiles on the village children's faces. It's all relative, our safety. I am deeply grateful for the clean towels in the little house. The warm water, the first in days, even though we still can't drink it. The toilet paper. The flush toilet. Kleenex. White linen sheets. A bed. The mattress. I look around in wonder. There are signs along the walkway following the river to watch out for crocs at night. A watchman with an AK-47 walks beside me. "Good evening, madam."

Daniel and Julia charge past me in the other direction, calling back, "The pool is open at night!"

I root around in my pack for my suit and slip it on. By the time I reach the pool, the kids are out again, having discovered the snooker table. I am thankful for our children's smiles. I slip into the cool, cold pool water at dusk, rinsing away layers of dust. Erik is waiting for me. We look up at the stars of this southern hemisphere together, alone in the dark, Scorpion blessing us with a wag of its tail. Every part of me tingles as if I'd just emerged from a sauna and dove into a cold bath. I am acutely aware of where I am at this moment, Erik's touch underwater, the crickets, the children's laughter, the warm desert air, the song of stars above.

DAY 8, LIANSHULU LODGE, MUDUMU NATIONAL PARK, NAMIBIA

The next day at 4 P.M. we're back at the lodge and we climb into a barge. Two of the handsome local guides come with us, this time with rifles on board. This is called a sundowner cruise. In deep, Africa-rhythm voices, they tell us the names of the rare birds flitting along the riverbank, point out crocs as they slip into the water, and warn of hippos around the corner. Just before the sun starts to slip below the horizon, one of the guides says he's run out of fuel and coasts to a stop along the riverside. He laughs a deep rumble of joy so we know he's teasing, as he pulls out an ice chest and we break out the drinks. Grass rustling, yellow, amber, gold. Two elephants crash down to the opposite bank. Sunset on the savanna.

The youngest guide takes a chair next to Julia, right in front of me, and I'm thinking: *He makes his move*...I eavesdrop mercilessly.

"You are from Holland? Is that near Germany?"

"Yes. And you are from here?" my daughter asks.

"Yes, I went to guide school nearby, but my village is twenty k's north of here. Can you tell me about Holland? I have never left Namibia."

"We have stone houses."

"Not made from grass?"

"No, stone. And we share the walls with our neighbors. We have no game around us."

"None? Not even impala?"

She looks at him to make sure he isn't teasing her, then gives him her sun-and-moon smile. A rare gift. "No, only sea-gulls. And in the winters the rivers freeze. Like ice cubes. The rivers are full of ice cubes, and we put skates on, like knives under our shoes, and run on the rivers."

I'm memorizing every word. No one is making fun here; these two young people are looking straight into each other's eyes, and sharing from their hearts in terms the other can understand.

The young guide shakes his head. "You're lying to me."

"No, really. It's called skating. And everyone has electricity."

"Their own generators?"

"No, one big generator for a whole region. And all the houses have television. Do you know what that is?"

"I have never seen one."

Ah, I think. *The charms of Namibia.*

DAY 9, VICTORIA FALLS, LIVINGSTONE, ZAMBIA

We enter the rainforest, mist from the falls filling the air around us with humidity. We hike to different cliffs, staring at the falls from a different perspective now. I'm hoping Daniel will calm down, hike out his frustration. If we were home, he'd be out hitting tennis balls. We finally reach the Zambian bridge. The view is incredible. Rocks fall far below us, water on three sides, the mist on our eyelashes.

I stand next to Julia and she's crying. I start crying. "What is it?" I'm almost afraid to ask.

"The beauty. It's like you said, Mama, part of heaven." Erik comes up behind us and puts his arms around us, his girls. Daniel is there, swallowing his anger because I won't let him leap from the tallest bungee jumping point in the world. Stupid bungee jumping almost spoiled one of the most special family moments we've ever had. You see how easily joy is stolen?

Day 10, Victoria Falls, Zimbabwe

(At the street market) Dark voices around me, "My sister, sister, please look at this."

"My best friend," they call Erik and Daniel. "My young, best friend, look at this." Daniel spends most of his money on drums. I'm not kidding, he becomes the proud owner of three drums. I buy baskets.

Daniel then buys figurines of the big five most dangerous to man (rhino, hippo, lion, leopard, elephant). He starts his bargaining with the line, "This is your lucky day, my best friend." A good time is had by all. Sunlight plays off of stone and shiny wood and smiles and eyes, proud of fine craftsmanship.

"Where did you learn this?" I ask a young man.

"At school."

I tell him of an exhibit of Zimbabwean art I saw at the Tate Gallery in London. He nods. "Yes, the world knows of Zimbabwe because of our art."

I say to myself, *And because of the AIDS.*

Which brings me to the sad comment that AIDS is everywhere in this country. Why are there so few young men? Dead. It is not a disease for people with many partners. Here it is the disease of children, born with AIDS, doomed to die before they reach eight. Men and women, every family has been touched by death in this way. In some communities nearly all of the adults twenty to forty-five have been wiped out by AIDS. In Zimbabwe alone, 25 to 30 percent of the population is HIV-positive. You can't picture it. There's just an absence of men and women of my generation. Gone.

Day 11, Hwange, Zimbabwe

We decide to combine the two-day drive to Jo'burg and our friends' house in nearby Hekpoort and push the whole way in one day. It will be a full day of driving but on asphalt roads we tell the kids, as if it were McDonald's or something. We have to drive the length of Zimbabwe, cross into South Africa, and drive another four hours to Hekpoort. If we make it, it will be 1300 kilometers. We roll out at 8 A.M., knowing if we have no trouble, we'll arrive at Martien and Brenda's place around 9 P.M. She's back from Holland now and Julia and I can't wait to see Sophie and Sara again. The memories of Pemba and the beach in Mozambique are still among our most treasured from last year.

The kids are in the back of the truck. We have three drums, so I drum a message, and they drum the reply. It's a credit to Erik that he puts up with this for thirteen hours.

We play the kids' tapes in the truck: Oasis, Verve, and a tape of Christian rock. One of the songs has a verse that explores the idea of God being one of us, just a stranger who's trying to make His way home.

I'm thinking about this, watching the African landscape fly by when suddenly all at once, I see a man walking along the road with a ten-foot cross over his shoulder. I hardly dare to breathe. The kids are asleep in the back, Erik is looking tired. I look in the rearview mirror and see the man walking on. Then we're over the hill and he's gone. He was white, dressed in shorts and desert boots, black hair. "Did you see that man?" I ask Erik.

He nods at the truck parked along the highway ahead of us. "Looks like he lost some lumber," he says.

"No, he was carrying a cross," I say. "He looked like Jesus."

Erik looks at me funny, then uses the same tone he uses on the kids. "You shouldn't mock God like that."

I protest, "I'm not mocking God. Remember what the song said, about God being just like one of us? If Jesus were walking along this road, why wouldn't He look like that man? The only clue we have is that he was carrying a cross. Why couldn't it have been Him? He visited Abraham and Sarah."

My kind husband looks at me and just sighs. "Okay, you weren't mocking God, I take it back."

I'm thinking if there's anywhere I'll see God, it will be in Africa. I'm almost tempted to ask Erik to turn around and go back, but check the mirror instead to see if my face is glowing.

The hours and the miles and kilometers roll by. There's a lodge somewhere off the road around lunchtime, but Erik has the same look he gets on the German autobahn: don't stop unless we have to go to the bathroom. We can buy some food at the petrol station, drive, drive, drive. Finally we roll into the border post with South Africa. I remember all over again how I don't like this country. While Erik is filling in the papers, I stay in the truck. Street kids all around us, like a flock of birds, hustling, watching, waiting to pickpocket or steal something. A policeman shows up and the kids scatter like sparrows.

We drive to the Shell on the other side of the border and find spotless bathrooms, toilet paper, warm water. Incredible. Lately I rejoice when a toilet can flush. And because these clean flushing toilets make me so happy, everyone makes fun of me.

I recount the kilometers, it's only 1200 kilometers from Hwange to Hekpoort. As it gets dark, we're driving through Pietersburg. Our Danish friends live somewhere nearby, in the mountains by Kruger Park. Erik's GSM phone works again and he's a happy camper, calling Holland, checking in with his brother Mark who codirects our company, calling difficult clients with fishing net problems in Mauritania and Scotland. He really loves his work and it seems a multiple blessing that he can do business while driving a 4-by-4 through Africa with a wife, two teenagers, and three drums in the truck.

He calls Martien in Hekpoort and warns him we'll be arriving a day early. "We'll bring the food, all you have to do is give us some carpet for our sleeping bags." Now we need to go shopping for tonight, so we pull into a township. Somehow, he drives straight to the market, but we've forgotten again that this is South Africa. In Botswana or Zimbabwe we just did what we needed, but here whites aren't supposed to enter the townships.

We park the truck and the blacks walk around us staring with open hostility. Daniel and Julia continue drumming back and forth to each other, the windows rolled down, and don't pick up on the tension. Then they try to drum to the beat of the music twanging from the loudspeakers attached to the lampposts. The hostile glances turn to smiles. I say to one man who is staring at us, "They're not very good, are they?" I make sure he hears my accent, to know that we're not South Africans.

He smiles, "No, they're not."

When Erik returns with his food for Martien, we stuff the plastic bags between the drums. We have zero leg room and drive off, heading for Pretoria. Erik calls Martien again, how to get through Pretoria? He gives us directions. It's dark. Pretoria is not a friendly city. Stark contrasts with expensive bank offices within three streets of the red-light district and a ghetto township. We won't be driving through Soweto, but it couldn't be much different.

"Windows up," I say, remembering the last time I issued such a warning was when we parked beside the three lionesses. Predators all.

Erik is tired. Eleven hours of driving. I try to be a good navigator. Left, right, straight here, there should be a stoplight. Okay, now another twenty kilometers, check your counter, mark. I tell the kids stories about our drives into Poland in the eighties when they were small: six hours to Berlin, two hours to the border, two hours at the next border, six hours to Gdynia. Now I can drive the distance in fourteen hours straight. Poland seems very, very far away, even though less than a month has passed since I last hiked the mountain passes on the Ukrainian border. *Lord, get us to Brenda's safely, I* pray. Maybe this marathon day was not such a good idea.

We leave Pretoria on a country road. So far, Martien's directions have been flawless. We drive and drive, no lights on the road; blindly we head in what we hope is the right direction. More townships, more black stares, what are we doing in their areas? It reminds me of the Indian reservations where I went to high school in Federal Way. Same stares, same get-out-of-here eyes.

We pass the turnoff to Brits, I know we're close, then it's Hekpoort, a country village. Brenda has told us her neighbors could belong to the KKK, they're old-apartheid whites and won't even drink coffee in the same room as blacks. I think: People here don't hate us for no reason. It's my Polish Zaneta's hatred of the Russians again. It's evil on earth.

When we finally grind the gravel in Martien's driveway, I'm beat.

DAY 13, JO'BURG AIRPORT, SOUTH AFRICA

Off we go, drums and statues and figurines and little backpacks as hand baggage. The flight to Durban is ninety minutes, heading east to the Indian Ocean. We fly over snow-covered mountains, there was frost on the windshield that morning. But in Durban it's a pleasant twenty-five (centigrade) and sunny.

The hotel is old and colonial, the last in a line along the boardwalk. The surf is gorgeous, fantastic! *I'm back in California. San Diego here we come!* Erik and I end up with a room overlooking the Indian Ocean, the sound of the surf all around us. Give my Dutch husband the sea and some boats and he's happy. We take off for the beach and end up at a place called Joe Kool's, ordering a late lunch. The sun! I love the beach! I read that this is the number three surf spot in the world. Durban turns out champion surfers with the regularity of Sydney and Maui. Daniel gives me the assignment of finding where we can rent boards for the next few days. I look around at the young men with tangled hair and surfboards under their arms and feel like I'm back in California. I tell the others, this is surf culture, beach boys all.

DAY 14, DURBAN, SOUTH AFRICA

We're on the beach when I go over to Julia's towel and sit beside her. I've waited all summer for this moment. In Poland I bought two silver and amber rings and now I give her one. I put the other on my finger where I usually wear my Stanford ring. When she and I went to London in July, she told me she had asked Jesus into her life—quietly, alone, in her bedroom, earlier that year. This ring is to celebrate that decision.

"Our rings," I tell her, "the triple *S*. Solidarity, her Sixteenth summer with a support Stone reflecting the Light of her life. We will always pray for you, always love you, always be there for you." I tell her, to have her choose as she has, in the privacy of her own heart, this is an answer to prayer from when we were pregnant with her. I was sixteen when I chose our Lord's path, too. She and I are both crying and now, instead of wiggling our hands at each other, which has been the secret sign of the trip, we show a fist, our rings twinkling, light. He is Light of our life, shining through Polish amber into South African golds and reds, silver lining my finger, my daughter's, one together in love and life. She was mine and now is God's. The plan for her life is set in stars on a night sky blinding in its darkness.

This night we discover the terrace, sun and sirens through the night, we've been warned by waiters and other hotel guests not to leave the hotel at night. During the day, though, Daniel is SO HAPPY! He does nothing but surf. He surfs alone; he surfs with others, hour after hour, his stomach burning with a rash, feet cut by the flippers. He's found his wave.

DAY 15, DURBAN, SOUTH AFRICA

This morning we stand outside waiting for Julia when the bomb squad clears us off the street.

Daniel! Panic rises in my throat as I remember he's left for the open market already. I grab Erik's shoulder and almost scream, "Daniel! He's out there." Soldiers from a South African SWAT team are swarming through the lobby. They have closed off the entrance, trained sniffer dogs at the steps.

Erik pushes past the special units calling, "My son is out there. My son!"

I'm shaking. Typically me, I'm thinking, *Now I'll lose both Erik and Daniel.* Erik goes after him while Julia and I wait in the hotel. I think, *Now, now it will happen, the tragedy I've been waiting for.*

When they tell us we can go outside again, I wait and watch until I see them walking toward me. Only then do I let myself think, *Not this time. I won't lose them both.*

Later, coming home from taking the boards back, Daniel and I pass a taped-off Holiday Inn. Police line the street. I ask an agent, "What's going on?"

"NAM conference, Non-Affiliated Member-states."

I'm not sure if I've heard him correctly. Then I remember the headlines in the hotel's paper that morning. In other words, *the countries that don't belong to a club.* Their own club. "Who's here?" I ask.

"Gadaffi from Libya, Arafat, Hussein. Mandela is here already."

Great, I think. *Cape Town had a bomb last week. If Clinton wanted to nuke his enemies in one blow, Durban would be this week's target.* The papers are full of his bombing of the pharmaceutical factories earlier that week, a reaction to the bombings of U.S. embassies in Nairobi and Dar es Salaam a few months earlier. The Dow Jones dives 512 points. *What's happening?* I wonder.

That night is our wedding anniversary and I wear my green malachite necklace and earrings I bought at Vic Falls. Erik and I are close, the rush of the surf at night on the terrace, the stars still with us, we watch as sirened motorcycles escort my country's enemies from reception to reception.

Day 16, Durban, South Africa

Now I'm sitting in mist, lulled by waves. Erik and Daniel wait and choose just the right waves to ride. Wave motion across the sea. Choose, choose, timing, *now.* Sea breeze from the opposite side, sun setting over land instead of sea. Trees rustling in the wind, biting sand gritty covered with a layer, watching Daniel and Erik ride and crash on waves pounding sand, waves curling, waves riding water movement.

Don't forget the sound of African wind and sea. Balcony door opens and I smell and see a world of ships and waves, surf everywhere, in the dull gold sky at sunset, the smiles of light-skinned blond boys in shorts and thongs, the language of the people around us. Wave height, tidal times, lunar phases. The sea and ships. Durban sunshine and wind, a modern baptism of fire complete with rock and roll and expensive brand-name clothing.

Crime at night, the added glamour of statesmen infamous the world around. I think, *NAM must really mean Non-Affiliated-Murderers.* On our last morning I learn in the elevator, from a woman wearing a sari, that yesterday, while we were at the beach, the entire hotel was evacuated for another bomb.

It's time to bring our children home.

ABOUT THE AUTHOR

Anne de Graaf has sold over 4 million books worldwide. Her latest novel series is based on her travels into Africa. In the past five years, she has trekked through sub-Saharan African countries, interviewing villagers and UNICEF personnel, visiting various camps for refugee children. Her exciting new trilogy, The Negotiator (Tyndale), tells of one woman's passion for peace that carries her from Africa to Ireland to the former Yugoslavia, where she hears the children in each of these places tell their own stories. This short story is based on Anne's most recent journey into Africa with her family.

HAWAIIAN SUNRISE

Lauraine Snelling

Leaving is always hard.

Maddy Morton glanced around the decrepit, empty apartment one more time. She stared at a familiar crack in the wall and listened for the continuous drip in the kitchen sink. The management, if you could call their landlord that, hadn't fixed anything in the two years they'd been there. No, leaving this shabby place wasn't hard, but friends...friends were a different matter.

But you never left your memories. Memories, both good and bad, came along whether you wanted them to or not.

"Come on, Nicholas, it's time."

"I don't want to go, and you can't make me."

She stared at her ten-year-old son. Right now Nicholas reminded her so much of his father, she could scream in frustration. Instead, she clamped her jaw shut and anchored her hands on her hips. She leaned forward, looking him square in the eye. And waited.

Her teeth ached from the clenched jaw.

Nicholas stared right back, his jaw a miniature of her own. Gray eyes that matched hers flashed to storm-cloud hue, and a lock of dark hair flopped forward over his left eye.

She started to brush it back and stopped. In the last few weeks, he'd avoided her touch. Gone, too, was the merry laugh that made her life worthwhile. In its place slunk this sullen caricature of her son.

Fear sucked the moisture from her throat. Would he turn out like his father in spite of her efforts? Gabino, better known as Gabe, Hernandez now occupied a cell in the state penitentiary for spousal abuse and illegal possession and sale of drugs. She and Nicholas were safe for ten years, according to the judge. At that time Gabe would be up for parole, if he could behave himself in the interim.

Since the notion of Gabe controlling his temper had yet to be even a possibility, Maddy was counting on her ex-husband's inability to change. She only let his threat to "get them when he got out" intrude on her mind in moments of utter despair. This wasn't one of them—yet.

She waited.

First Nicholas's shoulders drooped. The motion was so faint she'd have missed it were she not looking for that reaction.

"Why can't we stay in Honolulu? All my friends are here." His voice transformed from defiance to a plaintive whine.

She knew she'd won. Accepting his defeat gracefully, she went down on one knee so they could be eye-to-eye. "Nicholas, you know why. I can't pay the rent and—"

"We could move in with Juan. His mom said it was okay." He switched to reasoning mode.

Oh, to gather him in the shelter of both arms and heart! But the skinny arms he locked across his chest still kept her at bay.

"Rita didn't mean permanently, just for a night or two." Maddy waited again. It seemed like she'd spent half her life waiting. Waiting had never been her strong suit. Getting in and getting it done was more her style, no matter what "it" was.

"I hate you." His eyes narrowed to slits. "You're the meanest…" He then used a local word that she had forbidden. His lashes flickered and he sniffed, fighting to maintain his tough-boy facade.

Maddy debated between throwing him over her shoulder or paddling his behind. She knew how badly he needed a hug just now but feared he would resent it all the more. Inside she wasn't sure who needed the hug more—she or Nicholas.

If only she could hold on to her own temper long enough. "Sorry about that, son, but right now I'm not liking your behavior too well either. So you just go get your backpack and help me carry these last things down to the truck—Rita's waiting. We'll be on our way before they come and kick us out." She stood and looked down at him, shaking her head.

"It's going to be all right, Nicholas, I promise." Her voice had dropped to a whisper.

He shot her a look that told her quite clearly what he thought of her promises and stamped off to the bedroom.

She breathed a sigh of relief. Another skirmish done. The language he'd used was just one more reason to be leaving Honolulu; the gang he'd taken to running with, another. Life on the Big Island, living on her father's ranch, would be much slower and would give her renegade son enough to do to keep out of trouble. The cows would be calving now, and there was always at least one calf that needed bottle feeding, a good job for Nicholas.

If Pop would let them stay.

She brushed a lock of dishwater blond hair back from the corner of her eye and put that thought as far out of her mind as she had others. At least there they would be safe. She'd taken back her maiden name after the divorce was final, and neither Gabe nor his "friends" would look for them there...she hoped. He knew how she despised anyone running home with her tail between her legs. He also believed she was *his* property, to knock around when he wanted, divorce or no. Thinking of others was as foreign to Gabe's nature as the sun rising in the west.

What Gabe didn't understand was that she'd do anything to save her son, even broaching her father—something she'd sworn never to do.

Nicholas stomped by her, his pack slung over one shoulder, eyes averted. The long, furry ear of Mr. Mops hung out from the pack. The rabbit had been his constant bed companion since the Easter he turned three. Like the Velveteen Rabbit, Mr. Mops wore the patina of love.

With only a cursory glance around the place that had been their home for two years, Maddy closed the door and followed her son down the two flights of stairs. She felt like stamping her feet as he did, but that took far more energy than she had at the moment.

If only she hadn't dumped that man's drink in his lap, she'd still have a job. But he'd been trying to pick her up all night, and when he pinched her rear as she carried a tray of orders out, the camel's back had broken. Even though her boss had shaken his head sadly, she'd known a parting of ways was coming.

She slung her pack into the back of the pickup and climbed in the passenger side.

"You sure about this?" Rita asked for the umpteenth time.

"Sure as I'll ever be." Maddy reached to tousle Nicholas's hair as he hunkered in the narrow space between them, but he ducked away. "We'll miss our flight if we don't get a move on."

"There's always another." Rita shifted into first gear, and the pickup whined its way down the steep grade.

Maddy didn't have much to say as they drove out to the Honolulu airport. While she watched the passing palm trees and gigantic hibiscus blossoms, she felt nothing. Honolulu had never been home.

"Where will you go if he won't let you stay?"

Rita voiced the thought that had kept Maddy awake more nights than she cared to count.

"He'll let us." Maddy knew that in spite of himself, her father wanted to see his only grandson. She was counting on that being enough incentive. How could she ask Nicholas to put on a happy face if only to gain them a home where they weren't wanted? Anyone, including her father, would be able to tell that her son didn't want to be there. It was a shame she hadn't told Nicholas more about the ranch and his family, but whoever dreamed *she'd* be skulking back home?

She shook her head at the memory of her arrogant answer to her father's threat of cutting her out of his will if she ran off with Gabe Hernandez. As if she were leaving that much behind. Besides, the baby she was carrying made staying impossible.

She shook her head. Why did her father always have to be right? He'd said Gabe would end up in jail one day.

It was only unfortunate it hadn't been a whole lot sooner. She was now finally gaining back the strength in the arm he'd broken the last time he got mad at her, just before his trial. One lesson she'd learned with impeccable success through all this mess was there'd be no man in her life from now on. Men were far more trouble than they were worth. And to top it off, they always left.

"Here we are, then." Rita swung the truck into an empty space in front of the airline's open-air ticket counter. "You call if you need me?"

Maddy nodded. "Come on, Nicky, let's get our gear."

"Don't call me that." He shoved out the door and slung his pack on his shoulder again.

"Thanks, Rita, we'd never have made it without you." Maddy lifted their four boxes from the pickup bed and set them on the sidewalk. "Get me a cart, Nick, please."

He snagged one of the luggage carriers some departing guest had left loose and trundled it over.

After stacking the boxes on the cart, Maddy gave Rita a hug and, with promises to write or call, pushed all their worldly belongings up to the check-in counter. The horn honked and she waved. Looking down, Maddy saw her son's lip quiver. Rita had been like another mother as the two women swapped baby-sitting, meals, and anything else one had that the other needed, including a shoulder to cry on if necessary. Rita's son, Juan, had been Nicholas's best friend.

Once the scramble to board the plane was over, Maddy lapsed into memories again. She hadn't been home since her mother's funeral. If her mother had still been alive, there would be no doubt as to their welcome home. In fact, she'd probably have come for them if the news of Gabe's trial had made the Hilo paper. What would it be like without her waiting at the door? What if Pop really didn't let them stay?

Maddy stared at Mauna Kea, the highest peak on the island of Hawaii, as the plane circled to land at the Kona airport. The ranch lay on the eastern slopes, the leeward side of the island. A cloud hid the mountaintop and cottoned its flanks. Most likely it was raining in Waimea, the town nearest the ranch.

Maddy knew she didn't need to count the bills in her wallet again—hiring a driver to take them to the ranch would empty it completely. Why, oh *why* hadn't she kept in contact with any of the people she'd grown up with?

Get over it, she told herself. *The milk is all spilt and crying over it won't do any good.* She took a deep breath. *God, let him take us in.*

Her sigh was loud enough to make Nicholas turn from staring out the window and look at her with both questions and fear in his eyes. She'd given up on praying a long time ago and never planned on going back.

That one had sneaked up on her.

Once on the ground a short time later, with their packs and boxes around them, she shook her head at the man offering to drive her to the ranch.

"But I don't have that much." She raised her hands in defeat. So close and yet so far. Should she call her father to come get them?

That would happen the day a snowball rolled down the new lava flow. As the man walked back to his van, she glanced up to see a tall, familiar-looking Hawaiian looking her way. His broad smile invited one in return, but right now she was fresh out of smiles. In fact, she had been for quite some time, but he wouldn't know that.

She turned away when he began threading his way between the luggage and passengers toward them. Surely she'd known him from high school, though he was older. What was his name?

He didn't take the hint. "I heard you ask about Waimea. I'm going to Hilo and can drop you off in Waimea on my way."

Maddy stared at his scuffed cowboy boots, then followed creased khaki pants up to a turquoise shirt with peach hibiscus that covered a wide chest. Her perusal stopped at his smile. Wide and warm, just like the look in his eyes.

"I don't have much money." The words sounded flat, even to her ears. Who was he? *Come on, brain, what's left of you?*

"No matter. My name's Kam Waiano." He waited, the smile never leaving his face. It broadened when he looked down at Nicholas.

"I know! You played football." *But you wouldn't know me.*

"That was a long time ago."

Maddy understood Hawaiian courtesy. She'd been raised by it. He wouldn't take anything for the extra effort. She gestured to herself. "I'm Maddy, and this is Nicholas."

"Nick." Her son hadn't left his shoulder chip on the plane.

"Aloha, Nick and Maddy. Welcome back to the Big Island." He took a box under either arm, making Maddy feel petite. At five-feet-eight, she never felt petite. She picked up one of the remaining boxes, refusing to grunt in the process. All of them were heavy. Books and personal things weighed up quickly, but she found she couldn't leave all of her life behind. Just the hurtful parts.

After depositing the first boxes in the bed of the white pickup, he took hers and lifted up the rest. "I have to swing by Holuakoa."

When neither answered, Kam showed them into the pickup cab and slammed the door behind them. "How long since you been here?" He turned the ignition as he asked.

The warmth in his voice and its musical tone made Maddy want to answer. He was only being his friendly Hawaiian self, she reasoned. Aloha was a way of life among the Hawaiians, not just a polite greeting. After all, she wasn't a *haole*, a visitor from the mainland. She'd grown up on the island. And left.

"Ummm. Long time." She looked out the window, doing all in her power to discourage small talk. Nicholas had retreated into the shell he'd become so expert at closing around himself. She could tell the man was trying to place her.

Kam hummed a tune as he drove, glancing at her frequently but honoring her silence. Even though she stared out the window, she felt each of his glances as if he brushed every nerve end she owned with the tip of an ostrich feather.

"I'll just be a minute," he said, getting out of the truck in front of a weathered building that looked like a giant had put a foot on one side and lightly pushed. He was whistling when he returned.

Maddy brought herself back from the land of *what if* and nodded at his greeting.

"You want a cup of coffee?" Kam pointed to a ramshackle restaurant off to the right.

"No, thanks." *One more cup of coffee and I might shatter,* she thought, trying to still her already shaking fingers. *Hurry up and go. Take your time and wait.* The two contradicting schools of thought warred in her head.

By the time they'd stopped at one of the shrimp farms and started up Highway 19, the sun had disappeared beyond the horizon banked by dark masses of clouds.

They drove right into the rain cloud, huge drops pummeling the windshield and creating rivers of red beside the highway. Nicholas slumped against her side, his backpack on his lap, his mouth slightly open in sleep. By the time they drove through Waimea, dusk was drowning in night.

The huge eucalyptus tree that marked the ranch turnoff was nearly undecipherable in the torrent. The headlights glistened briefly on the silvery bark.

"Up there." Maddy indicated the road they had to follow. When the truck stopped in front of a picket fence that had certainly seen better days, Maddy dug in her purse.

"Don't even think about it." The firm tone in his voice left no room for argument. "Hey, you aren't Mark Morton's baby sister, are you?"

She ignored the question. After all, it was none of his business.

"Thank you for the ride." Maddy stepped out into the downpour, studying what she could see of her father's place by the headlights. The gate hung off one hinge, and the rose arbor, her mother's pride and joy, tilted to one side, propped up by two sticks rammed in the red clay soil. A light shone faintly at the window.

"C-come on, Nicholas, we're home." She shook him awake with one hand and pushed a soaked strand of hair back from her eyes. She pointed her son toward the front door and, ignoring the sheeting rain, hoisted one of her boxes out of the truck bed. Kam came around and helped her carry them to the lanai that circled the front of the low building. Like other houses on the islands, posts held the floor up off the ground to allow both air circulation and the water to run by.

At their arrival a dog had crawled from under the porch and stood barking.

"Amos?" Maddy asked softly.

The barks turned to a whine of welcome, the stiff stance to a dance of delight. The mottled gray, tan, black, and white cattle dog yipped and wriggled, spattering Maddy's sodden clothes with red mud. She set the boxes down and, using both hands, rubbed the dog's ears and whatever part of him she could grab onto.

"Nicholas, this is Amos—and he obviously remembers me." She glanced up to see her son standing just under the porch roof, arms again across his chest.

"He 'bout bit me."

"Oh, he was just doing his job, weren't you, fella?" More wriggles and yips, plus a flashing tongue that tried to clear the rain from her cheeks.

Kam cleared his throat. "You sure you'll be all right?"

"Yes, thank you." Maddy stood from her tussle with the dog. When Kam turned to leave, she almost reached out a hand to draw him back. *What's with you, girl?* she silently questioned. *First man who's nice to you, and you want to keep him near? Where's your backbone?* She resolutely turned toward the house again and began petting the dog, who put muddy paws up on her leg to reach her hand better. She waited until she heard the truck slosh out the lane.

Maddy flung her dripping braid over her shoulder and straightened to her fullest height, hoping the action would put some steel in her reluctant backbone. "Well, here goes nothing." She mounted the stairs and, with one hand on Nicholas's shoulder, walked to the door.

"Who in tarnation...?"

She heard him muttering even before she could knock. The door opened before her hand struck it. "Hi, Pop, we've come home."

Only her foot in the door kept it from closing in their faces.

ABOUT THE AUTHOR

Lauraine Snelling is an award-winning author of forty novels for both young adults and adults. The preceding story is an excerpt from Lauraine's novel *Hawaiian Sunrise* (Bethany House).

Favorite Novelists Tell Tales about Home

A great idea is always worth repeating! In one volume, Christian readers' favorite fiction authors—including Randy Alcorn, Terri Blackstock, Angela Elwell Hunt, Melody Carlson, Nancy Moser, and Karen Kingsbury—offer delightful new short stories about hometown faith and foibles. This hard-to-put-down book, which features story settings all around North America in a variety of time periods, reminds readers about what values really spell 'home'. And the contributors celebrate a home-based ministry by donating their royalties to Prison Fellowship!

ISBN 1-57673-820-5

The Prison Fellowship Ministries Connection

When ChiLibris authors collaborated on our first book of short stories, *The StoryTellers' Collection*, we decided to designate all the royalties to reaching the lost and needy for Christ. Those royalties continue to go to the *JESUS Film Project*, bringing the good news to the far corners of the earth. With this second book we wanted to support an equally Christ-centered and strategic ministry.

After nominating a number of worthy organizations, we chose Prison Fellowship Ministries. Prison Fellowship is the largest and most extensive association of national Christian ministries working within the criminal justice field. By the grace of God and the labors of more than fifty thousand volunteers, prisoners worldwide are being evangelized, discipled, taught God's Word, counseled, and linked with local churches. Men and women are being delivered from emptiness and despair and are learning a new way to think and live.

We consider this an investment in eternity and look forward to seeing in heaven the exciting results of the Holy Spirit's work, not just through this book, but through the proceeds given to Prison Fellowship.

Each of the contributors to this second *Storytellers' Collection* is honored to partner with Prison Fellowship and delighted that 100 percent of the royalties from this book will go to this outstanding ministry.

We encourage readers to pray for and consider supporting Prison Fellowship. For information, visit **www.pfi.org** or contact **Prison Fellowship, P.O. Box 17500, Washington, D.C. 20041-7500 (703-478-0100).**

As ChiLibris authors, we hope you enjoy *Storytellers' Collection 2: Tales from Home*, and that your heart is drawn to our Lord and King. We also hope it encourages you to know about the powerful ministry your purchase is helping support. Thank you, from all of us, for sharing in this important outreach.

Printed in the United States
by Baker & Taylor Publisher Services